HIS TO DEFEND

—

Rhenna Morgan

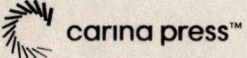

If you purchased this book without a cover you should be aware that this book is stolen property. It was reported as "unsold and destroyed" to the publisher, and neither the author nor the publisher has received any payment for this "stripped book."

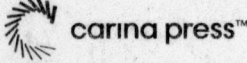

ISBN-13: 978-1-335-53437-8

His to Defend

Copyright © 2019 by Rhenna Morgan

Recycling programs for this product may not exist in your area.

All rights reserved. Except for use in any review, the reproduction or utilization of this work in whole or in part in any form by any electronic, mechanical or other means, now known or hereinafter invented, including xerography, photocopying and recording, or in any information storage or retrieval system, is forbidden without the written permission of the publisher, Harlequin Enterprises Limited, 22 Adelaide St. West, 40th Floor, Toronto, Ontario M5H 4E3, Canada.

This is a work of fiction. Names, characters, places and incidents are either the product of the author's imagination or are used fictitiously, and any resemblance to actual persons, living or dead, business establishments, events or locales is entirely coincidental.

This edition published by arrangement with Harlequin Books S.A.

® and ™ are trademarks of the publisher. Trademarks indicated with ® are registered in the United States Patent and Trademark Office, the Canadian Intellectual Property Office and in other countries.

www.CarinaPress.com

Printed in U.S.A.

Also available from Rhenna Morgan and Carina Press

Rough & Tumble
Wild & Sweet
Claim & Protect
Tempted & Taken
Down & Dirty
Guardian's Promise
Healer's Need

Coming soon

Hers to Tame
Mine to Have

Also available from Rhenna Morgan

Unexpected Eden
Healing Eden
Waking Eden
Eden's Deliverance

For those of you currently slogging through challenging times. Never forget that the clouds will run their course, the pain will eventually pass and the light of happiness will once more shine upon you. Until then, one step at a time and believe in happily-ever-afters. They *do* happen.

HIS TO DEFEND

Chapter One

$480.

Evette pinched the business-size check from her former employer a little tighter and glared at the cleaning company's logo in the top corner. On any other Friday, the money would have meant inching closer to some semblance of security for her and her son, Emerson. A step toward unraveling the mess she'd created for her life. Today, the unexpected termination that had come with her weekly pay felt more like a sucker punch to the gut. Yet another obstacle to overcome after too many damned years running the gauntlet and never even glimpsing the finish line.

Maybe she could get a job cleaning at one of the hotels. God knew the French Quarter was packed with them, and she was pretty sure she could count on regular shift work, like the office cleaning crew she'd been on. Though, how she was going to land one by Monday when it was already close to 4:30 on a Friday afternoon was beyond her. And landing something quick was the only way this latest setback wouldn't force her into dipping into Emerson's school fund. Plus, there was the hurdle of what would happen if they called her old company for references and found out she'd been fired for a security breach.

Not. Good.

The commuter bus swung onto Tulane headed toward Mid-City, and Evie's spirits sunk a little lower. If someone had told her when she was growing up that she'd be a single mom living in one of New Orleans's rougher parts of town at twenty-eight years old, she'd have laughed in their face. She was going to be a fashion retail buyer—or at least have some kind of career in fashion. She was going to travel the world. See things. Know people. Adventure her way through life and suck it dry.

Then her mom had died, and she'd gone off the rails.

She sighed and slunk a little farther down onto the hard plastic bench, the run-down stores, bars and restaurants along the roadside passing in a blur while the vibrations from the bus's engine rattled clear to her bones.

Get knocked down seven times, stand up eight.

If she had a dollar for all the times her momma had said it and all the times Evie had echoed it in the last eight years, she'd be driving a Porsche toward the Garden District right now instead of a barely livable apartment.

But her momma had made it.

Mostly.

Raised Evette through her tumultuous preteen years after her daddy's death and made it look easy. It hadn't been until a year after Emerson had been born and Evie had found the courage to read some of her mother's journals that she'd realized just how much of a challenge her mother had really faced. How much she'd given up and how alone she'd felt through every second.

Evie understood it now. Knew to her very marrow the sacrifices that had been made on her behalf.

And she'd thrown it all away nursing her grief.

Resolve and a whole lot of stubbornness revved her energy and forced her taller in her seat. Pity was what had gotten her into this mess to begin with, and she'd be damned if she went that route again. Labadie women didn't quit. Didn't give up. They faced whatever they needed to face, and they smiled doing it. Eventually, she was going to find a way to give her and Emerson the world. She just might have to scrimp a little longer and get more creative to make it happen.

The bus's brakes whined, and the older lady seated next to Evie leaned into her.

Evie braced herself enough to keep them both upright and smiled down at her fellow passenger. "You gettin' off here, Miss Arnold? You know Dorothy's Friday specials are always the best ones of the week."

Miss Arnold beamed a smile at Evie and hugged her grocery bag a little tighter to her chest. Her blue eyes might have turned murky in the last few years and the wrinkles lining her pale skin etched a little deeper, but her kind heart was still as strong as ever. "No, no, Evette. Trips to the grocery aren't as easy as they used to be. Better I get my tired bones on to the home before the sun goes down."

A smart move. Especially in this part of town, because a woman like Miss Arnold after dark was a mugging waiting to happen.

Once certain the older woman had her balance again, Evie stood, shouldered her purse and took another stab at the same argument she'd been having with the neighborhood woman for the past year. "Seems to me, you could use that fancy shuttle van all the other residents use for your errands and not have half the hassle."

Miss Arnold lifted her chin a little higher, the epitome of a Southern woman with an iron core. "Seein' to myself is a privilege. Gonna take advantage of it as long as the good Lord'll let me." She dipped her head toward the door at the front of the bus. "Best get yourself to Dorothy's and that handsome boy of yours."

Damn. Shut down again. "All right, but don't think we're not gonna talk about this next time."

"Lookin' forward to it, beautiful girl."

Evie shook her head and headed to the door.

"Evette." Miss Arnold's sharp voice halted her just before she took the first step down. She waited until Evie met her steady stare before she spoke again. "Gonna be all right. Whatever it is…it's not gonna beat you. You just keep on remembering that."

A tightness noosed around Evette's throat, and tears tingled along the bridge of her nose. Maybe she *wouldn't* have another chance to talk Miss Arnold out of taking the bus to the grocery store. Not unless her next job took her to the same part of town she'd been working in. She clenched the handrail beside the steep steps and forced a smile she didn't feel. "Don't you worry, Miss Arnold. Gonna take more than a kick or two to keep me down."

The older woman nodded as if she'd expected such an answer, then went back to staring out the window opposite her seat. "Good girl. Now get on to that boy of yours and tell Dorothy I said hello."

Outside, the temperature still hovered near eighty-five degrees. Not exactly an unbearable number at the tail end of September, but the humidity from the gulf and the subtle stench that last night's rains had stirred from the Quarter didn't exactly make for an ideal stroll on the streets either. She hurried past a cheesy souvenir shop, a convenience store and a pub—the latter leaving the faint scent of cigarette smoke on the sidewalk despite the front door doing its best to trap the conditioned air inside. At the end of the block, Dorothy's Diner sat like a neighborhood beacon. The entrance was right at the corner, two long walls of windows stretching for a good twelve feet on either side so those moseying past could get an easy view of the crowd inside.

And there was always a crowd at Dorothy's. As diners went, it was an institution. A safe haven in the middle of hell and a slice of soul food heaven all rolled into one. Per usual, Emerson was at the soda-shop-style counter perched on the barstool closest to the front door, his shoulders slightly hunched forward and his forearms around his plate like a linebacker braced to protect his food. His dirty blond hair was a nod to her daddy's side of the family and was a tad too long and tousled like any other seven-year-old boy's probably was at the end of the school day, but his expression was far too empty. His hazel eyes too void of emotion for someone so young.

She forced another bogus smile and shoved the glass door open. The bell overhead gave a cheerful jingle, and two or three of the waitresses on the floor called out a greeting.

Evie gave them all a polite wave, but went straight

to her kid and added a little extra mess to his hair with a playful ruffle. "Hey, champ. How was school?"

For the briefest of seconds, her little boy stared back at her. Not much more than a hint of a smile, but enough to let her know the kid who had curled so innocently in her lap a few years ago was still in there somewhere. The openness was gone again in a blink, the sullen scowl she'd grown to hate aimed back at a plateful of turkey and dressing. He shrugged and stabbed a bite of turkey. "Just a day."

"Yeah, but it's a *Friday* and everyone knows Fridays are always better by default." She slid onto the barstool next to Emerson and let her purse drop to the raised step beneath her feet. "Anything big go down at recess?"

Emerson shook his head.

"Any surprise tests?"

Another shake.

"Meet any cute girls?"

To that, he simply lifted his head and looked at her like he was torn between walking home without her and suggesting she have her head examined.

"Well, at least that got your attention," she said. "You know, when I was your age, my momma couldn't get me to shut up."

Emerson pushed a green bean that had strayed too close to his dressing back to the exiled portion of his plate. "No point in talking if there's nothing going on."

"Hmm." She crossed her arms and pretended to check out the rest of the diner's patrons while her brain scrambled for any clue on how to engage with her son. He might be only seven, but he talked with more sophistication than most adults. Barely any slang. No

Creole mannerisms and definitely no profanity. More like a gentleman stuck in a child's body. So, why she thought some shocking revelation on how to talk to him at his level was gonna plow its way to the forefront of her thoughts right this second after over a year of searching was beyond her. "Well, if you're not gonna talk to me, maybe Miss Dorothy will. You seen her?"

Emerson politely wiped his mouth with his napkin and dipped his head toward the kitchen. "She disappeared in there right before you came in. Table seven didn't like their special."

Evie glanced at the turkey and dressing on Emerson's plate. "Someone's complaining about the cooking? Are they high?"

Miracle of miracles, Emerson's mouth twitched with a smile that didn't quite break free. "Not everyone has good taste, Mom."

"True dat," she fired back, wishing with everything in her she could get her kid to let go and be a kid again. She swiveled toward the kitchen and waved her hand at her bag. "Watch that for me. Don't want our payday finding legs and running off without us."

"Yes, ma'am."

Yes, ma'am.

Evie meandered toward the kitchen, her son's perfect reply echoing in her head. If she'd been that proper growing up, her momma would have celebrated with street parties and however many charitable contributions for the offering plate their bank account would allow. Instead, she'd been sassy. Never disrespectful, of course. That would have earned her a butt whoopin' or boxed ears. But an *okie dokie pokey* or a *you betcha* was way more common than a proper *Yes, ma'am*.

The scrape of metal chair legs against the black-and-white industrial tile shot through the diner.

Evie paused at the end of the counter and turned toward the sound.

Backing away from the popular round booth in the back corner was a slightly balding fortyish-looking man with a short-sleeve checked button-down barely covering his paunch. His black pants were a tad too short in the length, but they were clean and well-pressed. He clenched some papers in his hand and executed a semi-bow that could have been interpreted as fear or extreme respect. Maybe a little of both.

One glance at who was sitting in the booth and the tense gesture made sense.

Sergei Petrovyh.

She'd missed seeing him on the way in. Which said a lot about how distracted the new twist in her life had left her because just thinking his name made her flush. Actually looking at him made her and three-quarters of the female population too tongue-tied to talk. The other quarter mostly threw themselves at him and prayed to any god who would listen for a chance to hear that deep Russian accent of his up close and personal. Preferably in a situation where no clothes were involved.

Rather than butt into Dorothy's rant with the chef in the kitchen, Evie waited near the register and straightened a stack of menus.

The balding man said something to Sergei, took two more steps backward, then turned and quick-stepped it toward the front door.

Her gaze drifted back to Sergei, though she covered her leisurely perusal by thumbing through an order pad near the register. Dark wavy hair to his shoulders, sharp facial features, one of those sexy-as-hell tightly cropped beards and a deliciously tall and fit body to go with it.

But it wasn't just his looks that left women wanting. It was his power. A charisma burning behind his dark blue eyes and a graceful yet predatory edge behind every movement. In short, Sergei Petrovyh was the kind of man who could make any female forget her problems for at least a few precious moments with a single look.

Actually, if she was honest, Sergei could eradicate her problems completely. It was what he'd done for a long list of people in her neighborhood since he'd moved to New Orleans a little over a year ago—traded fixing untenable situations in exchange for obligations owed.

More to the point...he was a mobster.

A damned good-looking one, for sure, but a seriously dangerous man all the same.

Footsteps and muffled grumbling registered a few seconds before Dorothy's droll voice cut through Evie's ogling. "Girl, I've seen star-struck groupies act less obvious than you right now."

Evie crushed the urge to flinch like a guilty schoolgirl and gave Sergei another thorough once-over just to prove to both of them she could. Seriously, the man was like a Greek god. Maybe it was all that olive skin. Or the fact that he moved like a panther. The custom-tailored suits he wore definitely made the fashion lover in her want to stretch out and purr.

So, yeah. She was old enough to ogle all she wanted and wasn't about to apologize to anyone for doing it. Especially not after the day she'd had. "Nothing wrong with looking." She faced her momma's lifelong friend, leaned a hip onto the counter and braced one hand on the other. "And lookin' at him is a damn sight better than tryin' to figure out how I'm gonna pull off a major miracle between now and Monday."

Dorothy tucked her order pad inside the pocket of her white apron. Her daddy had named her after Dorothy Dandridge purely because he'd had a crush on the actress when Dorothy had been born, but she'd grown into a woman as beautiful as her namesake. At sixty-eight years old, her skin was wrinkled and her hair a soft gray, but her near-black eyes were still sharp as ever. She eyeballed Evie the way only a mother could. "What kind of miracle are we talking about?"

"The kind where I find a job."

"I thought you were goin' for a supervisor position with the cleaning gig. What happened?"

Evie threw up her hands, then crossed her arms across her chest. "Damned if I know. Something about a security breach and my badge being used to access an attorney's office after hours last weekend. Which is complete crap. Aside from me and Emerson going to the Farmers Market and the church potluck last Saturday, me and my badge were home all weekend. It had to be a mix-up."

"You tell 'em that?"

"'Course I did. But they weren't listening. Said they didn't have a choice but to let me go with their security policy."

Dorothy frowned and ambled behind Evie to the back countertop and the tub of clean silverware waiting to be rolled into napkins. She laid out the first napkin and got to work. "Not sure how that constitutes an emergency. I know you, Evie. You're always bracin' for a storm. Don't tell me you don't have savings."

"All of that's going to Emerson's tuition."

"I thought he was on a wait list. No point in scrimping now if you need it and have time to build it back."

"He's not on a wait list anymore." Evie moved in beside her. She'd been rolling napkins at Dorothy's place for as long as she could remember and had worked through countless crises with the simple task. "The dean called this week and said one of the kids is moving. I can apply for a scholarship, but I have to pony up the tuition to hold the spot while they process it."

"How much is it?"

"$900."

Dorothy's head snapped her direction and her voice rose enough a good amount of the diner's chatter ceased. "$900? Are you insane?"

"Dorothy!" she whisper-scolded with a pointed look in Emerson's direction. "Emerson needs this. All his teachers say he needs this place. Say he's bored to tears in public schools and that a Montessori school is perfect for a kid like him."

"Pshht." Dorothy shook her head. "That much money just to hold a spot, that school better pave him a gold path to heaven and wipe his ass, too." She paused long enough to let a comfortable silence stretch between them, then aimed a sideways look at Evie. "So? What you gonna do?"

"Well, I was hopin' maybe you could let me work for you a little while I look for something else."

Dorothy sighed. A genuine one that said she didn't like sharing the words that came next any more than Evie wanted to hear them. "Can't do that, baby girl.

These ladies I got now are quality and if I scrimp on their schedules, they'll go find someplace else to work. Best I can do is give you a call if one of 'em calls in sick, but that ain't gonna happen. They need the money too bad."

Well, shoot.

So much for Plan B.

She placed a perfectly rolled set on top of Dorothy's growing pile, turned, leaned her butt against the counter and crossed her arms on her chest. "This is such absolute crap." Fear tried to push its way up from her chest, fueled by a healthy dose of long-ignored desperation and frustration. "I can't blow this chance for Emerson. He needs it. He needs…" To smile. To play. To be able to be a kid and just enjoy himself a little while. "He needs *something*. If this school is gonna give it to him, then I'll take up workin' the streets if I have to."

"Not gonna come to that," Dorothy said with all the quiet confidence of a woman who'd already forged her way through raising her own kids. "Lord's gonna give you what you need when you need it. He always does."

"Hmmph." Evie chewed on the inside of her lip to keep from saying what she really wanted to. Namely, that if the Lord was gonna give her what she needed, it'd sure be nice if he'd tell her how he planned to do that sooner rather than later.

Like a magnet, her gaze shifted back to Sergei. The two men she often saw him with at the diner and around town now sat flanked on either end of the round booth. Kir Vasilek was big and intimidating like Sergei, but had beautiful blue eyes and blond hair. He used both to his advantage and had created a heck of a reputation in Mid-City as a supreme playboy. Roman

Kozlov, on the other hand, rarely interacted with anyone. Probably because his big, imposing body, menacing features and hard facial structure made people think he was the devil incarnate.

Sergei could eradicate her problems completely.

The thought was a little subtler this time. A murmur uttered with the silken voice of temptation. "What about him?" she said to Dorothy under her breadth.

Dorothy twisted and studied Evie's face, then followed her gaze to Sergei. After years keeping a diner open in a rough part of town through every kind of hard time imaginable, not much drew her old friend up short, but in that second, Dorothy showed genuine concern. She covered it almost as quickly as it had come up and went back to her silverware. "Don't think you need protection, doll. I think you need a *job*."

"Well, maybe he knows someone. Could give me a lead or a reference. One look at those clothes he wears and that slick BMW outside, you know he's loaded. That means he's gotta know other rich people."

"He might know 'em. Might even give you a leg up with 'em, but in case you missed it—a man like him does you a favor, you'll end up owing for what you get."

"You did it."

It was a childish response. Something more appropriate for when she'd been sixteen and arguing with her mom and Dorothy about what a girl should and shouldn't wear. Not when she was twenty-eight and figuring out how to pay her bills.

But if Dorothy felt the slight, she didn't show it. Just kept right on rolling. "Lesser of two evils, child. I had thugs taking over my diner. Sergei took care of that and in exchange I give him a place to do business. A small price to pay to keep my place safe, but don't let that handsome face fool you. He's got dark in him. A lot of it. And he's not afraid to let it out." She paused a moment, the look on her face that of a woman searching for the right words to share next. She finally paused and faced Evie, lowering her voice. "Right now, you've got money troubles. You bring him into your life, you'll solve one problem, but might end up with an even bigger one."

"Out of the frying pan into the fryer, huh?"

Her eyes softened, a whole wealth of wisdom Evie couldn't begin to comprehend staring back at her. "Something like that."

Evette sighed and chewed the inside of her lip. The only other option she could think of would have made her momma roll over in her grave, but she threw it out there anyway. "I guess I could ask Uncle Carl for some cash. He was wavin' a big wad of it around here the other day. He's crazy as the day is long, but he's always offering to help me and Emerson."

"No." Dorothy's retort was so hard and fast, Evette felt it like a jolt. While she softened her tone almost as quickly, her hands shook when she picked back up with the napkins. "Your momma had reasons why she kept her distance from Carl. It's best you do the same."

It wasn't the first time Dorothy had expressed her dislike for Carl. *Why* she and her mother didn't like him had never been something they'd been willing to share, but considering Evette didn't like being around him either, she'd never pushed it.

Evette braced her hands on the counter behind her and stared at Sergei.

Sergei turned and caught her gaze.

Trapped it.

Owned the connection so completely Evie would have sworn he'd overhead her entire conversation.

Which was absolute bull-hockey. He couldn't have. He was just an intimidating man with a good sense of intuition.

But he could help her.

Way faster than anyone else in this neighborhood.

She shifted her attention to Emerson, now done with his dinner and staring out the window to the street beyond. "Any chance I can talk you into a hot fudge sundae for Emerson?"

"Any chance I can talk you out of what you're thinkin' about doing?"

"Not unless you can tell me how to get a job by Monday and where I can find another $500 in time to hold that spot for Emerson."

Dorothy kept her silence.

"Come on, Dorothy. You said yourself he's not a complete bad guy. Heck, I remember you actually mentioned you liked him once. You've never even said you liked Father Manny and everyone likes him."

"Yeah, but I *love* you. Same as I loved your mama. You mark my words, you tangle with Sergei Petrovyh, there's no telling what you'll be in for."

"Well, if it makes my boy smile for once, I'm thinking it'd be worth it."

Dorothy shook her head, picked the heavy tub up like it weighed nothing and slid it under the counter. She faced Evie, studied her for long seconds, then nodded and headed for the kitchen. "I'll make two sundaes. Have a feelin' that boy's not the only one who's gonna need a pick-me-up before this day is through."

Chapter Two

She was looking at him again.

Every time Sergei came to Dorothy's and Evette was there, she looked her fill at him and never once feigned bashfulness about it. Her boldness intrigued him. Challenged him with the subtlety of a matador with a red cape and a death wish. If she were anyone else, he'd have made it his mission to conquer her months ago. Would've slaked the hunger and burn her leisurely perusal always ignited in him over and over again until both of them were boneless and spent.

But she wasn't just anyone.

She was Evette Labadie. The neighborhood darling everyone adored and doted on. To take her all the ways he wanted was counter to his mission—namely, to earn the loyalty of those who lived on the most dangerous streets of New Orleans, control the vast majority of the enterprises that went with it and snuff out the competition in the process. Hard to earn respect and loyalty if you sullied a woman as respected as Evette.

Plus, she was Dorothy's goddaughter. Sergei might have traded his protection in exchange for a public place to do business with the locals, but he actually liked Dorothy, too. Respected her hard-earned wisdom and tough-as-nails tenacity. He wasn't about to dishonor that respect by bringing the ugliness of his world down on someone so bright and open.

From his place at the end of the round booth, Kir leaned forward enough to intercept Sergei's focus on Evette and grinned. "You should just fuck her."

If anyone else had said it, Sergei would have gutted them on the spot without a second thought. Fortunately for Kir, he was one of the few men Sergei fully trusted, so he settled for a warning. "The word *fuck* or any semblance of it will not cross your lips or enter your thoughts around Evette again. Let alone act on it." He forced his gaze away from Evette and gave his brother-in-arms a cold stare. "She is safe. From me. From you. From everyone."

Roman's throaty chuckle bore a close semblance to the idle of a Triumph Rocket. "You notice the warning toward you was specific, brother. The rest of us just got a generality."

One corner of Kir's mouth curved in an unconcerned and devious grin. "That's because he knows I could win her if I set my mind to it."

"You might." Sergei's gaze drifted back to Evette. She was a petite little thing. A few inches at most over five feet with impish features and short, yet stylish chestnut-colored hair that made him think of a fairy who'd just bounced out of bed from a spirited tumble. Sergei had drawn enough details from Dorothy to know Evette's father was from a white family, and that her mother had deep Creole and Native American roots, and her personality was equally vibrant. No one was a stranger to Evette, and she treated everyone as equal. Valued. Important.

He raised his coffee cup from the table and sipped it with deceptive casualness. "Be that as it may, your success would be short-lived."

"What?" Kir said. "You think I can't keep her attention?"

"No. I think I'd cut your cock off, bury it in your throat and watch you suffocate on it."

It wasn't an empty threat and the speed with which Kir's grin slipped said his old friend knew it. "Duly noted." He sat back, crossed one knee over the other in a pose that belied the cold killer he was and studied Evette. Whatever she and Dorothy were talking about had escalated to Evette using emphatic gestures. "Though, if you ask me, it's only a matter of time before you break your own warning."

He wouldn't.

Much as he'd honor and savor the touch of someone so light and good, the darkness in him was too thick. Weighted with too many bodies and tainted with too much blood to be worthy of such a gift.

"What did Smitty want?" Roman's none-too-subtle redirect proved how adept he'd grown at reading Sergei over the years.

Unfortunately, he'd chosen a topic that only soured Sergei's mood further. Particularly, since he knew the grocery owner from only a block north of Dorothy's Diner to be a positive presence in the community and a solid family man. "Steven Alfonsi's upped his recruiting."

"He went for Smitty?"

Sergei shook his head. "He's courting Smitty's son, Jamie. Using another boy close to his age. Smitty's seen the kid visit the store while Jamie's working."

Kir frowned, leaned in and crossed his arms on the table. "That's not Alfonsi's normal play. Jamie's a college boy. Smart. Follows the rules. Alfonsi doesn't like smart pawns. They're too hard to control."

"He wants closer ties to the neighborhood," Roman answered before Sergei could. "We've taken over nearly half his business. He wants to know how we're doing it and he needs bodies on the inside to help him figure it out."

"He won't get it." Of that, Sergei was certain. Those who lived and worked Mid-City and the Seventh and Eighth Wards knew beyond the shadow of a doubt Sergei was the beast among them, but he was *their* beast. The one ruthless enough to rid them of the tyrants who had overrun their world. They didn't care that he demanded tribute in return. Only that he'd treated them fairly. Protected them when they couldn't protect themselves. In that, he'd earned their loyalty.

"And what does Smitty want?"

Sergei tapped the edge of his coffee mug. "What all good fathers would want for their child. To clear temptation from the boy's path."

Kir looked to Roman, the unspoken directive picked up without hesitation. "You want this one, or can I have it?"

Roman kept his silence, but the malice bleeding off him was palpable. Of the three of them, he detested *kozels* like Steven Alfonsi the most. The man had no honor. Had built his image around the stereotypical Mafia movie and forced unnecessary power plays to instill fear. Traded in secrets and used them to bend good people to his will.

Just another reason the people from the most dangerous streets had willingly accepted him as one of their own. Sergei's realm was one of choice not force. A dance willingly accepted and honored with a debt. An act of trust and tribute.

It was only a matter of time before all of New Orleans was behind him for exactly that reason.

Sergei answered Kir before Roman could claim the opportunity to slake his bloodlust. "You will handle it."

Behind the counter, Dorothy twisted enough to rake Sergei with a look that could only be described as resignation, then said something to Evette before she stole into the kitchen.

Evette stared at him. Her arms were crossed and her expression void of its usual lightness. Whatever was on the *feya*'s mind, it was serious.

He didn't like it.

Not one bit.

He forced his attention back to Kir. "Don't overdo it. Something small. Enough to send a message, but not enough to start a war. We'll face Alfonsi when the time is right."

Kir jerked a single, terse nod and picked up his coffee.

Evette pushed off the back counter and rounded the bar, her steps slow but purposeful.

And her trajectory was headed straight toward him.

He caught the urge to sit up a little taller in the booth a second before his muscles engaged and focused on keeping his demeanor unfazed. If it were a killer approaching him with a gun in hand, the mask would have been second nature. Just another face-to-face with death.

But with Evette moving toward him, it was a whole

different experience. A foreign pressure behind his sternum. A flood of adrenaline that left his skin hypersensitive and made his surroundings inconsequential.

Disturbing responses.

Dangerous ones for a man like him.

Roman's low voice barely penetrated, the Russian cadence of their mother tongue a calming stroke. *"Two audiences in one day. And this one a lamb."*

Kir's mouth twitched. *"I wouldn't call her a lamb. Though, it will be interesting."*

"It won't be interesting for you," Sergei said as she neared their table, *"because you won't be here."*

This time Kir didn't try to hide his smile. Even dared to chuckle as he stood and looked to Roman, who was already on his feet. *"As I said, only a matter of time."*

Evette stopped squarely between them at the edge of the table. As tiny as she was, she made Kir and Roman look like giants, but she eyed each of them with an applaudable fearlessness. "Am I breaking something up I shouldn't?"

Roman offered her the closest he ever came to a smile and motioned her into the space he'd vacated. "No, *madám*. Please, have a seat."

For a handful of seconds, she studied the place indicated, the two men beside her and all the diners seated behind her. Then, with the same conviction he'd noted during her talk with Dorothy, she squared her shoulders and slid into the space to his right. "Thank you."

"Of course." Roman dipped his head toward Sergei. *"Best of luck, moy brat."*

Kir mirrored the respectful action, but his eyes gleamed with enough mirth to promise he'd be pushing for details later. *"Lucky bastard."* He jerked his head toward the sidewalk and shifted to English. "We'll wait outside."

Sergei ignored the taunt and shifted his attention to Evette as the two of them ambled away. "Miss Labadie. Your visit is unexpected."

"You know my name?"

"You pick up your son here every day after school. You visit Dorothy often on other occasions and sometimes work for her as well. I would be remiss not to ask your godmother for the name of a beautiful woman I see so often."

She pursed her mouth to one side, just enough chagrin and irony to show she had a quick sense of humor. "Dorothy failed to mention you're charming, too."

So, he'd been the topic of their conversation. Interesting. He supposed that also explained the resignation on Dorothy's face before she'd disappeared into the kitchen—his *feya* needed something. Something tangible enough she was willing to tangle with the devil and her godmother hadn't done anything to stop it. "I can be." Calling out his other, more frequently called-upon capabilities wasn't necessary. It hovered between them like a reaper wavering on the wind just waiting for his next assignment.

Evette fidgeted in her seat and slid Roman's abandoned coffee to the edge of the table. "You know, my momma used to work here. Almost from the day Dorothy and her husband opened it." She motioned toward the counter where Emerson still sat, now working on his homework. "I used to sit right where Emerson was while I waited for her to finish up her shift. If I didn't have homework, Dorothy would put me to work filling salt and pepper shakers, restocking the sugar packets or rolling silverware."

She was also an only child and a single mother who lived in a run-down apartment building that Sergei had tried to buy twice in the last three months. Who Emerson's father was, not even Evette knew, but sitting here beside her—hearing her voice and being in such close proximity to her stubborn goodness—his motivation to pay whatever it took to finish the deal went through the roof. "I know this."

Genuine surprise lit her face. "You do?"

"Dorothy is very fond of you. She's shared many things. Including how your mother stood by her through her husband's murder."

A little of the guardedness she'd brought with her to the table slipped and a somberness filled her hazel gaze. She braced her forearms on the table and traced the line of one fingernail with her forefinger. "That was a tough time. It was maybe a month or two after Katrina hit and everyone was on edge. I don't think any of us ever thought it would get so bad someone would get shot for food."

But Dorothy's husband had. Sergei had looked up the details of the shooting himself. An after-hours break-in by a man desperate to feed his family. Dorothy's husband had been the only thing that stood between the shooter and a highly sought-after commodity. "You were fifteen."

The detailed insight caught her attention in a single heartbeat, a street-smart wariness registering in her bright gaze.

Yes, malen'kaya feya. I know all about you.

He didn't have to say it. She felt it and respected the danger it represented.

All the better for both of them. If she had a request, she'd be wise to remember who and what she was dealing with before she made it.

He let the uncomfortable silence settle between them a moment before he prodded her forward. "Was there something you wanted to talk to me about, Miss Labadie?"

She held his stare. Her eyes were expressive. Transparent to the emotions shifting beneath. Fear. Caution. Desperation and hope.

Her gaze slid to Emerson at the counter and when she spoke there was a thread of awe in her angelic voice. "Do you have children?"

An unexpected pain stabbed between his ribs. *"Nyet."*

She faced him. "A wife?"

"Nyet."

"A girlfriend?"

An interesting turn. And for the life of him, he had no idea where she was headed. A woman like Evette wouldn't be interested in a man like him. Not in the way her questioning seemed to indicate. And yet, his physical reaction was instant and eagerly on board with the idea.

His silence or expression must have conveyed the direction of his thoughts, because she straightened and blurted, "I was trying to figure out if you had someone special in your life. Someone you'd go to great lengths for."

Ah, so it was Emerson she was worried about. Now *that* made sense. Anyone watching her interact with her boy would know she'd move a mountain range if it made her son's life better—or stoop to dancing with the devil.

He nodded, thoughts of the woman he considered his sister, Darya, and Anton, the man who'd been more of a father than his own blood, easily coming to mind. "I have a few."

She studied him, her focus narrowed as though gauging the honesty of his answer. Whatever she saw must have been enough to fuel her courage because she swallowed the last of her fear and plowed forward. "Emerson is my everything. The only family I have left."

"Family is, indeed, important." He waited. If she wanted something, she'd have to ask. He already had enough on his conscience to keep him locked in hell for eternity. He wasn't adding her descent to the list.

She went back to tracing her nails, her attention aimed toward the table, yet obviously somewhere else. "The last few years have been hard for him. It was like he went from being a kid to an adult trapped in a kid's body almost overnight. His teachers say it's because he's bored at school. Or underchallenged." She lifted her head and a proud smile curved her lips. "He's smart, my Emerson." The smile slipped. "But he's having a hard time, and the teachers all think if I can get him into the Montessori school over in Uptown it would help him."

As if he'd felt the shift in conversation move to him, Emerson looked up from his books and locked eyes with Sergei.

Pain.

Confusion.

Frustration.

Emptiness. The kind created when a valuable part of a boy's life was missing.

Sergei knew that emptiness. Had walked the same path of pain, frustration and confusion until Yefim had found him and introduced him to Anton. Evette could take him to the finest school in the country and it wouldn't fill the void her son was wrestling. He needed a mentor. A man to lead him and help him model his life.

But that wasn't Sergei's wisdom to share. Especially, when it was a need Evette couldn't fill. "Then perhaps you should give this school an opportunity."

"I want to. I will. In fact, they just had a slot open up on the wait list. The dean says he's got a good shot at qualifying for a scholarship, but I have to front the money for his tuition to hold his place."

"So, you need money to secure the registration." An easy enough request to honor, and one that would prevent her from seeing the ugly side to his life.

"No. No loans. I want help finding a job. A reference or a lead if you have one. And the sooner the better."

Interesting. Of all the times people had come to him and asked for help, not once had an offer of money been turned down.

He leaned forward, somewhat matching her posture with his forearms on the table but with his hands loosely clasped rather than fidgeting as hers were. "A job."

"Yes."

"What kind of job?"

She shifted in the booth so her torso was squared to

his, her leg closest to him slightly cocked and resting on the outside. As if she'd warmed up to a healthy conversation with an innocent man rather than a known entity in the criminal world. "Well, you know I can work in a place like this. At least out front. I've never worked a kitchen, so that would be a hard sell, but I'm good with people. My last job was on a commercial cleaning crew. We worked professional buildings—mostly office spaces. That's worked great since it's day work and I'm off right after Emerson gets out of school. Though, I'm thinking it's going to be hard to get another one if a new employer wants a reference from my old one."

"And why is that?"

"Because they fired me for breach of security."

Everything inside him stilled, his predatory instincts triggered with the same forcefulness he'd have felt if one of his most hated enemies had walked through the diner's door. "Explain."

Evette's eyes narrowed and she cocked her head just a fraction. When she spoke it was with the caution of a woman very aware she'd just tripped some kind of trigger, but wasn't yet sure what that trigger was. "I don't really know. They said my badge was used last Saturday in one of the attorney's offices, but I know that's not right. My badge was at home. Emerson and I only went out a few times on Saturday—to the Farmers Market and to church for a potluck. There's no way it could have been me."

"And you told them this?"

"Of course. But it was my word against a computerized tracking system, so my boss didn't listen."

He'd bet he could make her boss listen.

And suffer.

For a very long time.

But that wouldn't work well for her long term and a tempting, yet dangerous idea was taking shape in his head. An advantageous one for both of them, but pure torture for him.

He reclined against the booth's seat back once more and studied her.

She stared right back, those gold flecks interspersed with green and blue made that much more fascinating by the indomitable spirit firing behind them.

Helping a respected woman like Evette and her son would buy him significant trust, respect and loyalty from the locals. The more loyalty and trust—the faster he'd reach his goals.

A win for her and a win for him.

For that, surely, he could handle a little torture.

Decision reached, he made a mental note to find out the name of the company where she'd worked and the alleged security breach, then snagged a business card from his pocket. He wrote an address on the back of it and slid it across the table. "Be there Monday at nine in the morning."

With an adorable jaunt of her head, she picked up the card and scrutinized the formalized print on the front—a simple reference to Bogatyr Industries with a phone number that went to a call center—before flipping to the back. She frowned and looked up. "They'll help me find a job?"

"No, they'll give you a job."

"But they don't know me."

There it was. The innocence. The goodness miraculously untainted by the hard life she lived. But there was an iron will to her, too. A strength he couldn't help but feel.

If he went through with this—if she accepted the leg up he intended to give her—he'd be beguiled constantly.

But she'd benefit greatly. Perhaps finally find the footing she needed to jump-start the fashion career Dorothy had told him she'd left behind when she'd found herself pregnant with Emerson. He slid out of the booth, straightened his suit coat and buttoned it. "You asked for my help, Miss Labadie. Be at that address at 9 a.m. and you'll get it."

She gaped up at him, her pretty pink lips slightly parted and her eyes wide with wonder. As if she'd just seen a knight ride through the diner on a unicorn. After a few dumbstruck seconds, she shook herself free of her stupor and stood as well. She held out her hand. "Thank you."

Bozhe, but she was tiny. With him at six foot four, the crown of her head barely reached the top of his chest, but with the wonder and genuine gratitude on her face beaming up at him, he felt like a giant.

He took her hand in his, the sheer size of his grip engulfing hers completely.

Pull her closer.

Let her feel your strength.

Show her how safe you can make her.

He shook the unwanted thoughts off and released his hold. "Don't thank me yet, *malen'kaya feya*." He turned and strode toward the door and his men waiting on the street outside.

"Wait."

At the sound of her urgent voice, he halted with the door partway open and faced her.

She hustled to him. "What does that mean? The *feya* thing."

Emerson sat on the barstool, his homework long forgotten in favor of the interaction between Sergei and his mother.

Sergei shifted his gaze to Evette, and for the first time in longer than he could remember, he couldn't fight back a smile. "*Malen'kaya feya* means 'little fairy.'" Not waiting for a response, he nodded to Emerson and walked outside.

His men fell in on either side of him, the three of them headed to the navy blue Alpina BMW parked at the end of the block.

Kir made it until he opened the back door for Sergei before curiosity won out. "Well, what did she want?"

"A job. She needs one by Monday." Sergei slid into the back seat, knowing full well he wouldn't get away with such a vague answer. They'd been together too long to keep secrets. Fought for too many years side by side to take only the bare minimum on answers.

Sure enough, Kir hit him with a follow-up as soon as he hit the driver's seat. "Are you going to find her one?"

"I already did."

Kir looked to Roman.

Roman twisted enough to eyeball Sergei over his shoulder and raised an eyebrow.

"She's experienced in cleaning," Sergei said. "She's competent and trustworthy, so as of Monday morning, she's running my estate."

Chapter Three

Evette double-checked the address on the card, then the number etched on the fancy plaque hung on the wrought iron fence.

Yep. Definitely the right place.

Her gaze drifted back to the massive plantation house towering in front of her. With its white finish and classic round pillars, it was the stereotypical architecture every visitor to New Orleans's Garden District expected, complete with a second-story gallery perfect for sipping mint juleps while the sun went down.

And it was huge.

Gorgeous and staggering in its majestic beauty.

The question was why was she here instead of at a commercial building? Yeah, she'd known the address Sergei had given her was in the Garden District, but until she'd hopped off the Saint Charles streetcar, she hadn't realized the address would lead her to a house.

No, not a house, Evie. A house was for normal people. This thing was a mansion, and a part of her was terrified to even knock on the front door.

She stared up at the massive chandelier hanging over the huge mahogany front door. That door was the only thing that stood between her and a job. She could either stand on the sidewalk gawking like a tourist, or she could pull up her big-girl panties and get on with it.

"Well, the former option ain't gonna take care of my boy," she murmured out loud. She clamped her lips shut and straightened a little taller. *Way to go, Evie. They've probably got cameras pointing right at you. Let 'em see you talking to yourself right out of the chute.*

She strode forward with the same confidence she'd faked since the first day she'd come home from the hospital with Emerson and realized she'd bitten off a whole heck of a lot more than she could chew. There was some serious value in the old *Fake it till you make it* phrase, though. One day at a time and a whole lot of grim determination had helped her make it this far and she wasn't about to turn back now.

She punched the doorbell and a sound similar to a single church bell rang behind the thick door. She gave her outfit a quick once-over—skinny black pants cuffed to her ankles, a pretty cream crocheted tank with a sweetheart neckline and faux pearl buttons down the front, a matching casual blazer with the sleeves rolled to her forearms and snappy but low tan heels. Every bit of it was top-quality stuff she'd picked up over the years at thrift and secondhand shops, but no one else would know it was pre-owned. At least not unless they actually saw where she lived. She'd thought the look would convey her spunky can-do attitude, but considering the looks of the place, she might've done better to go with a traditional suit.

Oh, well.

She was here and, judging by the heavy footsteps

against a hard surface on the other side of the door, it was game time.

The knob turned.

Evie lifted her chin, sucked in a breath and blasted one of her trademark smiles toward the door.

It wavered a second later, the sheer shock of seeing Sergei staring down at her surpassed only by the fact that, for the first time since he'd started coming around the diner a year ago, he was minus his suit jacket.

And holy mother, was he a beautiful sight. Some men needed a suit to make them look powerful, but not Sergei. If anything, the lack of the jacket and the stretch of his fine dress shirt across his broad shoulders only put his prime torso on better display.

Today his shirt was a very pale lavender paired with perfectly tailored gray pants. While he'd always favored suits when she'd seen him before, he seldom wore ties and today was no exception. The look made it tempting as heck for a woman to slide her fingers beneath the crisp fabric to see if he was the fuzzy- or smooth-chested variety.

"Miss Labadie."

The humor in his voice snapped her gaze to his. Had she been staring?

Um, duh. Of course, you were. You always do.

Right. And now her cheeks were on fire and she was gawking all over again. She cleared her throat. "I didn't expect to see you here." She twisted just enough to motion toward the houses lining the block. "Actually, I didn't expect to be here at all. I thought I'd be going to a commercial place."

"A commercial place?"

"Yeah. You know. Like a placement agency or something."

He stepped back, waved her inside and shook his head. Though, with the smirk on his face, she was pretty sure the shake was more about humor and less about rejecting her assumptions. "I'm afraid not."

Wow.

The entrance was everything wonderful about plantation homes. Not so presumptuous as to waste space like some of the McMansions she'd seen online, but exacting enough in their details to make an instant impression. The walls were a comforting buttery yellow and the white baseboards and moldings were at least seven inches tall with details to make a master carpenter preen. A six-inch border of rich hardwoods framed small, octagon-shaped tiles in ivory with details that looked like an old-fashioned cross-stitch worked into the design. "This place is beautiful."

"It is a landmark." Sergei closed the door behind her, then paced forward. "I understand that the renovation kept the details remarkably close to when it was originally built in 1867."

She paused beside a massive painting framed in an ornate gold frame—the same house she'd walked into only moments ago, but set in an entirely different era. Something about it calmed her. As if all the technological advances of the present day were eradicated in a single instant and took the chaos of their instant-access world along with it.

"Come," he said from beside the sweeping staircase beside him. "I'll give you a tour."

Not many things left Evie tongue-tied. Not even some of the fancier houses she'd visited. But the details of this one left her floating. Brought all manner of delightful images of days gone by to mind.

Ornate, crystal chandeliers. Custom-made rugs. Fanciful drapes that covered nine-foot windows and pooled tastefully on the floor. It reminded her of the French palaces she'd looked at online, only with a Creole flair.

"There are seven bedrooms and eight bathrooms," he said as he stepped off the elevator into the kitchen. "All of which will require regular care. The ballroom and the living areas also. There is a groundskeeper and a cook, but you'll coordinate their responsibilities."

She would?

She stopped behind him. "Mr. Petrovyh."

"Sergei."

She nodded. "Sergei." She scanned the rich gray granite countertops paired with all the finest stainless steel appliances. Bit by bit, the fascination that had held her spellbound thus far wavered enough for reason to take a go behind the helm. "Why am I here?"

"I'm showing you the house and sharing my expectations."

The way he said it, there was an undercurrent of *don't be dense*, but for the life of her she couldn't see the huge elephant in the room. "Because..."

He anchored his hands in his pant pockets and cocked his head, challenge pinching the corners of his eyes. "You said you wanted a job, Evette. As of fifteen minutes ago, this estate and everything that goes into running it officially became that job." Not waiting for a response, he turned and strode toward the kitchen's back door. "Come this way and I'll show you the grounds and the pool."

She followed without a single thought, too stunned by his casual declaration to even think about digging in her heels. The second she laid eyes on the backyard, her brain pretty much went kaput and settled for accepting the fact that nothing was going to make sense. At least not until she had a chance to sit and give her mind time to catch up.

Perfectly trimmed hedges formed a classic boundary around a crystal-clear pool, and the grass that stretched along the backyard was golf course worthy. A balustrade delineated the raised stone porch from the winding sandstone path to the pool, and marble statues that were probably imported from Italy accented the many tasteful flower beds featuring everything from crepe myrtles to rosebushes.

Sergei finished the litany of instructions she hadn't heard a word of, planted his hands on his hips and faced her. "Any questions?"

Can you repeat all that?

Particularly the part where I'm running this place?

Probably not the smartest response considering the opportunity on the table. Honesty was good and all, but sometimes a girl just needed time to make heads or tails out of reality. "I have a ton, but they're going to take a little while to take shape."

He jerked a single nod like her answer was not only acceptable, but expected, then turned and headed toward a building to one side of the yard and at the end of the driveway. "Good. Then follow me and we'll cover compensation."

For the briefest of moments, her practical mind perked up for some action, but was quickly knocked aside by curiosity as they neared the detached structure. "What's in here?"

"It's the carriage house." He opened the quaint Dutch door that served as the main entry and motioned her in front of him. "Unlike the main house, the former owner took significant liberties here. It still has the same charm as everything else, but with more modern details."

Gorgeous.

Absolutely gorgeous.

Patina wood floors. Whitewashed walls. Rich hardwood stairs and wrought iron details. All of it accented with state-of-the-art appliances and rustic details. Like a farmhouse that'd butted up against the modern age.

She padded through the open living/kitchen area combo with its soaring ceiling and stopped at the long trestle dining room table with a bench along one side. She glanced up at the two bedrooms off the catwalk that ran overhead. "Who lives here?"

"You do." Sergei picked up a manila envelope from the table and poured out its contents—a small stack of papers clipped at one corner, a thick white envelope, a set of keys and a pen. He picked up the thick envelope and handed it to her. "You'll be given a signing bonus, of course, and time to secure Emerson's school registration this morning. After that, my men will help you move this afternoon."

She'd heard the words. Knew deep down that she really needed to get a grip and start doing her best to process them, but she was having a heck of a time doing more than just staring at the keys in front of her. "I'm supposed to live here?"

"A stipulation of the job. Nonnegotiable."

A place to live.

A really, really freaking nice one.

One where she wouldn't be terrified of Emerson getting killed on the walk home or recruited to join a gang.

Rather than reach for the keys like she was tempted to, she pulled the stack of papers closer.

A contract.

Numbers and details jumped from between the legalese. A thousand dollars a week. Rent and utilities included as part of the package. Three weeks' time off. Insurance provided.

And all that was required was that she see to keeping the house clean and manage all other service providers.

It was amazing.

Exactly the break she needed to give Emerson the life he deserved and get her career back on track.

"Mr. Petrovyh..." She licked her lips and stared down at the contract. Some deals were too good to be true, and she'd be twenty different kinds of foolish if she didn't do her part to find out if this was one of them. She forced her gaze to his. "Whose house is this?"

His grin was that of a wolf. A hungry, cunning and devastatingly handsome wolf. "Mine."

The admission should have terrified her. Should have sent her straight out the door and back to the streetcar that had brought her here.

Instead, it anchored her. Made locks and gears she didn't have a prayer of understanding settle into place.

"Is that a problem, Miss Labadie?"

Working for a Russian mobster.

Living with him.

Well, not *with* him. Not exactly. But close enough one had to wonder what the probability of bullets and kidnapping might be. She slid the contract out from in front of her. "I just didn't… I didn't realize housing was included. Or that I'd be working for you."

He stalked from his side of the table toward the end, then rounded it headed toward her. The way he looked at her with those deep blue eyes, it finally made sense why a predator's prey didn't flee when they could. They were too mesmerized. Too taken in by the hunter's beauty to take action to protect themselves. "I'm a very demanding employer, Miss Labadie. I expect much of those who work for me. In exchange for their skills and their loyalty, I provide excellent compensation. But make no mistake." He slid the contract back in front of her. Tattoos marked the tops of his fingers—odd symbols that made no sense to her—and intricate patterns circled his wrist before disappearing under his shirtsleeves. "This is my world and you will play by my rules."

There it was. A warning and an ultimatum all rolled up into one. The offer was generous. Beyond generous. If she took it, she'd finally have a way out of the never-ending struggles she'd created when she'd lost her way grieving for her mother and found herself pregnant.

But she'd also owe a very dangerous man a significant debt. More than that, she wouldn't just owe the devil. She'd be living with him. And with that, came certain danger. "I have a son. I have to take care of him. I can't…" She swallowed hard, trying to find a way to convey her concerns without insulting him.

No small task when just the thought of what she was considering terrified the living daylights out of her.

Apparently, her fear was written all over her face, because he answered the question anyway. "No harm will come to you. Or Emerson. Those who work for me are untouchable."

Untouchable.

Spoken with absolute confidence.

An unbreakable finality that reverberated through the beautiful space with all the subtly of a judge's gavel.

Logic said he couldn't guarantee such a thing, but looking at the resolution on his hard features and the implacable way he held his formidable body, she imagined even fate gave a second thought before crossing him.

With trembling hands, she picked up the contract and read it, this time forcing herself to absorb every single detail.

Sergei stayed perfectly still. No unspoken or spoken attempts to force her into a decision. Just a patient hunter confident in the trap he'd built.

The signing bonus would give her more than enough to hold Emerson's spot at the school. She'd actually have money left over at the end of each week to save and pay for her own schooling. Emerson would be able to walk to and from school in a safe neighborhood, and she'd have time in the evenings to take more than one class per semester.

A flutter moved through her belly and her arms felt so light they actually tingled.

Hope.

It'd been years since she'd felt it. Had given up believing a chance like this would come her way. But it was here now if she was brave enough to take it.

Dorothy had trusted him and Sergei had lived up to all of his promises. Eradicated the thugs who had overrun her diner and had threatened her safety on a daily basis for years.

Her gaze slid to the pen on the table. No ordinary pen. One of those fancy silver ones that probably cost a hundred dollars or more. She picked it up, the metal against her palm and fingers blissfully cool. The crackle of the papers in the open space as she flipped to the back page and laid the stack down on the table was overloud in the otherwise silent moment. Before she knew it, her signature stared back at her.

Evette Labadie.

Every line elegant and well-practiced. A signature she'd one day vowed would be used to contract big things.

She hadn't been wrong. She just hadn't imagined it would be on a deal that could cost her everything.

Straightening, she flipped the pages back into place and handed them to Sergei.

He took them, his steady perusal that of a contented man who'd just cemented exactly what he wanted. "A wise choice, Miss Labadie." He dipped his head in what felt like a formal rite, but held her gaze as he did so. As soon as he straightened the tense moment was over, replaced with the assumptive confidence he'd had all morning. He turned for the door and strode toward it, giving his first command as her formal employer. "Go. See to your son and his school. You have today to move and my men at your disposal. Tomorrow you begin your regular duties."

Pausing at the open door, he scanned her head to toe, cocked one eyebrow and grinned. "That's a tall order, Miss Labadie. I suggest you get busy."

Chapter Four

Sergei had spent much of his life in the United States. Enough to earn a double major in English and business then on to a master's in business after that, but he'd enjoyed his time in New Orleans by far the most. Russia was a beautiful place, but New Orleans was brimming with life. Rich, flamboyant life. With a half-moon shining down from a cloudless dark sky onto him, Kir and Roman seated around the patio table overlooking the pool, he couldn't help but be pleased with his decision to start his family here.

Cigar smoke drifted up and mingled with the moon's glow. At nearly ten o'clock the temperature was just now reaching eighty.

On October first.

He smiled to himself. If he were in Saint Petersburg right now, the high would have been midfifties at most. A veritable balmy temperature compared with winter when temperatures dipped well below freezing.

To one side of the back courtyard, the lights from upstairs in the carriage house shined bright. The windows on that side of the house were intended more for letting in light than visibility—which was just as well. Spending the morning with Evette and knowing she was only a quick walk from his office had been a challenge. More than he'd anticipated. Especially when she aimed those big, innocent eyes his direction.

He was loath to break the quiet. Even more hesitant to broach the subject that had taken up far too much space in his head all day long. But he needed to know. Needed to find his balance quickly if he had any hope of keeping himself in check going forward. "How did the move go?"

Roman shifted from his contemplative study of the sky to lock stares with Kir.

Kir smirked back at him. An unspoken communication Sergei knew all too well to mean he'd been the topic of much conversation today. Or, more to the point, his steps to bring Evette and Emerson into the family. Kir's gaze shifted to Sergei. "It's good you took action. A woman such as her should not be living in a hovel like that."

"Moving her was easy," Roman added. "Limited belongings."

An unwelcome itch of irritation sparked beneath his skin. "Explain."

"Only enough dishes for the two of them. One small couch. A few lamps. Two twin beds. Some clothes." Roman shrugged. "We got it all in one trip and didn't fill up half the truck."

"She's got taste, though," Kir said. "She might not have much, but the place was clean. Comfortable."

Not surprising. Nothing she ever wore when she picked Emerson up at the diner was over the top, but she always had a stylish air about her. It made sense that her love of fashion and practicality would extend to the home she kept. "Any spectators?"

Kir's mouth curved in a sly grin. "*Da.* The move was easy, but we took our time. Took a large moving truck and made a show of it."

Excellent. That meant word would spread that much faster. "And the school?"

"The boy's place is secured," Roman said. "The administrator was uncomfortable not telling Miss Labadie that your payment in full was one of their scholarships, but we overcame that obstacle. Emerson starts next week."

"I assume the obstacle was overcome with an additional donation?"

"A charitable contribution to the new gymnasium they're building."

Sergei nodded, not surprised the administrator had managed to wrangle additional funds out of the deal. If it made them feel better about the arrangement, he'd work with it. He'd also use it to his advantage later.

Roman's gaze cut to the carriage house and his voice dropped to an even lower pitch. "The boy is quiet. Observant." He shifted his attention to Sergei. "He is like us."

He'd seen it, too. Felt the intensity and wisdom burning behind the boy's eyes. He might be only seven, but he had an old soul who'd already seen too much. Perhaps when he realized that there were now other adults ready and able to look after his mother, he could find his way back to being a child again. "Shield him anyway. When he's grown, he'll make his choices, but for now he stays innocent."

He tapped the ashes from the tip of his cigar and zeroed in on Kir. Where Roman handled the muscle and execution of their plans, it was Kir who saw to security and intelligence, including technology. "What did you find on her old job?"

"Their claim was valid. Her badge was used to access the building after hours. If it wasn't her, then someone else had access to her badge."

"Close enough access to return it to her before work the following Monday," Roman added.

"Someone in her apartment building?" Sergei asked. "Friends?"

Kir made a circular motion with his cigar before he took a casual drag from it and sent the smoke from it airborne. "Everyone is a friend of Miss Labadie. Every tenant. Every person on the block. No one is a stranger."

A good thing when it came to earning the trust of the locals by taking her in, but a haystack when trying to find who might have had direct access to her home. Regardless, she was safe now. And, going forward, no one would get close to her without him or his men knowing about it. "I want guards on them. Neither leave the grounds without a man. Nothing overbearing, but enough to protect and send an unmistakable message."

Kir and Roman traded a long stare loaded with echoes of conversations Sergei hadn't been privy to. It was Roman who broke it first and looked to Sergei. "What kind of message are we sending, *moy brat*?"

A respectfully delivered jab against Sergei's motivations, but a jab nonetheless. Much as he hated to admit it, his brothers had good reason to be concerned. If his intent was truly just to win favor within the neighborhood by giving Evette a break, he could have done so with far more distance.

But he didn't want distance. He wanted the sun to shine on his dark life. To see and feel its presence even if it never shone directly on him. "I am following my instincts, and my instincts say that she and Emerson belong here." It was as close to the truth as he could get. At least as close as he could admit out loud.

"None of your other employees have guards." Like Roman, Kir took pains to deliver his words with the utmost care, but there was still unbreakable iron behind them. "If you take this route, you'll mark them both. You're claiming them whether you admit it or not. In our world, that's dangerous. It creates risk for them and liabilities for us."

He knew this. And yet, he could muster no resolve to change his course. He stared up at the windows high on the carriage house and the same certainty he'd felt the day Yefim introduced him to his mentor and father figure, Anton, settled in his gut. "They are protected. They are family." He looked to Kir, then to Roman. "And if anyone touches them, they die."

Chapter Five

Evette turned off the fancy stainless steel kitchen faucet, stared at it and waited.

No drip.

Neither of the bathtub stoppers leaked either, a fact she still had a hard time adjusting to after a solid week of living in Sergei's carriage house. Equally sweet was the fact that she and Emerson both had their own bathtub. And hers was one of those big ones with jets that were like heaven after a day of working and kept the water warm.

Two small perks on top of a host of other luxuries that shouldn't mean as much as they did, but felt like a lottery win all the same. And as of today, Emerson wouldn't be walking through dangerous areas to go to school anymore. The question that remained was if the price for so many blessings would be worth it. Sure, the accommodations were beyond anything she'd ever had before, but with them came guards. Lots of them. Some stationed around the estate and at least one or two who followed her and Emerson anytime they went anywhere—no matter how many times she tried to convince them to do otherwise. Never once did they overstep or get in her or Emerson's way, but they were a constant presence that reminded her of the world she now moved within.

Outside the kitchen window, the view wasn't much. Just a tiny courtyard framed in by tall Italian cypress trees and accented with well-tended hibiscus bushes that would no doubt be beautiful in late spring and summer. But holy cow, was it nice to go and sit on the Adirondack chairs on the pleasant nights they'd been having. Never in her life had she had such a luxury. And with the early morning sun just lightening the sky, it was tempting to go and steal a little slice of quiet just for herself. But it was Emerson's first day of school and she wasn't about to risk their being late.

She wiped her hands on one of the kitchen towels that had been delivered along with a whole host of other kitchenware and gadgets the day after she'd moved in and shouted up the stairs. "Emerson, you up?"

"Yes."

Ugh. One word but the tone of it said he was still in a foul mood. He'd acted curious—even a little hopeful—when he'd learned of her new job and seen the living quarters that came with it, but the second he'd learned he'd be moving to a new school, he'd clammed up tighter than a love-struck woman who'd lost her crush to her best friend.

Maybe she could bribe him into a good mood with food. "You want anything special for your big day?"

"Yeah, how about I go to my old school?"

"Not gonna happen, big man. The teachers all agreed this place was perfect for you."

He strode into view, the basic tan pants and maroon button-down required for all male students making him look even more like a grown-up stuck in a kid's body. Slinging his backpack over one shoulder, he stomped down the stairs. "Easy for them to say. They're not the one having to start all over and make new friends."

Except Emerson didn't have any friends. Never talked about anyone, never went to anyone's home or invited anyone over. That'd been another thing his teachers had been watchful of. Her boy just couldn't seem to tolerate other kids his age. He was usually more inclined to have conversations with the teaching staff. "Well, if anyone can start fresh and do it up right, it's you." She waited until he was at the bottom of the stairs, slung an arm around his shoulder and pulled him in for one of those awkward walking hugs boys always seemed to hate. "You never know, kiddo. This could be the beginning of big things for you."

Emerson's gaze slid to the window that looked out toward the main driveway and his expression shifted, an alertness and inquisitiveness more in line with what she'd expect for a seven-year-old boy shifting his features. "Maybe for both of us."

Hmm.

Interesting.

Sullen Emerson she was used to. Crabby Emerson she could tolerate. But Mischievous Emerson would be an absolute delight. She opened the pantry door, scanned the contents—also stocked without any request from her a day after they'd moved in. "What are you looking at?"

Emerson's attention cut to her, his unreadable expression back in place. "Nothing."

Lie.

She dipped her chin and gave him that trademark don't-you-mess-with-me look her momma used to use on her. "You know there's a built-in lie detector feature that's triggered in a woman the minute they give birth. Doesn't matter how a kid tries to outmaneuver it, we always know the truth."

Emerson's eyes crinkled at the corners and, holy Mother of God, was that a smile? Not one big enough to show teeth or anything, but definitely a marked lift of his lips and tweaked with some sass.

She gripped the pantry door's handle a little tighter, soaked up the moment and went for broke. "Now are you done pullin' my leg? 'Cause we got breakfast to eat before it's time to skedaddle for school."

"I'm done." He ducked his head and pretended to look for something in his backpack, but that grin was still there.

"Good, then what's it going to be? Lucky Charms, Pop-Tarts or Froot Loops?"

"Mom, you know those are all loaded in sugar."

God help her. How many mothers had to try to talk their kids into eating junk food? "Yeah, I know it. I also know if you don't enjoy eating pure sugar now, you'll miss out on it entirely. So, which one?"

Emerson shrugged. "Lucky Charms, I guess."

Evette grabbed the monster-size box and a bowl and got to work on the pouring. "Good choice. After all, they're magically delicious."

The chuckle that sounded from the farmhouse-styled table nearly made her slosh the milk all over the countertop.

A smile *and* laughter.

Neither huge, but a step in the right direction.

And the answer to the question that had kept her up way too late every single night for the last week. Gambling on Sergei Petrovyh was totally worth it. Especially if it meant lifting her boy out of the dark place he'd been.

Breakfast done and dishes tucked into the dishwasher—an appliance that was not only a novelty to have, but was also astonishingly quiet when it ran—Evette picked up her purse and tugged on a light sweater to combat the morning's chill. "Come on, champ. Let's get this new adventure underway."

He scowled and grumbled something she knew would piss her off if she tried to sort the meaning of, so she ignored it and waited for him at the front door.

The three men who'd taken turns walking her and Emerson everywhere the last week stood roughly ten feet beyond her doorway. It had taken some adjustment having someone always on her heels, but given whom she worked for, she'd rationalized and even come to appreciate the safety precaution. What she hadn't expected to see this morning was Sergei standing beside his badass BMW talking with Kir and Roman and looking as fine as ever. Today, his gray suit was paired with a crisp white shirt and his longish hair was pulled back in a ponytail. Part biker and part executive, all wrapped up in a killer mob boss attitude.

She felt Emerson move in beside her a second before he spoke. "You know he knows when you watch him, right?"

The kid was way too perceptive for his age. She'd be wise to remember that and keep her ogling eyeballs to herself. "Can't blame a woman for appreciating a fine man. One of these days when you're all grown up and loaded down with swagger, a woman's gonna give you the once-over and you'll agree with me."

"Hmph."

"Hmph," she mimicked back and opened the door. "Let's do this."

Ignoring Sergei completely, she breezed right past her guards. "Starting a new school today, guys. All good terrain between here and there, so we're good."

After the repeated arguments they'd given her through most of last week, she expected at least a little lip in response. Instead they stayed where they were.

Emerson called back to them, "See ya, Tony. Bye, Reggie. Bye, Mikey."

At the sound of his familiar, almost chipper goodbyes, Evie nearly tripped looking back at her son.

Emerson hitched his backpack higher on his shoulder. "What?"

She shook her head and turned back to watch where she was going—and stopped one step before colliding with Sergei. She held up her hands and staggered backward. "Oh, hey." She glanced at Kir and Roman just slightly behind him on either side. "We're just on our way to school."

"Indeed." Sergei motioned toward the rear door of the BMW. "But you're not walking."

Silent as ever, Mikey moved in behind her and opened the door wide.

While she'd had plenty of opportunities to appreciate the exterior of the high-priced sedan—one Emerson had taken great pains to educate her as being an Alpina and the most prestigious of the BMW lineup—she'd never seen the inside. It was equally impressive. Pale tan leather stretched over plush seats accented by gleaming dark wood. TV screens were embedded in the two front seat backs, and every inch of the insides was showroom ready.

She straightened from her obvious perusal and faced Sergei. "We don't need to drive. It's a nice neighborhood and the weather's good. We can walk."

"You will ride."

"Mr. Petrovyh, that's not necessary."

He cocked one eyebrow.

"Sergei," she corrected. "Really. We're good walking. It's healthy."

"Perhaps another day." He prowled one step closer and lowered his voice. "My domain, Miss Labadie. My rules."

Part of her wanted to plant her hands on her hips and give him a piece of her mind about his high-handed tactics. The more reasonable part of her knew when to pick her battles and digging in her heels in front of Emerson probably wasn't the place to do it. So, she lifted her chin and waved Emerson into the back seat. As soon as Emerson began to crawl inside, she whisper-scolded over her shoulder. "Why do I have to call you by your first name if you call me by my last?"

She didn't really expect an answer. Just wanted to get a dig in before she followed her son into the back seat. She definitely didn't expect Sergei to stall her entry with an arm around her middle, the feel of his big body along her back and his low, heavily accented voice in her ear. "Because, *malen'kaya feya*, I like the sound of my name on your lips."

His touch was gone as fast as he'd moved in, his towering body a polite yet steady presence behind her.

But the impact of his touch and his message still rattled through every inch of her.

She braced one hand on the top of the car, torn between looking back at him to see if she'd imagined the whole thing and hiding inside the vehicle.

Truly, she was a glutton for punishment, because she craned her head just enough to glimpse his face.

Nope. She hadn't imagined it. The smirk was too prominent, the look of a man extremely pleased not only with his actions, but the response he'd won.

Heat blasted across her cheeks and she ducked inside, her normally fluid movements so shaky she nearly whacked her head on the top of the car doing it. She smoothed her hands over her jean-covered thighs and let out a shaky exhale.

He's just messing with you. Nothing to read into it. Just blow it off and get on with your day.

Without a word of warning, Sergei slid in next to her, forcing her to the center of the wide leather seat.

The door slammed shut and the two front doors opened. Mikey got behind the wheel and Roman took the front passenger seat, neither man sparing them so much as a backward glance.

"What are you doing?" she snapped a little too sharply to Sergei.

Unruffled as ever, he merely crossed one leg over the other as only a luxury sedan would allow in a back seat. "I would think it's obvious, Miss Labadie. I'm going with you."

"I don't need help taking my son to school."

"Of course you don't. But you did say it's an exceptional school and I'm a staunch supporter of education.

It's also a part of the neighborhood in which I live, so I'd like to familiarize myself with it."

The car started down the drive. "You're a supporter of education?"

His lips twitched, but he kept his gaze trained out the front windshield. "I have a double major in English and business. I also have a master's in business. So, yes. I'm a firm believer in scholarly pursuits."

On her right, Emerson chuckled.

Two chuckles, a smile and sassy behavior from her son, and what she could only perceive as a seriously sexy come-on from her deadly boss—all before eight o'clock in the morning. At this rate she was going to need wine and a nap before noon.

Emerson leaned forward enough to look at Sergei. "Why an English major?"

"Because I enjoy literature."

"Hmm. Makes sense." With a nod, her son slid back in his seat. "Mom likes it, too. Especially the quote, *Most men lead lives of quiet desperation and go to the grave with the song still in their heart.* That's why she named me Emerson."

Sergei cocked his head ever so slightly, his gaze shifting to the seat back in front of Emerson. "That quote is Henry David Thoreau."

"Right, but she said Henry and David were too plain, and Thoreau for a first name is awful, so she went with Thoreau's mentor, Emerson."

An expression she'd never seen before moved across Sergei's face. Thoughtful. Surprised. Maybe even a little moved. His gaze slid to hers. "You are a fascinating woman, Miss Labadie."

"Dorothy says she's a handful," Emerson said.

And now her son had turned into a Chatty Cathy. With Sergei Petrovyh.

What the heck was going on?

Sergei's mouth didn't move, but the way his eyes gleamed down at her before he turned and stared out the front window again, Evie would have bet good money he was laughing on the inside. "I don't doubt that for a moment."

The rest of the drive passed in silence, save for the barely detectable drone of the car's tires against the pavement and the clang of the Saint Charles streetcar as it went trundling by.

It was weird living in this part of the city. Where the parts of town she'd grown up in were nearly always bustling with some kind of noise or activity, the rows of nineteenth-century homes with their wrought iron fences and mature trees casting thick shade on the streets below seemed perpetually peaceful. Like the quiet magnificence of the plantations that had once stretched across the area still held everyone now living upon their soil under a genteel spell.

Ahead, the prestigious facade of Emerson's new school crept into view, the ten-foot iron fence that lined the massive front courtyard and the row of oak trees in front of it standing guard against the rest of the world. The wide double gate stood open and Mikey turned into the circle drive with its perfectly maintained hedges.

The architecture was beautiful, a mix of Old English charm and Deep South flair. The entire first floor of the U-shaped structure had covered patios held aloft by white pillars, where the top two floors put its soft tan brick and maroon shutters on display. Even Emerson, who'd avidly absorbed every detail the day she'd enrolled him, seemed spellbound all over again, his wide eyes locked on the angelic statue with its arms opened wide and welcoming above the main entrance.

Before she could say anything to nudge Emerson out of his concentrated focus on the angel, Roman was out of his seat and had the back door open.

Emerson's gaze snapped to the students slowly making their way into the building, the vast majority of them avidly studying the obvious newcomer with the fancy wheels. By the time Emerson slid out of his seat and had taken two steps away from the door, Sergei was already out and offering his hand to help Evie out.

Evie frowned up at him. "What are you up to?"

He cocked his head and concocted an innocent look. "I'm giving my employee and her son a ride to school on his first day and demonstrating interest in my neighborhood. What else would I be doing?"

She showed him her own version of an arrogantly raised eyebrow, ignored his outstretched hand and pried her way out of the sedan. "I don't buy it." She straightened and marched toward Emerson waiting with Roman at the edge of the drive. "A man like you doesn't do anything without more than one purpose. I just haven't figured out what all of yours are yet."

She'd meant to say it under her breath, but it must have carried farther than she'd meant because both Roman and Emerson averted their faces.

Not before she'd caught them grinning, though.

Too much testosterone. That had to be the problem. *Note to self: Hire more women.*

After all, Sergei had said she was in charge. She

might as well take advantage and hire an all-female staff to even out the hormonal balance.

The rest of the school grounds were as fabulous as the exterior. Marble floors, arched cathedral ceilings in the chapel with exceptionally detailed molding and statues tastefully placed amid meticulous landscaping. In a nutshell—lots of history and some seriously old money.

She walked up to the office desk, Emerson beside her. While she tried to pretend Sergei and his men weren't there at all, she had to admit, their impenetrable presence behind her gave her own nerves a little extra courage. "Hello, I'm Evette Labadie and this is my son, Emerson."

A woman in a classic navy blue suit came striding out of her corner office. "Miss Labadie, how nice to see you."

Interesting. Evie had never seen this woman in her life, and there was no way she'd have forgotten anyone with such enviable strawberry blonde hair. Though, if she had that color hair, she'd have sure done more with it than pin it up in a French twist. Yeah, it was a classic style, but classics were better for evening gowns and cocktail parties.

Evie held out her hand. "I don't think we've met."

The woman shook it—not too soft and not a manly grip either. Which was nice because Evie hated either. "I'm Dean Benedict, but you can call me Caroline. We're so very glad to have Emerson joining our school." She glanced at the office door behind her and her smile grew wider. "And this is Emerson's homeroom teacher, Maddie Smith."

In a swirl of greetings and handshakes, Evie and

Emerson were out the door and headed to his classroom. Sergei and his men didn't follow, and oddly, she was mildly disappointed by the development.

Miss Smith proved to be a bright, energetic woman who clearly loved working with kids.

Emerson was polite, yet reserved, all of the casual humor he'd shown on the ride over stuffed back under the mask he'd worn for the last two years.

With a quick wave she hoped wouldn't embarrass him too much, Evie said goodbye to the teacher and stepped out into the now quiet hallway. Her pale blue Keds whisper-squeaked against the marble floors on the way back to the office, and for the first time since Sergei had stepped into her path this morning, her heart settled into a calm rhythm.

First day down.

Now if she could just keep her worrying to a minimum between now and when she picked Emerson up this afternoon...

Her thought died off at the sight of Sergei through the wide windows surrounding the main office. The dean, both ladies who'd manned the front desk and a man dressed in a security uniform formed a loose arc around him. The ladies were, not surprisingly, sporting dazed looks appropriate for love-struck women everywhere. The man had his thumbs tucked in his utility belt and his shoulders pushed back.

He's not interested in school. He's interested in making a point. A very strong, and unmistakable point.

That was why the dean was there to greet her. Why all of Emerson's paperwork had already been processed and his teacher personally came down to escort him to his classroom.

Standing there dumbfounded outside the window, she couldn't decide if she was happy for the protective statement, or madder than hell for the troubles it might cause her son if other kids picked up on it.

Maybe both.

Sergei turned and their gazes locked.

Quick to pick up the loss of his attention, Dean Benedict followed his line of sight, beamed a delighted smile at Evette and quickly hustled her way.

The goodbyes were brief and essentially a repeat of the greeting she'd been given.

Happy to have you and your son with us.

Always here if you need us.

Anything you need at all, just call or come by.

All of them snippets of conversation intermingled with vigorous handshakes and a personal escort back to the circle drive and Sergei's waiting car.

Evette barely caught any of it. She was too aware of Sergei's presence tight at her back. Particularly when he rested a possessive arm around Evie's shoulders and shook the dean's hand himself. "It appears you run a fine school, Ms. Benedict." His sharp focus cut to the security guard who'd stepped outside with them and waited on the entrance steps, then back to the dean. "It's good to know Emerson will be in a place where safety and education are the primary focus."

Dean Benedict noted Sergei's hand resting on Evie's shoulder and the already megawatt smile on the dean's face grew brighter. "Oh, yes. A safe environment is critical for quality education. You can rest assured our students are protected at all times."

"Good." Sergei's hand slid down Evette's spine and rested low on her back, scattering what was left of her wits. "Now, we'll let you get back to your duties. Thank you for welcoming us today."

"Of course. We're delighted to do so."

Getting into the car was a blur, Sergei's lingering touch up until the last possible moment seeping into her bloodstream as effectively as an opiate. When he slid into the back seat beside her, he was still close. So close her body practically begged her to scoot the few inches between their thighs and make contact.

It took a few blocks and several steady breaths for her to even out and find her voice. "What's going on?"

Silence stretched long and dense between them before he spoke. "I told you, Miss Labadie. Those inside my domain are untouchable. I find it better to communicate my expectations early and clearly so that there are no assumptions or opportunities for misinterpretation."

So, she'd been right. He was sending a message. She just wasn't sure what kind of message he'd given. "I put on my application that I work for you."

"And she knows that this is true as I confirmed it today." He paused long enough to look from the windshield to her. "But I also made it clear that I consider you and Emerson family, and as such, are under my protection."

Family.

That was all the contact and posturing meant. A physical show intended for her and Emerson's safety. Nothing more, and nothing less.

And yet the word struck a powerful chord inside her. A song filled with more reverberation than she'd felt in a very long time. Aside from her chats with Dorothy and a smattering of uninvited drive-bys from her uncle, it'd been only her and Emerson for years. Before that it had been only her and her mother, the two of them grieving her father's untimely death in a driving accident when she was fifteen.

She held his steady gaze, the depth of the blue irises just as mysterious and decadent as a moonlit midnight sky. Yes, he was a predator. A wolf barely contained by the human confines of flesh. But she sensed something else beneath as well.

A lost soul.

One aching like everyone else.

The buzz of her phone in her back pocket jolted her from her thoughts. Shrugging off Sergei's stare, she retrieved it and thumbed in her code.

Uncle Carl: Where are you? Just went by your house and your landlord said you moved out. You can't just move and not tell your family where you are.

Um, yeah, she could. And if she could manage it, she was gonna stretch the time before her uncle actually paid her a visit out as long as possible. She'd never been comfortable around him and, while Emerson never said as much, she was pretty sure he felt the same. But a visit where Uncle Carl might run into Sergei?

She shuddered and typed out a response.

Yep. Just haven't had time to text. Can't talk. At work. Will send info later.

Not exactly a long-term fix, but she figured she could "forget" to send any follow-up info for a day or two. That would give her enough time to come up with a better reason to keep him at a distance.

She tucked her phone back in her pocket and glanced up to find Sergei scowling down at her.

"Everything all right, *feya*?"

Well, it was better when he wasn't talking like that within touching distance. Really, the man had no idea how a rumbling deep voice affected a woman. "I'm fine." She made a show of casually taking in the scenery floating by her window. "Just family stuff."

While she couldn't see him directly with her feigned perusal of the neighborhood, she could sure feel his eyes on her.

"Miss Labadie." He didn't say anything else, which meant he was waiting on eye contact before he said anything more.

She inhaled deep, lifted her chin and gave him what he wanted with raised eyebrows.

"Remember what I told you," he said. "Those who work for me are untouchable. If someone should cause you any concern, I expect you to share that concern with me at once."

Whoa, boy. Definitely not a good idea to let Carl cross paths with Sergei anytime soon. If she was having a hard time hiding how uncomfortable her uncle made her feel via text, it'd be impossible to conceal it in person. And she had a feeling Sergei saw everything that went down on his turf.

She nodded, crossed her arms with as much sass as she could manage—which was a lot—and resolutely stared out the window. "Crystal clear, Mr. Petrovyh. Crystal clear, indeed."

Chapter Six

He should be working. Should be out and visible on the streets working the deals he had cooking through every means possible. And he would.

Eventually.

But right now, the security feed from the kitchen displayed on Sergei's monitor was simply too entertaining to walk away from. He nudged his computer volume a little higher.

"Really?" Evette looked up from the grocery list Olga had handed her only seconds before and aimed the hefty woman a flabbergasted look. "You expect me to go to the most expensive grocery in town to get things I could buy at somewhere else for less?"

Olga wasn't the least bit intimidated. Didn't even glance away from whatever she was stirring on the stove. And from the lack of passion in her thick Russian accent, she wasn't anywhere close to budging on Evette's tirade. "It is where best ingredients can be found, so it is where I want them from."

"But it's a waste of money."

Olga shrugged. "It is not my money, but it is my food."

Evette straightened to the top of her five-foot-two

body and jammed her hands on her hips. "No, it's *Sergei's* money and it's my job to make sure his house is being run efficiently. That includes how his money is spent."

Olga froze, waited all of a heartbeat, then tapped her wooden spoon on the edge of the pot and sat it gently aside. She faced Evette slowly, an unflinching determination pinching her hard, wrinkled features. Since she was six feet tall with a body as stout as a barrel of Scotch, the move and expression would have made some of his more seasoned men take a cautious step backward.

But not Evette.

She just stood there, as resolute as ever, and matched Olga's glower.

"My *pakhan* will not eat cheap food," Olga said.

"And I'm not asking him to. You can get all of this at the Farmers Market on Thursday at almost half the price."

"I don't need the items Thursday. I need them today."

"Then change your menu."

"No." Olga hmmphed and turned back to her stove. "You get the ingredients, or you talk to the *pakhan*. I will not."

Well played, my old friend. With a simple sentence, the crafty woman had gotten her way because—if the last few weeks were any indication—hell would freeze over before Evette willingly sought him out.

What he couldn't decide, though, was whether he was relieved or irritated that someone other than himself had noticed her evasive behavior.

Clearly, Evette wasn't pleased with the outcome of

her head-to-head with Olga because the hands at her hips ended up fisted at her side for all of two seconds before she marched out of the kitchen.

Chuckling, Sergei muted the volume and sat back in his chair tracking her progress through the house via the cameras. Of all the people who worked his estate—his soldiers included—Olga was the only one not eating out of Evette's hand. On the other hand, he was the only one who couldn't gain her attention.

Perhaps he'd pushed her too far on Emerson's first day. Frightened her with his touch. After all, she was an angel and he was the devil. Two sides of the spectrum fated never to meet.

But a man can dream.

Loaded up with a case of cleaning supplies, Evette shut the storage door behind the kitchen just a little more forcefully than normal and hustled down the main hallway and up the main stairs, then hung a right—headed directly toward his office.

He barely had time to straighten from his casual observation and get his hands on the keyboard before she stormed into view.

She stopped dead in her tracks, then staggered back two steps. "Oh. Sorry. I thought you were out with your guys. I'll come back later."

His pulse thrummed stronger at his throat. An irritating response that nearly allowed him to hold his silence. A challenge leapt from his tongue instead. "And why would you do that?"

Ah, there it was. His tenacious *feya* digging in her heels and bracing to prove herself. The woman truly had the most indomitable spirit. It called to him. Dared him to push her just a little more.

"I am here. You are here." He motioned to the leather couches and chairs arranged in comfortable seating areas around the wide room in front of him. "There is nothing to stop you. Is there?"

One second. One infinitesimal speck of time that he'd have missed if he'd blinked.

But he hadn't. And in that raw moment he glimpsed the unexpected.

Hunger.

Maybe not the raw animalistic kind that had drawn him one too many nights to the patio where he stared at the carriage house windows and remembered the press of her body when he'd pulled her close. The subtle scent of an exotic flower against the skin at her neck when he'd whispered in her ear. The shudder it had drawn in response.

But there was something there.

Maybe she wasn't frightened.

Maybe his angel wanted a dance with the devil.

His pulse deepened. Pounded with the same determined anticipation that came before a confrontation. "Miss Labadie?"

She cleared her throat, strode to one of the floor-to-ceiling shelves full of classic books and sat her cleaning supplies on the floor beside the coffee table. "I didn't want to disturb you, but if you're okay with me being here, then I'll get on with my business."

It was good she was too intent on demonstrating her indifference by turning and dusting the shelves. Otherwise, she'd have caught his quick smile. Even before he'd laid eyes on her, Dorothy had called her a firecracker. He'd seen glimpses of it for himself watching her traipse in and out of the diner over the last year, but in the three weeks since she'd come to work for him, he'd seen loads of it.

He forced himself to focus on his screen. Even managed to read the first few lines of a business contract.

And then his gaze drifted over the top of his monitors.

Evette's back was still to him. Her jeans were simple—no fancy embellishments like some women liked to wear, but the hem was rolled up a little past her ankles and the cut accented her ass and hips perfectly. The pale pink tank she wore accented her toned arms well-accustomed to regular labor. With her hair as short as it was, the curve of her neck was perfectly exposed, a delicious stretch of skin he'd often fantasized of tasting for himself.

She stopped, pulled her phone from her back pocket and checked the screen.

Sergei shifted his gaze back to his monitors, but caught her glancing at him in his periphery.

She typed out a message, tucked the phone back in her pocket and went back to work.

A few moments later, the whole process repeated. Then again, each text preceded by a quick check of what he was doing.

The smart thing to do was ignore it. To dodge temptation altogether. But he liked tangling with Evette. More than he cared to admit. "Is there something wrong, Miss Labadie?"

She looked up from the coffee table she'd just sprayed with some citrus-scented solution and paused mid-wipedown. "Excuse me?"

"Your phone. You've checked it three times now. Is there something you need to see to?"

A sheepish expression blanketed her face a second before she averted it and started wiping the surface down again. "It's nothing."

Bullshit. If it was nothing, she'd have ignored the conversation entirely and damned sure wouldn't have looked away so quickly when he'd asked about what was going on. While she didn't seem nearly as concerned as when she'd received the text message in the car two weeks ago, she was still antsy. And while he hadn't caught who it was that had texted her that day, he'd glimpsed the phrase *Where are you?* clearly enough. If his *feya* had some reason she didn't want to be found, he needed to know. "I've made it clear on two occasions I don't like it when those under my protection have concerns of any nature. Are you sure there isn't anything you wish to share with me?"

She threw down her rag, straightened and planted her hands back on her hips as she had with Olga. "No, Mr. Petrovyh. I don't. Not unless you plan to terrorize my kid or his teachers for having homework."

Normally, nothing shocked him, but the surprising topic caught him completely off guard and he was certain his face showed it. "Homework?"

"Yeah, you know. That annoying stuff every person thinks they've left behind when they graduate from school, but learn they get to do it all over again when they have kids?" She frowned, grabbed the spray she'd used before and doused the end table next to a beautifully upholstered leather wingback. "This school might be the sweetest thing since sliced bread, but they don't scrimp on homework."

Tempting as it was to smile at her sass, he kept it

in check and refocused on his computer. "No, I don't imagine they do."

Silence settled in the room, broken only by Evette's brisk cleaning and sporadic clicks from his keyboard when he typed. Her phone stayed in her back pocket, but given the periodic scowls on her face, he'd bet Emerson hadn't slowed on his text messages.

It made sense, actually. The boy might be mature for his age, but patience in a seven-year-old wasn't exactly the norm.

Sergei closed his document, locked his computer and stood. "I have something to take care of."

Rather than answer, Evette simply nodded and kept moving, avoiding eye contact.

Down the stairs, through the hallway and kitchen and a direct trek across the backyard, and he was where he needed to be. He knocked on the main door to the carriage house.

It opened all of ten seconds later, and from the surprise on Emerson's face, Sergei had been the last person he'd expected to find on the opposite side.

"Hey," Emerson said, then shook himself and straightened as tall as his little body would allow. "I mean, hello, Mr. Petrovyh."

"You're doing homework?"

Emerson's eyebrows pinched inward to form a sharp V. "Yes, sir."

"What kind?"

"Math."

"You're having a hard time with it?"

The boy's mouth twisted to one side, the truth clearly distasteful on his tongue. "The teacher said my class is probably a grade or two faster than my old school. I've got some catching up to do."

No complaining. No whining. Just a simple statement of fact. Sergei stepped back and waved Emerson toward the main house. "Come. You'll show me what you're working on and I'll help you until your mother is done."

The boy's eyes narrowed, wariness dancing behind eyes the exact same color as his mother's. "You will?"

Sergei nodded. And waited.

Emerson glanced at the kitchen table where his book sat open next to a three-ring binder, then over to the main house. "Do you have cookies?"

"Olga always has tea cakes."

"Tea cakes?"

"A Russian favorite and better than cookies. Lots of sugar and walnuts."

Emerson didn't look like he was buying it, but at least took the time to consider his options. "Mom hasn't taken me in the big house. She says it's a place where she works. Not a place to look around."

"Yes, but the *big house* is mine. If I invite you, then you're my guest."

With only a few more seconds of hesitation, Emerson shrugged, collected his books, then pulled the door shut behind them. "Okay, let's go."

He thought it might be awkward working with a child, but Emerson was easy to interact with and relate to. Especially once Olga laid eyes on him and started plying him with Russian sweets.

The homework was done no more than forty-five minutes later.

"So," Sergei said, dusting the confectioner's sugar off his fingers from his own tea cake, "how is school?"

"Good," Emerson said around a mouthful. "Haven't really made any friends yet. Expect one kid. He's in my class. Really shy and quiet, but nice. Otherwise, I'm just playing catch-up."

"Things will change." At least Sergei hoped they did. His younger years hadn't exactly been teeming with friends. Most of the boys around him either gave him grief and said he had a leg up only because of Anton, or maintained a feigned relationship with Sergei *because* of Anton. Very few did he consider real allies. "In time, you will adjust and meet new people."

The quick traipse of soft-soled shoes on the hardwood floors sounded only a moment before Evette came sailing into the kitchen. Her head was down, her case of cleaning supplies hanging on one forearm and her thumbs texting rapid-fire on her screen. She was well into the room before she realized she wasn't alone, and her head snapped up.

One glimpse at Emerson and she halted on a dime. "Baby, you haven't been answering my texts." She frowned and glanced at Sergei and Olga. "And why are you here? I told you this was Mr. Petrovyh's home."

"He invited me."

Her head snapped backward as though she'd been slapped, and she blinked with all the vigor of a person who'd just been thrown into the daylight after days in the dark. "He did?"

"Mmm-hmm."

She looked to Sergei. "You did?"

"Indeed."

"Why?"

"He helped me with my homework." Emerson slid his three-ring binder to the empty space at the table beside him. "Check it out. The Russian knows math."

Olga chuckled and murmured in Russian, *"The Russian. I like it. The boy's got balls, just like his mother."*

Sergei held back his smile, but only barely. He'd suspected Olga's stubbornness with Evette was more for show than the territorial play it appeared to be on the outside, but with that little quip, she'd confirmed it.

Evette sidled up to the pub-height table and studied her boy's homework. Once satisfied, she shut the folder and met Sergei's gaze. "Thank you."

"You're most welcome."

She picked the folder up and started to hand it to Emerson, but noted a folded gold piece of paper peeking from the top. She plucked it free and opened it. "What's this?"

Emerson snatched it. "It's nothing."

"It's not nothing if I can't read it." Evette took it back, unfolded it and scanned whatever was written on the surface. Her face softened a second later and her gaze lifted to Emerson. "A father and friends breakfast?"

"They're stupid." Emerson pulled the paper from Evette's now loose fingers and set it to one side. "Almost no one ever goes anyway. It's not a big deal."

But it was a big deal. And given the depth of emotion in Evette's eyes, it had been a big deal on other occasions as well. "You could ask your uncle Carl to go."

"No." Emerson stacked his textbook on top of his binder and hopped from the high seat. "Last time we tried that, I couldn't look at anyone for weeks."

"Who is Uncle Carl?" Sergei asked.

"My dad's brother," Evette answered on an exasperated sigh. She followed Emerson, who'd started toward the back door that led to the patio and the carriage house beyond. "Emerson, mind your manners and tell Mr. Petrovyh good night."

Emerson stopped at the back door and faced Sergei, a frown still marring his features. "Thank you for helping. And for the cookies. Or tea cakes. Or whatever they're called. Sorry I got in such a mood."

"Math can do that to a man," Sergei said. He dipped his head in farewell, then focused on Evette. "The next time your son needs help, my house can wait."

It was the first unguarded smile she'd given him since—well, perhaps the day she'd sat down at his table at Dorothy's. "Thank you." She nudged Emerson through the door and waved goodbye to Olga. "See you both tomorrow."

And with that they were gone, leaving an uncomfortable silence in the kitchen.

Olga laid her folded apron on the kitchen island and shuffled to the door that led to her private rooms beyond the kitchen. *"I'm taking a rest. Dinner will be ready in an hour."*

She didn't wait for an answer, just left Sergei alone with his thoughts and the lingering energy of a little boy and his fairy mother.

On the table, the gold paper sat folded near the center.

Sergei picked it up and read it.

Fathers and Friends Breakfast
8 a.m. Friday, October 26

For some unfathomable reason, Evette's unguarded smile before she'd ducked out the back door hit him all over again, followed quickly by the sheer wonder on her face when she'd learned he'd helped Emerson with his math.

Finally, he'd gotten just a taste of the light and tenderness everyone else in his household save Olga had earned.

He liked it.

Very much.

He folded the paper lengthwise once more, tucked it inside his suit coat pocket and strolled toward his office. One way or another, he'd find a way to earn even more.

Chapter Seven

3:28 p.m.

Evette's watch wasn't much—just a pale pink faux leather band with a plain face and gold-plated trim that she'd got on clearance at Penney's a few years ago—but it was rock solid on keeping time. And right now it was telling her she needed to kick things into a power walk if she wanted to be waiting outside Emerson's school with the surprise she'd planned.

Her guard's footsteps picked up their pace to match hers. The guards never crowded her. Never tried to stop her from going where she wanted. But off the estate, they were always there.

For the most part, she'd gotten used to it. Had even taken advantage of it a time or two while out running household errands by asking them to carry bags.

Still, every now and then she wished she could meander at the Farmers Market a little longer. Or take some side trips while out and about to see what styles were hitting the stores and if there were any good markdowns she could take advantage of. Not exactly the best thing to do when you were on the clock and the boss man's eyes and ears were always on you.

The fancy church-style bell over the main school

building gonged, indicating the end of the school day just as she hustled across the street and through the main gate.

About three seconds later, kids alighted from the doors of all three buildings. Watching them going into and out of the building always made Evie smile. Not just because it was refreshing to see their enthusiasm, but also because they still found creative ways to make the school uniforms unique. No matter what adults tried to do to rein them in, kids were going to find a way to stretch their wings.

She loved it.

Loved their expressiveness. Their energy. Their optimism.

Lungs chugging a little heavier than they probably should, she stopped at the bench to one side of the circle drive where she always waited for Emerson.

A cluster of kids just a little shorter than Emerson burst through the front door on a blast of giggles. Right behind them, Emerson walked into view.

And lo and behold, he had a monster smile on his face.

It was beautiful. The kind that made a boy's whole face light up and his eyes dance. He laughed loud enough she could hear him from twenty feet away, then looked up and over his shoulder—at Sergei.

Every muscle in her went rock solid, teeming with an electrical current that could have likely powered the entire school.

What in the ever lovin' name of God was he doing here?

With her boy!

A dangerous wave of righteous indignation and fury

got her legs into motion, her lungs heaving for an entirely different reason this time around.

Be calm.

Don't overreact.

Ask questions first.

Rip the overbearing Russian a new asshole later.

Right. Good plan. Assuming she could maintain it.

She stopped in front of them both and pasted on what she was absolutely certain was a noticeably fake smile. She focused on Emerson first and clutched her purse in front of her. "Hey, you two." She looked up to Sergei. "Kind of surprising seeing the two of you together."

"Sergei came to Fathers and Friends for me," Emerson said, drawing her attention back to him. "Isn't that cool?"

Presumptive was a better word.

Arrogant and *overbearing* were two other favorites.

"It was very thoughtful." Gaze back on Sergei, she felt her smile slip. "Probably something that would have been good for his momma to know in advance, but thoughtful."

He knew she was mad. The knowledge was right there in every smug line on his face. And still he smiled down at her and dared to use that sinfully sexy voice on her. "You are correct. It was impulsive of me. An idea that came to me at the last moment, but should have run past you, regardless." He bowed. Not a full bend at the waist, but a courtly dip of his torso with a casual hand placed on his belly. On anyone else, it would have looked preposterous. In his fine navy blue suit that perfectly matched his seductive eyes, it was panty-melting hot.

Or would have been if she wasn't primed and ready to tear his head off. "Right, well." So much for having to cushion the blow of not having a male figure at a class function again. She looked to Emerson. "Guess that means my after-school surprise will just be icing on the cake to an already awesome afternoon."

"What surprise?"

She pulled the tickets she'd purchased earlier in the day out of her clutch and held them up. "Two tickets to that new superhero movie you've been wanting to see. Reserved recliner seats and everything."

"Wow!" Emerson snatched the tickets from her hand and studied them like he didn't believe a word she'd said. "This is awesome! And at the good theater, too."

Wow indeed. Her son wasn't just happy. He was in full-scale kid euphoria. "Yep. No dollar seats. Not today."

Emerson beamed his megawatt smile up at Sergei. "Wanna come? The hero's what they call an antihero. You'd *love* him."

She was so stunned by Emerson's response that it took a few extra beats before reality kicked in and made her realize her son had just invited the very man whose ass she wanted to kick to join them.

Emerson pinned his puppy dog eyes on her. "He can go, right, Mom?"

Shit.

Shit, shit, shit.

She cleared her throat and scrunched her nose at Sergei. "I'd be happy for you to join us, but they're reserved seats. Not sure if they'd still have a seat next to us, but we could try."

Please say no.

Please say no.
Please say no.

Sergei's mouth twitched. Knowing that crafty bastard, he'd probably found some way to bug her brain and had heard her thoughts loud and clear.

He shifted his attention to Emerson. "While I believe I would find this antihero most intriguing, I have other plans for the afternoon." His gaze slid to Evette and this time his lips lifted in a smirk. "Perhaps we could all go another time. I suspect you are a good pair to share movies with." Glancing over her shoulder, his expression blanked. He took a polite step back from Emerson. "Thank you for letting me share your day with you."

"Thanks for coming! That was really awesome."

His blue BMW pulled up in front of the three of them. The man riding up front hopped out just as it came to a stop and opened the back door for Sergei. Sergei slid in and the fancy sedan rolled away with barely any downtime.

A smooth getaway for sure, and one Evette was glad he'd arranged because the whole debacle had her shaken in a way she didn't completely understand.

She pushed through it, though, and asked all the usual questions she did on their walk home—only this time they used the streetcar to cut across the Garden District to the theater where she'd prepurchased the movie tickets. It might have been only her imagination, but she could have sworn her guard hung back a little farther than normal. And once, when they'd just hopped off the streetcar and were waiting to cross the street a short way from their destination, she thought she glimpsed Sergei's car.

Sheer stubbornness and lingering anger kept her focus trained on the theater down the street. If he wanted to spend his day skulking around after them, then that was his prerogative. Right now was for her and Emerson and no one else.

On the tail of that thought her conscience whispered, *No one else? Sounds a bit like the green-eyed monster has its teeth in you.*

She wanted to shake it off. Wanted to ignore the implications that came with it, but it was hard when every reasonable thought was carried on her mother's voice.

Inside the lobby, they got the popcorn deal and some candy, then meandered through the crowd to their movie. Emerson's lighthearted mood had softened a little over their long trip, but for the most part the carefree sound in his voice remained. He even shared about a showdown between a boy and girl in class in a somewhat animated voice, which made it hard to hang on to the dregs of her anger.

The lights in the room dimmed.

Emerson dipped his hand in the giant popcorn bag and rooted around for a handful. "He was just a friend, Mom. He didn't act like he was my dad."

Evie froze with a handful of popcorn halfway to her mouth. She covered it and got herself back in gear with chowing down about two seconds later.

"It was nice," Emerson said, still not taking his eyes off the screen. "Having a guy there, I mean. And it's not just Sergei either, but the rest of the guys. Olga and the rest of the workers at the house, too. Like we finally have a family. A really weird one, but a family."

And there it was. The nerve that seeing Sergei walking out of the school beside Emerson had struck. Only this time when the family button had been poked, it had threatened rather than warmed her.

Like I said—green-eyed monster.

She snatched their shared Coke and washed down the popcorn in her suddenly very dry mouth. Her kid had finally had a man he could be proud of show up at a class function and she'd doused his afterglow. Had bungled what could have been a doubly awesome day for him by getting territorial instead of seeing Sergei's actions for what they were—good old-fashioned family support.

And Emerson was right. It wasn't just Sergei who'd been supportive. It was all of his men. All of the people who worked the estate. Even Olga, in her own bossy, opinionated way. It'd been nice. The longest stretch she could remember with people not only looking out for her and her boy, but working as a mostly cohesive unit. Emerson had seen it way before her. Had seen it and embraced it and had tried to say thank you by inviting Sergei to join them.

Evette set the drink back in its holder, grabbed his hand and gave it a squeeze to get his attention. She waited until she had it. "You're right, kiddo. It's a weird family, but a good one."

The movie was great. All the effects, wry humor and attitude Emerson appreciated the most in a movie. Evette enjoyed it, too, but it was hard to shake her revelation, or the earnestness Emerson had shared it with. He'd been right to say something. To call her out and state the truth. By the time they got home and she tucked him in to bed, her own truth had settled in.

She'd been here nearly a month. Taken their generosity and kindness and showed politeness in return.

But she hadn't really opened up. Particularly not with Sergei. And if her boy was astute enough to see and honor their inclusion, then she could do the same.

Downstairs she waited thirty minutes, watching the ten o'clock news without really seeing a single thing on the screen while she paced on the inside, wondering about how to best apologize for the way she'd behaved. Eventually, sitting still was impossible. She pushed from the comfy flannel sofa and padded out the main door to the estate's backyard.

The pool lights were always on, and with the subtle landscape lighting built into the lush details, the space was a perfect nighttime oasis. A perfect place to think.

She rounded the first hedge that lined the backyard and stopped dead in her tracks.

Sergei sat on the porch alone. His pose was casual, one ankle perched on the top of his opposite knee and his elbow braced on the edge of his patio chair. His suit jacket from earlier today was long gone and the shirtsleeves from his crisp white shirt rolled up to his forearms. Smoke from the thick cigar pinched between two fingers drifted upward in a lazy curl before it disappeared into the night sky.

She wished she could be like those smoky tendrils. Just fade away into the night so she'd have more time to think about her next steps.

But his eyes were locked on her.

Well, you wanted to apologize. No time like the present.

Right, but she'd at least have liked to have a plan. Some predefined context to guide her when he inevitably jumbled her thoughts with that devilish smirk of his.

Forcing herself back into motion, she made her way along the winding path, pretending to appreciate the beauty around her when in reality she was acutely aware of his attention locked on her every step. At the two long sandstone steps that led up to the raised porch, she met his stare and tried for a smile. It was shaky at best. "Hey."

He dipped his head in acknowledgment, dark curiosity dancing in his eyes.

She clasped her hands in front of her and scanned the backyard. "Do you come out here a lot?"

He cocked his head slightly, as though her question was the last one he'd expected.

Well, duh. The last time you saw him you probably looked like you wanted to stab him.

She cleared her throat and jumped right back in before he could answer. "I mean, with a place like this, it would make sense. I just didn't really ever picture you as the type to sit and enjoy the outside at night."

Oh, good. Now you're gonna dig yourself a deeper hole.

"I mean, not that you don't appreciate it," she said quickly. "I just always picture you as someone who's always got a million things to do and wouldn't have time to kick back and enjoy a quiet cigar."

At that, one corner of his mouth lifted in a cockeyed grin. "What is it that brings you out this late, Miss Labadie?"

So smooth. Direct and to the point, but delivered on that deep voice that never failed to quiet all the other background noise in her head. Plus, he'd teed things up for her quite nicely. All she had to do was grab the Russian by the horns and jump in. "Well, for starters, could we talk about you being so formal with me? Maybe negotiate you calling me Evie like everyone else?"

An emotion she couldn't quite capture moved across his face, an expression there and gone so quickly, she'd have thought it was a cloud casting shadows in the moonlight if it hadn't been a perfectly clear night. The intensity with which he studied her was electric. A palpable connection even though he sat nearly five feet away and had hardly moved a muscle. "Evette."

"Well, most people use Evie. Except my momma, God rest her soul. She usually called me Evette since I was usually in trouble."

"Ah, but I think we've established—I'm not most people." He thumbed the end of his cigar and sent a big chunk of ash to the sandstone patio. "I will call you Evette."

Right. Probably a good idea to take what she could get on that point and call it a win, especially with the challenge burning in his eyes. "Okay. Fair enough."

The chirp of crickets peppered the awkward silence.

"Was there something else you wanted to talk about?" He paused only long enough to make sure his next word stood out. "Evette?"

She frowned and motioned to the pile of ashes on the ground. "Would you be open to me getting you an ashtray for your trips outside? It might make cleanup in the morning a little easier." Not that she'd ever caught evidence of any other late-night cigar activities.

"I gave you complete control as to the care and maintenance of my home," he said. "If you feel an ashtray is warranted in my backyard, then by all means, purchase whatever you see fit." The cigar didn't need it, but he tapped the end of it again anyway, then lifted it for a casual drag. He exhaled a stream to the heavens. "You seem to be on a roll. Was there anything else you needed to negotiate this evening?"

Whether it was his casual demeanor, or her nerves getting tired of too much adrenaline, she blurted out, "I need to ask your forgiveness."

His head snapped back, and his eyebrows shot high, his cigar hand frozen midtrek to his mouth. He lowered it a heartbeat later and schooled his features. "And why is that?"

"For starters, because you did a kindness for my son. You showing up today to be with him at the school thing was really nice for him. The first time he's had someone be there where he wasn't ashamed." She paused long enough to let her thoughts form into the right words. "I should have thanked you, but I was angry."

"Protective," he said. "As a mother should be. A man beyond blood invited himself somewhere without reviewing that invitation with you first. It was wrong of me. One could say I should be apologizing to you."

"But you didn't." It jumped out before she could censor it.

Given his sly grin, she hadn't needed to. "Because I'm not sorry. If I had it to do over again, I would."

Well, at least he was honest. Bold to the point sometimes she wanted to kick him on principle, but honest.

She nodded and crossed her arms. "Well, if you do it again, I'd like to know in advance."

He mimicked her nod. "Duly noted." He took a drag off his cigar and studied her through narrowed eyes.

"You said *for starters*. What else brings you out tonight?"

He really was an incredibly handsome man. That enviable tightly groomed beard, wavy thick hair and golden skin stretched over a proportionate and well-toned body. But it was his eyes that drew people in. The mysterious dark blue paired with male ferocity.

"Evette?"

Shoot. See? This was why she needed a plan around him. Or a script. Heck, even some note cards would be handy. She licked her lower lip. "I haven't been as…open…as I should. You and your…family…have been wonderful to Emerson and me. He's adjusted to it quickly. Seen it for what it is much more quickly than me. But I just wanted you to know—I see it now, too. And I appreciate it. More than you know."

She'd surprised him with her first admission, but this time around she'd apparently left him stupefied, because his lips parted as though at a complete loss of words.

An idea popped into her head. One that was either divinely inspired, or a fast track to trouble. Either way, she'd gone this far, so she might as well go for it. "I figured since you and your family have opened up to me and Emerson, it'd be nice if we opened up our family to yours."

He cocked one eyebrow. "To my knowledge, you have one uncle and neither you nor Emerson seem too fond of him."

She uncrossed her arms and waved dismissively into the air. "No, not Uncle Carl. I'm talking about the neighborhood I grew up in. Dorothy's having a block party tomorrow night. She always does something this time of year." She shrugged and jammed her fingertips in her back pockets. "I thought you and a few of your guys might like to go."

As soon as she said it, she wanted to shrivel up into a tiny ball and roll back to the carriage house. After all, what kind of idiot invited Russian badasses widely known as Mafia to a neighborhood block party? It was like inviting a shark to a bloodbath.

Surprisingly, Sergei slowly uncrossed his leg, stood and paced toward her. "That's a very kind offer, Evette." He stopped right in front of her and smiled the smile of a hungry wolf. "I accept."

Chapter Eight

In his lifetime, Sergei had been known to wait days—weeks, months or even years—for anticipated events to come to pass, and not once had he been impatient. Yet, here he was…less than twenty-four hours past the time when Evette had offered her invitation, already dressed, ready to go and staring at his computer screen in a halfhearted effort to work while he waited.

It was pathetic.

A behavior he was as uncomfortable with recognizing as he would be detonating a bomb with no knowledge of its wiring.

Outside his office windows that looked down on the backyard, the sun had already dipped beneath the horizon and a deepening stretch of blue reached toward the heavens. Only a hint of the deep red that had marked the sunset remained.

He'd watched it go down. Watched and ruminated on his behavior. On the response Evette's presence around him created and the interesting choices he'd made because of that response. He'd needed inroads within the local neighborhoods. To build trust and create solid connections on that trust. Evette and Emerson had been with him only a month, but helping the mother-and-son team had already done much to accomplish his goals. Tonight, he'd be seen as an invited guest at a popular event among the neighborhood. It was everything he'd set out to do.

But it wasn't his real driver.

He could dance around the truth all he wanted, but only a fool denied their true motives, and he was no fool.

He wanted her.

Had been intrigued by her from the first day she'd all but bounced into the diner and ruffled Emerson's head. Kir and Roman were right. The life of the *bratva* wasn't for relationships. Relationships created liabilities. Leverage to be used by enemies.

And yet he'd still been dressed and ready to go thirty minutes early and had zero intention of walking away from the opportunity she'd offered him—whether it marked Evette and Emerson or not.

The kitchen door downstairs closed with a muted *chunk* and Evette's happy voice drifted in behind it. The conversation was unintelligible at such a distance, but there was no mistaking her excitement. He'd watched her enough to know that whatever she was saying was also animated by wild hand gestures and her expressive face.

Fully alive.

Bright. Fearless and passionate.

Emerson's matter-of-fact boy voice volleyed back, and Evette's laughter followed.

No. He definitely wasn't changing his mind. He'd put more guards on her if he needed to and would do his part to keep his hands to himself, but Evette and her son were staying.

From the muffled yet quick sounds on the carpeted steps, Emerson apparently darted ahead of his mother, headed straight for Sergei's office. Sure enough, he rounded the open door only a beat later dressed in jeans and a Venom T-shirt, his hair wild, his lungs churning and raw anticipation on his face. "Hey, Sergei."

"Mr. Petrovyh," Evette corrected as she came into view behind him. Like her son, she'd kept to jeans and a T-shirt, but her jeans clung to every inch of her curves and ended at her ankles. The tee was a vivid coral color he'd expect to find at a tropical resort and had an enticing V that drew a man's eyes too easily to her breasts.

She aimed an apologetic smile at Sergei, then firmly grabbed her son by the shoulder just inside the doorway. "And you might want to give him a second before you just barge into his office. What if he'd been on a call or talking to someone?"

"Oops." On any other boy his age, the single word might have sounded disingenuous, but Emerson clearly meant it sincerely. "If you're busy, we can wait in the kitchen."

"Nyet." Sergei locked his computer and stood. "If my door is open, you are welcome."

As soon as he stepped out from behind his desk, Evette scanned him from head to toe and frowned.

Emerson did as well.

Surprised by the candid perusal, Sergei checked his jeans and his black button-down. "Is something wrong?"

"You're wearing jeans," Emerson said. It was a factual statement but there was a bite of disbelief worked into the words. "You never wear jeans."

"No, but you should." Where Evette's voice had been light and playful before, now it was lower. Distracted. Clearly, the change registered in her own ears, because she flinched as soon as she spoke and blinked as though she'd been startled awake. "I mean, casual looks good on you." Her gaze drifted over him again and a reaction he couldn't quite interpret moved behind her eyes. "It makes you...more approachable."

For some reason, he didn't think *approachable* had been the word she'd wanted to use, but he'd go with it. Particularly if it meant she kept aiming those wide, wonder-filled eyes at him. "Suits are for business, are they not? And, if I understand the goal for tonight, business is not on the agenda."

The devil inside him purred in agreement, but he quashed it down and motioned them both back out into the hallway. "If you're both ready to go?"

"Yes!" Emerson bounded back down the hallway with an enthusiasm Sergei had never seen from him before and called back over his shoulder. "Dorothy's block parties are the best. She does a ton of jambalaya and red beans and rice, but lots of other people bring stuff, too. Even the ladies from the retirement place down the street. They bring homemade beignets, cakes and bananas Foster." At the base of the staircase, he glanced back and made a face, but kept moving forward. "I don't like the bananas Foster, but the ice cream's good."

Sergei followed them both through the kitchen and out the back door to the driveway. Through it all, Emerson kept chattering, telling him all he should expect for the night, who would be in attendance and the projected lineup for entertainment. His excitement was palpable. Enough even to jump-start his own adrenaline, which hadn't been ignited in too long to remember.

More fun than listening to Emerson was watching Evette eyeball her son. As wide as her eyes were and the slackness at her jaw, one would think her son had grown three heads and was speaking solely in tongues. By the time they reached his car and Kir and Roman waiting beside it, she seemed nearly in a trance.

The trance snapped, though, as soon as Roman moved forward and opened the back door to the BMW.

"Oh, no." She held up a hand and faced Sergei. "We can't go to a block party in a car that costs over a hundred grand."

Sergei cocked his head. "You know about cars?"

"No, my son knows about cars and felt duty bound to explain to me all the features that come with this one along with its ridiculous price tag." She paused long enough to scrunch up her face. "We walk."

"It's over an hour walk," he said, forcing calm and reason into his voice. It was one thing to allow her to walk to a school or a market that was a short distance away, but walking all the way to Mid-City was out of the question. "Surely, you don't want to waste time that could be spent with your friends when we could easily drive."

"It's less than that if we take the streetcar."

"By fifteen minutes at most." He straightened and clasped his hands loosely in front of him. "Perhaps we could reach a compromise."

She cocked one eyebrow.

"We drive to Tulane and walk from there," he said.

Her mouth pursed and she sucked in a slow breath.

"And your men don't follow us. They can join in the fun, but no guards. Not tonight."

There would always be guards. Whether she knew it or not, hell would freeze over before he left her or Emerson unprotected. He gave her a short bow, then looked to Kir and Roman. "Tonight, everyone enjoys themselves." Then added in Russian, *"I want shadows. At least three at all times."*

The two men nodded in unison.

Evette narrowed her gaze, considering for all of a heartbeat, then nodded and made her way to the open car door. "Emerson, you sit in the middle."

Emerson grinned and sent a sidelong glance at Sergei as he moved to comply. Clearly, he'd picked up on his mother's crafty move to buy herself some distance, too.

They made it to Tulane in fifteen minutes, Roman's muted instructions in Russian to his men via phone mostly drowned out by Emerson's chatter. The three-block walk to Dorothy's was a pleasant one, the classic R&B strains of "Mustang Sally" from a live band drifting down the street.

It was a perfect night for a block party. The evening temperatures had held in the low eighties for weeks, making the humidity more bearable than in the summer months, and the lack of rain for the last several days kept the unpleasant smells that could sometimes drift from the French Quarter at bay. Mini lights had been strung from outside Dorothy's Diner to the businesses on the opposite side of the street in a zigzag pattern and a sizable buffet lined the sidewalk. Traffic had been barricaded from the entire block as well, allowing people to mingle at one end of the street and dance at the other where the band had set up.

Emerson lifted his chin, scented the air and twisted to Sergei without missing a step. "See? I told you Dorothy would have jambalaya. You wanna be sure and eat it first before it's gone."

Just as Emerson's words died off, their presence seemed to register with most of the people lined up at the buffet and standing in the street. While the band never missed a beat and those dancing in front of them had no hint of their arrival, the rest hesitated as though a pack of wolves had just stepped into view.

Sergei was used to it. Kir and Roman were as well, but Emerson and Evette both reacted—Evette by subtly lifting her chin, smiling huge and forging right into the thick of things, and Emerson by shifting to Sergei's side and grabbing onto his hand.

"Come on," Emerson said, tugging him forward. "If we're lucky, Miss Arnold's hash brown casserole isn't gone yet. I could eat all of it, but Mom says I can only have a spoonful or two."

And that was all it took. A show of spunky defiance from the neighborhood darling, and a physical stamp of approval from her son, and the crowd went back to their business.

Sergei shared a look over his shoulder with Kir and Roman.

Kir smirked and strolled toward the outskirts of the crowd where a cluster of late twenty- to early thirty-year-old women were gathered. Never a big fan of social events in Russia and even less in the US, Roman shook his head and followed his friend.

In the end, the night proved highly entertaining. The

band was excellent. The food, as Emerson had promised, even better. Kir and Roman did their part to blend in even if they did move like predators among lambs.

And all the while, Sergei was surrounded. If not by curious neighbors bold enough to introduce themselves and share conversation with him, then by Evette or Emerson when someone aimed a wary or unfriendly glare his way.

He was on his second helping of bananas Foster—the portion Emerson had cleverly passed off after a well-meaning older woman had handed the boy a plate—when Evette came back from one of her conversational promenades and sat next to him on the low window ledge outside Dorothy's Diner. She glanced at Sergei's near-empty plate and grinned. "He pawned it off on you, huh?"

So, she'd seen that. And here he'd thought she'd been totally engaged in the conversation with the woman Kir appeared to have picked up. "Indeed."

He scooped up one of the last few remaining bites.

Evette chuckled. A low throaty sound that sounded dangerously sexy with her sitting so close. "When are you going to tell him you don't like bananas either?"

He placed his spoon on his plate, slowly grabbed the napkin off his thigh and wiped his mouth. "What makes you think I don't like it?"

"Because you ate everything else almost as fast as Emerson, but the dessert was very slow going." She bit her lip as though trying to stop her self-satisfied smile from growing bigger, but failed miserably. "You might wear exceptionally tailored suits and have impeccable manners, but you still eat like every other man." She glanced down at the plate. "Unless you don't like it."

Clever, clever woman. She never failed to surprise him. He laid the napkin over what was left of the food and set the plate down on the ground beside him. "I agree with Emerson. Bananas don't belong in dessert."

The band ended their song and those gathered to dance in front of them sent up a decent amount of applause.

"So, tell me something else about you." It was said so tentatively—so quiet—that he almost missed it.

What he didn't miss was the reaction her interest created. A stirring in the pit of his devil's belly that wasn't good for either of them. And yet, he answered anyway. "What would you like to know?"

Gaze directed at the dancers, she shrugged, for all appearances nonchalant. But there was something in the way she held herself...an intensity or an awareness that made him think she was more interested than she acted. "How about what it was that brought an educated man from Russia to New Orleans?"

He watched the dancers. Listened as the lively music from the band's new song lifted into the air. He could either give her the truth, or pacify her with something more generic.

Truth.

The direction from his gut was crystal clear. But if he gave it to her, there'd be no going back. No more pretending he was only a powerful businessman with merely a dangerous image.

A calm as steady and certain as the day he'd first met Yefim settled inside him. "I broke away from my family in Russia to build a family of my own. I wanted to settle somewhere warm. Somewhere with much life, color and history. I picked New Orleans."

She nodded and leaned forward, resting her elbows on her thighs and clasping her hands in front of her. "Family as in people you grew up with?"

He waited. Listened for any indication from his instincts he should change his path.

Nothing came.

"No, Evette. Family as in *bratva*. Or as you would know it, *Mafiya*."

Her hands tightened so her knuckles turned white, but she took a slow, steady breath and twisted her head to meet his eyes. "Did something happen? To make you break away?"

"*Nyet*. It was a reward."

"A reward?" The question seemed genuine. Interested and engaged.

For some reason, it cracked the door to his past open a little farther. "I'd grown restless with the politics among the families in Russia. I've long believed the foundations of what it once meant to be *bratva* have been lost. I wanted to return to those foundations. My *pakhan* knew this. There was something he needed. Something many families needed. I fulfilled that need and, in exchange, I was given permission to build my own family here."

Her expression sobered. "Do I want to know what that need was?"

So sweet. An angel staring into the darkness. He shook his head. "No, *malen'kaya feya*. You do not."

She considered him a moment, her gaze drifting over his features. "How did you end up…" She frowned, either at a loss for words, or uncomfortable putting words to the images she'd formed. "…doing what you do."

Beneath his tan Italian loafers, the sidewalk was cracked, but clean. It was one of the things he most appreciated about the business owners in this part of town. Their clientele might not be top-end and their profit margins meager, but they had pride. Determination and grit. It reminded him of the streets he'd grown up in. The life he'd led before everything changed.

He didn't want to remember the past. Let alone talk about it. But Evette needed to know. Needed to understand how long he'd been a part of this life. How deeply it was etched on his soul.

"My father worked in a shipyard. His skills were limited, and he refused my mother's offers to work, so our income was minimal. My mother contracted pneumonia when I was five." The cold from that winter seeped into his bones just as it had all those years ago. "She died."

Beside him, Evette sat perfectly still. Riveted and impervious to the crowd around them.

Sergei wasn't. He needed the reality of other humans and the night's warmth to ground him against the memories. "After her death, my father was worthless. Drank much and only worked enough to pay for what he drank. I needed money to eat, so I learned to steal. One day I set my sights on a wealthy man leaving a building in the business district. That man was Yefim Mishim and, while I might have been good at picking pockets, he was better at protecting them."

He felt the smile on his lips. Remembered all over again the terror as he'd looked up into Yefim's stern face, his guards all around him, and expected the worst. "He held me by my wrist and stared at me for the longest time. To this day, I do not know what it was he searched for, but in the end, he cuffed me on the back of my head, dragged me into his limousine and kept me with him as he went from one meeting to the next."

"He didn't turn you in?"

At her question, Sergei couldn't help but let go of the past and focus on her. "Boys like me didn't get turned in by men like Yefim. They were either ignored completely or taught a lesson."

She swallowed. "Which one did you get?"

"Neither."

Across the street, Emerson stood in front of two older ladies, the expression on his face as they shared a conversation as somber and focused as a fully grown man's.

Sergei understood it. While he had no doubt Evette had done her best to shield her son from as much as possible, nothing made a boy grow up faster than harsh reality. "When the day was over, Yefim demanded my address. I thought he would drop me off and, perhaps, demand some type of punishment from my father. Instead, he walked right inside. My father was passed out on the sofa. The kitchen was empty and the house a mess, though I'd managed to keep my own space clean. Yefim stood in the center of my small room, looked down at me and told me to pack my things."

"What did you do?"

"I packed. Took some clothes and a picture of my mother and walked out the door behind him. I stayed with him for two weeks, following him everywhere. Two weeks later, he took me to a man named Anton Fedorov, the *pakhan*—or boss—for one of the most powerful families in Russia. Yefim told me, *He will*

*be your father now. He will give you a chance. What
you do with that chance is up to you."*

"I take it you capitalized on that chance."

"With everything in me, and with no regrets. Anton treated me as his own. Started me from the very bottom of his organization and gave me everything. In return, I served him as *kryshas*."

"What's a *kryshas*?"

He hesitated, hating the truth for the first time in his life. But he forced himself to look her in the eye. "It means, *feya*, that when my *pakhan* had something he needed enforced or...*resolved completely*...he sent me to do the job."

Understanding registered behind her beautiful eyes, the gold flecks among the sparkling green dimming as it did. "I see."

"Yes. I believe that you do." He pulled in a long steadying breath and soaked up the warmth around him. The laughter and the music filling the air. "Now, I am the *pakhan*. My destiny is mine."

"And you want something more...old-fashioned?" As soon as she said it, comprehension or inspiration fired on her face. "Like those flashback scenes in *Godfather II*? The parts with Robert De Niro as a young Vito Corleone when he was helping the neighborhood?"

The chuckle slipped out before he could stop it. Leave it to Evette to find a way to tie their discussion back to lighter ground by bringing up classic mob movies. "Something like that."

Her bright smile was redemption in physical form. Absolution given without price attached. The smile softened a second later and her voice dropped to a near whisper. "I'm sorry you lost your mom. I know that's hard. I was fifteen when I lost my dad and twenty when I lost my mom and both almost killed me. I can't imagine if I'd lost them when I was five."

He'd known they were both gone. Knew that Evette's mother was one of Dorothy's dearest friends before her unexpected death, but had no clue how the father had died. "What happened to your father?"

Her mouth scrunched up to one side before she ducked her head and studied her white Keds. "An accident in his truck." She lifted her head. "He worked for a delivery service. Was out late on a route in winter. We don't get bad roads in winter often, but when we do, the black ice catches lots of people off guard. Dad's truck went off the road on an iced-over bridge. They found the truck easy enough, but it took about a week to find his body downstream."

"And your mother?"

This time her expression turned darker.

The hairs on the back of his neck bristled and the alertness that had saved him from death on too many occasions to count danced across his shoulders.

"They really don't know," she said. "From all appearances, it looked like she just went to sleep one night and never got up. No signs of foul play and she hated drugs and alcohol, so with her age, they put it down as natural causes."

But Evette didn't buy it. No matter how much she portrayed it as such, her voice was thick with disbelief.

And pain.

Much of it.

She stared out at the crowd and scrunched up her nose. "I kind of went crazy when Mom died. Was starting the second half of my sophomore year and just stopped going to classes." She scoffed and hung her head. "Actually, strike that. I was too hungover to go to class." She twisted her head to Sergei. "Got hammered every chance I could. Lost my part-time job… everything." She shrugged and found Emerson in the crowd and a misty smile tilted her lips. "One of those benders got me him, though. Much as it shames me to say it, I couldn't pick his daddy out of a lineup, but finding out I was pregnant sobered me up. Got me focused again." She smiled up at him. "Now, here I am."

"All the more reason to like your son."

The delight on her face was pure sunshine. "Did you just flirt with me?"

He wasn't entirely sure what he'd done. In truth, the shock that he'd even remotely said such a thing to her was still rattling beneath his skin. "I just shared with you the nature of my work in sufficient detail to scare most people. I assure you, I'm not a man who flirts."

"Mmm." Even with her lips pressed tight together and fighting back laughter her eyes practically sparkled with mischief.

The band finished one song and launched right into another, this one a zydeco piece that sent cheers up from the crowd and drew even more people to the makeshift dance floor.

Evette shot to her feet and clapped her hands. "All right! Now we're talking!" She turned to him and held out a hand. "Come on, Big Man. You can't come to a street party and pass up a chance for a little Cajun two-step."

Oh, he could pass it up. Under normal circumstances he wouldn't ever be in a position where *Ser-*

gei and *dancing* occurred inside the same thought. But with Evette practically bouncing in front of him and her outstretched hand just waiting for him to take it, *no* wasn't an option.

He took her hand and stood. "You realize, me dancing may be the fastest way to bring the party to a standstill."

"Or the quickest way to mark it in the history books." With that, she practically dragged him toward the still-growing crowd and swung around to face him with a playfully dramatic flair. He might not have surprised her by accepting her invitation, but the fact that he deftly pulled her in with a hand at her shoulder and steered her straight into the stream of two-stepping couples did.

"You know how to dance!" she said.

"I spent nearly ten years gaining my education in America," he answered with only enough volume for her to hear. "I assure you those years were spent learning far more than literature and business."

Evette threw back her head and laughed to the skies, drawing curious yet happy stares from the couples around them. Even after the throaty sound had died out, her smile never wavered.

And for every note, all of her attention was locked on him. Her enjoyment infectious. Her body close to his.

It was addictive.

An innocent seduction that tempted him to shove aside years of discipline and simply take without thought. Without reason or assessment of the risk it created.

The song ended too soon. A frustration further exacerbated by the fact that the band opted to take their break on a high note—right up until Evette finished her applause, spun back toward him and wrapped her arms tight around the waist.

It wasn't sexual. More of a friendly bear hug. The kind Darya—and only Darya—would dare give him.

But he couldn't breathe for the ferocity behind it. The genuine acceptance and connectedness conveyed behind the simple act.

He closed his arms around her, gently, as though too much might shatter the illusion and send him crashing back to reality.

Mine.

Logic told him to ignore it. To set her carefully away from him and garner himself precious distance. Even now, there could be enemies watching. Marking her and, by association, Emerson.

Mine. The thought came louder this time and his arms tightened around her.

She lifted her head, a curiosity burning in her expression that said she'd somehow sensed the turmoil inside him.

Seldom in his life had he acted without thought. Without a well-placed strategy complete with contingencies and backup plans. But in that second, with the echo of his possessive thought still ringing in his head, he clasped her hand and pulled her alongside him toward the sidewalk.

Kir and Roman stood just twenty feet away, both watching. Passive in their stance and expression, but their sharp gazes taking in every detail.

They knew.

They'd warned him.

But they wouldn't stop him. He was the *pakhan*. His decisions would be supported no matter the cost.

Roman dipped his head in a barely perceptible nod.

Kir smirked and rubbed the back of his hand along his jaw.

"Sergei, where are we going?" Evette quickened her steps to stay beside him. "I need to keep an eye on Emerson."

"I have eyes on Emerson." With that, they reached the shadowed service alley that ran between Dorothy's building and the pub next door. He spun her with far more vigor than he'd shown on the dance floor, backed her against the brick wall and pressed himself tight against her, his hands braced on either side of her head.

Evette's chest rose and fell in a heavy rhythm from the pace he'd taken to get them there, but the breathiness in her voice and her wide eyes had nothing to do with fear. "I don't think you can see him from here."

He saw plenty. "I see everything, *feya*. I see Emerson waking up. I see the way you keep your distance, but still watch me when you think I'm not looking. I see your curiosity and your light."

So long, he'd wondered what it would be like to touch her. How her body would feel against his. If her lips would be as soft as they were full. He gave in to temptation and traced them with the pad of his thumb.

They parted at the bold contact, her breath whispering against his skin and her pupils dilating to the point it was almost all black that stared up at him. "I see desire. Awareness and need." He slid his hand to the back of her neck, held her steady and lowered his head. "I'm going to feed those needs—whether it damns us both or not."

He claimed her mouth. Swallowed her startled gasp and took what he wanted. What he *needed*.

And fuck if she didn't taste divine. Better than any sweet confection that had ever passed his lips. And her body—she was everything a man craved. Lush curves. Soft and pliant. And so damned petite compared with him, the devil inside him practically roared with the need to protect her. To curl himself around her, wrap her up tight and hoard her away where no one else could find her. Could dare to lay eyes on or touch her. At the very least, he wanted to drag her farther into the alley and take his fill of her until he was the only thing she knew. The only thing she could think about.

Footsteps sounded on the sidewalk, the scratch of dirt against concrete dimly warning him that a passerby had stopped walking.

Sergei shifted on instinct, putting himself between whoever watched and Evette even as he struggled for the will to break their kiss.

But Evette wasn't having it. With a ragged sound somewhere between a moan and a whimper, she rolled up on her toes, slid her hands from his pecs to the back of his neck and deepened the kiss.

Or did, until a masculine voice he'd never heard before spoke from behind them. "Evette, is that you?"

Chapter Nine

This was bad. Very bad. As in the worst of the worst situations.

Evette slowly but firmly pushed against the hard wall of Sergei's chest and forced her eyes open.

Sergei stared down at her, every bit the predator he'd admitted to being only minutes before and obviously unhappy that a lesser being had dared to interrupt them.

"Evie?"

At the sound of Uncle Carl's voice, Evette winced and scrunched her eyes closed. Definitely shit timing. Kissing her boss had been bad enough. Having Uncle Carl waddle into the picture while she'd been practically crawling her way up Sergei's body and kissing him with everything she had in her...*that* was the mother of all bad combinations.

"I know that's you, girl," Carl said. "Don't you hide from me. Why haven't you answered my texts?"

Sergei's expression went from irritated to fuming. *Shit. Shit. Shit.*

He'd seen the texts and asked her point-blank if she had a problem. Which, of course, there hadn't been—and wouldn't ever be one—if she'd kept her scheme-concocting, pain-in-the-ass uncle from ever crossing paths with her deadly employer.

She tried for a playful smile, but was pretty sure it came out as shaky. "Sorry," she whispered, then leaned out from behind Sergei the best she could with him still holding her firmly at her hips. "Hey, Uncle Carl."

"Don't you *Hey, Uncle Carl* me." He tottered closer, though wisely sputtered and stopped two arm spans away as soon as Sergei twisted and gave him a death glare. While the glare also helped to downgrade Carl's irate tone, his words were still aggressive. "Why haven't you answered my texts? I been worried about you for weeks."

More like he hadn't had a place to loiter or a polite audience to listen while he expounded on all his grand adventures. And by *grand adventures*, she meant droning on and on about how he'd blown his latest earnings and how he planned to make it rich on his next wild idea.

Before she could plow past her frustration and muster a response, Sergei turned so he stood partially in front of her. "If she wanted you to know, I have no doubt she would have told you."

"And who the hell are you?"

"Her boss."

Okay, she'd been wrong. *Now* it was the worst situation ever. She hustled out from behind Sergei, cast a silent yet wide-eyed plea for Sergei to butt out over her shoulder and grabbed her uncle by the forearm. "I manage his estate." She kept moving, steering her annoying and highly embarrassing family member out into the street, though she felt Sergei not far behind. "He hired me a month ago."

"A month ago?" Carl stopped dead in his tracks and jerked her back a few steps in the process. "But you had a good thing with that big cleaning company. Good connections."

Only Carl could call a cleaning gig with a commercial cleaning company *good* and make it sound like she was the CEO. "Yeah, it was good, I guess. Until I got fired."

A weird look crossed his face, there and gone again in a blink. Not surprise—that much she'd have expected. This looked more like panic. "What do you mean you got fired?"

"I mean they pulled me aside on a Friday afternoon and told me my access card had showed up on reports saying I'd been in one of the legal offices when I shouldn't be." Behind Carl, Sergei waited a respectful distance away, but also braced as though he was prepared to charge at the drop of a hat. Kir and Roman had waded in to flank him and, while they had that patented bored Russian badass mask on their faces, their body language said they were prepped to be anything but passive. "I needed a job and Sergei helped me out way faster than anyone else could have and he's given me a sweet deal."

"Sergei?"

She dipped her head toward the deadly trio behind Carl. "My boss."

A whole different demeanor crept over her uncle. Namely, the one that said new and highly embarrassing ideas were percolating in his head. He faced Evette. "Sergei Petrovyh?"

"You know him?"

Carl chuckled. A low, almost evil sound that made

her skin crawl. "Cher, everyone in New Orleans knows him. The man's got money and connections. Lots of them. He'd be a big help to your uncle Carl. You should introduce us."

"No way. He doesn't like outsiders on his estate, so if you want to see me and Emerson, you're going to have to arrange dinner or lunch with us at Dorothy's or something."

Carl's eyes shot wide. "You're living with him?"

Okay, maybe there *was* still room for things to get worse. "Not with him, per se. There's an apartment on the property, and it's a heck of a lot better than where I was. Plus, it's part of my pay." She paused long enough to lower her voice and loaded up the rest of her message with what she hoped was sufficient sincerity to make Carl back off his questions. "This is a good chance for me and Emerson. A *great* chance. It gave me enough money to get Emerson enrolled in that school his teachers recommended and gives me enough money to pay for classes to finish my degree, too. Not to mention more time to go to class. I *can't* screw this up."

Her uncle didn't move. Just stared at her with that distant expression reserved for people who were thinking about something entirely different while they pretended to be interested in the conversation happening in front of them.

"Uncle Carl?"

He shook himself out of his stupor, glanced back at Sergei, who'd now crossed his arms and was glaring at Carl, then looked back to her and cleared his throat. "You know…you ask me…that clinch you were in when I found you two—I'd say you could bend the rules however you wanted."

Evette jerked, the same shock she'd have processed if he'd slapped her moving down her body. "What? It's not like that."

"Oh…" Carl said with a dirty chuckle. "I'd say it's *very* much like that." He chucked her on the shoulder. "Nothing to be ashamed of, darlin'. A girl's gotta use her assets."

Her hand was in motion without conscious thought, the sting against her palm as she slapped her only living relative quickly crawling up her arm in a painful vibration. "Do not *ever* disrespect me like that again."

The crowd around her went silent, the lack of music from the band making the silence that much more tangible.

Carl gently covered the space where she'd landed the blow with his own hand, his jaw slack with surprise.

She didn't dare let her gaze drift over Carl's shoulder. One look at Sergei and she had no doubt Carl would end up with far worse. Better for her to keep the upper hand and close down this debacle while she could. She could always hide in Dorothy's kitchen until it was time to go. Or, better yet, nab Emerson and take the Saint Charles back to the carriage house before Sergei and his men could catch her.

She scanned the people still avidly watching all around them with a look that politely told them to mind their own business and straightened as tall as her short stature would allow. "When you're ready to apologize, you let me know. Until then you keep your distance."

With that, she spun on her Keds and made a beeline to Dorothy's.

Chapter Ten

Sergei's pulse pounded in his ears and his muscles strained to move. He was going to kill Evette's uncle. Or at the very least beat the fucker until he wished he was dead. Knowing the details of their conversation didn't matter. His *feya* had sealed her uncle's sentence as solidly as a gavel the second she'd struck him.

Carl still stood in the middle of the street, dumbfounded and staring after Evette. His height was average, but his middle indicated he had a love for food, alcohol or both. His dirty blond hair was the same as Emerson's, but was cut in a style more popular in the eighties and looked like he'd not washed or combed it since he slept last. Given how wrinkled his white guayabera shirt and tan pants were, Sergei imagined they'd been on him in bed, too.

A wastrel. A user. A leech.

In short, the man was trouble.

Even before he'd watched Evette slap the odious man, Sergei's instincts had told him as much. Had bristled at the whine and entitled demand in his voice.

Carl snapped out of his stunned trance, clocked Sergei and his men watching him, then took note of the crowd waiting to see how he'd respond. It took him all of two heartbeats to find someone he recognized, lift his hand in a familiar greeting and stroll their direction like nothing had happened. "Hey, McKensie. Where you been keepin' yourself lately?"

No apparent remorse.

No concern for his niece.

All the more reason to make him hurt.

"Do you know him?" Kir asked in Russian.

As tight as Sergei had ground his jaws together, loosening them enough to answer was a challenge. *"Her uncle. Carl. My guess, from her father's side of the family."*

"She's never mentioned him," Roman offered.

She hadn't. Though, he'd surmised her uncle had been the one who had upset her with the text messages. And what made Evette upset made him furious. He nodded toward the diner. "I'm going to Evette. The two of you find Emerson. We're going home." Just before he got in motion, he gave each of his men a look they knew all too well how to interpret. *"And then you find me everything there is to know about the uncle."*

Chapter Eleven

A girl's gotta use her assets.

Every time her uncle's words rounded through her head, Evie was tempted to find the ass and smack him all over again. And considering the number of loops the replay had made in her head all day Sunday and most of this morning, it was truly a miracle she hadn't followed through. Especially when she'd gotten almost no sleep for two nights in a row replaying everything that had happened.

The skies on the walk back from dropping Emerson off at school were as gray as her mood. Really, she should be relieved. Not only did she not have to worry about hiding things from Uncle Carl anymore, but he'd probably saved her from doing the one thing guaranteed to screw up the opportunity she'd been given—namely, sleeping with the boss. Yeah, her only living relative had also shown what a sexist pig he was, but that wasn't life altering. Getting personal with Sergei?

Totally life altering.

How, she wasn't sure, but she'd had plenty of time to think about it since Saturday night and not once had she come up with a rainbows-and-hearts outcome.

She veered off the sidewalk and up the driveway.

Rather than follow her into the house as her guard normally did, Reggie silently kept strolling toward the front of the house, jogged up the steps to the front porch where one of his peers was already stationed and gave her a wave.

Odd. Usually the men huddled in Sergei's office after she got home from school.

She shrugged and meandered toward the backyard and the kitchen entrance, only to find two more men poised at either corner of the patio.

Honestly, she'd been a little shocked at how quiet things had been since Saturday night. How matter-of-fact. No more than ten minutes after she'd slapped her uncle, Sergei had found her in the diner, calmly announced it was time to go and driven the whole crew back to the house. In the mood she'd been in, she hadn't argued, but a part of her had thought—or maybe hoped—he'd have at least been interested in trying for another kiss. Or at least shown her physical attention. He'd been kind. Courteous. Even helped her into and out of the car.

But otherwise, no touch. No conversation. Not even a glimpse of him since they'd pulled into the drive that night and he'd walked her and Emerson to their door.

Definitely, no more breath-stealing, toe-curling kisses.

Good Lord-a-mighty...that man could kiss. Just thinking about it drew a flush to her cheeks and fired all kinds of curious thoughts. No doubt, he'd be a thorough, demanding lover. The kind a woman would feel for days after and wish for all over again for much, much longer.

A girl's gotta use her assets.

And there it was again. The gut-punch part of the vicious circle. Maybe that was why Sergei hadn't done or said anything about their kiss. Maybe he saw her the same way. After all, she was a single mother and she made no secret that there was no dad involved.

She shut the kitchen door behind her a little harder than she should have and strode toward the massive granite island. "Olga?" Usually, the bossy cook was armed with her apron and either manning the stove or whipping up some new mouthwatering baked goodie. She might be as argumentative as they came and opinionated to boot, but she was a wicked cook.

Silence surrounded her. No television audio. No sounds from the landscaping crew. No voices from upstairs or the living area beyond the kitchen.

She padded toward Olga's rooms off the kitchen. As it usually did when the cook was either in the kitchen or out running errands, the door stood open. "Olga, you there? I need to get this week's grocery list."

Nothing.

Hmm.

The countertops were perfectly clean. No notes. No covered bread rising. Just a show-ready dream kitchen ready for action, but minus a cook.

"Okay, fine. So, I'll do the groceries later." She marched to the supply closet and gathered up what she needed to get a cleaning pass done on the kitchen while Olga was out. Basket of supplies in hand, she flipped the light switch, backed out of the closet—and shrieked loud enough the neighbors could have heard at the sight of Sergei standing squarely in her path.

She covered her chest with her free hand as if it might calm the startled heartbeat beneath it into something a little less painful. "Good grief. You scared me half to death."

"You were humming and didn't hear me."

She'd been humming? Figured. She tended to make up inane tunes that went nowhere and had no rhyme or reason to them when she got distracted.

She took a step back to gain a little distance, but ended up backed against the closet doorjamb. The distance only helped to bring what he was wearing into focus—another casual pairing of jeans and a quality button-down with the sleeves rolled up his forearms. This time the color was a pale blue that made the color of his navy eyes seem that much darker. Somehow, seeing him so casual made the tattoos that wound along his wrists and dotted the backs of his fingers seem that much more sinister. As if his usual dress clothes were only a tool to hide the deadly man underneath.

"Where is everyone?" she said.

"Off."

A single word, but it rattled through her with all the subtly of the world's largest gong.

Oh, no you don't, girly. You just barely skirted danger last time. Don't even think about snuggling up next to it again.

Shooting for breezy attitude, she sidestepped, went around him and set her supplies on the counter, keeping her back to him as she unpacked them. "Why would everyone be off? Is there some holiday I don't know about?"

"They're off because I have business to attend to." He moved in tight behind her, braced one hand on the counter and covered her hand with the other, stilling her from unpacking the can of granite cleaner. "Because *we* have business to attend to."

A shudder moved through her. One so powerful he probably felt it in his own torso. Holding herself perfectly still, she closed her eyes and tried to ignore the immediate and eager response from her body. "I wasn't aware we had business."

God, was that her voice? So low and raspy?

"Yes, *malen'kaya feya*. We have business." Sergei dragged in an achingly slow breath and his hand tightened atop hers. A heartbeat later, he released his hold and stepped back. "We'll start by you sharing what it was your uncle said to you Saturday night."

The loss of his heat at her back and the press of his hard body against hers nearly drew a whimper past her lips. She licked them instead and steadied herself with both hands on the countertop, keeping her back to him. "What do you mean?"

"Don't play innocent, Evette. Something provoked you enough to slap him. I gave you time and space to process whatever it was. Now it's time for you to tell me what happened."

"No, it's not." She faced him and braced herself to dodge whatever questions Sergei had ready. Uncle Carl might have proven himself a dick, but he was still the only family she had left beyond Emerson. Telling her boss what Carl had said would drop that family count by half. "It was a family thing. Nothing you need to worry about."

"You recall, Miss Labadie, my policy on harm coming to those under my protection."

"I do. And, if you'll recall, it was me doing the harming. Not the other way around."

His lips twitched. "He provoked you."

"Yes."

"How?"

"I'm not talking about it. It was just a case of Uncle Carl being Uncle Carl. I dealt with it. End of story."

"And why wouldn't you tell him where you lived?"

"Because I didn't want to."

"Does he harm you?"

"No!" It came out a little too emphatically. Enough so, Sergei might be tempted to act if she didn't add details. She softened her voice and forced her shoulders to relax. "He's just a jerk, okay? Always has been." She pinched her lips together, the truth sour on her tongue. "He shows up unannounced, eats my food and rambles on and on and on about the things he's been up to. When he doesn't show at home, he shows at the diner either bragging about how he's made a big score of money, or hitting people up for a new scheme. It's embarrassing."

"And you did not want him here."

"I didn't want him at my last place. Or the place before that." She waved her hand dismissively in the air. "Seriously, it's not a big deal. He's done the same thing forever. Everyone knows it. He used to drive my mom batty with the same behavior. After Dad died, he'd show up all the time and make himself right at home."

Sergei cocked his head slightly and studied her, his eyes narrowed.

It was unnerving. An assessment that made her want to squirm or hightail it back to the carriage house. "Stop looking at me like that," she said instead. "I told you, it's not a big deal. Just me addressing a pain-in-the-ass relative."

Sergei still didn't move.

She planted both hands on her hips and went for the sass she used with Olga. "Are we done? Because if everyone's off today, I'm going to make the most of it and get some serious cleaning in."

"No."

"No, I'm not cleaning?"

"No, we're not done."

She threw her hands up, the adrenaline and hormones that had kicked into overload the second he'd pressed himself against her pushing her to exasperation. "Well, can we get on with whatever else is on your agenda, then? Because I've got things to do."

"Yes." He prowled forward. "We can proceed."

He was in her space in all of two steps, the wide and deliciously hard chest she'd happily explored in the alley so up close and personal, her hands went to his pecs on reflex. "What are you doing?"

His hands settled on her hips and his voice dropped to the low rumble that did dangerous things to her reasoning. "Getting on with my agenda and finishing what we started Saturday night."

Abort.

Abort.

Abort.

Step back.

Get some distance.

GO HOME!

Her body—traitorous bitch that it was—ignored every word of it and stayed right where it was. Even her mouth and lungs got in on the rebellion, because the little bit of logic she was able to voice came out disingenuous. "That's a bad idea."

His fingers tightened at her hips and he pulled her closer.

"Seriously." She wanted to push him away, but instead her hands moved down just enough to appreciate the flex of his muscles as he held her in place. "We can't do this again. I need this job. I need to get my life back together. I can't do that if we get personal."

God, he smelled good. Earthy, sensual and all man.

She forced herself to look up. To meet those deep and seductive blue eyes of his.

Determination.

Relentlessness.

A hunter with no intention of stopping.

"We need to stop," she rasped, the conviction behind her words distracted and lacking. "Pretend it didn't happen and move on."

His hands roamed to her back, one sliding up the length of her spine to just between her shoulder blades and the other pressing firmly high on her ass. "Ah, but it did happen." He pulled her flush against him, blatantly letting her feel the very tangible erection behind his jeans. "And now that I've had a taste, I have no intention of going without." The hand between her shoulder blades glided higher, cupping the back of her neck. "And you, *feya*..." He lowered his head, his lips ghosting against hers in a teasing brush she felt clear to her toes. "You will not go without either."

He sealed the words with his mouth. Held her steady and kissed her with the same ruthlessness he had Saturday night. Bold strokes from his tongue. The skilled, passionate press of his mouth. The unyielding way he held her in place. The tightly coiled strength of his arms around her and the hard press of his body.

to one side and slid the top drawer open, all the while holding her gaze. "Will this meet your needs?"

Her gaze dropped to the contents inside the drawer. Specifically, the dozen or more gold foil packages waiting and ready for use. "Um." She leaned a little closer for a better look. No. Not a dozen. More than that. Which meant either today was premeditated as hell, or he'd had a lot more action going on in this house than she'd noted in the month since she'd moved in.

She straightened, but couldn't quite manage to meet his stare. Not with her cheeks flaming as hot as the asphalt on Bourbon Street in August. "That's probably overkill."

"You underestimate the power of your kiss, *feya*." He moved in, anchored her against him with a hand at her hip and cupped the back of her head. His voice as he lowered his mouth to hers was everything dark and wonderful mothers warned their daughters about. "And the depths of my determination to see how the rest of you tastes."

Wow.

It was bad enough that his kiss made her stupid. That the taste of him made her drunk and the commanding way he held her brought all those white knight moments from her youth galloping back to life. But words, too? At this rate, they'd find her months from now still overdosed and grinning in his bed.

So what if it was a royal screwup? It wouldn't be her first, and likely not her last, but it felt so good to be touched. To have physical contact from a man who not only seemed to know what he was doing, but that fired every circuit in her system just looking at him.

He lifted his head, the loss of his kiss taking her

breath with it. In the near month she'd worked for him, she'd caught glimpses of the man behind the mask he showed the rest of the world, but in that second, the beast showed through. A wolf intoxicated by its spoils and still hungry for more.

Forcing her hands at the back of his neck to relax, she smoothed them across his shoulders. "Why are you stopping?"

"Not stopping." He tugged her T-shirt free of her jeans. "Appreciating." Not missing a beat, he lifted the shirt up and over her head and let it fall to the floor.

And that was when it hit her. When the realization whispered through her mind as silkily as the room's cool air dancing against the skin he'd bared.

This wouldn't be a quick tumble.

No fumbling in the dark.

No morning after she could slip free of before anyone was the wiser.

This was all out in the open. A tangle she'd never be able to hide from. Even if nothing else happened between them after today—and nothing else *could* happen—he'd leave a mark. A memory she'd be hard-pressed to ever outdo.

He traced the skin above her waistband, the backs of his knuckles teasing her pebbled flesh. "You're thinking too much."

"One could argue I'm not thinking enough."

He smiled at that, a soft curve of his lips she doubted many people ever witnessed. "The angel is having second thoughts about dancing with the devil?"

Her answering bark of laughter filled the room. "Me? An angel?"

His smile slipped. So smoothly there was no mistaking he had ample experience in these situations, he skimmed his fingertips up her spine, slipped the fastener on her bra free and gently peeled the fabric from her shoulders. His gaze dropped to her bared breasts and an unmistakable hunger deepened behind his dark eyes. "Compared to me, yes."

So much contempt. Such self-loathing and scorn. The urge to pull him against her and simply hold him made her palms itch, but she'd had enough experience with male pride to know that was the wrong move. She smoothed her hands down his arms, taking time to appreciate the muscles bunched beneath her palms. "You're not the devil either. You've been nothing but kind to Emerson and me. Protective and thoughtful."

His expression hardened, the sharp edge of the beast she'd glimpsed pushing its way free. Despite his gentle touch, there was unmistakable power and hunger in his voice. "Make no mistake, Evette. There is darkness in me." He unfastened her jeans and slipped his hands beneath the denim at her hips. "Enough that I'm taking your light and will suffer no conscience for it."

The confession should have given her pause. Or at the very least pushed her to demand further explanation, but paired with the gravelly rumble of his voice and the way he lifted her by her ass, dropped her on the side of the bed and pulled her panties and jeans free in one seamless maneuver, it sent her reasoning on a detour she had no intention of missing. Especially when he lasered his attention on her exposed sex, palmed her knees and pried them up and wide, growling a string of Russian words that sounded filthy.

"What does that mean?"

The dirty smirk that tilted his lips made him look

every bit the devil he claimed to be. He cupped her ass and lowered his head, holding her gaze even as his warm breath danced across her flesh. "It means I'm going to devour your sweet pussy until you come on my tongue."

Her sex clenched, the combined jolt of his words and the wet heat of his mouth closing around her clit shoving her straight into the deep end of sensation. There was no coyness. No leisurely buildup or pause to reconfirm the consent she'd already given.

He took.

Feasted as though he'd hungered for years. Explored every inch of her with an unabashed thoroughness. His wicked mouth. His talented tongue. He used them both, deftly following each whimper or lift of her hips to give her more of what she craved. Built the roiling need until all she could do was ride the swelling wave and accept the release barreling toward her.

He pressed one hand to her belly, stilling her rolling hips even as he pressed a finger inside her.

Holy hell.

When she'd grown so emboldened to spear her hands in his hair, she hadn't a clue, but they were there now. Holding him steady. Reveling in the vibrations his hungry sounds created against her swollen, aching clit.

It'd been so long.

Too long.

He added another finger, the fullness welcome and yet not nearly enough. A poor imitation for what she really craved. "Sergei."

She tried to lift her hips, eager for more and dancing at the edge. Her pussy fluttered around his fingers, release so close it hurt. "Sergei, please."

A feral sound rumbled from his chest. He shifted his fingers, brushing his fingertips against the tender stretch along her front wall, and sucked her clit deep.

And she was gone.

Her sex pulsing around his fingers and her blood pounding in her ears. It was exquisite. Every inch of her bared body rippling in the wake of a climax unlike anything else she'd ever felt before. Channeling pure sensation as warm and bright as a summer sun and as powerful as a hurricane. In that moment she was invincible. Whole and free of both the past and the future. There was only right here. Right now. And the decadent feelings sweeping through her.

How long she lingered she didn't know. And for the first time in her life, didn't care. Only knew that Sergei's fingers continued to glide in and out of her. Slower than before, but still present and drawing out the aftershocks with the combined pressure of his thumb at her clit.

Definitely a man with a lot of experience.

And patience.

And exceptional oral skills.

She rolled her head to one side, forced her climax-weighted eyelids open—and spied one seriously smug Russian staring back at her.

As if he had all the time in the world and no inclination to resign his task, he held her gaze and gave her one last thorough lick.

"You look rather pleased with yourself," she said, the huskiness in her voice undeniably thick with the aftereffects of an exceptional climax.

Pushing himself up with one hand, he skimmed a calloused palm over her hip, then inward toward her belly. "Your cries were loud, *feya*." His thumb fanned through the curls she kept tightly trimmed atop her sex. "The house is empty, but the grounds are not."

Fuck.

The men outside the house.

She'd forgotten about them. Actually, she'd forgotten about everything. Which was amazing considering her mind wasn't the type that appreciated the art of relaxation. She scooched her bottom closer to the pillows, centering herself on the bed. "I wasn't that loud." She paused a beat, trying to remember. "Was I?"

Grinning, Sergei pushed off the bed, straightened and started casually releasing the buttons on his shirt as he toed off his shoes. "If you think they were protective before, I'm afraid you'll find them intolerable now."

Well now, that didn't make any sense at all. Razzing her, she'd understand. Or maybe acting awkward and unable to look her in the eye a few days, but more protective? That didn't make any sense.

She opened her mouth to ask him what he meant, then snapped it closed at the sight of his bared chest.

She'd known he was fit. Had savored the feel of his arms and torso when she was holding on for dear life through one of his devastating kisses. Had even expected to see more tattoos given those she'd seen on his knuckles and wrists, but this...

He was a work of art.

Literally.

Swarthy skin stretched over well-defined muscle and the vast majority of it was inked with elaborate tattoos in black and red. And it wasn't one massive piece of art work either. More a collage of inspiration added bit by bit, but done so well it all fit together. Epaulets on each shoulder, five-pointed stars with intricate shading atop each pectoral, a dagger that appeared embedded in his skin, a winged creature that seemed part bat and part dragon. The imagery was fascinating and made her itch to explore.

The muted *zritch* from the zipper on his jeans ripped her from her stupor just as he pushed them past his hips. Either he'd snagged his briefs or boxers on the way down, or he was a commando man because when he straightened, he was completely naked and ready for action.

"Oh." From some dim corner of her mind, she noted she'd actually spoken the single, breathless syllable out loud, but at that particular moment she didn't give a damn. She was too fascinated. Too riveted and tongue-tied for pride to have any say over her actions. Yes, he'd unveiled more tattoos. Lots of them. Detailed ones combining dragon scales, weapons and armor that coiled around his hips and continued to his muscled thighs. But the real focus—the thing that left her jaw slack and her mind on pause—was the thick erection straining toward his navel.

"Oh?" He paced to the edge of the bed, the pleased glint in his eyes belying the nature of his words. "I don't believe I've ever heard you at such a loss for words." He put one knee to the mattress and crawled toward her, a panther inching close enough to strike. "Does that mean you're disappointed, *feya*?"

He kept coming. Braced his knees on either side of hers and leaned in until gravity and his kiss took over and she found her head cushioned by thick down pillows.

She sighed into his mouth, the hot contact of his skin against hers and his delicious weight pinning her to the bed the most beautifully tactile experience of her life. The faintest trace of her release still lingered on his lips, and his tongue stroked against hers with the same masterful deliberation he'd exercised on her sex.

And his hands. Good Lord, his touch was divine. Purposeful. Passionate. Reverent even as it demanded a response. Every rasp of his calloused palms against her sensitized flesh sent tingles rippling in all directions. Awakened that part of her she'd thought forever buried years ago.

Never in her life had she felt anything remotely this erotic. This overwhelming and yet peaceful in the same breath. She was floating. Buoyed on a sensual cloud by his drugging kiss, his hypnotic touch and his sinful taste.

He shifted, dragging seductive kisses along her jawline and down the side of her neck as he slid one knee between hers and nudged it wide. "You never answered my question, *feya*."

Questions?

There'd been questions?

She whimpered and arched her back, encouraging him to speed up the leisurely trek his mouth was making toward her breast. "Stop talking."

His low chuckle was pure delighted wickedness, the warm tickle of his exhalation drawing her already straining nipple to an agonized peak. He grazed the distended tip with his teeth. "How long has it been, *feya*?"

Fisting her hand in his hair, she tried to guide his

mouth where she wanted it. When her words came out, they were surprisingly gruff. "It doesn't matter."

He licked the tip, an agonizingly slow motion that made her breath catch and her heart skitter. "Oh, but it does." He shifted again, bringing his other knee between hers, and forced her thighs wide with his own. One minute press of his hips and his shaft glided against her clit.

"No, it doesn't." She rolled her hips, angling for more of the delicious friction. "Trust me, it doesn't."

His fingers at her hip dug into her skin. "Look at me."

Her eyes snapped open, a demand for more ready on the tip of her tongue.

It fizzled in an instant, the sheer magnificence of the man above her commanding her silence.

A dark knight.

One poised to claim his due.

His voice was like midnight. Low, lush and endless. "How long has it been?"

Why it was so important, she couldn't imagine. She'd given birth, for crying out loud. There was no way he'd hurt her. But the vehemence in his tone stirred the truth. "Since Emerson."

Something moved behind those mysterious eyes of his. Something so raw and primitive goose bumps lifted along her skin.

"Nightstand drawer, Evette. Now."

Oh, boy.

She threw out a hand and fumbled for a condom, no small task considering how badly her hands shook from the adrenaline coursing through her and how he refused to let her go. Even once she managed to snag one of the packets, she nearly dropped it on the hand-off. "Hurry."

Keeping one hand at her hip, he held her gaze and tore the packet open with his teeth. *"Nyet."*

Not just a no, but a hard no.

"You've been without for seven years." He rolled the condom into place, palmed the back of one thigh and leaned forward so he braced his other hand beside her head. "There will be no hurry this time." He pulled back just enough the head of his cock nudged her entrance. "You will remember it." He pressed inside, just the tip of him gliding easy through the slickness of her release. "Every stroke." Deeper. Fuller. Every inch gained earned while his stare stayed locked to hers. "Every sound. Every sensation. You will remember who it was who gave them to you."

Holy freaking *wow*, she'd forgotten how amazing it felt to be connected with a man. To the delectable stretch as her body adjusted to him and the unique fit of his body. And with him gazing down at her—studying every reaction as if his every move was driven off her response—it was off-the-charts intimate. Her words came out ragged and breathless. "I think it's a safe bet I'm not going to forget them no matter what tempo you set." She dragged her foot up the back of his thigh and used her heel to urge him the rest of the way home. When his hips met hers and the heavy weight of his balls lay flush against her, she sighed. "But I promise you, I won't break."

The wolf she'd glimpsed before returned and smiled down at her. "You mistake me, *malen'kaya feya*. I said I wouldn't hurry." He lowered his head and murmured against her mouth. "I didn't say I wouldn't take you hard."

A flutter rippled through her sex, the dirty promise in his words a mere precursor to what he delivered in reality. There was no planning. No seduction. No run-of-the-mill step-by-step playbook learned from *Men's Health* or *Penthouse*. It was animalistic. Glorious in its unscripted beauty and driven solely on physical sensation. And through every second, his focus was riveted on her. On her response to each touch. Each moan or sigh. The reaction garnered from each position he guided her through. As if his pleasure was contingent on hers.

It was freeing. Empowering and humbling all at once.

In one smooth move, he pulled free of her sex, flipped her to her belly and drove back inside her. His warm breath coasted against her neck and his voice was as rumbly as thunder at midnight. "You will come for me." His pelvis pounded against her ass and his balls slapped against her labia with each thrust. "You will give me your release and cry my name while you do it."

Under any other situation, she'd have laughed. It was so like him to command such a thing. So blatant and defiant of any obstacles that stood in his path.

But with his weight blanketing her...his scent all around her and the delicious shuttling of his cock through her sex...all she could do was whimper and accept it. To latch on to the tightening low in her belly. Surrender to the growing climax stomping closer by the second.

He gripped her wrists, his fingers like manacles

pinning her to bed. And yet, his words were pure velvet. A seductive beast luring her toward its shadowed den. "I felt it, *feya*. Already know how tight your pussy clenches when you come. Now I want to feel my sweet angel milk my cock."

"Oh my God." Pleasure speared straight to her core and her hips lifted higher on pure instinct.

His cockhead brushed her G-spot. Once. Twice.

And that was all she wrote.

She was soaring. Riding uncharted highs. Relishing each squeeze of her sex around his thick shaft and bucking against each of his increasing thrusts.

He groaned into her neck and murmured a string of words she had no hope of understanding against her skin.

And then he bit her.

Made her pussy fist him all over again as he speared to the hilt and his cock jerked inside her.

So perfect.

Dangerously so.

A hedonistic moment so powerful even the most pious person would relinquish every vow simply to delight in its pleasure. And she was just a normal woman. A mother who'd gone too many years without touch or intimacy.

An addict just waiting to happen.

He licked the tender spot where he'd bitten her neck. Then kissed it. Languorously, undulated his hips against hers and explored the delicate stretch of skin from her neck to her shoulder with more tender, affectionate kisses.

Such gentleness. A reverence in stark contrast to the unforgiving, dispassionate demeanor he showed the rest of the world. He skimmed one hand over the curve of her hip. "You are all right, *malen'kaya feya*?"

"I'm peachy," she sighed, savoring his heat as the room's chill began to settle on her sweat-misted skin. Her bed at the carriage house was comfy—old as the hills, but soft and familiar. Comparatively, Sergei's was probably what they had stocked in heaven. "Snug as a bug in a rug."

He chuckled near her ear, the smile in his low voice when he spoke mingling with the aftereffects of her release to create a quiet, peaceful cocoon. "I like you sated and pliant." He kissed the spot he'd bitten again and lingered there. "I like even more how I got you there."

A prodding from somewhere in her conscience told her to make note of the statement. To perk up and make sure he wasn't assuming there would be any future encounters.

But his warmth was too tempting. The gentle rasp of his beard against her skin as he rolled them both to their sides and pulled the thick comforter over them too much to heed direction from anything but the heavy peace settling over her.

She mumbled something. Or she assumed she did because he chuckled again and spooned her with his arm cradling her head. "Go to sleep, Evette. I've got you."

So nice.

So warm.

She couldn't remember the last time she'd been this warm. This protected. Surrounded by the strength of a capable, intelligent man.

The weight of sleep pressed harder. Lulled her to let go and trust.

She could fight it.

Probably should.

But she'd think about that later.

Right now, she was safe. And happy.

Just this once, she'd take it.

Chapter Twelve

Night and day.

To Sergei's mind, it was too common of an expression to be worthy of anything to do with the woman curled on her side, fast asleep in his bed, but apt for the moment nonetheless. He was shadows. Secrets. Death.

But she was everything bright, positive and hopeful in the world.

Pure sunshine.

And she was his.

She'd accepted him. Shown him what it felt like to touch heaven. To taste it and hold it. He'd known where they were headed. Had acknowledged it as soon as he'd walked her and Emerson to the carriage house door Saturday night and forced himself to give her distance all day Sunday. But he hadn't anticipated the change their physical connection would create. The ruthless possessiveness that would follow or the speed with which he was inclined to take things.

He'd touched the sun. Claimed it for his own.

And he wasn't giving it back.

Seated in the plush leather wingback to one side of his bed, he shifted just enough to pull his phone from his back pocket and double-check that he'd silenced it.

3:37 p.m.

He smiled to himself, tucked the phone back in his pocket and stood. He'd never seen someone sleep so soundly. Certainly never experienced it for himself. But she was completely relaxed. Her features beautifully unguarded and her plump lips slightly parted. The last thing he wanted to do was wake her, but she'd be furious if he waited any longer to do so.

He paused by the side of the bed.

The sheets and blankets he'd pulled over her when he'd slipped out of bed an hour after she'd fallen asleep barely covered her breasts, leaving the upper swells exposed. Her skin was exceptional. A tactile indulgence he'd happily gorged on.

Perhaps a furious Evette wouldn't be such a bad thing. He'd already gotten a taste of her attitude, but taming her anger in a highly sexual fashion would be a worthy challenge. One he'd make sure they both remembered for a very long time.

He put a knee to the bed and stretched out beside her.

Rather than wake at the movement, she sighed and rolled a little closer.

It was tempting to take advantage. To peel off his clothes, slip between the sheets with her and stake his claim all over again. But Emerson would be ready for her soon and she'd need time to get herself in order. He cupped the side of her face. "It's time to wake up, *solnyshka*."

She started, her eyes snapping open and shooting straight to him. Almost as quickly, she relaxed and gave him a shaky smile. "Wow. I was really out." For a moment, she looked her fill at his face, a unique expression that said she was as much uncertain as to what to do with her current situation as she was pleased to be there. She shook herself into focus, pulled away from him and patted the covers. "Where's my phone?"

He nodded to the clothes he'd folded and placed on the dresser along one wall. "There."

It was a good distance away. One she'd be forced to take without anything covering her glorious body. Her eyebrows dipped inward on a playful pout that said she'd intuited the direction of his thoughts. But, true to her spirited form, she threw the covers aside and gracefully slid from the bed. "Well, what time is it?"

"Nearing 3:45."

She froze in her tracks. "What?"

There it was. The fury surfacing in a single moment.

Before he could calm her with the actions he'd taken on her behalf, she shot the rest of the way to the dresser. "Emerson was out of school at three."

"He was, and my men were there to get him."

She straightened from pulling on her panties and snatched her bra. "What? Why didn't you wake me?"

While the show was entertaining on a certain level, the possessive drive that had ridden him all afternoon wouldn't let him sit still any longer. He stood and prowled her direction. "You were peaceful. Resting. Waking you when I could see to the responsibility on your behalf and give you more of what you needed made no sense." He caught her hand just as she reached for her T-shirt. "Relax, *solnyshka*. He is in the kitchen studying for an American history test. He will text me when he's ready to be quizzed."

There was genuine curiosity in her voice, but also

lingering panic. She jerked her hand free and pulled the shirt over her head. "You're helping him with American history now?"

"I am from Russia, but I studied many years in America. I know American history better than most people who live here."

She frowned and glanced over her shoulder at the bright afternoon skies. "He doesn't know where I am, does he?"

He might not have flinched outwardly, but his insides stung as though she'd shocked him. "He thinks you're running an errand for me."

"Right." The little puff of air that followed the single word could be interpreted only as relief. She shook out her jeans and wrangled them on.

He should leave things alone. Let her lay eyes on her son and know that he'd take care of her as he should. As he always would. But for the first time in more years than he could remember, impulsiveness guided his mouth. "It bothers you your son might think you've spent time with me?"

"No, it bothers me that my son might think I missed picking him up at school because I was asleep in a man's bed."

Emerson.

True, he was an impressionable boy, but he was also wise. Much more so than she gave him credit for. And while he understood her reasoning, it didn't warrant the fear radiating off her. "There is something else wrong."

She fastened her jeans, her lips pinched tight together.

"You will tell me what it is."

Her gaze shot to his for all of a second before she

stomped to her shoes by the bed. "Sergei, we can't do this again." She shoved one foot in her Keds and wedged her finger in the back to pull it on. "Nothing's changed. I work for you. It's unprofessional. I can't..." She repeated the process with the other shoe and straightened, an expression on her face that made his beast furious. "People will draw all kinds of horrible conclusions and that's going to blow back on me. On my son."

"Horrible conclusions?"

"That I'm sleeping with you for money. For a job. For a place to live."

The fury morphed to a blazing rage. When he spoke, his voice was so low he barely heard it himself. "You think people will call you a whore."

"Yes!"

"And have I ever made you feel this way?"

"No! Never! But you have to understand—perception is reality, and people can be cruel. Especially kids. Who knows what they'll say to him at school?"

"You don't know people will think this."

She let out a wild chuckle and threw her hands up in exasperation. "Actually, I do. My own uncle thought it Saturday night."

The slap.

That's what the whole altercation with her uncle had been about.

A fiery heat crept up Sergei's neck and his palm itched for the weight of his Glock. "He called you a whore?"

"No, he caught me in a clench with a man he later found out was my boss, then he promptly encouraged me to use *all my assets*." She blew out a breath and visibly fought to wrangle her emotions before she paced toward him. "You have to understand—I enjoyed today. Very much. More than…well, ever." She stopped in front of him, braced her tiny hands on his biceps and lowered her voice. "But I have to think about Emerson. I can't afford for those lines to get blurred again."

She hadn't understood.

Not what today had signified for him, or where he planned to take them. Yes, she'd given herself freely, but she hadn't yet grasped what he wanted. What he needed.

But she would.

Her and everyone else. "The lines will not be blurred, *solnyshka*. They'll be crystal clear. I promise you."

She frowned, stepped back and crossed her arms over her chest. "Why do I get the feeling we're saying two very different things? And what does that word mean anyway? It's new."

His phone buzzed in his pocket. He took it out, saw the notification was the text he'd been waiting on and used her curiosity of Russian to dodge any more questioning. "It's an endearment." He put the phone back in his pocket and pulled her flush against him, affectionately squeezing her shoulders and holding her in place when she tried to push away. "The literal translation is small sun, but your equivalent would be sunshine."

She ceased her attempts to flee and cocked her head, something beyond curiosity moving behind her sparkling hazel eyes.

Before she could ask whatever question went with her thoughts, he distracted her with the best tool at his disposal. One that would keep her busy all night and give him time to set his plans in motion. "Now, your son advises he's ready to have someone quiz him. Shall you do the honors, or shall I?"

Chapter Thirteen

"Baby, hurry up. We're gonna be late!" Evette raked her fingertips through the long bangs on her pixie, checked the effect in the fancy mirror hanging over her even fancier lavatory and listened for Emerson to head toward the stairs. Normally, it was him calling on her to hurry up, but she'd had a crap time sleeping last night for replaying the hot-as-hell interlude with Sergei. She'd finally given up tossing and turning at six this morning and decided to get an early start on the day. Add to that, her boy had been groggier than normal waking up and didn't show any signs of kicking things into high gear anytime soon. "You stay up too late or something?"

Finally, his footsteps sounded on the thick carpet lining the catwalk that ran between their rooms on the top floor. From how heavy those footsteps were, one would think he was headed to a guillotine instead of to school. She rounded out of her bedroom in time to catch him shrug and head down the stairs. "Was talking to a friend online. Should have gone to bed earlier, but I didn't want to be rude."

By some crazy miracle, Evie kept the surprise out

of her voice and didn't trip down the stairs. "Oh, yeah. Which friend was this?"

See? Totally smooth. Nowhere near the *You have a friend?* she wanted to ask.

Emerson hit the first floor, snatched a banana off the trestle table and unhooked his backpack from the chair he'd left it on. "I guess. One of the kids at school. Different grade." He paused at the front door and glanced back at Evette with a *come on already* glower. "I thought you said we were going to be late?"

Okay. Something was definitely up. Staying up late shooting the bull...late getting into his normal morning routine...snippy with his momma. And what was with the untucked polo shirt? She grabbed her purse on the way to join him. "I thought you had to keep your shirts tucked in."

"You're supposed to, but not all the guys do."

"Hmm." So distracted with wrangling what had her boy clicking to a different rhythm, she nearly plowed into two of Sergei's men waiting just outside the door. She held up both hands and took a short step back. "Oh, hey!"

Two more men she'd never seen before stood another ten feet away surrounded by boxes and tool chests.

She zeroed in on the two more familiar men. Neither were her usual escorts to school or around town, but they'd waved or nodded to her and Emerson on the grounds or in the house a time or two. "What's going on?"

"The boss wants some upgrades to security," the taller of the two advised. While she'd never asked Sergei directly, she assumed most of his employees were recruited from the local scene because Sergei, Kir and Roman were the only ones with Russian accents. This guy's Cajun lilt definitely marked him as a native to her part of Louisiana. "Shouldn't take too long. Maybe a few hours. You okay if we get on it while you're walking Emerson to school and working?"

"He wants upgrades?" She glanced at the main house, over to her guard waiting halfway down the driveway, then back to the man who'd spoken. "This place is already pretty fortified as it is."

"Hey, I don't ask. I just do."

Right. Because mob bosses didn't exactly expend a lot of energy explaining the ins and outs of why they did things. "You've got a point." She shook her head and waved them into the house. "Help yourself. I've got plenty to keep me busy in the main house when I get back."

The trip to school was quieter than normal. Granted, Emerson was never a huge talker, but this morning he seemed distracted. Puzzled or pensive.

Not that she minded. She had her own issues to wrestle. Like how she was going to keep things platonic with her boss when all her mind seemed to be capable of remembering was his touch, the sound of his voice murmuring things in a language she didn't understand and his devastating kiss. Before she knew it, Emerson was dropped off and she found herself meandering back down the driveway, only moments from having to put her game face on.

Piece of cake. Just be polite and friendly and pretend yesterday never happened.

Per usual, the kitchen was a beehive of activity. Kir and Roman sat at the round table, each of them manning a computer and a giant cup of coffee. A few more men she'd seen before but didn't really know stood near the island talking about something she couldn't quite make out, while Olga had both hands on her hips giving what-for to the specialized butcher who, in Evette's opinion, was grossly overpriced.

Olga noted Evie's arrival, dropped her hands to her side and exclaimed, "You were right. The man is a thief. Give me the name of your man again."

Evette stopped dead center in the kitchen.

Kir and Roman stopped talking.

The two men by the island did, too.

The butcher's face turned a scary red and he aimed a deadly scowl at Evette. "You called me a thief?"

She probably should have gone into political soothing mode at that point, but Evette was too shell-shocked from Olga's outburst to get in the game. She focused on the feisty cook she'd gone head-to-head with for nearly a month. "Did you just say I'm right?"

"He brought me a choice prime rib and charged me prime price."

"It's a prime!" the butcher said. "You pay the prime price."

Olga rewrapped the huge cut of beef and shoved it back into his hands. Her accent was so thick it was hard to make out the words, but the meaning was crystal clear. "I do no such thing."

One of the men who'd been standing near the island edged closer to the butcher. "Come on, man. I'll see you out."

For all of a heartbeat, the butcher looked like he'd argue. Then he reevaluated, hugged the infant-size package to his chest and harrumphed as he stomped to the door.

Evette waited until he was gone before she tried again. "You love that guy's product. What happened?"

Maybe it was the way the sun came through the back kitchen windows, but Evie could have sworn Olga blushed. "Nothing happened. He simply will not be used any longer." She smoothed her apron down and cleared her throat. "You want coffee?"

Whoa. An agreement and an offer for coffee? Maybe she'd hit her head before bed and had woken up in an alternative universe. "Um…sure."

The kitchen door opened, and the gardener hustled in, one of his helpers tight on his heels. "Miss Labadie, I need to know what flowers you want planted in the front beds."

"Excuse me?"

"The front flower beds—what flowers do you want? Pansies are nice, but I think a mix of primrose and winter jasmine would look better with the house."

It was way too early for this. Way too early and way too weird. She scanned the room's occupants.

The man still at the counter looked away.

Olga hustled toward her with a fresh cup of coffee.

Kir and Roman both watched her with knowing smirks.

"Why on earth would you ask me?" Evette said to the gardener. "I just man the schedules and pay on Fridays."

"Mr. Petrovyh said you're to make those decisions going forward."

Olga handed over the coffee mug, the smile on her flushed face shockingly pleasant. "Cream and sugar."

Through some miracle, Evette didn't drop the mug. "How do you know I like cream and sugar?"

"Sergei, of course." She bustled back to the stove like it was common knowledge their employer knew everything.

Evette sampled the coffee and, lo and behold, Olga had nailed the combination of cream and sugar. "So, I'm supposed to tell you what to plant now?" she said to the gardener.

"Yes, ma'am. Whatever you think would look best."

"Um..." Putting her in charge of flowers was like putting her in charge of automotive care. "Okay, primrose and jasmine sound nice." So did a do-over for the morning, because right now she was pretty sure she'd woken up in the twilight zone.

The gardener nodded and hurried back outside.

She probably would have stood there nursing her coffee and staring after him for a solid five minutes if Kir hadn't cleared his throat and nudged a large manila envelope across the kitchen table. "Sergei left this for you."

Oh, goodie. At the rate her morning was going, it was probably tax returns that needed preparing or some other accounting nightmare. She set her coffee on the table and opened the package to find a stack of brochures.

Parsons School of Design.

Savannah College of Art and Design.

Rhode Island School of Design.

Pratt Institute.

She looked to Kir and Roman. "What are these?"

The doorbell rang, and Kir went back to staring at

his computer, but Roman at least managed a shrug and a "Not my business."

Hmm. *Not his business* her ass.

Footsteps sounded from the foyer.

Evette spun to Olga. "Olga, do you know what these are for?"

"Nyet," she said, not looking up from her pot on the stove. "He left it for you early this morning."

The man who'd escorted out the butcher led a team of three into the kitchen. "Here she is." He paused, focused on Evette and motioned toward the newcomers. "Miss Labadie, these people are here to see you."

They were? She locked eyes with the woman at the front of the pack. "And you are?"

"Mary Thompson." She held out a business card. "Mr. Petrovyh contacted my company and said you'd be instructing us on what you wanted done."

The simple bold text on the plain white card nearly knocked her over.

Magic Rags Cleaning Service.

What. The. Hell.

The disoriented vibe for the morning lasered to a finite point in a heartbeat. "You work for a cleaning service?"

"I own it," Mary said, pushing her shoulders back and beaming a proud smile. "This is our fourth year in business. We have very good references."

Of course they did. Sergei wouldn't hire anyone who didn't. Except her. Her he'd hired on a whim. Though, what role she was filling now, she didn't have a clue.

She was about to find out, though. She handed the card back to Mary. "Would you excuse me?"

"Oh, yes. Of course."

Evie aimed a stern look at Kir and Roman. "Where is he?"

"Who?" Kir said, though the grin on his face said he knew damned well whom she wanted.

"Don't mess with me, Kir. I've had a weird morning."

Roman chuckled at that and apparently decided to take pity on her. "You will find him in his office."

She nodded and went for a Hail Mary with Olga. "Olga, any chance you could get these people a coffee while I go see what's going on with the big guy?"

Olga might have pretended to be busy with her cooking, but she spun around and got busy on the request fast enough to make it clear she'd been homed in to everything that had been going on. "Yes, of course."

The rooms went by in a haze, the drone of the normal goings-on muted beneath the tirade going on in her head. He'd lost his mind. Lost his ever-lovin' freaking mind. Or maybe he'd just taken her words yesterday to heart and found someone to replace her.

No, that didn't make any sense. Why replace her and then have the gardener come to her for decisions?

See? Totally insane.

The door to his office stood open so she stomped right in. "What's going on?"

Sergei looked up from his computer, but took his sweet time doing it. For a man who'd just had his domain infiltrated by a woman practically vibrating with a pending storm, he seemed awfully calm. Actually, relaxed. "You'll have to be more specific."

"There are people here to clean the house."

"Yes."

"That's my job."

"Not anymore."

Her stomach pitched as if someone had yanked a trap door out from underneath her and her throat got so tight breathing was sketchy. "What do you mean, *not anymore*? I have a contract that specifies I'm responsible for taking care of this place."

"Correct." He sat back in his chair, anchored his elbows on the slick leather arms and tented his fingers in front of him. He was every bit the boardroom executive—only with a deadly presence. "They are here to do the work. You are here to direct them."

"But why? It's not necessary. Not to mention, it's a waste of time and money."

"It is not a waste of time. You have other things to do."

She did? "Like what?"

His attention dipped to her hands.

The pamphlets.

She'd forgotten about those.

She raised them up and waggled them back and forth. "That's the other thing. What's this about?"

"Your schooling."

"You don't have anything to do with my schooling. I work on it as I have time."

"And now you have more."

She strode to the front of the desk and slammed the fancy brochures down on top of it, sending three or four unanchored papers flying. "Stop circling the point of this conversation."

He grinned. Actually freaking *grinned*. "I'm not circling anything, *solnyshka*. You are."

Oh, no.

He did *not* just play that card.

The tops of her ears and cheeks burned with the heat of holy feminine fire. If he wanted to play head-to-head, then she'd more than happily play along. "Fine. You want direct, I'll give you direct. I've got four men swarming the carriage house and setting up security to rival Fort Knox. Olga's not only decided she agrees with me about the butcher, but she poured me coffee. *With cream and sugar.* My employer's suddenly taken an interest in my fashion career, the gardener wants to know which flowers I want in the front flower beds and there's an unnecessary army of people here to clean a house I'm supposed to clean. Now, I want to know what's going on."

His lips twitched as though it was all he could do to take her seriously, but he nodded and stood, gently pushing back his desk chair as he did. "Very well. I'm updating the carriage house, because the security wasn't to my satisfaction and it needs to be impenetrable until we're to a place where Emerson has a chance to get accustomed to the changes between you and me." He rounded the back of the desk, moving with that panther grace that both fascinated and terrified her. "Olga acted as she did because she is loyal to me and, by extension, is therefore loyal to you. The gardener is asking your direction because this house is yours to do with as you please and the design schools are because it's unacceptable for you to wait to achieve what you want in a career—which is also why the cleaning crew is here."

He stopped within touching distance, smoothed his hands from her elbows to her shoulders and tried to pull her in.

She stopped him with a splayed hand at his sternum. "What changes between you and me?"

His eyes sparkled. Not the sweet and innocent kind meant for knights in shining armor or angels, but the wicked kind from the devil himself. "You were correct yesterday, *solnyshka*. If we continued on as we were, people might misinterpret your place. Today, we are making it clear to everyone and anyone who might be interested exactly what that place is."

"Well, would you mind telling me? Because things are a little hazy from where I'm standing."

His demeanor shifted in a second, the amusement and patience he'd shown swept away in the space of one gasp as he cupped the back of her head and tugged her flush against him. "Mine."

He kissed her.

Consumed and claimed her as devoutly as his single possessive word still purring through her mind. All night long she'd remembered. Marveled at how natural it had felt to let go with him. To simply surrender and let him build the sensations until all she could do was feel and enjoy.

But that was yesterday. And while she'd made her share of mistakes, repeating them wasn't wise. No matter how good those mistakes felt.

She pushed against him. Tried to ignore the warmth of his body and the comforting earthy scent that clung to him. With his arms unrelentingly bound around her, gaining enough distance to murmur, "Sergei," was a challenge.

At her broken voice, he gave her only enough space to peer down at her.

"What you've done is sweet." She rubbed her palm

up and down his sternum. "I get what you're trying to do, but it's not going to work. People are still going to take things the wrong way, no matter how much control you give me."

He stared down at her so long, his gaze so fixed and inscrutable, she wasn't even sure he'd heard her. When he finally moved, he still kept her close, but reached for something on his desk. "They might misconstrue some things, *solnyshka*. But they will not misconstrue this."

He held up a box.

A tiny blue velvet one the color of his eyes.

A ring box.

"What is that?" Considering what kind of box it was, her question was ludicrous. Rather like looking at a snake curled up right in front of her and asking the same.

He released her and opened it.

Holy crapola.

Not just a snake, but a really freaking big snake.

Or ring.

Same thing.

The sun streaming through the French doors that led to the balcony caught in the facets and made the cushion-cut diamond and the halo diamonds surrounding it even more brilliant. "That's a ring."

"Yes, it is."

She took a step back, the pounding of her pulse in her ears drowning out all but its rapid thud. "A big ring."

"Three carats," he said, gliding forward to pick up the distance she'd created. "Exceptional quality." He plucked the ring from its velvet bed. "Perfect for my bride and an unmistakable message to those who might question your place in my life." He captured her wrist and lifted it. "Even to you."

No.

No, no, no, no, no.

Panic flooded her system. Scampered beneath her skin like a swarm of frantic rats and put her feet in motion. Out of his office. Down the stairs and through the main hallway.

She needed air. Lots of it.

And sunshine.

Someplace—any place—without walls.

She jerked the front door open and strode across the front porch.

Masculine voices sounded behind her. Footsteps, too. But she blocked them out. Kept going. Kept forcing herself to breathe past the near-painful constriction at the base of her throat.

The late October air whispered across her skin. Warred against the sweat misted along the back of her neck and sent shivers down her spine. He was out of his mind. People didn't just get married to prove a point. Didn't fall into bed one day and decide to have a life together the next. That was crazy. Impulsive and stupid.

But that's not what's bothering you is it, baby girl?

The thought murmured on her mother's voice slowed her steps just a block from the Saint Charles Streetcar. She didn't want to think about her mother. Didn't want to think about the pain that had followed her death, or Evie's actions after.

The easy chuckle she'd always earned from her mother with her crazy antics growing up rolled through her mind. *You were plenty impulsive then. Always have been. That's how we Labadies are. We live. We love.*

She didn't love. No one but Emerson. And maybe Dorothy. It hurt too bad when you lost them. Cut pieces out of your soul and left you scarred and broken.

The streetcar clanged to a stop.

Evette climbed on board and slid onto the plastic bench at the back. The only other passengers were her guard who barely made it on board on time and a family clustered near the front. The father pointed out a majestic house to his daughter beside him while the mother rested with a dozing toddler on her lap.

She'd had that once. A family. The warmth of her father's protection and the love of her mother. Then she'd lost them both and thrown her dreams away in her grief.

She barely knew Sergei.

Okay, so, yes, he'd made her feel alive for the first time in forever. Had shown her a physical connection beyond anything else she'd ever experienced. Had given her every comfort and provided for her needs at a time when she wasn't sure how she was going to pull through. But that wasn't grounds to get married. Certainly not to an overbearing, presumptuous man who, by his own admission, was creating his own criminal family and was her boss to boot. She'd be insane to agree to something like that.

Mmm-hmm. Almost as insane as going to work for him in the first place, but you took that leap, didn't you?

The streets streamed by her. Houses. Businesses. Locals and tourists meandering the streets. Before she knew it, she found herself outside Dorothy's, staring through the wide window at the empty barstools lining the front counter. It'd been a second home for as long as she could remember. Her safe space. A bevy of memories of her mom and Dorothy together, so many of them earned while she sat on that same barstool Emerson favored.

The tiny bell that hung over the front door jingled as she entered and the rich scents of bacon and coffee from the morning crowd surrounded her in an instant. A few patrons sat at booths and tables farther back, and both of the waitresses manning the floor turned and gave her a polite wave.

But it was Dorothy's voice from the kitchen that she followed, the familiar warmth in her Cajun lilt drawing her the same way her mother's had when she was little. She rounded the wall that separated the diner from where the bulk of the work was done.

The new cook Dorothy had hired three months ago stood at the end of the island. Both hands were on his hips and pure dismay etched on his face as he stared at Dorothy hunched over the counter going to town on what Evie surmised was either the week's coming menu or the newest order list.

Dorothy looked up, sized Evette up in all of two seconds and straightened. "Not gonna work the way you have it." She slid the paper back in front of the cook, but never shifted her gaze from Evette. "Change Saturday's and Sunday's specials so we're not orderin' double the meat. I'll come look soon as I'm done with Evette."

"But I gotta be somewhere at noon."

Dorothy never looked back, just kept her knowing stare on Evette, grabbed her by the shoulder as soon as she got within touching distance and steered her toward Dorothy's office. "You wanna go at noon, you figure that out and get it to me quick. Looks of my girl, I got other business to take care of."

She shut the door behind them and pointed toward the old diner chair next to her cluttered desk. "Sit."

"I can wait until you're done."

"Don't need to wait. That boy's gotta pull his own head out of his ass this time. Been teachin' him long enough." She sat in her own chair and dipped her head toward the still-empty seat beside her desk. "Don't make an old woman crane her head, child. Sit and tell me what's wrong."

Evette slid into the chair as easily as she had when she was little and she'd come to ask Dorothy's opinion on how to deal with a trio of bullies in fourth grade. "What makes you think something's wrong?"

"Only time you're not smilin' is when something's wrong, and you're not smilin'."

The soft buttery yellow from the old gooseneck lamp Dorothy kept on her desk was the only light, making the oversize storage space Dorothy had claimed for her own years ago more like a secret hideaway than an office. Two file cabinets sat against the wall behind Dorothy and a bookshelf full of cookbooks and supply catalogs crowded the wall to her right.

Looking at the details—the history and the memories that went with them—was easier than looking at Dorothy. When she couldn't avoid the woman's gaze any longer, she stared at the invoices cluttering the top of the desk. "I slept with Sergei."

Dorothy grunted. One of those tell-me-something-I-don't-know sounds reserved for mothers and grandmothers who'd not only heard it all, but had done most of it, too.

Evette folded her hands in her lap and hung her head. "I screwed up."

"Not sure any other woman who's laid eyes on that man would call gettin' tangled in the sheets with him a screwup. Hell, most of 'em would be in here braggin' about it instead of staring at their lap like a guilty teenager."

The jab did what Dorothy had likely intended it to do, and Evette lifted her head. "He wants to marry me."

Not much surprised Dorothy. In fact, in all the years Evette had known her, only the death of her husband had truly broken through her even-keeled demeanor. But for a second, her eyes widened in surprise. She nodded a moment later, reclined against her seat back like the weight of the world had finally grown too heavy to fight and sighed. "Not surprised."

This time it was Evie's turn to be shocked. "What do you mean, *you're not surprised*? That's insane. He barely knows me."

Dorothy stared at her. Studied her the way a mother did when considering whether to rip the veil off one of life's ugly truths or just to let them keep living unaware of a hard reality. On a heavy exhale, her gaze slid to her desk. "I saw him, child. Saw the way he looked at you when he thought no one else was looking." A sad smile tilted her lips. "Like an angel had come tiptoeing into hell with a ray of sunshine just for him. A little spark in the darkness."

She shifted her attention to Evette. "A man like Sergei—goodness has a hard time getting through. Thinks they're not worth it. I have to imagine if the good ever did get through, he'd fight the whole damned world to keep it."

The already muted sounds from the kitchen and the patrons from the dining area faded to nothing. Even Evie's heart seemed to still, her ears straining as if that might somehow make the words her lifelong friend had shared clearer. "What are you saying?"

"I'm saying you stomped into the arena. Waved a big old red cape in front of the bull's face and did it knowing full well you were in the ring with the baddest of the bad." She hesitated only a heartbeat, then plowed ahead. "Before you jab your blade into his hide, you might ought to take a look around and see if that bull's charging you, or trying to level the obstacles in your life."

"You think I should marry him?"

"You asking my opinion?"

"Yes."

Dorothy pulled in a long, audible inhale, then let it out hard. As if with the exhalation, she was releasing thoughts long ago buried. "I think when your daddy died, you started buildin' up a wall. I think when your momma died you finished building it. And I think, underneath all that wild rebellion that came after your momma's death, a part of you was looking for Emerson. To find a way to rebuild a family for yourself in a way it couldn't be taken away from you. Least not as easily." She cocked her eyebrow in that knowing way she'd done countless times to all her children over the years. "You ask me, it seems you've got a whole new family, whether you like it or not. You haven't had anyone in your corner in a long damned time and for a self-sufficient woman like you, that's a big change."

Holy crap. "You agree with him."

Dorothy shrugged, stood and shuffled toward the closed door, her movements slow and indicative of the pain that came from years of being on her feet for breakfast, lunch and dinner. "You asked me what I think. Well, what I think is that Sergei's big enough to stomp out any threat that comes your way and pry those dreams of yours out of the trash heap."

He *had* done that.

Had listened to her concerns about what people might think and taken action. Thought about her future and her career. Had even factored how Emerson might feel about the situation and what time he might need to adjust.

She spun toward Dorothy's retreating form. "What do I do?"

"Don't know, child." She opened the door, took one step through and paused with her hand on the jamb long enough to meet Evie's stare. "What I do know is, running's not your style. And if there's anyone on this planet with a heart big enough to love the devil himself, it's you."

With that she was gone, leaving Evette alone in the shadowed room with nothing but her thoughts.

Chapter Fourteen

Not even twenty-four hours since Evette had stormed out of his office and Sergei was already sorely tempted to break his self-imposed vow to give his *feya* space. Evette wasn't stupid. When the initial shock he'd thrust upon her yesterday finally cleared and she began to move through all the ramifications of being tied to a man like him, she'd quickly zero in on negatives.

But she was also an instinctive creature. One nimble enough to raise a smart boy with very little help and as street smart as they came. His hope was that, if he gave her the time and room to process both the pros and the cons of a life with him, she'd opt to give him a chance. To explore the explosive passion between them and welcome the safety and comforts he offered.

Until then, the best thing he could do was avoid any and all opportunities to break his vow—which meant diving as deeply into his business interests as he could and praying fate didn't ply him with temptation before Evette had at least had enough time to center herself.

He stared out the back seat window of his BMW, the deeply tinted windows doing little to stifle the colors beyond it. Every city had a feel to it. A uniqueness born from the people who lived there. To Sergei, New

Orleans's style was one of life and the love of self-expression. A city willing and able to sample and appreciate a variety of styles and histories.

The South Shores of Lake Pontchartrain were no exception. Palm trees, red brick sidewalks and electric-blue streetlamps fashioned with a contemporary flair lined the streets, giving it a hint of the tropical elements you'd expect to find in Florida or some other seaside venue while still holding on to its Cajun flair.

Pulling into one of the many parking lots facing Lake Pontchartrain's choppy waters, Roman looked into the rearview mirror and met Sergei's gaze in the back seat. "You sure you want in the restaurant business?"

Sergei wanted in all kinds of businesses. Construction, gambling and bars had been the first he'd ventured into over the last year, but he wanted more diversity. More avenues to fully cement himself in the home he'd chosen.

Sergei shifted his attention to the wide, weathered sign with evergreen lettering that said simply *André's*. The building beneath it was even less impressive—a single-story building in red brick with a simple black door and black shutters on either side of wide windows. "People are our business. The more varied our businesses, the more extensive our connections will be and the more influence we will hold."

Kir chuckled from the front passenger's seat. "And here I thought it was just because you liked Italian food."

Both men opened their doors and got out.

Kir went to the restaurant's front door, while Roman opened the car's back door for Sergei.

The anticipation that went with any new business venture left Sergei exhilarated. Focused in the same way a hunter prepared for a hunt or crept through a forest. Only Sergei's hunt was one of acquisition. A financial pursuit where camouflage, scents and stealth were replaced with suits, money and collateral.

Inside the building, the dim dining area with its midseventies crimson-and-black décor was empty. Smoking had been banned years ago, but it was all too easy to imagine the patrons that had frequented in the early days lingering at their tables over a cigarette and coffee or cocktails. Women would have worn dresses and heels and their men would have all been in suits.

It was simply that kind of place. A throwback feel to a time long gone.

Sergei loved it.

Couldn't wait to create a place of his own just like it, albeit with a modernized kitchen and a focus on the younger generation.

With Roman and Kir preceding him, they made their way toward the office at the back of the building. A blast of water sounded from the kitchen followed by the clang of a metal pan on something sharp.

The office door stood open and Henri Trahan sat behind the scarred black desk that had likely been here since his father, André, had opened the restaurant's doors forty-three years ago. The fact that a traditionally Cajun family had not only started but maintained a successful Italian restaurant for nearly half a century still amused Sergei greatly.

Henri looked up, obviously startled. Where he'd normally met Sergei dressed in crisp pants and button-downs, today he wore jeans and a Saints T-shirt. From the looks of his mussed black hair and tired face, he'd either been on one hell of a bender, or had a crisis on his hands. "Mr. Petrovyh." He shot to his feet, glanced at Kir and Roman on either side of him and wiped his hands on his jeans at his hips. "Sorry, I lost track of time."

Not good.

Not good at all.

In all the years since he'd first begun working for Anton, he'd learned to deal with many character traits and personalities, but a lack of focus was intolerable. The only trait that trumped it as a deal breaker was dishonesty. "Lost track of time, or forgot?"

Henri swallowed hard. "I didn't forget. I just…" He planted his hands on his hips and hung his head a beat. When he raised it there was pure determination behind his eyes. "I've got a problem and I got caught up trying to find a way out of it."

Truth.

He could deal with honesty. Though, he'd likely get to the bottom of whatever was troubling his intended business partner more quickly without Kir and Roman putting the fear of God in the man.

"Go," Sergei said to Kir and Roman. "I will talk with our associate privately."

Both hesitated long enough to consider each other, then quietly turned and disappeared into the hallway.

Henri let out a relieved breath, the action taking the tension in his shoulders with it. "Thank you."

"There is nothing to thank me for. Not yet, anyway." Sergei seated himself in one of the midcentury American-styled chairs opposite Henri's desk and casually crossed one leg over the other. "I take it the troubles you've run into have something to do with our arrangement?" Said arrangement being the planned renovation of the original Andre's and two new expansions under the same name—one in the Quarter and another in Baton Rouge.

Henri studied Sergei's relaxed posture, then slid into his own seat with the same caution a man might use when cozying up to a snake. Only when he was situated and seemed convinced his afternoon wasn't going to end in bloodshed or pain did he anchor his forearms on his desk, clasp his hands tightly together and clear his throat. "You know I have a daughter."

Sergei nodded. He also knew Henri had a son named after his grandfather and that both children had grown up accustomed to a ready supply of money in their parents' bank accounts, most of which had come from André's long-running success.

The hands Henri had clasped in front him fisted together tighter. "Well, Amy's first year in high school was a tough one."

"You're referring to the situation that caused her to be sanctioned for theft and put on probation through her junior year."

Henri's eyes went wide. "How did you know about that? Her records were sealed."

"We've discussed and agreed upon entering into a business venture together, Mr. Trahan. I make it a point of knowing everything there is to know about someone before I move forward."

Henri kept his silence.

"I also know that your son had some issues with a sophomore girl only a few months ago," Sergei said matter-of-factly. "This resulted in a very quietly conducted medical procedure and a sizable payment made to her family. Both of these events have caused stirrings with your wife's involvement in several charitable organizations and the two of you have been somewhat estranged as a result."

Red flooded Henri's face and neck.

Sergei kept going. "Given your demeanor today, I'd guess all, or some part, of these details have come to light with other individuals and they are causing you problems?"

"If I follow through on our plans, it will all be made public," Henri said on a rush, the emphasis as the words came out thick with panic. "My kids would be devastated, and my marriage won't make it through the carnage."

Sergei hadn't met Henri's children. Had only seen pictures and heard the details from Kir when he and his crew had completed their research. Personally, he was a fan of consequences earned from a person's choices, but to each his own.

He took time to consider Henri across the desk. That he'd have to do something to deal with his business partner's latest issue was certain, but Sergei had learned long ago that a few extra minutes to let a man soak in his troubles tended to make them more agreeable long term. "Who is it?" he finally said.

"Pardon?"

"The person holding this information over your head—who is it and why are they taking this action?"

Henri's gaze shot to the desk. "Please don't ask me that." His fists opened and closed twice before he realized what he was doing and pushed back all the way in his seat. "I'm in a dangerous enough situation as it is."

"I see." Probably more so than Henri realized. "Have you...had previous dealings with this person?"

"No." Spoken so quickly and vehemently there was no question in its honesty. "I have no idea why they sought me out. I've never spoken to them before."

"But they don't want you doing business with me, and they want to prevent our venture bad enough they're willing to drag your family's ugly secrets out into the open."

It took several more heartbeats, but Henri finally answered. "Steven Alfonsi."

Of course, it was. Of all the competition Sergei had had to deal with since setting down roots in New Orleans, the local man who portrayed himself among the locals as a classic Cosa Nostra had made it his personal mission in recent months to undercut Sergei wherever he could.

Sergei sighed, more irritated than angry at having to deal with the poorly dressed thug. "And if this... threat...were to go away. The deal would resume as planned?"

"Yes," Henri said. "I want this deal. I've always wanted to expand. Plus, you helped me with my refinancing when no one else would. I appreciate that. I want to repay that. But not at the expense of my wife and kids."

"That pleases me to hear." Sergei stood. Where his meeting with Henri had originally served as a pleasant distraction from the waiting game of seducing his bride-to-be, now he was eager to be home with room to pace.

He straightened his suit jacket and pulled his shirt sleeves down. "You will say nothing more to anyone.

Nothing about our agreement and no meetings with Alfonsi. We will meet again in one week. At that time, you will be prepared to close the deal as planned."

"But my family—"

"Will not suffer. The issue will be dealt with and you and your family will have no involvement." He turned for the door, but stopped at the threshold enough to turn slightly toward Henri. "A note for future reference. Should anyone come between you and me on business deals in the future, you will come to me immediately. I will handle obstacles. You will deliver. Understand?"

Henri finally shook himself from the stupor that gripped him and stood. "Yes. Absolutely."

Sergei dipped his head once in acknowledgment and resumed his departure, casting a clipped, "One week," reminder over his shoulder.

Kir and Roman waited in the middle of the building with their backs to the wide U-shaped bar. At the height of dining hours—particularly on weekends—the bar was always crowded, predominantly by couples waiting for their table and nursing the classic cocktails André's was known for in addition to its exceptional food. While he had no plans to change what had clearly worked for many years, he did intend for the new restaurants to have a larger bar with more opportunities for waiting guests to run up their tabs with drinks.

Sergei kept moving and the two men fell in step on either side of him.

"You don't look like a man who's just entered the restaurant industry," Kir murmured.

"We have a slight delay that needs to be dealt with."

Roman pushed open the main door and the vibrant

afternoon sun sliced through the shadows. "A practical delay, or something more tactical?"

"Tactical." Sergei scanned the parking lot for signs of any eyes on them and slid into the back seat as soon as Roman opened the door. Only when his two *avtoritets* were seated as well and the car started and in motion did he continue. "It seems our friend Steven Alfonsi has moved beyond simply gathering information on my interests to taking action."

Kir twisted in his seat enough for direct eye contact. "A competing offer with Trahan?"

"*Nyet.* He seeks to block the deal entirely. His leverage is the information you found on the children."

Roman locked stares with Sergei in the rearview mirror. "Secrets are his trade."

Sergei nodded, well aware of his competitor's penchant for forcing people to his will through whatever dirty details he could find. It was one of the reasons those in the Mid-City and Seventh Ward had been so ready to welcome Sergei into their midst. Deals built on choice rather than coercion were not only more palatable to most, but garnered long-term loyalty. A concept Steven Alfonsi didn't seem to comprehend.

Sergei focused on the choppy waters across Lake Pontchartrain. Thus far, he'd avoided direct conflict. Had simply demonstrated his strength and determination through solid positioning with the community and targeted strategic business. The timing for escalating with Evette and Emerson just coming into the picture wasn't ideal, but not dealing with a direct threat wasn't tolerable. "It's time to send a message. Show the *kozel* that we do not bend to threats and how deeply our reach extends."

"And Henri?" Kir said.

"Deal with all evidence against his children. Ensure that those who might support any circumstantial claims will not do so."

Kir shrugged and faced forward, his demeanor that of a man slightly disappointed he hadn't been given a more meaningful or complicated task. "Done."

Quiet settled inside the vehicle, broken only by the highly muted purr of the performance engine. Business after business sped by on either side of the street, the unremarkable details interspersed with moderate traffic and people walking along the sidewalk creating a near-meditative space for his mind to unwind.

Or it did until the light at a major intersection brought them to a halt and drew his attention to a public school on his side of the street. The architecture marked it as a building erected sometime in the 1920s, its deep red brick and Romanesque revival design giving it a prestigious air amid all the other more modern buildings around it. Only a few students walked into or out of the main building, but the parking lot was full of cars. "Emerson's trip to school this morning was uneventful?"

Kir and Roman traded sidelong glances.

Kir smirked and did a decent job of holding in his laughter. While Sergei couldn't see any more of Roman's face beyond his eyes in the rearview mirror, it was still enough of a view to know his smile was there as well. "No issues. Mikey took them."

"And Evette?"

"Went back to the house for an hour, tried to work with the cleaning crew for another hour, then gave up and went to the mall."

"The mall?"

Kir actually chuckled this time. "The mall. And from what Mikey shared, she's the only woman alive who can make such a trip look like torture."

Interesting. He already knew from the man who'd followed her yesterday after she fled that she'd had a long talk with Dorothy, after which she'd taken her time getting home and hadn't ventured out of the carriage house except to retrieve Emerson at school. The men had described her demeanor as pensive. Thoughtful and considering. "Did she buy anything?"

"No," Kir said. "Mikey said she looked like she would a time or two, but seemed to talk herself out of her selections."

A reasonable behavior for a woman who'd made do with limited means her whole life. He'd break her of that eventually, but until then he'd take heart in the fact that she hadn't bolted altogether and might actually be settling into accepting that she wouldn't be doing labor at the house anymore.

"Emerson appears to be making friends," Roman said. "Mikey mentioned a group of boys were with him when Evette picked him up yesterday and were waiting for him this morning as well."

Friends were good. Even without Evette's insight, it was clear the boy had spent too much time alone in recent years. Though, he'd also have to instruct his men to be watchful of those who struck up a friendship with Emerson in the future. Sergei knew all too well how opportunistic people could be with people in positions of power, and as soon as his engagement with Evette became public, Emerson would definitely become a target. "Find out more about them. Who they are. Their parents...anything that might be a cause for concern."

"We will look," Roman said, "but Emerson has good instincts. If they are not worthy, he will handle it. The same way you did growing up." His gaze lifted to Sergei's in the mirror once more. "He will be a good heir."

Kir chuckled low and cast a smirk at Roman. "Best you not share that opinion around Evette. Sergei will never get her to the altar."

An astute observation and a realization he'd be wise to do what he could to steer Evette away from until he could convince her that she and Emerson belonged with him. With all of them. "We have many years before that becomes a consideration, and he will join us as a brother only if that is his wish."

Sergei zeroed in on Kir. "What do you have on the uncle?"

"On paper, he's a consultant for offshore drillers. Reported anywhere from forty to fifty thousand a year on taxes over the last ten years. Those in his neighborhood say he disappears for weeks or months at a time, then shows with impressive sums of cash."

"More than what he's reporting?"

Kir nodded. "He's known to boast of his income when he surfaces. Talks of investment schemes and gambling but never drilling. Bank accounts and credit cards in his name show limited activity."

"He sticks to cash?" Sergei said.

"So it seems." Kir shifted enough to meet Sergei's gaze. "We did have one mention of him seen with Alfonsi."

One mention was enough. Especially when the man in question had a history of flaunting cash and lived largely without a monetary footprint. "Keep on it. Start hacking into Alfonsi's accounts, too, and see if we can find any ties there."

"Word is," Roman said, "Alfonsi's technical sources aren't as good as Kir's, but if they catch a break and find we're digging in their accounts, things will escalate. Quickly."

A very good point. Fortunately for him, he had an outside source Alfonsi would be hard pressed to catch. He pulled out his phone and thumbed through his contacts.

Knox Torren.

A hacker in the truest sense of the word. A genius in the cyber world and a man who knew what it meant to protect family at all cost. It had been Knox, his wife, Darya, and the rest of those they considered family who had helped Sergei earn the right to build his new life in the city of his choosing.

Both of them would help him in a second.

He hesitated with his thumb over Knox's number.

As it had all day, the ring still inside its box sat heavy in his pocket. A constant reminder of the hurdles in front of him to overcome.

Yes, Knox was brilliant, but why solve only one problem when he could solve two at the same time?

He shifted to Darya's number instead, pushed Connect and settled in while the call rang through. Darya was a born-and-bred Russian. Not only charming and fashionable, but accustomed to the *bratva* way of life. What better way to ply his suit with Evette than to call in reinforcements who'd help stack the deck in his favor?

Darya's melodic voice answered on the third ring.

"Sergei! It's about time you called. How's my favorite overbearing big brother?"

It was an honorable title only. One earned years ago before she'd caught the eye of a *vor* and fled the country with Sergei and Anton's help.

But he valued the titles as he valued few others. "I'm afraid I find myself in need of your assistance."

She giggled at that, a light, happy sound that never failed to make him smile. "Mine? Or my husband's?"

"Actually, both." In the distance, a large airliner came in for a landing at the New Orleans International Airport. "How would you feel about the two of you coming for an impromptu visit? There's someone I'd like you to meet."

Chapter Fifteen

God, she hoped she had enough candy. Throwing one bulk variety pack of high-end candy after another into the cart this afternoon, Evette had been sure she'd bought enough for the night's trick-or-treaters, but now that she'd dumped it all into the giant cauldron Olga had produced a few hours ago, Evette was having second thoughts. Especially on a perfect fall night in the Garden District.

The kitchen door opened and shut behind her, and Emerson's breathless voice followed a beat later. "Are they here yet?"

If any topic could throw her off her worry, the reminder that Emerson would be trick-or-treating without her for the first time ever was the thing to do it. That he'd be doing it with a pack of boys Emerson had actually referred to as *friends* who also happened to be five years older than her son only added extra kick to the walloping shock. "No. Not yet. But shouldn't they meet you at the carriage house? This is Sergei's house and we shouldn't lead people to believe it's ours."

"Yeah, that's what I told 'em, but they've never been here, so I wasn't sure where they'd go first."

Suddenly, it struck her what her son was wearing. "Where's your costume?"

Emerson held out his hands to both sides, an empty pillowcase instead of the plastic jack-o'-lantern he'd used every other year dangling from one fist. The black New Orleans Saints jersey with the large gold number nine in the center hung well past the knees of his jeans. "This is my costume."

"No, your costume was a green army man. I know because I had to sew that green plastic jacket by hand for three months."

A sheepish look crept across her son's face and red dotted his cheeks. "I changed my mind."

"Changed your mind, or were trying to fit in with your new buddies?"

Emerson shrugged, which was basically budding man speak for begrudging agreement.

"Baby, they're twelve and thirteen years old. You sure you're comfortable hanging around with a group like that?"

"Only Jeb is thirteen. Todd and Remmie are eleven and twelve. And you always say I'm old for my age."

She had said that. Too many times to count. Now she wanted to take every single instance back. "Okay, so, you're what now? A football player?"

He turned and jabbed a thumb at the name at the top of the jersey's back. "I'm Drew Brees. See?"

"And where'd you get that?"

"Jeb loaned it to me." He faced her once again and grinned big enough it made Evette's heart ache. "He says he's got one for Cam Jordan and Michael Thomas, too, so he didn't mind me borrowing this one."

"Mmm." Well, girls traded purses. And shoes.

Maybe trading jerseys between boys for Halloween was okay. "His momma know you're using it?"

"I guess." Emerson shrugged and threw his pillowcase on the kitchen table. "Where's Sergei? I wanna show him my costume and see what he thinks before the guys get here."

Sergei's low, accented voice sounded from the kitchen's main entrance. "He's right here."

Evette and Emerson both spun to face him.

Standing squarely in the wide opening and dressed casually in jeans and a black T-shirt, a faint smile to match the amusement in his voice softened his features, every bit of his attention aimed on Emerson. "Not as creative as a green army man, but still worthy of much candy." His gaze lifted to Evette behind Emerson. "And my home is yours as well. His friends are welcome to meet him wherever he likes."

Sneaky bastard. She should have known the distance he'd given her for the last twenty-four hours was more to refortify his game plan than to retreat completely. "That'll make them draw conclusions and you know it. Better to have friends who like you for who you are than what they think they can get out of you."

Sergei's expression shifted, an indefinable emotion drifting across his dark features. As if she'd unintentionally tripped over a long-forgotten or buried memory better left undisturbed. His focus shifted to Emerson and he prowled toward them both with the confidence of a king. "This house is yours. I trust your judgment." He stopped in front of them. "But your mother is right. There are many in this world who will try to take advantage of who you are."

Emerson stared up at Sergei, a mix of wonder and

confusion on his innocent face. "I'm not anything special. And I don't have anything to take advantage of."

Sergei crouched in front of him and studied Emerson's face for three long heartbeats. When he spoke, his voice was hushed, but thick with solemnity. "You are Emerson Labadie. You are your mother's son. Those alone are enough for others to covet." His voice dropped even deeper and he held out his huge calloused hand between them, palm up. "But you are also my family."

Oh, shit. "Sergei—"

She gripped Emerson's shoulder, part of her wanting to pull him away from Sergei and drag him all the way back to their old apartment and pretend the last month hadn't happened.

But the way Emerson stared at Sergei's outstretched hand stilled her. Made her remember how much her son had come out of his shell since moving here. How hard he'd studied. How he'd smiled and laughed and actually seemed like a kid again instead of an adult trapped in a little boy's body.

Her son wasn't stupid. Even if he hadn't heard talk of Sergei Petrovyh and his reputation throughout the neighborhood, no other boys needed guards to go to school. Didn't require high-end security systems or men patrolling the grounds they lived on twenty-four hours. And yet he still lifted his little hand and placed it solidly in Sergei's. "Family."

Sergei's fingers closed around Emerson's, the reverence in the action so poignant that goose bumps fanned along Evette's skin just watching it. He stood a second later. "Now, perhaps we should heed your mother's wishes and wait for your friends in the carriage house."

"You're not gonna pass out candy?"

"Later." Sergei started for the back door, her son happily tagging along right beside him and snatching his pillowcase off the table along the way. "I'll help your mother after we see you and your friends off."

The claim forced her to pry her attention off Sergei still holding her son's hand. "Actually, Olga can hand out the candy." She hurried after them. "You and I are going to talk."

"Is that so?" He held open the door.

Emerson plodded right on through, either totally unaware of the tension brewing between his mother and Sergei, or completely in league with her manipulative boss.

"I have no problem spending time alone with you, *solnyshka*. It's you who's been avoiding me." Sergei smirked and motioned toward the carriage house. "After you."

"Don't you *solnyshka* me," she whisper-growled as she stormed across the threshold. "That meant something to him."

He caught her by the waist before she could get past him and pulled her back flush against his front. His voice was all growl in her ear. "It meant something to me, too." His hand splayed wide on her belly, just low enough to send her insides spinning and yet high enough it wouldn't seem completely improper if Emerson were to look back and catch them. "And I never make promises I can't keep."

He released her before she could draw a steady breath, but captured her hand in his and guided them both along the winding concrete path toward the carriage house.

She tried to surreptitiously wriggle her hand free, but while his grip wasn't painful, there was also no getting away from it. "Sergei, stop. Emerson really likes you. It's one thing for the two of you to be friends, but I don't want to get his hopes up about us."

"First, he will not be a friend. He will be my son."

A simple statement, but one shared with such certainty it fired through her with the finesse of an electric shock. She stopped, halting Sergei beside her. "Your son?"

"As soon as you both agree to give me that privilege, yes. My son along with every advantage that goes with it." He waited only long enough to let the weight of his words sink in, then pulled her back into motion.

Well ahead of them, Emerson made it to the carriage house door, opened it and ducked inside.

"Second," Sergei said, "it is obvious you are troubled, and my men tell me you have been distracted ever since you picked Emerson up from school." His gaze slid to their joined hands and his thumb shuttled across the pulse point at her wrist. "My touch is to remind you that you are no longer alone."

It was the last thing she'd expected him to say. And while the way he'd chosen to deliver it was just as overbearing and assumptive as everything else that had come out of his mouth since she'd known him, there was a raw vulnerability beneath it. A vow given without subterfuge.

It was strangely comforting and gently touched something deep inside her. Her hand softened within his hold and her steps slowed until she was stopped once more and staring up at his hard features.

For the world beyond this estate, he wore a mask.

But here he smiled. Opened his home to those he trusted and gave without strings or obligations save loyalty and honesty.

For her, he'd given more. Turned her whole world on its head in mere days and offered to lay the world at her feet.

A man like Sergei—goodness has a hard time getting through. Thinks they're not worth it. I have to imagine if the good ever did get through, he'd fight the whole damned world to keep it.

He was a dangerous man. A killer. But Dorothy's words had kept her up much of the night and woven through her thoughts most of the day. Now—hearing him and seeing the sincerity behind his dark blue eyes—they made sense. "You really want this, don't you?"

One corner of his mouth lifted, the wry grin of a man who'd not only found himself in a predicament he'd never expected, but who'd fully resigned himself to embracing it. He cupped the side of her face with his free hand. While the sun was just beginning its final descent over the horizon, his voice was pure midnight. "*Moy solnyshka*...we are an inevitability."

The chatter of youthful, masculine voices drifted on the cooling evening air. Happy voices. Boisterous and full of laughter. A sound that felt incongruent with the seismic shift ripping through her. As if the rest of the world was utterly unaware of the massive clockwork pieces reformulating her life in a single moment.

Dorothy was right.

She'd been the one to topple the first domino. The one who'd set her present course of events in motion by sitting down at Sergei's table. But she'd always been drawn to him. And according to Dorothy, the same had been true for him. Maybe some other circumstance would have brought them together eventually.

Maybe they *were* an inevitability.

And why did that have to be such a bad thing? She knew what he was. The life he'd chosen to lead. But did that negate what they were or could be together?

He edged closer, the heat from his body an intimate and welcome caress. A comfort that gently reminded her of all he'd done, not just for her, but for her son. "Tell me what's troubling you, Evette. Let me help you."

The voices grew louder and mingled with the subtle patter of tennis shoes coming up the concrete driveway. It drew her attention away from Sergei to the trio of boys.

Jeb was the tallest and the oldest, and while his strawberry blond hair and freckles gave him a gangly, innocent appearance, his sharp hazel eyes reminded her of every bully she'd suffered through in high school. Todd and Remmie were the polar opposite—both average height with dark hair and innocent faces, but the way they looked up to Jeb said neither would serve as the voice of reason.

The three of them spied Evette and Sergei, and the same chill she'd felt meeting them yesterday afternoon at school scampered down her spine. "Them." She pushed away from Sergei, forced a calm yet polite mask into place and started back toward the carriage house, but muttered low enough for Sergei to hear, "They worry me."

The boys beat Evette and Sergei to the front door as did Emerson answering their knock. By the time she rounded the corner, there was already much young boy high-fiving going on and a level of rambunctiousness she'd forgotten was possible with so much budding testosterone in one room.

It was Sergei who brought some semblance of calm to the group simply by wading in and asking Emerson to introduce him to his friends. From there he stated his expectations as to when Emerson was to return and how all of the boys should behave on their night out with the same perfunctory direction she'd seen him use on his men.

And it worked like a charm.

In less than two minutes, all four of the boys were dutifully nodding their heads and moving toward the exit with Sergei a steady presence behind them.

Not surprisingly, Emerson was at the rear of the group.

Sergei took advantage of the moment when the three visitors filed through the front door to hold Emerson back with a hand at his shoulder. "Mikey and Daniel will be with you. They will not intrude, but their presence is nonnegotiable."

A look that lasted all of a second passed between them.

Emerson nodded and Sergei released him, the interaction completing so quickly none of the other boys was the wiser.

Evette stepped outside to join them and watch her baby boy trundle off with not-so-baby boys in time to witness Jeb pointing at the main house and saying to Emerson, "Hey, aren't you gonna show us the big house first?"

"No." Evette's quick and cold reply probably

wouldn't win her any Mother of the Year awards, but her instincts were fully in charge in that second and she wasn't about to ignore them. She moved in a little closer to the kids and crossed her arms in a pose reserved for stubborn mothers everywhere. "Not tonight. It's Sergei's house and he has enough going right now. We're not adding to it. Maybe some other time if he gives his permission."

She half expected Sergei to contradict her—or at least offer up an alternative to placate the boys and help Emerson save face.

Instead, he moved in tight behind her, coiled his arm around her waist like they'd been a couple for years and simply declared, "No later than ten o'clock, boys." He locked stares with Emerson. "The phone I gave you stays on at all times."

The comment caught her off guard enough she jerked in his hold and craned her head to meet his gaze. "What do you mean you gave him a phone? What's wrong with the one he has?"

His eyes sparked with laughter and his mouth softened, but his response was matter-of-fact and hushed enough the boys couldn't hear as they tromped away. "The one he had had outdated security and tracking features. He's had a new one for two days—given with specific limits for usage and with significant parental controls and updated security in place." He turned her so she faced him completely and pulled her flush against him. "And before you reprimand me for taking such an action without consulting you, you were clearly in need of space to think and I did it for the added safety of tracking his whereabouts."

"I haven't even seen it!"

"Then he's not using it for anything other than emergencies, as I instructed."

"Or he's hiding it from me!"

This time he did a far worse job of hiding his amusement. "That, too."

"Ugh." She shoved her hands against him, for all the good it did her. "You're not gaining any points going around me."

In an instant, the lighthearted gleam in his eyes was gone, replaced with the intensity he'd shared the moment he'd handed her the ring. "Let me in and there will be no need to go around you."

The rest of her arguments whooshed right out of her and that disconcerting flutter in her belly took wing all over again. "How is it you always manage to say things that should piss me off, but make me want to kiss you instead?"

Damn.

Had she actually said that?

Out loud?

"If you want me to kiss you, *solnyshka*, I am happy to oblige." Rather than do as he insinuated he would, he backed away and nudged her toward the carriage house with a hand at the small of her back. "But first you will tell me what troubles you about the boys."

Inside, all was quiet, the sounds from the neighborhood completely muted by the thick walls. The silence had been the first thing she'd noticed when she'd moved in. How isolated and soothing the safe space he'd given her truly was compared with the paper-thin walls she'd known her whole life.

He guided her to the couch.

Rather than sit beside her, he sat on the heavy farmhouse-styled coffee table in front of her, rested his elbows on his knees and cradled her hands in his. "Tell me." The words were so simple, and on the surface as demanding and expectant as those he'd shared with the boys. But there was concern in them, too. A genuine desire to hear what she had to say.

"They're older than Emerson."

He dipped his head.

"Much older."

He held her gaze, still listening.

"Jeb is thirteen. The others are eleven and twelve. You don't think that's weird? Or at least suspicious?"

His hold on her hands tightened and his thumbs shuttled across her skin, the touch as comforting as his low voice. "You don't think he has enough experience and wisdom to see if he should avoid these boys?"

"I think he's *seven*. How good could anyone's judgment be at his age?"

A sad smile lifted the corners of his mouth. "Do you remember the story I told you? About the day I met Yefim? And later Anton?"

The room's temperature was pleasant and the heat from his hands soothing, but at the melancholy sound of his voice, a chill settled beneath her skin.

"I was seven then," he said. "Dealing with these boys and gauging their value in his life is only the first of many situations Emerson will face, but he will face them. He is capable. Intelligent. Wise. And he will not face his choices alone."

Seven years old.

Faced with hardships and life-altering decisions at a time when she'd been focused on Barbie dolls and

with. Until they prove themselves, they are not to be trusted."

From the trajectory of Kir's voice behind him, he still hadn't budged from the passenger's side of the car. "Where are you going?"

"I have ice cream and a woman relaxing in a hot bath." He glanced over his shoulder. "Where do you think I'm going?"

Kir chuckled and shook his head. "You're whipped."

Perhaps he was. God knew he had no patience where Evette was concerned. Only a hunger that had grown steadily out of control since that night in the alley. As if her touch—her kiss and her scent—had infected him with an unquenchable lust. A pleasure that left the rest of the world in boring shades of black, white and gray when she wasn't beside him. He paused at the door and locked eyes with Kir. "Watch Emerson."

All humor fled his friend's face. Kir had seen firsthand the bloodshed Sergei was capable of when someone dared to cross him and, companionable razzing aside, both of his *avtoritets* knew what Evette and Emerson meant to him. Knew what fury any harm to either of them would ignite.

Kir nodded. "He will be safe."

It was all the reassurance Sergei needed. A handful of steps later, he was in Evette's kitchen and unloading his purchases in the freezer.

Upstairs, all was quiet. So much so, he wondered if perhaps she'd snuck out while he'd been at the store. But then, if she'd done so, one of his men would have notified him.

He shucked his suit jacket, tossed it onto the kitchen table and quietly stole up the stairs. The master bedroom was empty, but the clothes Evette had been wearing were neatly folded on the flannel chair in the corner and the door to the master bathroom was closed. While the wide window on the far wall was high enough no one could directly see inside, the blinds were still tilted so the sunlight would fill the room during the day. With nightfall in full swing, the only light at this point was the soft white of the moon through the slats. He padded to them, closed them completely and turned on the small bedside lamp.

A warm buttery glow filled the space. What had once been a simple room with soft grays, dark charcoals and white furnishings now had teal and yellow pillows and random knickknacks that gave the space a Bohemian feel.

It fit Evette perfectly. And while he enjoyed the sophisticated décor of his own home and the rich colors that went with it, he couldn't help but find himself rethinking his selections. Maybe, once Evette and Emerson moved into the main house, she would make it her own as well. Give it the homey and welcoming feel that she'd created in her own private haven.

The soft tinkling of water spilling on water sounded through the closed door followed by a muted sigh.

Still bathing.

Still lingering in the warm water he'd imagined her in the whole drive to the store and back. While arguing with Kir had definitely tried his patience, the picture his mind had created the second she'd mentioned taking a bath had left him tense and preoccupied. Narrowly focused to a degree that could prove dangerous to him if he didn't get a grip on his response to Evette soon.

He toed off his Italian loafers and rid himself of his socks. Beneath his feet, the thick, plush carpet was soft and delicate. Perfect for the woman who walked on it each day.

The smooth brushed-steel knob turned easily. Silent.

Candlelight danced against the walls emanating from four votives spaced along a wide tile inset just above the soaking tub. Like her room, the olive and scarlet glass holders gave the grays and whites in the room much-needed warmth.

But the most striking feature in the room was Evette. As deep as the tub was, all he could see from the doorway were her arms draped along either side, her head resting on a deep red towel she'd rolled and wedged behind her neck and one slender, toned leg perched on the tip of the faucet. Every inch of her skin glowed in the soft light.

He loved her skin. Loved how the unique color embraced the many facets of her heritage and amplified her mysterious fairy image. As if the tone were a reflection of how the woman inside couldn't be categorized into one race or persona.

The flames flickered, stirred from the air moving through the open door.

Evette slowly opened her eyes. She noted the agitated state of the candles, turned her head to the door and gasped. "Sergei." Whether it was instinct, fear or modesty, she covered her breasts and sunk a little lower in the water. "I thought you were getting ice cream."

"I did." He unbuttoned his shirtsleeves and rolled them to his forearms. "Three pints of Ben & Jerry's."

Rather than demand he leave as he'd anticipated, her eyes narrowed. "Which kind?"

"Half Baked, The Tonight Dough and Chocolate Fudge Brownie."

"Thank God. I was afraid you were going to bring Cherry Garcia." She relaxed a little, but kept her suspicious gaze on him and her arms across her chest.

"Really? I have it on good authority that Cherry Garcia is preferred by most females."

"Which authority?"

"Kir." He unfastened his watch and set it on the vanity.

"Hmph." She shook her head. "Not this female. Fruit doesn't belong in ice cream."

"I see." For a moment he considered sitting on the edge of the tub, but he wanted full access to her. Wanted to look his fill and teach her what she could expect from him. He crouched beside the edge and rolled to his knees. Bubbles floated across the water's surface, a thin layer that had slowly dissipated in the time he'd been gone and now let the faint outline of her curves bleed through. He traced the backs of his knuckles from her elbow to her wrist, banded his fingers around it and guided her hand back to the tub's edge. "Why do you hide yourself from me, *solnyshka*? There is no part of you that I have not seen." He repeated the gesture with her other arm. "No part of you I have not touched."

A ragged breath slipped past her slackened lips and a shudder moved through her. A tiny one that sent subtle ripples through the water around her torso. Her breasts weren't overly large, but ample enough the water lifted them, leaving the darker tips peeking just above the surface. Tempting him to touch and taste. "There's not a woman alive who wouldn't cover herself if they saw you standing in a doorway looking at them like that."

"Like what?"

She hesitated a moment, studying his face. For what, he had no clue, but it felt important. "A wolf."

A wise assessment. One she might be smart to heed and run. "I am a predator. It's who I've been for most of my life." He dipped his hand beneath the water. Let his fingertips trail the path along one hip and up to the side of her breast. "You can focus on that part of me if you choose, or you can see the other side." He fanned his thumb along the outward swell of her breast. A tender, teasing touch that made her nipple harden farther, straining toward him. "What belongs to you and Emerson and no one else."

Her back arched ever so slightly, the movement betraying the impact of his touch and her growing need in the most natural way possible. Her voice was deeper when she spoke, raspy and distracted. "What's that?"

"Your protector."

Another shiver, this one so palpable he slipped his other hand beneath her neck to steady her.

Her body gave way to his. Surrendered and molded itself to his guidance as he lifted her. Brought her mouth closer to his. "You do not have to fight me." He teased her parted lips with his own. "You have nothing to fear from me."

Her hands pressed against his chest, the lingering wetness from her fingertips seeping through the fine fabric. The gold in her hazel eyes flickered in the candlelight, but the fear behind them was a living thing.

A monster bared in an intimate moment. "It's easier being alone. There's nothing to lose."

Death.

He'd felt its freezing sting at an early age. Had watched his father drown himself in liquor and pity because of it.

But he'd found a family because of it, too. A merciless and dangerous one at times, but a family nonetheless. Loyal people who would come to his side no matter the distance. Anton. Yefim. Kir and Roman. Darya and now her family as well.

Beyond Dorothy and Emerson, she'd lost that.

The monster behind her eyes taunted him. Coiled in on itself and challenged him.

But he had no problem with monsters. He welcomed their ugliness and took great pleasure in choking the life from their vile bodies. Keeping his grip on her neck, he pulled the towel out from beneath her head, shook it out, then guided her to her feet. "You have me. My family and their loyalty." Once she was out of the tub and steady on her feet, he wrapped the crimson fabric around her shoulders, cradled the back of her head and pulled her flush against him. "Fight it as long as you need to. Watch and learn if that's what it takes. But your days of being alone are over."

He kissed her.

Sealed his vow with all he had in him.

Willed her to feel his determination. His absolute resolve to win her. To protect and provide for her. She'd want for nothing. Know no hardship save what was unpreventable by sheer existence, and even that, she would not experience alone.

He would be there.

His family would be there.

And she would be *his*.

"Sergei." Her arms shook as she pressed against his chest. The monster in her eyes was gone, replaced with questions. Uncertainty, yes, but openness, too. A door opened, if only a crack. As if she realized the vulnerability she'd offered him, her gaze dropped to his chest and her voice shook with adorable shyness. "I'm getting you all wet."

Inside his arms, she was so tiny. Completely engulfed by his size and his strength. And yet she fit perfectly. Had melted into him every single time he'd touched her. "Indeed."

He loosened his grip and guided the thick, soft towel across her shoulders. Down her arms and up along her sides. He crouched and rubbed the fabric over her hips and along the outside of her thighs and shins. At her ankles, he released the towel and skated his thumbs upward. A mirrored path he'd taken to the outside of her toned legs, only more delicate and skin-to-skin along the inside.

At her knees, he paused. Circled slow patterns and savored the silky texture of her skin. Allowed himself to look his fill at her sex. The flushed and swollen folds and the slightest hint of her clit peeking out from behind her hood. He exhaled through his mouth. Let the warmth of his breath ghost across her sex.

She gripped his shoulders and whimpered.

Bozhe, but he loved that sound. Craved the responsive tremors that moved through her every time he earned it. The way her skin heated beneath his touch and her breath quickened.

Her nails bit through the fabric of his shirt. "You've got that wolfish look on your face again."

"Do I?" He nudged her feet farther apart and splayed his hands against her inner thighs. Her scent hit him instantly. Musky, yet sweet. Even in the dim candlelight, her pussy glistened with wetness. Not just ready for him, but eager. "Perhaps it's because I'm hungry and in need of a treat."

"Oh, God." One hand at his shoulder shifted to the top of his head, whether to push him away or pull him closer, he couldn't be sure. But he could certainly influence her decision. Influence her and take what he wanted.

"Hold on, tight, *solnyshka*. I promise you, I will not break."

He licked her. Blatantly ran his tongue along her labia and savored her juices. Circled her swollen clit with his tongue and sucked it into his mouth. Fingered her drenched pussy while he worked her until her cries and moans ricocheted off the bathroom tiles like a symphony.

She fisted his hair. Clutched his shoulder and rolled her hips against his mouth with complete abandon.

Wild.

Beautiful.

Completely unrestrained.

And all his.

Her legs shook, and her pussy quivered around his fingers. A gratifying response that had signaled her releases before, but a shitty location and position for her to enjoy one now. In one smooth move, he pulled his fingers from her wet heat, stood and lifted her up, guiding her legs around his waist.

The shout that filled his ears as he stalked out of the bathroom was decidedly less pleasant than the others he'd earned. "You did *not* just stop right before I was about to come."

"Not stopping. Only delaying." He gently tossed her on the bed, slid his hands under her perfect ass and pulled her pussy back to his mouth. "But now that I see the reaction denying you gets me, perhaps I should tease you a little longer." He licked her slit, the taste of her sweet on his tongue. "A little harder."

She pushed up on her elbows, her breaths churning short and choppy. Her gaze sharpened, and her tone was that of a woman readying for battle, but the muscles in her legs relaxed, widening her knees for better access. "You wouldn't."

In answer, he licked her again, holding her gaze through every second. "You've accepted I'm a predator." Another pass through her folds and a rush of honey on his tongue. "Everyone knows how we like to play with our prey."

Her mouth parted and her eyelids grew heavy. While the independent, strong woman in her might not like the idea of being delayed her release, the sensual side to her clearly enjoyed the visual and his aggression because her voice turned to velvet. "You know that saying? The one about turnabout being fair play?"

His cock, already aching and straining for release, jerked and lengthened farther behind his pants. Fuck, just the idea of her full lips anywhere near his shaft made him want to show her just how primitive he could be. "You are always welcome to put your beautiful mouth on me, *solnyshka*. As much or however long you want to." He smiled and let her see the real wolf inside. The merciless one who was tired of its confines and ready to run free with its mate. He circled her clit with his tongue. Nudged the base of it and let his warm breath dance across the swollen surface. "Of course, the harder you push me, the more I'll be driven to dominate you." Another circle paired with the slow insertion of two fingers. "To take control and force your surrender."

Her head dropped back on a moan and her hips undulated against his mouth. If he'd had any doubts as to whether the idea of domination appealed to her before, the fingers she speared in his hair and the desperation with which she urged him for more pressure from his mouth wiped them away. "Don't you dare tease me. Don't you dare."

Oh, he'd dare.

Plenty.

He'd just make sure he had his ring on her finger and his last name behind hers before he took it there. "Shhh," he crooned against her flushed skin. His lips grazed her clit over and over and he pumped his fingers in and out of her with aching slowness. "I will not tease my bride." A tiny lick to the very tip of her clit. "Not yet anyway."

It was the last quiet sound in the room, the low, grated sound that rolled up the back of her throat as he closed his lips around her and suckled deep like that of a feminine warrior embarking on the most pleasurable fight of her life. Her cunt fisted his fingers. Greedy, pulsing contractions that made him wish he'd had the foresight to rid himself of his clothes before he'd reengaged.

But this wasn't about him. Wasn't about proving

how potent their connection was or satisfying himself. It was about seeing to her needs. Demonstrating who he would be to her in and out of bed.

Plus, her taste was divine. His lungs filled with her musky scent and her low, throaty sighs of pleasure making the delay of his own pleasure worth the wait. Worth the challenge.

He let her ride her release. Kept the pressure at her clit to string the sensations out and savored the sweet aftershocks rippling around him. Only when her hips slowed and her moans turned into breathy sighs did he ease his fingers from her sheath.

"You see, *solnyshka*?" He gripped both of her hips and pressed a tender kiss to the tightly trimmed curls atop her mound before slowly shifting himself to cover her naked body. "I told you I had more efficient methods for relaxation."

Her eyes opened slowly, the weight of her lids over her hazel eyes enticing and seductive. A wry smile crept onto her face. "Certainly lower in caloric intake, that's for sure." The smile slipped and her gaze locked on his mouth. She traced his lower lip with her forefinger. "Do you keep your promises, Sergei?"

A sly question. That of a huntress baiting her trap. "I don't make promises I can't keep."

She let out a sound that was part hum and part sigh and lifted her stare to his. "That's good." Her fingers drifted to his shirt placket and, one-by-one began to loosen the buttons. "Because last time things went too fast and I didn't get to explore."

He'd been wrong.

One look at the mischief dancing in her eyes and he

knew it to the very core of him. Delaying his pleasure wouldn't be tonight's challenge.

But surviving it would be.

She pulled his shirttail free, released the last two buttons and smoothed her fingertips from his abs, to his pecs, then over his shoulders, pushing the fabric out of her way. Her gaze roamed the ink she'd bared. "These all mean something, don't they?"

"Many. Yes."

"Mmm." Not a sign of encouragement so much as acknowledgment of a noted piece of information tucked away for later. Once his arms were free of his shirt and she'd tossed it to the side of the bed, she braced her hand on his sternum and pushed with surprising strength.

He rolled to his back, potently aware not just of her energy and the sensual promise of her movements, but of the power he'd chosen to give her in that moment. Not once in all the lovers he'd known had he allowed a woman this space. To rise above him in any way.

But she wanted to explore. Wanted to learn him in the same way he'd learned her. The truth was right there, burning behind her eyes. She unhooked his belt. "You said I was welcome to put my mouth on you." The button and zipper came next, each move tentative yet determined. "As much or however long I wanted."

He'd endure torture for her if it meant seeing her blossom as she was right now. Would take an iron brand and suffer it without a sound if it meant feeling her sweet touch on his bare skin.

She hooked her fingers in the waist of his pants and briefs, locked stares with him and pulled them over his hips.

Her breath left her on a shaky exhalation before his pants had cleared his shins, and her mouth slackened.

He kicked his pants free and skimmed one hand up her forearm, needing the connection every bit as much as he imagined she did. "I also told you that the harder you push me, the more I'll be driven to dominate you."

She started, his word triggering a delightful tremor in her torso. With the grace of a feline, she knelt between his knees and skimmed her hands from his knees to his thighs.

"You like the prospect of that outcome, don't you, *solnyshka*? To have your man take control and guide you. To leave you free to simply feel."

Her hands drifted along his hip bones and beside his straining cock.

It jerked in response. Strained in anticipation of her touch.

Her gaze might have been riveted to his sex when she answered, but he felt her whispered answer in every part of him. "Yes."

"Then take it. Do what you want. But know there will come a time when payment will be due."

Moving only her eyes, she peeked at him from beneath her lashes, a delightful mix of coy maiden and devilish vixen beaming up at him. "Maybe." She held his gaze and lowered her head with aching slowness. Her warm breath whispered against his shaft. "Maybe I'll be good enough at my task you'll be too spent to demand payment when I'm done."

She didn't give him time to respond. Rather stole his breath and what was left of his plans with a gentle yet confident lick from the base to the tip of him. The wet glide against his flesh. The warmth of her mouth as she closed her lips around him. The questing touch of her fingers on his balls and the way her eager moan vibrated all the way through him.

The combined impact was exquisite. An experience so far beyond any other encounter he'd had that comparison seemed laughable. There was no sense of avarice in the act. No calculated glances to indicate she was angling for something in return. It was pure devotion. A gift of sensation that only pulled him deeper. Dragged him farther into the spell she'd cast the first day he'd laid eyes on her with all the mercy of a storm's undertow.

Release pushed closer. Tightened the muscles at his core and drew his nuts up tight. And given the eager pace she'd set with her mouth and firm, saliva-slickened fist she worked at the base of him, she had no intention of stopping. No goal save sending him over the edge just as fervently as he'd sent her flying.

He knifed upward, her startled gasp mingling with his growl as he lifted and flipped her to her belly, pulled her hips up and back and buried himself to the hilt.

Home.

Mine.

All. Fucking. Mine.

The words were a mantra. The only tether that kept him in check as he pumped his cock inside her. A guide and a promise as he focused on her moans. The flush that spread across her shoulders and back and the way her hips lifted and met his for each stroke.

He fisted his hand in her hair, pulled her up in what should have made her cry out in pain, but earned him a sexy groan instead. He splayed his hand on her belly and held her steady for his thrusts. Pounded deep so she'd never forget. "You think I would let you steal my come? Think I would let you drink it down when I could mark you with it instead? Claim you as my own?"

"Oh my God..." The whimper in her voice was just as tremulous as the flutters rippling through her pussy. She clutched his hand at her belly and squeezed. Her head dropped back against his shoulder and her back bowed for more. "Please. I'm right there."

"Of course you are. Because your body was made for me. Your pleasure a perfect match for mine."

Her legs shook and the muscles in her sex tightened.

"Give in, Evette. Come on my cock and accept my claim."

The breath she took was barely audible. Jagged and far too short to fill her lungs.

But the clasp of her cunt around his shaft was ferocious. A physical manifestation of the wildest scream that ripped his own release free. Milked him with a desperate demand he had no hope of ignoring.

His cock jerked inside her. Filled her sex as her pussy pulsed around him. Left him exposed and raw, yet strangely fulfilled and empowered. She was his weakness. The delicate chink in his otherwise insurmountable wall.

But she was also his redemption. His absolution, greater purpose and color in another otherwise drab and monochrome world.

Her body trembled against his, tiny aftershocks ricocheting through the muscles that still clutched him and sent her hips rolling against his. Minute, sensuous movements that perfectly matched each contented whimper and sigh.

He guided her to her belly. Brushed her neck and shoulders with reverent kisses and painted her back, sides and hips with soothing caresses. "You can't ignore that, Evette. This isn't something that will go away. Won't dim." He pressed his hips against her lush ass, the softening of his cock allowing his seed to trickle down her labia. "You belong to me."

Her head jerked up. "Oh, no!" She tried to wriggle out from underneath him, but his weight was too great. Her strength no match for his.

And, he'd been ready.

He manacled her wrists with his hands and pressed a single kiss to the top of her spine. "Shhh."

She shook her head and still tried to push up. "Don't you *shhh* me. We didn't use protection."

"No. We did not."

She stilled in her struggles, but craned her head enough to try to make eye contact. "And you don't think that's a problem?"

"I have never gone without protection with another woman before. You have not been with anyone since Emerson was conceived. And you are mine regardless."

Her eyes got even bigger. Flooded with fear. "And we could have *babies*!"

His cock stirred. And while he was wise enough to pull himself free of her before she could register the primitive response her reminder had created, he didn't stifle his growl in time. He nuzzled her neck and forced himself to focus on her scent. To recognize and honor her fear. All she'd been through without anyone there to help her. "We *will* have babies, *solnyshka*. Emerson will be a wonderful big brother."

"You're not helping!"

He chuckled at that. By no means his most intelligent response, but honest all the same. "You want to plan. I understand this. We will take those steps immediately to give you comfort, but we will not be using condoms again. I will not have anything between me and my bride."

"I'm not your bride yet."

This time when she tried to roll to face him, he allowed it, but guided her back underneath him as soon as her shoulders hit the mattress. "You are. My bride and my light."

Something in his tone stilled her long enough to study him. To connect with him and consider what he was saying.

He took full advantage, daring to release one of her wrists to cup the side of her face. "We will find other means. Wait until you are ready for children."

She opened her mouth, clearly ready to argue further.

He cut her off. "No matter what happens, you will not be alone again. Ever. Whether it happens tonight, or two years from now, our children will have us both."

"You're going too fast," she whispered. "Everything is going too fast. It's too big. Too much. Too powerful."

"The good things often are. Perhaps the answer isn't to slow down or try to stop the fall, but to go with it." He stroked the line of her jaw. Her collarbone and the apple of her shoulder. "Perhaps the answer isn't to fight it or wait, but to surrender to it the same way you surrender your body."

"That's different."

"How? Have I not been there? Looked after you? Provided for you? Offered you my vow and my name?"

Her eyes widened for a moment, then narrowed on a frown.

He captured the confusion while he could, rolled off her long enough to spoon her and pulled the covers over them both. "Or perhaps you could stop thinking altogether. Just allow me to spoil you and let you grow accustomed to the idea a little longer, hmm?"

"You're a bossy and manipulative man." Her words were sassy, but there was a distractedness to them that said she was still stewing on the idea. Ungrounded and scrambling for steady emotional ground.

"Yes. I am." He plumped a pillow under her head, slid his arm underneath it and pulled her closer. Her fit against him was perfect, the silky brush of her exotic skin a heavenly gift. "I'm also a man who not only bought you ice cream but intuited against Cherry Garcia. Don't forget to factor that aspect into your analysis."

She grunted. A cute little sound that all too easily allowed him to picture the little mew on her lips as she'd uttered it. "You should probably be handing me some of that ice cream when you say that. Especially after the risk we just took."

He smiled against the shell of her ear and kissed it. "You will forgive me. Eventually."

This time he got a *harrumph* and a wiggle of her pert butt that only served to remind his cock of better things to do besides getting ice cream. "Ice cream first. Sweet talk later. Then maybe I'll forgive you."

Oh, yes. They were inevitable. Inevitable and unstoppable together. He slipped from between the sheets, leaned into the bed and kissed her cheek. "Whatever my bride wants."

Chapter Seventeen

Sergei spread the design mockups for his new restaurants across his desk and compared them with the photos of Henri's existing restaurant below it. The coloring was right. Lots of crushed red velvet, black furniture and gold accents. But the feel of it was all wrong. More current contemporary than the Rat Pack era steeped in every detail of Henri's place.

Yes, the food was exceptional, but the other reason people went there was for the experience. The surroundings. The knowledgeable, competent staff and how things moved at an entirely different pace. Patrons immersed themselves in it. Dressed for the environment. Spying cell phones for anything other than necessity was a rarity. It was as if they were eager to go back in time—even if only for an hour or two.

If his expansions with Henri didn't provide the experience, they wouldn't succeed. And considering the lengths his men had gone to the last five days in sending a message to Alfonsi and wiping out all trace of Henri's children's past, he wasn't about to fail over something as controllable as décor.

He pulled up the email from the designer, reattached the actual photos from *André*'s and added a terse reply:

Authentic. 1960s. Make it happen or I'll find someone who can.

Footsteps sounded on the stairs down the hallway from his office. More than one set, both with a heavier tread and clipped purpose—which meant his *avtoritets* were either on their way to give him news they were eager to share, or shit had hit the fan.

He clicked Send on the message, pushed his keyboard away and sat back in his chair. For the comfort of his household, he hoped it was good news. After a pleasant weekend of minimal work and free time spent with Evette and Emerson, he'd grown a liking for the warm and comfortable peace of domestication. The first person who made him step too far from his newfound comfort zone was likely to feel his bite rather than his bark.

Kir strode through the doorway first, the black shirt and charcoal suit a stark contrast to his blond hair and playboy looks. Roman had skipped formal attire altogether and wore jeans and a simple gray T-shirt that made it clear he had muscle to back up any threat, which meant he'd likely been out in the field and developing his troops. Neither had the blanked expressions typical when they were coming to deliver bad news, though, so that was a plus. If anything, Kir looked downright pleased with himself.

Rather than angling for one of the two chairs positioned in front of Sergei's desk, Kir headed for the leather sofa opposite Sergei's end of the room, snatched the remote control off the coffee table and aimed it at the huge flat-screen mounted on the wall. "I have a gift for you, brother."

Roman turned one of the two leather chairs sideways so he could keep Sergei in view on his left and the television on his right and dropped down into the seat. "He is insufferable when he gloats. But I must confess, this one will be enjoyable enough I can tolerate hearing him tout his success."

The tail end of the opening graphics for the local noon news came on and the news anchors began their usual chipper welcome spiel. The dark-headed male on screen looked like he'd been riding the station desk for at least ten years, and his suit was one he'd probably bought at the beginning of his career. The blonde woman next to him, though, was fresh and stunning with a shrewd gaze that said she was as smart as she was beautiful.

Kir ambled back to the remaining chair in front of Sergei's desk and turned it so it mirrored Roman. He thumbed the volume lower, unbuttoned his suit jacket and settled in.

Sergei listened for all of fifteen seconds, then turned his attention on Kir. "Your gift is the news?"

Kir shook his head, but kept his gaze trained on the screen and his hand poised with the remote, ready to raise the volume when necessary. "*Nyet*. Just an extra follow-up to the actions we took against Alfonsi."

"Kir's conquests appear to have served a handy purpose," Roman said, nodding to the screen. "He met the blonde last Thursday. Turns out our brother can be subtle when he wants to be if it means adding public embarrassment to the other steps we took with Alfonsi."

Right on cue, the camera panned to the blonde and a string of videos played beside her showing the variety of complications Alfonsi's enterprises had encountered over the last four days.

"*Native businessman Steven Alfonsi has had a hard streak the last several days. Troubles started bright and early Thursday morning when a popular family restaurant that had been in the Alfonsi family for generations suffered a kitchen fire. The fire was quickly put out and the building saved, but the damage was significant enough to force the restaurant's closure until repairs and renovations could be made. Later that day, health inspectors at other restaurants Alfonsi is known to have a majority interest in reported numerous violations and hefty fines.*

"*But the restaurant industry isn't the only place Alfonsi is suffering. Many of the other ventures that make him one of New Orleans's most notable businessmen took a hit as well with gaming workers walking out of his casinos in protest of unsatisfactory work conditions and his most sizable company—Alfonsi Construction—having all of their jobs put on hold pending research of unsafe building practices alleged by local building code authorities. As if those developments weren't enough for Alfonsi to juggle, a class action suit was filed at the New Orleans Civil District Courthouse today by lawyers representing new homebuyers who purchased homes built and sold by Alfonsi's real estate division. At least fifteen plaintiffs have alleged that Alfonsi had an undisclosed interest in the inspection companies used on the homes prior to closing, but that they used that interest to cover up defective workmanship that is now costing the homeowners thousands of dollars.*

"*Alfonsi has long been suspected of Mafia ties*

and illegal activities in the state of Louisiana, but no charges have ever stuck. Speculators state that Alfonsi's latest string of bad luck is likely a result of his alleged Mafia activities and that he's crossed the line with the wrong people."

Kir paused the TV with a click from the remote, leaving a straight-on view of Alfonsi's scowling face as he exited the back of his Cadillac and a slew of reporters rushed to interview him. "He's hurting..." Kir turned to Sergei, the grin on his face totally unrepentant. "And now everyone knows it."

It was a solid move. Legal hurdles and authorities digging into your business was one thing, but the press were like gnats—they came in droves and got into everything. Plus, Alfonsi's ego was so caught up in his public image, a hit to it wouldn't sit well at all.

Two quick raps on the door sounded a second before it opened just enough for Evette to poke her head through. She scanned the room, noted it was only Kir and Roman with him and pushed the door wider. "Can I interrupt you guys a minute?"

Given the consternation in her expression, Sergei's good humor vanished in an instant. He stood, as did Kir and Roman, and waved her into the room. "Of course. We were just watching the noon news. Is there a problem?"

She motioned Kir and Roman back into their seats and sashayed forward until she stood between them, squared perfectly with Sergei. "Well, that depends. Did you know there was going to be a horde of construction workers showing up today to do a renovation?"

"I did."

"Where exactly?"

"The two bedrooms at the end of the hall in the other wing."

Her mouth screwed up into that cute little sideways mew that said she was torn between laughing and ripping into him. "The cleaning crew just cleaned there this morning."

"So?"

"So, we pay them hourly. If we're sending a construction crew in to renovate them, that's wasted money. Not to mention, there's nothing wrong with those rooms."

His good humor rebounded in a heartbeat and he smiled even bigger than he had after watching the story on Alfonsi.

Apparently, Evette didn't care for his response because she planted her hands on her hips and turned her stern-mother glare to full bright. "Are you laughing at me?"

"No, *solnyshka*. I'm merely appreciating the fact that you've finally used the correct pronoun when referencing our home. And while I appreciate your focus on saving us money, I hardly think that the hour the cleaning crew spent cleaning those rooms will break us."

Her frown slipped and she fidgeted as though the realization she'd come to think of the home and finances as *theirs* wasn't altogether a comfortable one. She pushed her shoulders back and lifted her chin anyway. "Well, it's still a waste of money, and if you want me to run this house, then *you're* going to have to tell me when you've got big plans so I have a chance to sidestep that waste."

Bozhe, but she was adorable. Feisty and sweet and

fearless. "As you wish, *liubimaja*. In the future, I'll ensure all plans that might impact your scheduling or our household finances are shared with you in advance. Although, I'll have to ask you to keep everyone—including you—from that wing for the rest of the week."

"Why?"

"It's a surprise."

Her eyes narrowed and she gave him a sidelong look. "Take this in the spirit it's intended, but I'm not sure I can take many more surprises."

"Ah, but this one isn't for you. Though, I'm happy to think up more if that news disappoints you."

She volleyed her attention between Kir and Roman. "Did aliens land this morning and do a brain swap with him or something? He's never this playful and agreeable."

Always the charmer, Kir was the one to answer. "I believe his good mood is mostly your doing. But by all means, keep up with it. He's far more enjoyable to be around with you here."

Roman nodded and chuckled. "This is true."

"Hmm." Evette tried to keep up her irritated pretense, but as she lifted her gaze back to Sergei, a soft smile that spoke of fond memories and intimate secrets tilted her lips. "Well, far be it from me to ruin a good thing." She circled her hands on either side of her head. "You men carry on."

She turned and headed for the door, but stopped halfway there and cocked her head at the television screen. "What's Alfonsi doing in the news this time?"

"You know him?" Roman said.

With a beleaguered harrumph that sounded a lot like the one Dorothy used, Evette shook her head and looked back at the men. "Not for a very long time. He went to the same high school my dad and Uncle Carl did. When I was little they all used to come around for crawfish boils and such, but Dad and Mom said he was a loose cannon so they stopped inviting him. Only time I've seen him since was on the news." She twisted back to the screen. "I take it he's in hot water again?"

"A class action lawsuit." Sergei motioned for Kir to push Play on the remote. "Something to do with using inside contacts with inspectors to cover up shoddy workmanship."

"Ha! Sounds like him." She shook her head and finished her trek to the door, giving them all a backward wave. "I'll let you guys get back to your news. It seems I've got a construction crew to get started."

Kir punched Play on the remote and thumbed the sound down. "You wanted to know if Carl and Alfonsi had a connection. Now you know what it is."

"Or at least a history," Roman added.

"It could be a coincidence, but I doubt it." Sergei sat in his chair and crossed one leg over the other. "Knox is digging into Alfonsi's accounts. If there's a definitive connection with money, he'll find it. Until then, we keep looking, stay alert and keep the pressure on Alfonsi."

The mockups for his restaurants lay lined up on his desk. A reminder not just of the business deal that had been interrupted, but of Sergei's long-term goal to eradicate all competition. Louisiana and the states around it would be his and that meant decisive, ruthless intent in everything he did. "And up the detail on

Evette and Emerson. Alfonsi will either knuckle under or go looking for a target to strike back." He looked to Kir, then Roman. "No one touches who's mine."

Chapter Eighteen

Guests tonight.
7PM.
Dress nice, but comfortable.

Evette checked the text messages she'd received from Sergei for what felt like the fiftieth time, growled and scanned her walk-in closet. Her clothes took up only one half of it, which said a lot about the difference between not just where she used to live and where she lived now, but how drastically her world had shifted.

How out of place she was in Sergei's world.

"Dress nice, but comfortable," she muttered to the neatly lined-up hangers. "Does that mean semiformal? Business casual?" She forced herself to go slower this time around, carefully considering her options and replaying the rest of the unhelpful text messages she'd received on her way home from picking up Emerson at school.

Evette: Do I need to get with Olga and have food? Hors d'oeuvres? And how many people? What kind of event are you hosting?

His answer had been slow in coming, the little bubbles showing, then disappearing at least five times before his cryptic answer came.

I have handled everything. You need only arrive at seven.

Not helpful. Not even a little bit. Maybe if they'd spent more of the week and a half since Halloween night doing more talking instead of Sergei showing how inventive he could be in the bedroom, she'd have understood what was going on better. Was he expecting her to help host whatever he had going on? Was there protocol involved? Were these normal business negotiations, or *business* negotiations? And what the hell was she going to do if he did introduce her to… well…more dangerous people? Did she want that? Would Sergei do that?

She growled out loud, shook her head and refocused on her meager options. Her hand landed on the one little black dress in her closet. A classy three-quarter-length-sleeve affair with a wraparound design that hit at the knees and clung to her body. It was a total knockoff brand she'd found at a department store, but most men wouldn't know that, and somehow she couldn't envision any female mobsters showing up at Sergei's house anytime soon.

No, not mobsters. Bratva—the literal translation for which Sergei had informed her meant *brothers.*

God, what's happened to my life?

She pulled the dress from her closet and marched into her bedroom just as Emerson came striding in.

"Hey, Mom! Jeb and the guys wanna come over tonight and throw around the football in the backyard. That okay?"

The screen on her phone glowed a peaceful 6:15 p.m. in soft white letters. Forty-five minutes for a quick freshening up. She could totally pull that off. "Sure." She tossed the dress on the bed, stuffed her phone into one of her robe's deep pockets and hurried toward the bathroom.

"Yes!" Emerson fist pumped, spun and headed for the door.

Boys.
Playing football in the backyard.
Maybe with mobsters in the house.

"Wait!" Her panicked screech as she came to a dead halt was enough it hurt even her own ears. She faced her son. "Maybe not. I mean..." *Shit.* Conversation was definitely going to have to trump gloriously hot sex with her Russian employer/boyfriend for a while. "Sergei has something going on tonight. I don't think having a bunch of boys over will be such a great idea."

"You don't *think*? Or you know for sure?"

"I don't know what he's doing. Only that I'm supposed to be there at seven."

"Well, can you ask him?"

Pulled from her worries about tonight, the amount of time Emerson was spending with the older boys rushed in to fill the void. If she was smart, she'd use tonight to get her son some time away from his royal highness, Jeb.

Or you could ask Sergei how he feels about company and see if his answer gives you any clues about his plans.

Right.

A win/win opportunity.

She dug her phone out of her pocket.

Emerson's posse wants to bond over tossing around a football in your backyard. How would that go over with your guests?

Emerson crowded closer and surreptitiously tried to peek at her screen.

Evette tilted it away from him and gave him a warning look. "Hard limit, kid."

"You looked at mine."

After she'd confronted him, told him he was never to hide it from her again and that she would always have the password to it. "You got that right. And when you're paying the bill for your own phone, you can block anyone you want from looking."

His eyes narrowed. While he didn't say what he wanted to say, *You're not paying for this one* was written all over his face.

She planted her hands on her hips and frowned right back at him. "Don't push your luck, kid. Sergei might have given you that phone, but I can take it away from you twice as fast and don't think for a minute he'd stop me."

His face blanked in a heartbeat and his posture got military straight even faster. "I didn't say anything."

"No, but you thought it."

He might have argued further, but the ding on her phone cut them both off.

This is Emerson's home. So long as you are okay with it, he can play all the football he likes.

"Yes!" Emerson said, running out of the room. "I'll tell the guys."

Her shoulders sunk. A lose/lose—no info and more quality time with Jeb.

Goodie.

She dove back into her quick-fix-me-up routine. On the bright side, maybe this meant that Sergei's house wasn't going to be filled with a bunch of muscly, gun-toting Mafia guys tonight.

Thirty-five minutes later, she was all gussied up and downstairs, packing some essential lip gloss and breath mints into a small handbag. "Emerson, I know Sergei said the boys could play, but try to be polite, okay? He's got people coming over."

Emerson twisted from the TV long enough to give her a once-over. His eyes hopped high on his forehead. "Wow, Mom. You look nice."

"You act like you've never seen me dressed up before."

"Well, yeah. For church and stuff, but that dress is really pretty." He smiled in a way that said he'd learned a whole lot more from Jeb and other boys at school than she'd ever imagined. "You and Sergei gonna go on a date?"

"Sergei has guests coming over. I'm just there to help." Her voice wavered. "I think."

Emerson's smile got bigger. "You think too much."

Smarty-pants. "That does it. No more talking to Sergei for you."

This time he flat-out laughed, the rich sound of it blanketing her heart so completely she halfway decided maybe Jeb and the way her and Emerson's life had been turned on its head wasn't such a bad thing for her son. He went back to his TV watching, the deep cushions that lined the back of the couch making only the top of his blond head visible. But there was still a lot of happiness in his voice when he spoke. "You won't block me from Sergei. That'd mean you couldn't see him either. Or kiss him."

So, he'd caught those little stolen moments, had he? And here she'd thought she and Sergei were being creative. She zipped her purse shut and kept her voice as matter-of-fact as possible. "Where's your head on that?"

"On what?"

For some reason, saying it out loud felt big. Like admitting a deep dark secret for the very first time. "Me and Sergei."

The fight scene from the *Iron Man* rerun on the screen filled the silence and goose bumps that didn't have a thing to do with temperature fanned out along her forearms.

The TV went silent and Emerson twisted on the couch. He'd always been a somewhat serious kid. Cautious and pensive. But he'd also been a straight shooter nearly from the time he'd come out of the womb. No dillydallying about when it came to sharing his thoughts.

And tonight was no exception.

His hazel eyes locked hard with hers, a depth behind them that no seven-year-old should have beaming back at her. "You're safe with him. And happy."

"You saying that because we've got guards all the time and have a nice place to stay?"

He shook his head, a minute and gentle motion that

talking her momma into letting her spend her allowance on an Easy-Bake Oven.

A man like Sergei—goodness has a hard time getting through. Thinks they're not worth it.

"He will be safe, *solnyshka*. My men will never be far from him. You and I will watch over his actions and decisions together. If we need to, we will intervene. But I trust that he will see what needs to be seen."

"We." It was barely more than a whisper. A single word she hadn't meant to say out loud and that sounded even more foreign than it had in her head.

He shifted closer, his earthy scent and heat mingling with his already powerful presence. "It is inevitable."

Part of her wanted to lean in. To accept the contentment his nearness offered. But more than that, she desperately wanted to understand. "You don't even know me. Not really. I could have habits that you end up finding annoying."

Lightness crept into his dark gaze and a crooked smile graced his face. "Such as?"

"I don't know. Maybe I snore."

"I watched you while you slept in my bed. You do not snore."

"Well, maybe I've got a short temper."

"You do. It's adorable and I am not easily riled."

That much was true, and under normal circumstances his patience only fueled her ire higher. Tonight, though, he was a rock. An anchor when she wanted to emotionally flail and kick against all the turmoil blowing through her life. "This is too much. All of it. The job. Emerson changing schools. You. Me. What you want."

"What *will* be." He shifted both of her hands to

one of his and cupped the side of her face, stilling her rant and her breath with the single touch. "But there is no hurry. No rush. Only an intent stated clearly." He trailed his fingertips along her jawline and traced her lips with his thumb. "We will take time to learn each other. To uncover our quirks. Our likes. Our dislikes."

"Usually, people do that through dating. Not engagements."

"Ah, but you said people would talk. And you were right. An engagement is more definitive. More accurate for where we are headed." He smiled. An endearing one she suspected few if any ever saw. "Let me take care of you, *solnyshka*. Let me show you what it means to be my bride."

The swirl in her stomach came back with a vengeance and her heart kicked an unsteady beat. "That's not helping."

"Fine. Then tell me what you normally do to relax."

She frowned, taken aback at the change in topic. "I don't know. Probably spend an inordinate amount of time in the tub and overdose on ice cream."

He nodded. "What kind of ice cream?"

Okay, they were definitely off track now. And try as she might, she couldn't figure out where he was headed with his line of questioning. "The bad stuff. Heavy cream. High calories. Cookie dough, chocolate syrup and caramel. But I don't see how that applies to right now."

He stood, using his grip on her hands to pull her upright with him. "It applies because you are going to relax. You will trust that Emerson has good judgment and know that my men are with him should he suffer a lapse in reason and will guard him with their life." He

He toed off his Italian loafers and rid himself of his socks. Beneath his feet, the thick, plush carpet was soft and delicate. Perfect for the woman who walked on it each day.

The smooth brushed-steel knob turned easily. Silent.

Candlelight danced against the walls emanating from four votives spaced along a wide tile inset just above the soaking tub. Like her room, the olive and scarlet glass holders gave the grays and whites in the room much-needed warmth.

But the most striking feature in the room was Evette. As deep as the tub was, all he could see from the doorway were her arms draped along either side, her head resting on a deep red towel she'd rolled and wedged behind her neck and one slender, toned leg perched on the tip of the faucet. Every inch of her skin glowed in the soft light.

He loved her skin. Loved how the unique color embraced the many facets of her heritage and amplified her mysterious fairy image. As if the tone were a reflection of how the woman inside couldn't be categorized into one race or persona.

The flames flickered, stirred from the air moving through the open door.

Evette slowly opened her eyes. She noted the agitated state of the candles, turned her head to the door and gasped. "Sergei." Whether it was instinct, fear or modesty, she covered her breasts and sunk a little lower in the water. "I thought you were getting ice cream."

"I did." He unbuttoned his shirtsleeves and rolled them to his forearms. "Three pints of Ben & Jerry's."

Rather than demand he leave as he'd anticipated, her eyes narrowed. "Which kind?"

"Half Baked, The Tonight Dough and Chocolate Fudge Brownie."

"Thank God. I was afraid you were going to bring Cherry Garcia." She relaxed a little, but kept her suspicious gaze on him and her arms across her chest.

"Really? I have it on good authority that Cherry Garcia is preferred by most females."

"Which authority?"

"Kir." He unfastened his watch and set it on the vanity.

"Hmph." She shook her head. "Not this female. Fruit doesn't belong in ice cream."

"I see." For a moment he considered sitting on the edge of the tub, but he wanted full access to her. Wanted to look his fill and teach her what she could expect from him. He crouched beside the edge and rolled to his knees. Bubbles floated across the water's surface, a thin layer that had slowly dissipated in the time he'd been gone and now let the faint outline of her curves bleed through. He traced the backs of his knuckles from her elbow to her wrist, banded his fingers around it and guided her hand back to the tub's edge. "Why do you hide yourself from me, *solnyshka*? There is no part of you that I have not seen." He repeated the gesture with her other arm. "No part of you I have not touched."

A ragged breath slipped past her slackened lips and a shudder moved through her. A tiny one that sent subtle ripples through the water around her torso. Her breasts weren't overly large, but ample enough the water lifted them, leaving the darker tips peeking just

steered her toward the stairs, motioned her up them as soon as they reached the landing, then playfully swatted her behind. "Go."

"Go where?" she said, not moving an inch.

Sergei, on the other hand, was already strolling toward the front door, a certain swagger in his gait that did even wonkier things to her insides. "You're going to take a long hot bath."

"And what are you going to do?"

"My bride says she needs ice cream. So, I'm going to get it for her." He paused with the door open and his hand resting on the knob and aimed a wolf's smile her direction. "And then I'm going to educate her on other, more effective methods of relaxation."

Chapter Sixteen

Sergei loved many things about modern life. Particularly modern *American* life. But after fifteen minutes too long in the frozen foods section of the nearest grocer and Kir offering his opinions on which ice cream to select, Sergei had decided that Ben & Jerry's had officially taken things too far.

The growl of his BMW's engine as he pulled into the driveway more quickly than was wise matched his unspoken frustration.

If Kir had an issue with his aggressive driving, he didn't show it. Just casually unbuckled his seat belt before Sergei got the car in Park and dryly offered, "I still think you should have gone with Cherry Garcia."

"She didn't say anything about fruit. She said cookie dough, chocolate syrup and caramel."

Kir grunted as they both got out of the car. "It has fudge in it."

"Not enough." Sergei rounded the front of the car and angled toward the carriage house, the plastic sack full of three different pints of ice cream dangling from his fist. "I want regular check-ins with Mikey and Daniel. Evette is uncomfortable with the boys Emerson is

3:37 p.m.

He smiled to himself, tucked the phone back in his pocket and stood. He'd never seen someone sleep so soundly. Certainly never experienced it for himself. But she was completely relaxed. Her features beautifully unguarded and her plump lips slightly parted. The last thing he wanted to do was wake her, but she'd be furious if he waited any longer to do so.

He paused by the side of the bed.

The sheets and blankets he'd pulled over her when he'd slipped out of bed an hour after she'd fallen asleep barely covered her breasts, leaving the upper swells exposed. Her skin was exceptional. A tactile indulgence he'd happily gorged on.

Perhaps a furious Evette wouldn't be such a bad thing. He'd already gotten a taste of her attitude, but taming her anger in a highly sexual fashion would be a worthy challenge. One he'd make sure they both remembered for a very long time.

He put a knee to the bed and stretched out beside her.

Rather than wake at the movement, she sighed and rolled a little closer.

It was tempting to take advantage. To peel off his clothes, slip between the sheets with her and stake his claim all over again. But Emerson would be ready for her soon and she'd need time to get herself in order. He cupped the side of her face. "It's time to wake up, *solnyshka*."

She started, her eyes snapping open and shooting straight to him. Almost as quickly, she relaxed and gave him a shaky smile. "Wow. I was really out." For a moment, she looked her fill at his face, a unique ex-

Chapter Twelve

Night and day.

To Sergei's mind, it was too common of an expression to be worthy of anything to do with the woman curled on her side, fast asleep in his bed, but apt for the moment nonetheless. He was shadows. Secrets. Death.

But she was everything bright, positive and hopeful in the world.

Pure sunshine.

And she was his.

She'd accepted him. Shown him what it felt like to touch heaven. To taste it and hold it. He'd known where they were headed. Had acknowledged it as soon as he'd walked her and Emerson to the carriage house door Saturday night and forced himself to give her distance all day Sunday. But he hadn't anticipated the change their physical connection would create. The ruthless possessiveness that would follow or the speed with which he was inclined to take things.

He'd touched the sun. Claimed it for his own.

And he wasn't giving it back.

Seated in the plush leather wingback to one side of his bed, he shifted just enough to pull his phone from his back pocket and double-check that he'd silenced it.

The weight of sleep pressed harder. Lulled her to let go and trust.

She could fight it.

Probably should.

But she'd think about that later.

Right now, she was safe. And happy.

Just this once, she'd take it.

the rest of the world. He skimmed one hand over the curve of her hip. "You are all right, *malen'kaya feya*?"

"I'm peachy," she sighed, savoring his heat as the room's chill began to settle on her sweat-misted skin. Her bed at the carriage house was comfy—old as the hills, but soft and familiar. Comparatively, Sergei's was probably what they had stocked in heaven. "Snug as a bug in a rug."

He chuckled near her ear, the smile in his low voice when he spoke mingling with the aftereffects of her release to create a quiet, peaceful cocoon. "I like you sated and pliant." He kissed the spot he'd bitten again and lingered there. "I like even more how I got you there."

A prodding from somewhere in her conscience told her to make note of the statement. To perk up and make sure he wasn't assuming there would be any future encounters.

But his warmth was too tempting. The gentle rasp of his beard against her skin as he rolled them both to their sides and pulled the thick comforter over them too much to heed direction from anything but the heavy peace settling over her.

She mumbled something. Or she assumed she did because he chuckled again and spooned her with his arm cradling her head. "Go to sleep, Evette. I've got you."

So nice.

So warm.

She couldn't remember the last time she'd been this warm. This protected. Surrounded by the strength of a capable, intelligent man.

pinning her to bed. And yet, his words were pure velvet. A seductive beast luring her toward its shadowed den. "I felt it, *feya*. Already know how tight your pussy clenches when you come. Now I want to feel my sweet angel milk my cock."

"Oh my God." Pleasure speared straight to her core and her hips lifted higher on pure instinct.

His cockhead brushed her G-spot. Once. Twice.

And that was all she wrote.

She was soaring. Riding uncharted highs. Relishing each squeeze of her sex around his thick shaft and bucking against each of his increasing thrusts.

He groaned into her neck and murmured a string of words she had no hope of understanding against her skin.

And then he bit her.

Made her pussy fist him all over again as he speared to the hilt and his cock jerked inside her.

So perfect.

Dangerously so.

A hedonistic moment so powerful even the most pious person would relinquish every vow simply to delight in its pleasure. And she was just a normal woman. A mother who'd gone too many years without touch or intimacy.

An addict just waiting to happen.

He licked the tender spot where he'd bitten her neck. Then kissed it. Languorously, undulated his hips against hers and explored the delicate stretch of skin from her neck to her shoulder with more tender, affectionate kisses.

Such gentleness. A reverence in stark contrast to the unforgiving, dispassionate demeanor he showed

against her mouth. "I didn't say I wouldn't take you hard."

A flutter rippled through her sex, the dirty promise in his words a mere precursor to what he delivered in reality. There was no planning. No seduction. No run-of-the-mill step-by-step playbook learned from *Men's Health* or *Penthouse*. It was animalistic. Glorious in its unscripted beauty and driven solely on physical sensation. And through every second, his focus was riveted on her. On her response to each touch. Each moan or sigh. The reaction garnered from each position he guided her through. As if his pleasure was contingent on hers.

It was freeing. Empowering and humbling all at once.

In one smooth move, he pulled free of her sex, flipped her to her belly and drove back inside her. His warm breath coasted against her neck and his voice was as rumbly as thunder at midnight. "You will come for me." His pelvis pounded against her ass and his balls slapped against her labia with each thrust. "You will give me your release and cry my name while you do it."

Under any other situation, she'd have laughed. It was so like him to command such a thing. So blatant and defiant of any obstacles that stood in his path.

But with his weight blanketing her...his scent all around her and the delicious shuttling of his cock through her sex...all she could do was whimper and accept it. To latch on to the tightening low in her belly. Surrender to the growing climax stomping closer by the second.

He gripped her wrists, his fingers like manacles

one of the packets, she nearly dropped it on the hand-off. "Hurry."

Keeping one hand at her hip, he held her gaze and tore the packet open with his teeth. *"Nyet."*

Not just a no, but a hard no.

"You've been without for seven years." He rolled the condom into place, palmed the back of one thigh and leaned forward so he braced his other hand beside her head. "There will be no hurry this time." He pulled back just enough the head of his cock nudged her entrance. "You will remember it." He pressed inside, just the tip of him gliding easy through the slickness of her release. "Every stroke." Deeper. Fuller. Every inch gained earned while his stare stayed locked to hers. "Every sound. Every sensation. You will remember who it was who gave them to you."

Holy freaking *wow*, she'd forgotten how amazing it felt to be connected with a man. To the delectable stretch as her body adjusted to him and the unique fit of his body. And with him gazing down at her—studying every reaction as if his every move was driven off her response—it was off-the-charts intimate. Her words came out ragged and breathless. "I think it's a safe bet I'm not going to forget them no matter what tempo you set." She dragged her foot up the back of his thigh and used her heel to urge him the rest of the way home. When his hips met hers and the heavy weight of his balls lay flush against her, she sighed. "But I promise you, I won't break."

The wolf she'd glimpsed before returned and smiled down at her. "You mistake me, *malen'kaya feya*. I said I wouldn't hurry." He lowered his head and murmured

mouth where she wanted it. When her words came out, they were surprisingly gruff. "It doesn't matter."

He licked the tip, an agonizingly slow motion that made her breath catch and her heart skitter. "Oh, but it does." He shifted again, bringing his other knee between hers, and forced her thighs wide with his own. One minute press of his hips and his shaft glided against her clit.

"No, it doesn't." She rolled her hips, angling for more of the delicious friction. "Trust me, it doesn't."

His fingers at her hip dug into her skin. "Look at me."

Her eyes snapped open, a demand for more ready on the tip of her tongue.

It fizzled in an instant, the sheer magnificence of the man above her commanding her silence.

A dark knight.

One poised to claim his due.

His voice was like midnight. Low, lush and endless. "How long has it been?"

Why it was so important, she couldn't imagine. She'd given birth, for crying out loud. There was no way he'd hurt her. But the vehemence in his tone stirred the truth. "Since Emerson."

Something moved behind those mysterious eyes of his. Something so raw and primitive goose bumps lifted along her skin.

"Nightstand drawer, Evette. Now."

Oh, boy.

She threw out a hand and fumbled for a condom, no small task considering how badly her hands shook from the adrenaline coursing through her and how he refused to let her go. Even once she managed to snag

She sighed into his mouth, the hot contact of his skin against hers and his delicious weight pinning her to the bed the most beautifully tactile experience of her life. The faintest trace of her release still lingered on his lips, and his tongue stroked against hers with the same masterful deliberation he'd exercised on her sex.

And his hands. Good Lord, his touch was divine. Purposeful. Passionate. Reverent even as it demanded a response. Every rasp of his calloused palms against her sensitized flesh sent tingles rippling in all directions. Awakened that part of her she'd thought forever buried years ago.

Never in her life had she felt anything remotely this erotic. This overwhelming and yet peaceful in the same breath. She was floating. Buoyed on a sensual cloud by his drugging kiss, his hypnotic touch and his sinful taste.

He shifted, dragging seductive kisses along her jawline and down the side of her neck as he slid one knee between hers and nudged it wide. "You never answered my question, *feya*."

Questions?

There'd been questions?

She whimpered and arched her back, encouraging him to speed up the leisurely trek his mouth was making toward her breast. "Stop talking."

His low chuckle was pure delighted wickedness, the warm tickle of his exhalation drawing her already straining nipple to an agonized peak. He grazed the distended tip with his teeth. "How long has it been, *feya*?"

Fisting her hand in his hair, she tried to guide his

added bit by bit, but done so well it all fit together. Epaulets on each shoulder, five-pointed stars with intricate shading atop each pectoral, a dagger that appeared embedded in his skin, a winged creature that seemed part bat and part dragon. The imagery was fascinating and made her itch to explore.

The muted *zritch* from the zipper on his jeans ripped her from her stupor just as he pushed them past his hips. Either he'd snagged his briefs or boxers on the way down, or he was a commando man because when he straightened, he was completely naked and ready for action.

"Oh." From some dim corner of her mind, she noted she'd actually spoken the single, breathless syllable out loud, but at that particular moment she didn't give a damn. She was too fascinated. Too riveted and tongue-tied for pride to have any say over her actions. Yes, he'd unveiled more tattoos. Lots of them. Detailed ones combining dragon scales, weapons and armor that coiled around his hips and continued to his muscled thighs. But the real focus—the thing that left her jaw slack and her mind on pause—was the thick erection straining toward his navel.

"Oh?" He paced to the edge of the bed, the pleased glint in his eyes belying the nature of his words. "I don't believe I've ever heard you at such a loss for words." He put one knee to the mattress and crawled toward her, a panther inching close enough to strike. "Does that mean you're disappointed, *feya*?"

He kept coming. Braced his knees on either side of hers and leaned in until gravity and his kiss took over and she found her head cushioned by thick down pillows.

belly. "Your cries were loud, *feya*." His thumb fanned through the curls she kept tightly trimmed atop her sex. "The house is empty, but the grounds are not."

Fuck.

The men outside the house.

She'd forgotten about them. Actually, she'd forgotten about everything. Which was amazing considering her mind wasn't the type that appreciated the art of relaxation. She scooched her bottom closer to the pillows, centering herself on the bed. "I wasn't that loud." She paused a beat, trying to remember. "Was I?"

Grinning, Sergei pushed off the bed, straightened and started casually releasing the buttons on his shirt as he toed off his shoes. "If you think they were protective before, I'm afraid you'll find them intolerable now."

Well now, that didn't make any sense at all. Razzing her, she'd understand. Or maybe acting awkward and unable to look her in the eye a few days, but more protective? That didn't make any sense.

She opened her mouth to ask him what he meant, then snapped it closed at the sight of his bared chest.

She'd known he was fit. Had savored the feel of his arms and torso when she was holding on for dear life through one of his devastating kisses. Had even expected to see more tattoos given those she'd seen on his knuckles and wrists, but this…

He was a work of art.

Literally.

Swarthy skin stretched over well-defined muscle and the vast majority of it was inked with elaborate tattoos in black and red. And it wasn't one massive piece of art work either. More a collage of inspiration

A feral sound rumbled from his chest. He shifted his fingers, brushing his fingertips against the tender stretch along her front wall, and sucked her clit deep.

And she was gone.

Her sex pulsing around his fingers and her blood pounding in her ears. It was exquisite. Every inch of her bared body rippling in the wake of a climax unlike anything else she'd ever felt before. Channeling pure sensation as warm and bright as a summer sun and as powerful as a hurricane. In that moment she was invincible. Whole and free of both the past and the future. There was only right here. Right now. And the decadent feelings sweeping through her.

How long she lingered she didn't know. And for the first time in her life, didn't care. Only knew that Sergei's fingers continued to glide in and out of her. Slower than before, but still present and drawing out the aftershocks with the combined pressure of his thumb at her clit.

Definitely a man with a lot of experience.

And patience.

And exceptional oral skills.

She rolled her head to one side, forced her climax-weighted eyelids open—and spied one seriously smug Russian staring back at her.

As if he had all the time in the world and no inclination to resign his task, he held her gaze and gave her one last thorough lick.

"You look rather pleased with yourself," she said, the huskiness in her voice undeniably thick with the aftereffects of an exceptional climax.

Pushing himself up with one hand, he skimmed a calloused palm over her hip, then inward toward her

every bit the devil he claimed to be. He cupped her ass and lowered his head, holding her gaze even as his warm breath danced across her flesh. "It means I'm going to devour your sweet pussy until you come on my tongue."

Her sex clenched, the combined jolt of his words and the wet heat of his mouth closing around her clit shoving her straight into the deep end of sensation. There was no coyness. No leisurely buildup or pause to reconfirm the consent she'd already given.

He took.

Feasted as though he'd hungered for years. Explored every inch of her with an unabashed thoroughness. His wicked mouth. His talented tongue. He used them both, deftly following each whimper or lift of her hips to give her more of what she craved. Built the roiling need until all she could do was ride the swelling wave and accept the release barreling toward her.

He pressed one hand to her belly, stilling her rolling hips even as he pressed a finger inside her.

Holy hell.

When she'd grown so emboldened to spear her hands in his hair, she hadn't a clue, but they were there now. Holding him steady. Reveling in the vibrations his hungry sounds created against her swollen, aching clit.

It'd been so long.

Too long.

He added another finger, the fullness welcome and yet not nearly enough. A poor imitation for what she really craved. "Sergei."

She tried to lift her hips, eager for more and dancing at the edge. Her pussy fluttered around his fingers, release so close it hurt. "Sergei, please."

taking he had ample experience in these situations, he skimmed his fingertips up her spine, slipped the fastener on her bra free and gently peeled the fabric from her shoulders. His gaze dropped to her bared breasts and an unmistakable hunger deepened behind his dark eyes. "Compared to me, yes."

So much contempt. Such self-loathing and scorn. The urge to pull him against her and simply hold him made her palms itch, but she'd had enough experience with male pride to know that was the wrong move. She smoothed her hands down his arms, taking time to appreciate the muscles bunched beneath her palms. "You're not the devil either. You've been nothing but kind to Emerson and me. Protective and thoughtful."

His expression hardened, the sharp edge of the beast she'd glimpsed pushing its way free. Despite his gentle touch, there was unmistakable power and hunger in his voice. "Make no mistake, Evette. There is darkness in me." He unfastened her jeans and slipped his hands beneath the denim at her hips. "Enough that I'm taking your light and will suffer no conscience for it."

The confession should have given her pause. Or at the very least pushed her to demand further explanation, but paired with the gravelly rumble of his voice and the way he lifted her by her ass, dropped her on the side of the bed and pulled her panties and jeans free in one seamless maneuver, it sent her reasoning on a detour she had no intention of missing. Especially when he lasered his attention on her exposed sex, palmed her knees and pried them up and wide, growling a string of Russian words that sounded filthy.

"What does that mean?"

The dirty smirk that tilted his lips made him look

Funny. She'd always taken great pains to clean his private space when he wasn't home, but had also spent a good amount of the time caring for it wondering how he'd look here. How he'd fit with elegant yet masculine décor rich with its dark chocolates, golds and scarlet accents. A decorator's nod to more refined eras and prestigious enough for a king. But seeing him now—stealing toward her with the glide of a predator confident in capturing his prey—she realized her maneuvering had probably been an instinctual step toward self-preservation. Much the same way a human didn't go dancing around in the lion's cage.

"You're going the wrong way, *feya*."

Damn it.

She dug in her heels and her gaze skittered to the king-size bed with its sumptuous crimson comforter and thick bedposts. If the thing hadn't been such a work of art with the swirling ivy designs carved into the wood, she'd have hated the never-ending fight to keep the dust from settling into the details. "Don't you think we should talk?"

"About what?"

"I don't know." Maybe circle back to how this was a bad idea. Or what the repercussions would be to her job once they'd scratched their collective itch. For crying out loud—the last time she'd had sex she couldn't remember a single detail of the actual event and had ended up peeing on a little pink stick just over a month later.

"Protection," she managed on a surge of inspiration.

Sure enough, Sergei stopped an arm's length away and narrowed his eyes. "Protection?"

Okay, maybe it wasn't the sexiest topic to come up

with, but it was practical. And necessary. "I don't do things like this. I'm not prepared."

Sergei cocked his head like she'd completely lost him.

"I'm a mom. Single moms barely have time to take a bubble bath. Let alone go out on enough dates to warrant any action." When he just stared at her, seemingly at a loss for words, she blurted, "I'm not on the pill, so condoms are a must."

A dangerous expression moved across his face. Something so primal and possessive she was torn between rubbing up against him like a cat and jumping off the balcony beyond the French doors. "How long?"

Now she was the one lost. "What do you mean, *how long*?"

"How long has it been since you've been with a man?"

Whoa, boy. The heat coming off his words alone was enough to melt the wrought iron gates surrounding his estate. No way was she fanning the testosterone any higher. She braced her hands on her hips the way she would when going head to head with Emerson. "That's not the point. The point is, safe sex is important."

"Safe sex," he murmured and closed the distance between them.

"Yes."

"Mmm. A practical woman." Slowly, he manacled one of her wrists with his fingers and tugged her forward. Instead of pulling her against him as she'd expected, he turned and led her toward one side of the bed. "Let's see if we can accommodate your requirements."

By the nightstand, he faced her, casually dipped

Oh.
Holy.
Hell.
Sex.
With Sergei Petrovyh.

Her belly swirled in a dizzying loop de loop, and a mini-gasm that threatened to buckle her knees speared through her sex. And damned if her brain didn't conjure up some high-definition ideas about what *all of me* meant. "Yes."

It was probably the stupidest thing she'd agreed to in her life. Definitely the most dangerous. But she got all of one second to second-guess her answer before the world spun and she found herself in his arms. His long legs took up the distance in no time. Out of the kitchen. Through the living room. Up the stairs two at a time like he wasn't carrying a damned thing. Down the hallway.

His heavy footsteps pounded as powerfully against the thick carpet as her heartbeat, and as tight as he held her, she doubted she could have wriggled free even if she'd wanted to.

Little late for that, isn't it, missy?

The prod from her common sense bubbled up just as he crossed the threshold to his room. He eased her to her feet all of one step into the massive space, shut the antique door and threw the bolt.

The clack of the stout lock rounded through the room, which considering how lush the fabrics, furniture and carpet were in his domain, said he'd put some serious torque behind the action. Whether it was her nerves or pure instinct, she backed up a step. Then another. "Um…"

She was lost in seconds. Drowning in the taste of him. Surrendering to the sensual demands his body built in hers. Even her common sense acquiesced. Gave way to the onslaught the same as the earth reformed in the wake of a volcanic explosion. Nature simply didn't argue with what was. It flowed and accepted reality in whatever form it took, and her body reacted to Sergei in kind. Action and reaction. Fire and rebirth.

Yes, she'd experienced passion before, but never like this. Never something this primal. Where every touch…every shared breath and the crackling yet unseen connection between them overshadowed everything else.

It was frightening. Thrilling and terrifying all at once. She wrapped her arms around his neck. Let her fingers tangle in the thick mass of his hair and moaned into his kiss. Savored the press of her breasts against his chest and the unforgiving press of his cock against her belly.

He fisted his hand in her hair and pulled her head back, the mix of the aggressive act and his throaty growl ripping a startled gasp past her mouth. His eyes were so dark they were more black than blue and the harshness of his features made him seem more animal than man. "You will accept this."

Accept?

What was he talking about? And was he asking her or telling her? Because, her ability to rationalize and make decisions had been at half capacity from the time she'd found him standing behind her and had shut down completely the second his mouth had come into contact with hers. "What are we talking about?"

"You will take me. Willingly. All of me."

to one side and slid the top drawer open, all the while holding her gaze. "Will this meet your needs?"

Her gaze dropped to the contents inside the drawer. Specifically, the dozen or more gold foil packages waiting and ready for use. "Um." She leaned a little closer for a better look. No. Not a dozen. More than that. Which meant either today was premeditated as hell, or he'd had a lot more action going on in this house than she'd noted in the month since she'd moved in.

She straightened, but couldn't quite manage to meet his stare. Not with her cheeks flaming as hot as the asphalt on Bourbon Street in August. "That's probably overkill."

"You underestimate the power of your kiss, *feya*." He moved in, anchored her against him with a hand at her hip and cupped the back of her head. His voice as he lowered his mouth to hers was everything dark and wonderful mothers warned their daughters about. "And the depths of my determination to see how the rest of you tastes."

Wow.

It was bad enough that his kiss made her stupid. That the taste of him made her drunk and the commanding way he held her brought all those white knight moments from her youth galloping back to life. But words, too? At this rate, they'd find her months from now still overdosed and grinning in his bed.

So what if it was a royal screwup? It wouldn't be her first, and likely not her last, but it felt so good to be touched. To have physical contact from a man who not only seemed to know what he was doing, but that fired every circuit in her system just looking at him.

He lifted his head, the loss of his kiss taking her

breath with it. In the near month she'd worked for him, she'd caught glimpses of the man behind the mask he showed the rest of the world, but in that second, the beast showed through. A wolf intoxicated by its spoils and still hungry for more.

Forcing her hands at the back of his neck to relax, she smoothed them across his shoulders. "Why are you stopping?"

"Not stopping." He tugged her T-shirt free of her jeans. "Appreciating." Not missing a beat, he lifted the shirt up and over her head and let it fall to the floor.

And that was when it hit her. When the realization whispered through her mind as silkily as the room's cool air dancing against the skin he'd bared.

This wouldn't be a quick tumble.

No fumbling in the dark.

No morning after she could slip free of before anyone was the wiser.

This was all out in the open. A tangle she'd never be able to hide from. Even if nothing else happened between them after today—and nothing else *could* happen—he'd leave a mark. A memory she'd be hard-pressed to ever outdo.

He traced the skin above her waistband, the backs of his knuckles teasing her pebbled flesh. "You're thinking too much."

"One could argue I'm not thinking enough."

He smiled at that, a soft curve of his lips she doubted many people ever witnessed. "The angel is having second thoughts about dancing with the devil?"

Her answering bark of laughter filled the room. "Me? An angel?"

His smile slipped. So smoothly there was no mis-

with. Until they prove themselves, they are not to be trusted."

From the trajectory of Kir's voice behind him, he still hadn't budged from the passenger's side of the car. "Where are you going?"

"I have ice cream and a woman relaxing in a hot bath." He glanced over his shoulder. "Where do you think I'm going?"

Kir chuckled and shook his head. "You're whipped."

Perhaps he was. God knew he had no patience where Evette was concerned. Only a hunger that had grown steadily out of control since that night in the alley. As if her touch—her kiss and her scent—had infected him with an unquenchable lust. A pleasure that left the rest of the world in boring shades of black, white and gray when she wasn't beside him. He paused at the door and locked eyes with Kir. "Watch Emerson."

All humor fled his friend's face. Kir had seen firsthand the bloodshed Sergei was capable of when someone dared to cross him and, companionable razzing aside, both of his *avtoritets* knew what Evette and Emerson meant to him. Knew what fury any harm to either of them would ignite.

Kir nodded. "He will be safe."

It was all the reassurance Sergei needed. A handful of steps later, he was in Evette's kitchen and unloading his purchases in the freezer.

Upstairs, all was quiet. So much so, he wondered if perhaps she'd snuck out while he'd been at the store. But then, if she'd done so, one of his men would have notified him.

He shucked his suit jacket, tossed it onto the kitchen table and quietly stole up the stairs. The master bedroom was empty, but the clothes Evette had been wearing were neatly folded on the flannel chair in the corner and the door to the master bathroom was closed. While the wide window on the far wall was high enough no one could directly see inside, the blinds were still tilted so the sunlight would fill the room during the day. With nightfall in full swing, the only light at this point was the soft white of the moon through the slats. He padded to them, closed them completely and turned on the small bedside lamp.

A warm buttery glow filled the space. What had once been a simple room with soft grays, dark charcoals and white furnishings now had teal and yellow pillows and random knickknacks that gave the space a Bohemian feel.

It fit Evette perfectly. And while he enjoyed the sophisticated décor of his own home and the rich colors that went with it, he couldn't help but find himself rethinking his selections. Maybe, once Evette and Emerson moved into the main house, she would make it her own as well. Give it the homey and welcoming feel that she'd created in her own private haven.

The soft tinkling of water spilling on water sounded through the closed door followed by a muted sigh.

Still bathing.

Still lingering in the warm water he'd imagined her in the whole drive to the store and back. While arguing with Kir had definitely tried his patience, the picture his mind had created the second she'd mentioned taking a bath had left him tense and preoccupied. Narrowly focused to a degree that could prove dangerous to him if he didn't get a grip on his response to Evette soon.

above the surface. Tempting him to touch and taste. "There's not a woman alive who wouldn't cover herself if they saw you standing in a doorway looking at them like that."

"Like what?"

She hesitated a moment, studying his face. For what, he had no clue, but it felt important. "A wolf."

A wise assessment. One she might be smart to heed and run. "I am a predator. It's who I've been for most of my life." He dipped his hand beneath the water. Let his fingertips trail the path along one hip and up to the side of her breast. "You can focus on that part of me if you choose, or you can see the other side." He fanned his thumb along the outward swell of her breast. A tender, teasing touch that made her nipple harden farther, straining toward him. "What belongs to you and Emerson and no one else."

Her back arched ever so slightly, the movement betraying the impact of his touch and her growing need in the most natural way possible. Her voice was deeper when she spoke, raspy and distracted. "What's that?"

"Your protector."

Another shiver, this one so palpable he slipped his other hand beneath her neck to steady her.

Her body gave way to his. Surrendered and molded itself to his guidance as he lifted her. Brought her mouth closer to his. "You do not have to fight me." He teased her parted lips with his own. "You have nothing to fear from me."

Her hands pressed against his chest, the lingering wetness from her fingertips seeping through the fine fabric. The gold in her hazel eyes flickered in the candlelight, but the fear behind them was a living thing.

A monster bared in an intimate moment. "It's easier being alone. There's nothing to lose."

Death.

He'd felt its freezing sting at an early age. Had watched his father drown himself in liquor and pity because of it.

But he'd found a family because of it, too. A merciless and dangerous one at times, but a family nonetheless. Loyal people who would come to his side no matter the distance. Anton. Yefim. Kir and Roman. Darya and now her family as well.

Beyond Dorothy and Emerson, she'd lost that.

The monster behind her eyes taunted him. Coiled in on itself and challenged him.

But he had no problem with monsters. He welcomed their ugliness and took great pleasure in choking the life from their vile bodies. Keeping his grip on her neck, he pulled the towel out from beneath her head, shook it out, then guided her to her feet. "You have me. My family and their loyalty." Once she was out of the tub and steady on her feet, he wrapped the crimson fabric around her shoulders, cradled the back of her head and pulled her flush against him. "Fight it as long as you need to. Watch and learn if that's what it takes. But your days of being alone are over."

He kissed her.

Sealed his vow with all he had in him.

Willed her to feel his determination. His absolute resolve to win her. To protect and provide for her. She'd want for nothing. Know no hardship save what was unpreventable by sheer existence, and even that, she would not experience alone.

He would be there.

His family would be there.

And she would be *his*.

"Sergei." Her arms shook as she pressed against his chest. The monster in her eyes was gone, replaced with questions. Uncertainty, yes, but openness, too. A door opened, if only a crack. As if she realized the vulnerability she'd offered him, her gaze dropped to his chest and her voice shook with adorable shyness. "I'm getting you all wet."

Inside his arms, she was so tiny. Completely engulfed by his size and his strength. And yet she fit perfectly. Had melted into him every single time he'd touched her. "Indeed."

He loosened his grip and guided the thick, soft towel across her shoulders. Down her arms and up along her sides. He crouched and rubbed the fabric over her hips and along the outside of her thighs and shins. At her ankles, he released the towel and skated his thumbs upward. A mirrored path he'd taken to the outside of her toned legs, only more delicate and skin-to-skin along the inside.

At her knees, he paused. Circled slow patterns and savored the silky texture of her skin. Allowed himself to look his fill at her sex. The flushed and swollen folds and the slightest hint of her clit peeking out from behind her hood. He exhaled through his mouth. Let the warmth of his breath ghost across her sex.

She gripped his shoulders and whimpered.

Bozhe, but he loved that sound. Craved the responsive tremors that moved through her every time he earned it. The way her skin heated beneath his touch and her breath quickened.

Her nails bit through the fabric of his shirt. "You've got that wolfish look on your face again."

"Do I?" He nudged her feet farther apart and splayed his hands against her inner thighs. Her scent hit him instantly. Musky, yet sweet. Even in the dim candlelight, her pussy glistened with wetness. Not just ready for him, but eager. "Perhaps it's because I'm hungry and in need of a treat."

"Oh, God." One hand at his shoulder shifted to the top of his head, whether to push him away or pull him closer, he couldn't be sure. But he could certainly influence her decision. Influence her and take what he wanted.

"Hold on, tight, *solnyshka*. I promise you, I will not break."

He licked her. Blatantly ran his tongue along her labia and savored her juices. Circled her swollen clit with his tongue and sucked it into his mouth. Fingered her drenched pussy while he worked her until her cries and moans ricocheted off the bathroom tiles like a symphony.

She fisted his hair. Clutched his shoulder and rolled her hips against his mouth with complete abandon.

Wild.

Beautiful.

Completely unrestrained.

And all his.

Her legs shook, and her pussy quivered around his fingers. A gratifying response that had signaled her releases before, but a shitty location and position for her to enjoy one now. In one smooth move, he pulled his fingers from her wet heat, stood and lifted her up, guiding her legs around his waist.

The shout that filled his ears as he stalked out of the bathroom was decidedly less pleasant than the others he'd earned. "You did *not* just stop right before I was about to come."

"Not stopping. Only delaying." He gently tossed her on the bed, slid his hands under her perfect ass and pulled her pussy back to his mouth. "But now that I see the reaction denying you gets me, perhaps I should tease you a little longer." He licked her slit, the taste of her sweet on his tongue. "A little harder."

She pushed up on her elbows, her breaths churning short and choppy. Her gaze sharpened, and her tone was that of a woman readying for battle, but the muscles in her legs relaxed, widening her knees for better access. "You wouldn't."

In answer, he licked her again, holding her gaze through every second. "You've accepted I'm a predator." Another pass through her folds and a rush of honey on his tongue. "Everyone knows how we like to play with our prey."

Her mouth parted and her eyelids grew heavy. While the independent, strong woman in her might not like the idea of being delayed her release, the sensual side to her clearly enjoyed the visual and his aggression because her voice turned to velvet. "You know that saying? The one about turnabout being fair play?"

His cock, already aching and straining for release, jerked and lengthened farther behind his pants. Fuck, just the idea of her full lips anywhere near his shaft made him want to show her just how primitive he could be. "You are always welcome to put your beautiful mouth on me, *solnyshka*. As much or however long you want to." He smiled and let her see the real wolf inside. The merciless one who was tired of its confines and ready to run free with its mate. He circled her clit with his tongue. Nudged the base of it and let his warm breath dance across the swollen surface. "Of course, the harder you push me, the more I'll be driven to dominate you." Another circle paired with the slow insertion of two fingers. "To take control and force your surrender."

Her head dropped back on a moan and her hips undulated against his mouth. If he'd had any doubts as to whether the idea of domination appealed to her before, the fingers she speared in his hair and the desperation with which she urged him for more pressure from his mouth wiped them away. "Don't you dare tease me. Don't you dare."

Oh, he'd dare.

Plenty.

He'd just make sure he had his ring on her finger and his last name behind hers before he took it there. "Shhh," he crooned against her flushed skin. His lips grazed her clit over and over and he pumped his fingers in and out of her with aching slowness. "I will not tease my bride." A tiny lick to the very tip of her clit. "Not yet anyway."

It was the last quiet sound in the room, the low, grated sound that rolled up the back of her throat as he closed his lips around her and suckled deep like that of a feminine warrior embarking on the most pleasurable fight of her life. Her cunt fisted his fingers. Greedy, pulsing contractions that made him wish he'd had the foresight to rid himself of his clothes before he'd reengaged.

But this wasn't about him. Wasn't about proving

how potent their connection was or satisfying himself. It was about seeing to her needs. Demonstrating who he would be to her in and out of bed.

Plus, her taste was divine. His lungs filled with her musky scent and her low, throaty sighs of pleasure making the delay of his own pleasure worth the wait. Worth the challenge.

He let her ride her release. Kept the pressure at her clit to string the sensations out and savored the sweet aftershocks rippling around him. Only when her hips slowed and her moans turned into breathy sighs did he ease his fingers from her sheath.

"You see, *solnyshka*?" He gripped both of her hips and pressed a tender kiss to the tightly trimmed curls atop her mound before slowly shifting himself to cover her naked body. "I told you I had more efficient methods for relaxation."

Her eyes opened slowly, the weight of her lids over her hazel eyes enticing and seductive. A wry smile crept onto her face. "Certainly lower in caloric intake, that's for sure." The smile slipped and her gaze locked on his mouth. She traced his lower lip with her forefinger. "Do you keep your promises, Sergei?"

A sly question. That of a huntress baiting her trap. "I don't make promises I can't keep."

She let out a sound that was part hum and part sigh and lifted her stare to his. "That's good." Her fingers drifted to his shirt placket and, one-by-one began to loosen the buttons. "Because last time things went too fast and I didn't get to explore."

He'd been wrong.

One look at the mischief dancing in her eyes and he

knew it to the very core of him. Delaying his pleasure wouldn't be tonight's challenge.

But surviving it would be.

She pulled his shirttail free, released the last two buttons and smoothed her fingertips from his abs, to his pecs, then over his shoulders, pushing the fabric out of her way. Her gaze roamed the ink she'd bared. "These all mean something, don't they?"

"Many. Yes."

"Mmm." Not a sign of encouragement so much as acknowledgment of a noted piece of information tucked away for later. Once his arms were free of his shirt and she'd tossed it to the side of the bed, she braced her hand on his sternum and pushed with surprising strength.

He rolled to his back, potently aware not just of her energy and the sensual promise of her movements, but of the power he'd chosen to give her in that moment. Not once in all the lovers he'd known had he allowed a woman this space. To rise above him in any way.

But she wanted to explore. Wanted to learn him in the same way he'd learned her. The truth was right there, burning behind her eyes. She unhooked his belt. "You said I was welcome to put my mouth on you." The button and zipper came next, each move tentative yet determined. "As much or however long I wanted."

He'd endure torture for her if it meant seeing her blossom as she was right now. Would take an iron brand and suffer it without a sound if it meant feeling her sweet touch on his bare skin.

She hooked her fingers in the waist of his pants and briefs, locked stares with him and pulled them over his hips.

Her breath left her on a shaky exhalation before his pants had cleared his shins, and her mouth slackened.

He kicked his pants free and skimmed one hand up her forearm, needing the connection every bit as much as he imagined she did. "I also told you that the harder you push me, the more I'll be driven to dominate you."

She started, his word triggering a delightful tremor in her torso. With the grace of a feline, she knelt between his knees and skimmed her hands from his knees to his thighs.

"You like the prospect of that outcome, don't you, *solnyshka*? To have your man take control and guide you. To leave you free to simply feel."

Her hands drifted along his hip bones and beside his straining cock.

It jerked in response. Strained in anticipation of her touch.

Her gaze might have been riveted to his sex when she answered, but he felt her whispered answer in every part of him. "Yes."

"Then take it. Do what you want. But know there will come a time when payment will be due."

Moving only her eyes, she peeked at him from beneath her lashes, a delightful mix of coy maiden and devilish vixen beaming up at him. "Maybe." She held his gaze and lowered her head with aching slowness. Her warm breath whispered against his shaft. "Maybe I'll be good enough at my task you'll be too spent to demand payment when I'm done."

She didn't give him time to respond. Rather stole his breath and what was left of his plans with a gentle yet confident lick from the base to the tip of him. The wet glide against his flesh. The warmth of her mouth as she closed her lips around him. The questing touch of her fingers on his balls and the way her eager moan vibrated all the way through him.

The combined impact was exquisite. An experience so far beyond any other encounter he'd had that comparison seemed laughable. There was no sense of avarice in the act. No calculated glances to indicate she was angling for something in return. It was pure devotion. A gift of sensation that only pulled him deeper. Dragged him farther into the spell she'd cast the first day he'd laid eyes on her with all the mercy of a storm's undertow.

Release pushed closer. Tightened the muscles at his core and drew his nuts up tight. And given the eager pace she'd set with her mouth and firm, saliva-slickened fist she worked at the base of him, she had no intention of stopping. No goal save sending him over the edge just as fervently as he'd sent her flying.

He knifed upward, her startled gasp mingling with his growl as he lifted and flipped her to her belly, pulled her hips up and back and buried himself to the hilt.

Home.

Mine.

All. Fucking. Mine.

The words were a mantra. The only tether that kept him in check as he pumped his cock inside her. A guide and a promise as he focused on her moans. The flush that spread across her shoulders and back and the way her hips lifted and met his for each stroke.

He fisted his hand in her hair, pulled her up in what should have made her cry out in pain, but earned him a sexy groan instead. He splayed his hand on her belly and held her steady for his thrusts. Pounded deep so she'd never forget. "You think I would let you steal my come? Think I would let you drink it down when I could mark you with it instead? Claim you as my own?"

"Oh my God…" The whimper in her voice was just as tremulous as the flutters rippling through her pussy. She clutched his hand at her belly and squeezed. Her head dropped back against his shoulder and her back bowed for more. "Please. I'm right there."

"Of course you are. Because your body was made for me. Your pleasure a perfect match for mine."

Her legs shook and the muscles in her sex tightened.

"Give in, Evette. Come on my cock and accept my claim."

The breath she took was barely audible. Jagged and far too short to fill her lungs.

But the clasp of her cunt around his shaft was ferocious. A physical manifestation of the wildest scream that ripped his own release free. Milked him with a desperate demand he had no hope of ignoring.

His cock jerked inside her. Filled her sex as her pussy pulsed around him. Left him exposed and raw, yet strangely fulfilled and empowered. She was his weakness. The delicate chink in his otherwise insurmountable wall.

But she was also his redemption. His absolution, greater purpose and color in another otherwise drab and monochrome world.

Her body trembled against his, tiny aftershocks ricocheting through the muscles that still clutched him and sent her hips rolling against his. Minute, sensuous movements that perfectly matched each contented whimper and sigh.

He guided her to her belly. Brushed her neck and shoulders with reverent kisses and painted her back, sides and hips with soothing caresses. "You can't ignore that, Evette. This isn't something that will go away. Won't dim." He pressed his hips against her lush ass, the softening of his cock allowing his seed to trickle down her labia. "You belong to me."

Her head jerked up. "Oh, no!" She tried to wriggle out from underneath him, but his weight was too great. Her strength no match for his.

And, he'd been ready.

He manacled her wrists with his hands and pressed a single kiss to the top of her spine. "Shhh."

She shook her head and still tried to push up. "Don't you *shhh* me. We didn't use protection."

"No. We did not."

She stilled in her struggles, but craned her head enough to try to make eye contact. "And you don't think that's a problem?"

"I have never gone without protection with another woman before. You have not been with anyone since Emerson was conceived. And you are mine regardless."

Her eyes got even bigger. Flooded with fear. "And we could have *babies*!"

His cock stirred. And while he was wise enough to pull himself free of her before she could register the primitive response her reminder had created, he didn't stifle his growl in time. He nuzzled her neck and forced himself to focus on her scent. To recognize and honor her fear. All she'd been through without anyone there to help her. "We *will* have babies, *solnyshka*. Emerson will be a wonderful big brother."

"You're not helping!"

He chuckled at that. By no means his most intelligent response, but honest all the same. "You want to plan. I understand this. We will take those steps immediately to give you comfort, but we will not be using condoms again. I will not have anything between me and my bride."

"I'm not your bride yet."

This time when she tried to roll to face him, he allowed it, but guided her back underneath him as soon as her shoulders hit the mattress. "You are. My bride and my light."

Something in his tone stilled her long enough to study him. To connect with him and consider what he was saying.

He took full advantage, daring to release one of her wrists to cup the side of her face. "We will find other means. Wait until you are ready for children."

She opened her mouth, clearly ready to argue further.

He cut her off. "No matter what happens, you will not be alone again. Ever. Whether it happens tonight, or two years from now, our children will have us both."

"You're going too fast," she whispered. "Everything is going too fast. It's too big. Too much. Too powerful."

"The good things often are. Perhaps the answer isn't to slow down or try to stop the fall, but to go with it." He stroked the line of her jaw. Her collarbone and the apple of her shoulder. "Perhaps the answer isn't to fight it or wait, but to surrender to it the same way you surrender your body."

"That's different."

"How? Have I not been there? Looked after you? Provided for you? Offered you my vow and my name?"

Her eyes widened for a moment, then narrowed on a frown.

He captured the confusion while he could, rolled off her long enough to spoon her and pulled the covers over them both. "Or perhaps you could stop thinking altogether. Just allow me to spoil you and let you grow accustomed to the idea a little longer, hmm?"

"You're a bossy and manipulative man." Her words were sassy, but there was a distractedness to them that said she was still stewing on the idea. Ungrounded and scrambling for steady emotional ground.

"Yes. I am." He plumped a pillow under her head, slid his arm underneath it and pulled her closer. Her fit against him was perfect, the silky brush of her exotic skin a heavenly gift. "I'm also a man who not only bought you ice cream but intuited against Cherry Garcia. Don't forget to factor that aspect into your analysis."

She grunted. A cute little sound that all too easily allowed him to picture the little mew on her lips as she'd uttered it. "You should probably be handing me some of that ice cream when you say that. Especially after the risk we just took."

He smiled against the shell of her ear and kissed it. "You will forgive me. Eventually."

This time he got a *harrumph* and a wiggle of her pert butt that only served to remind his cock of better things to do besides getting ice cream. "Ice cream first. Sweet talk later. Then maybe I'll forgive you."

Oh, yes. They were inevitable. Inevitable and un-

Authentic. 1960s. Make it happen or I'll find someone who can.

Footsteps sounded on the stairs down the hallway from his office. More than one set, both with a heavier tread and clipped purpose—which meant his *avtoritets* were either on their way to give him news they were eager to share, or shit had hit the fan.

He clicked Send on the message, pushed his keyboard away and sat back in his chair. For the comfort of his household, he hoped it was good news. After a pleasant weekend of minimal work and free time spent with Evette and Emerson, he'd grown a liking for the warm and comfortable peace of domestication. The first person who made him step too far from his newfound comfort zone was likely to feel his bite rather than his bark.

Kir strode through the doorway first, the black shirt and charcoal suit a stark contrast to his blond hair and playboy looks. Roman had skipped formal attire altogether and wore jeans and a simple gray T-shirt that made it clear he had muscle to back up any threat, which meant he'd likely been out in the field and developing his troops. Neither had the blanked expressions typical when they were coming to deliver bad news, though, so that was a plus. If anything, Kir looked downright pleased with himself.

Rather than angling for one of the two chairs positioned in front of Sergei's desk, Kir headed for the leather sofa opposite Sergei's end of the room, snatched the remote control off the coffee table and aimed it at the huge flat-screen mounted on the wall. "I have a gift for you, brother."

Roman turned one of the two leather chairs sideways so he could keep Sergei in view on his left and the television on his right and dropped down into the seat. "He is insufferable when he gloats. But I must confess, this one will be enjoyable enough I can tolerate hearing him tout his success."

The tail end of the opening graphics for the local noon news came on and the news anchors began their usual chipper welcome spiel. The dark-headed male on screen looked like he'd been riding the station desk for at least ten years, and his suit was one he'd probably bought at the beginning of his career. The blonde woman next to him, though, was fresh and stunning with a shrewd gaze that said she was as smart as she was beautiful.

Kir ambled back to the remaining chair in front of Sergei's desk and turned it so it mirrored Roman. He thumbed the volume lower, unbuttoned his suit jacket and settled in.

Sergei listened for all of fifteen seconds, then turned his attention on Kir. "Your gift is the news?"

Kir shook his head, but kept his gaze trained on the screen and his hand poised with the remote, ready to raise the volume when necessary. "*Nyet*. Just an extra follow-up to the actions we took against Alfonsi."

"Kir's conquests appear to have served a handy purpose," Roman said, nodding to the screen. "He met the blonde last Thursday. Turns out our brother can be subtle when he wants to be if it means adding public embarrassment to the other steps we took with Alfonsi."

Right on cue, the camera panned to the blonde and a string of videos played beside her showing the variety of complications Alfonsi's enterprises had encountered over the last four days.

"*Native businessman Steven Alfonsi has had a hard streak the last several days. Troubles started bright and early Thursday morning when a popular family restaurant that had been in the Alfonsi family for generations suffered a kitchen fire. The fire was quickly put out and the building saved, but the damage was significant enough to force the restaurant's closure until repairs and renovations could be made. Later that day, health inspectors at other restaurants Alfonsi is known to have a majority interest in reported numerous violations and hefty fines.*

"*But the restaurant industry isn't the only place Alfonsi is suffering. Many of the other ventures that make him one of New Orleans's most notable businessmen took a hit as well with gaming workers walking out of his casinos in protest of unsatisfactory work conditions and his most sizable company—Alfonsi Construction—having all of their jobs put on hold pending research of unsafe building practices alleged by local building code authorities. As if those developments weren't enough for Alfonsi to juggle, a class action suit was filed at the New Orleans Civil District Courthouse today by lawyers representing new homebuyers who purchased homes built and sold by Alfonsi's real estate division. At least fifteen plaintiffs have alleged that Alfonsi had an undisclosed interest in the inspection companies used on the homes prior to closing, but that they used that interest to cover up defective workmanship that is now costing the homeowners thousands of dollars.*

"*Alfonsi has long been suspected of Mafia ties*

and illegal activities in the state of Louisiana, but no charges have ever stuck. Speculators state that Alfonsi's latest string of bad luck is likely a result of his alleged Mafia activities and that he's crossed the line with the wrong people."

Kir paused the TV with a click from the remote, leaving a straight-on view of Alfonsi's scowling face as he exited the back of his Cadillac and a slew of reporters rushed to interview him. "He's hurting..." Kir turned to Sergei, the grin on his face totally unrepentant. "And now everyone knows it."

It was a solid move. Legal hurdles and authorities digging into your business was one thing, but the press were like gnats—they came in droves and got into everything. Plus, Alfonsi's ego was so caught up in his public image, a hit to it wouldn't sit well at all.

Two quick raps on the door sounded a second before it opened just enough for Evette to poke her head through. She scanned the room, noted it was only Kir and Roman with him and pushed the door wider. "Can I interrupt you guys a minute?"

Given the consternation in her expression, Sergei's good humor vanished in an instant. He stood, as did Kir and Roman, and waved her into the room. "Of course. We were just watching the noon news. Is there a problem?"

She motioned Kir and Roman back into their seats and sashayed forward until she stood between them, squared perfectly with Sergei. "Well, that depends. Did you know there was going to be a horde of construction workers showing up today to do a renovation?"

"I did."

"Where exactly?"

Chapter Seventeen

Sergei spread the design mockups for his new restaurants across his desk and compared them with the photos of Henri's existing restaurant below it. The coloring was right. Lots of crushed red velvet, black furniture and gold accents. But the feel of it was all wrong. More current contemporary than the Rat Pack era steeped in every detail of Henri's place.

Yes, the food was exceptional, but the other reason people went there was for the experience. The surroundings. The knowledgeable, competent staff and how things moved at an entirely different pace. Patrons immersed themselves in it. Dressed for the environment. Spying cell phones for anything other than necessity was a rarity. It was as if they were eager to go back in time—even if only for an hour or two.

If his expansions with Henri didn't provide the experience, they wouldn't succeed. And considering the lengths his men had gone to the last five days in sending a message to Alfonsi and wiping out all trace of Henri's children's past, he wasn't about to fail over something as controllable as décor.

He pulled up the email from the designer, reattached the actual photos from *André*'s and added a terse reply:

stoppable together. He slipped from between the sheets, leaned into the bed and kissed her cheek. "Whatever my bride wants."

"The two bedrooms at the end of the hall in the other wing."

Her mouth screwed up into that cute little sideways mew that said she was torn between laughing and ripping into him. "The cleaning crew just cleaned there this morning."

"So?"

"So, we pay them hourly. If we're sending a construction crew in to renovate them, that's wasted money. Not to mention, there's nothing wrong with those rooms."

His good humor rebounded in a heartbeat and he smiled even bigger than he had after watching the story on Alfonsi.

Apparently, Evette didn't care for his response because she planted her hands on her hips and turned her stern-mother glare to full bright. "Are you laughing at me?"

"No, *solnyshka*. I'm merely appreciating the fact that you've finally used the correct pronoun when referencing our home. And while I appreciate your focus on saving us money, I hardly think that the hour the cleaning crew spent cleaning those rooms will break us."

Her frown slipped and she fidgeted as though the realization she'd come to think of the home and finances as *theirs* wasn't altogether a comfortable one. She pushed her shoulders back and lifted her chin anyway. "Well, it's still a waste of money, and if you want me to run this house, then *you're* going to have to tell me when you've got big plans so I have a chance to sidestep that waste."

Bozhe, but she was adorable. Feisty and sweet and

fearless. "As you wish, *liubimaja*. In the future, I'll ensure all plans that might impact your scheduling or our household finances are shared with you in advance. Although, I'll have to ask you to keep everyone—including you—from that wing for the rest of the week."

"Why?"

"It's a surprise."

Her eyes narrowed and she gave him a sidelong look. "Take this in the spirit it's intended, but I'm not sure I can take many more surprises."

"Ah, but this one isn't for you. Though, I'm happy to think up more if that news disappoints you."

She volleyed her attention between Kir and Roman. "Did aliens land this morning and do a brain swap with him or something? He's never this playful and agreeable."

Always the charmer, Kir was the one to answer. "I believe his good mood is mostly your doing. But by all means, keep up with it. He's far more enjoyable to be around with you here."

Roman nodded and chuckled. "This is true."

"Hmm." Evette tried to keep up her irritated pretense, but as she lifted her gaze back to Sergei, a soft smile that spoke of fond memories and intimate secrets tilted her lips. "Well, far be it from me to ruin a good thing." She circled her hands on either side of her head. "You men carry on."

She turned and headed for the door, but stopped halfway there and cocked her head at the television screen. "What's Alfonsi doing in the news this time?"

"You know him?" Roman said.

With a beleaguered harrumph that sounded a lot like the one Dorothy used, Evette shook her head and looked back at the men. "Not for a very long time. He went to the same high school my dad and Uncle Carl did. When I was little they all used to come around for crawfish boils and such, but Dad and Mom said he was a loose cannon so they stopped inviting him. Only time I've seen him since was on the news." She twisted back to the screen. "I take it he's in hot water again?"

"A class action lawsuit." Sergei motioned for Kir to push Play on the remote. "Something to do with using inside contacts with inspectors to cover up shoddy workmanship."

"Ha! Sounds like him." She shook her head and finished her trek to the door, giving them all a backward wave. "I'll let you guys get back to your news. It seems I've got a construction crew to get started."

Kir punched Play on the remote and thumbed the sound down. "You wanted to know if Carl and Alfonsi had a connection. Now you know what it is."

"Or at least a history," Roman added.

"It could be a coincidence, but I doubt it." Sergei sat in his chair and crossed one leg over the other. "Knox is digging into Alfonsi's accounts. If there's a definitive connection with money, he'll find it. Until then, we keep looking, stay alert and keep the pressure on Alfonsi."

The mockups for his restaurants lay lined up on his desk. A reminder not just of the business deal that had been interrupted, but of Sergei's long-term goal to eradicate all competition. Louisiana and the states around it would be his and that meant decisive, ruthless intent in everything he did. "And up the detail on

Evette and Emerson. Alfonsi will either knuckle under or go looking for a target to strike back." He looked to Kir, then Roman. "No one touches who's mine."

Chapter Eighteen

Guests tonight.
7PM.
Dress nice, but comfortable.

Evette checked the text messages she'd received from Sergei for what felt like the fiftieth time, growled and scanned her walk-in closet. Her clothes took up only one half of it, which said a lot about the difference between not just where she used to live and where she lived now, but how drastically her world had shifted.

How out of place she was in Sergei's world.

"Dress nice, but comfortable," she muttered to the neatly lined-up hangers. "Does that mean semiformal? Business casual?" She forced herself to go slower this time around, carefully considering her options and replaying the rest of the unhelpful text messages she'd received on her way home from picking up Emerson at school.

Evette: Do I need to get with Olga and have food? Hors d'oeuvres? And how many people? What kind of event are you hosting?

His answer had been slow in coming, the little bubbles showing, then disappearing at least five times before his cryptic answer came.

I have handled everything. You need only arrive at seven.

Not helpful. Not even a little bit. Maybe if they'd spent more of the week and a half since Halloween night doing more talking instead of Sergei showing how inventive he could be in the bedroom, she'd have understood what was going on better. Was he expecting her to help host whatever he had going on? Was there protocol involved? Were these normal business negotiations, or *business* negotiations? And what the hell was she going to do if he did introduce her to… well…more dangerous people? Did she want that? Would Sergei do that?

She growled out loud, shook her head and refocused on her meager options. Her hand landed on the one little black dress in her closet. A classy three-quarter-length-sleeve affair with a wraparound design that hit at the knees and clung to her body. It was a total knockoff brand she'd found at a department store, but most men wouldn't know that, and somehow she couldn't envision any female mobsters showing up at Sergei's house anytime soon.

No, not mobsters. Bratva—the literal translation for which Sergei had informed her meant *brothers*.

God, what's happened to my life?

She pulled the dress from her closet and marched into her bedroom just as Emerson came striding in.

"Hey, Mom! Jeb and the guys wanna come over tonight and throw around the football in the backyard. That okay?"

The screen on her phone glowed a peaceful 6:15 p.m. in soft white letters. Forty-five minutes for a quick freshening up. She could totally pull that off. "Sure." She tossed the dress on the bed, stuffed her phone into one of her robe's deep pockets and hurried toward the bathroom.

"Yes!" Emerson fist pumped, spun and headed for the door.

Boys.
Playing football in the backyard.
Maybe with mobsters in the house.

"Wait!" Her panicked screech as she came to a dead halt was enough it hurt even her own ears. She faced her son. "Maybe not. I mean..." *Shit.* Conversation was definitely going to have to trump gloriously hot sex with her Russian employer/boyfriend for a while. "Sergei has something going on tonight. I don't think having a bunch of boys over will be such a great idea."

"You don't *think*? Or you know for sure?"

"I don't know what he's doing. Only that I'm supposed to be there at seven."

"Well, can you ask him?"

Pulled from her worries about tonight, the amount of time Emerson was spending with the older boys rushed in to fill the void. If she was smart, she'd use tonight to get her son some time away from his royal highness, Jeb.

Or you could ask Sergei how he feels about company and see if his answer gives you any clues about his plans.

Right.

A win/win opportunity.
She dug her phone out of her pocket.

Emerson's posse wants to bond over tossing around a football in your backyard. How would that go over with your guests?

Emerson crowded closer and surreptitiously tried to peek at her screen.

Evette tilted it away from him and gave him a warning look. "Hard limit, kid."

"You looked at mine."

After she'd confronted him, told him he was never to hide it from her again and that she would always have the password to it. "You got that right. And when you're paying the bill for your own phone, you can block anyone you want from looking."

His eyes narrowed. While he didn't say what he wanted to say, *You're not paying for this one* was written all over his face.

She planted her hands on her hips and frowned right back at him. "Don't push your luck, kid. Sergei might have given you that phone, but I can take it away from you twice as fast and don't think for a minute he'd stop me."

His face blanked in a heartbeat and his posture got military straight even faster. "I didn't say anything."

"No, but you thought it."

He might have argued further, but the ding on her phone cut them both off.

This is Emerson's home. So long as you are okay with it, he can play all the football he likes.

"Yes!" Emerson said, running out of the room. "I'll tell the guys."

Her shoulders sunk. A lose/lose—no info and more quality time with Jeb.

Goodie.

She dove back into her quick-fix-me-up routine. On the bright side, maybe this meant that Sergei's house wasn't going to be filled with a bunch of muscly, gun-toting Mafia guys tonight.

Thirty-five minutes later, she was all gussied up and downstairs, packing some essential lip gloss and breath mints into a small handbag. "Emerson, I know Sergei said the boys could play, but try to be polite, okay? He's got people coming over."

Emerson twisted from the TV long enough to give her a once-over. His eyes hopped high on his forehead. "Wow, Mom. You look nice."

"You act like you've never seen me dressed up before."

"Well, yeah. For church and stuff, but that dress is really pretty." He smiled in a way that said he'd learned a whole lot more from Jeb and other boys at school than she'd ever imagined. "You and Sergei gonna go on a date?"

"Sergei has guests coming over. I'm just there to help." Her voice wavered. "I think."

Emerson's smile got bigger. "You think too much."

Smarty-pants. "That does it. No more talking to Sergei for you."

This time he flat-out laughed, the rich sound of it blanketing her heart so completely she halfway decided maybe Jeb and the way her and Emerson's life had been turned on its head wasn't such a bad thing for her son. He went back to his TV watching, the deep cushions that lined the back of the couch making only the top of his blond head visible. But there was still a lot of happiness in his voice when he spoke. "You won't block me from Sergei. That'd mean you couldn't see him either. Or kiss him."

So, he'd caught those little stolen moments, had he? And here she'd thought she and Sergei were being creative. She zipped her purse shut and kept her voice as matter-of-fact as possible. "Where's your head on that?"

"On what?"

For some reason, saying it out loud felt big. Like admitting a deep dark secret for the very first time. "Me and Sergei."

The fight scene from the *Iron Man* rerun on the screen filled the silence and goose bumps that didn't have a thing to do with temperature fanned out along her forearms.

The TV went silent and Emerson twisted on the couch. He'd always been a somewhat serious kid. Cautious and pensive. But he'd also been a straight shooter nearly from the time he'd come out of the womb. No dillydallying about when it came to sharing his thoughts.

And tonight was no exception.

His hazel eyes locked hard with hers, a depth behind them that no seven-year-old should have beaming back at her. "You're safe with him. And happy."

"You saying that because we've got guards all the time and have a nice place to stay?"

He shook his head, a minute and gentle motion that

echoed the sincerity of his words. "You'd be safe and happy with him even if he didn't have all that to give."

God, but her kid was smart.

Smart and wise beyond his years.

Maybe Sergei was right. Maybe it was time she trusted her kid's intellect and instincts and focused on letting him find his way the same way her momma had let her find her own.

"Yeah." She anchored the slim strap of her handbag over her shoulder. "I think you're right on that, kiddo." She winked and headed toward the door. "Try to stay out of trouble, would ya?"

From the direction of his voice when he spoke, it was obvious he'd flopped back on the big couch and had gone back to his TV. "It's just football, Mom."

Mmm-hmm. And boys were just boys.

But Emerson was right. She had bigger things to worry about right now. Like what was in store for tonight.

Outside the air was brisk, the early November night making her quicken her pace to the main house and sending sharp clicks from the heels of her peekaboo pumps into the otherwise quiet space. The guard posted on the back porch by the kitchen door nodded respectfully as she approached, though he looked almost as uncomfortable in a suit as she felt walking into God only knew what. "Guess I'm not the only one dressing up tonight, huh?"

He gave her a wry smile. "No, ma'am. Everyone's on full detail tonight."

"Wow." For a split second, she considered seeing what other tidbits she might get out of her unsuspecting informant, but scratched the idea almost as quickly.

Sergei not telling her things was one issue. Making other people aware of that lapse was something else. "Well, it won't last forever, right?"

"No, ma'am."

She opened the back door.

Inside, the kitchen was fully lit and spotless, but empty. A mix of voices sounded from the living room, though. First, Sergei's low accented voice, then another masculine one—sharper and warm but unfamiliar.

She laid her purse on the kitchen table and kept going. Whoever it was sounded friendly, the words unintelligible from her distance. Two steps from the wide arched opening that would bring the guest into sight, a delicate ripple of feminine laughter rolled over her.

Sweet.

Cultured.

Nowhere near as brash as her own.

Evette stepped into view and flinched, drawing to an immediate standstill.

A man stood to one side of the room—tall and dressed in a dark suit as fine as Sergei's. But it was the statuesque woman hugging Sergei who gripped her attention. Winter-white hair fell in elegant waves past her shoulders and her toned arms held him in a solid hug, her eyes closed and the embrace with which she held him that of a woman who'd missed him.

Evette's gut clenched, all kinds of emotions she didn't understand and didn't particularly want to figure out with an audience looking on clamoring behind her sternum. The woman was cover-model gorgeous. Even without speaking a word, it was obvious she'd be the polar opposite of Evette.

And Sergei clearly held her in high regard. Hugged her back with an affinity that spoke of much history.

Had he slept with her?

Had a relationship with her?

Evette wanted to disappear. Slink back into the kitchen and tiptoe across the courtyard where she could hide in her room. She was a maid, for God's sake. No matter how Sergei prettied it up, that's what she was. And this woman was...well...perfect.

As if her turmoil had sent an uncomfortable wave through the room, Sergei looked up and locked stares with Evette. While he didn't release the woman in his arms and flash a guilty expression at Evette like she'd been afraid he might, she didn't care much for the reaction he did respond with. Namely, that he smiled, hugged the woman tighter and murmured something in her ear, all the while grinning at Evette.

The woman gasped and pushed out of his arms. "This is Evette?"

Definitely perfection. Maybe even more so with a very slight, yet worldly Russian accent making her melodic voice that much more enviable.

She glided toward Evette, her long legs eating up the space between them but still giving plenty of time for Evette to process the simple yet chic designer dress clinging to her hourglass figure. The cobalt blue was perfect for her. Striking but not garish. And her heels were no doubt Prada or some other outlandishly expensive brand.

She wore all of it like a second skin. As if she'd been born in it. Rather than stop in front of Evette and offer her hand the way Evette had expected, the woman wrapped her up and held her tight. "You have no idea how happy I am to meet you." She pulled away enough to beam her angelic smile on Evette, but kept her hands firmly gripped on Evette's shoulders. "Sergei has told me so much about you."

He had?

Because she didn't have a clue who this was. Or how she was supposed to react.

Dimly, she noted both Sergei and the other man moving toward them, but it was the male she didn't know who spoke, his voice easygoing and full of laughter. He stopped right beside the startlingly beautiful blonde. "Sweetheart, you might want to introduce yourself first, 'cause I'm not thinking she knows either of us."

Surprise washed across the woman's face all of a second before she dropped her hands from Evette's shoulders and whipped her attention to Sergei. "She didn't know we were coming?"

Sergei stopped beside Evette and placed a hand on her shoulder. "She knew we were having guests. I wanted to keep who it was a surprise." With a tenderness she'd come to crave, he smiled down at Evette. "Evette, this is Darya Torren and her husband, Knox." He slid behind Evette and rested his hands on her hips in a possessive touch.

One look.

One touch.

And she'd not only forgotten all the terrible conclusions she'd almost drawn, but all the nervousness she'd carried into the room with her. So deep in the respite his touch created, she almost missed the rest of his introductions.

"Darya. Knox. This is Evette Labadie." Sergei kissed the top of her head. "My bride."

Okay, now that part she heard clearly enough, and the shock it generated must have been written all over her face, because Knox chuckled.

Darya laughed outright, but covered her mouth with her hand to try to stifle the sound as an afterthought. Which was silly really considering the merriment still in her eyes.

Evette *hmmphed* and held out her hand to Darya. "I'm not his bride. And it's nice to meet you."

Darya's laughter died in an instant. While she accepted Evette's outstretched hand, her gaze cut to Sergei. "I thought you said she was the one?"

"She is." Sergei squeezed Evette's hips, a mix of fondness and emphasis combined in the gesture. "She has not formally accepted yet, but she will."

Knox's grin grew bigger. While his attire was just as formal as Sergei's, he looked more like a rock star who preferred faded Levi's and had only begrudgingly agreed to wear the high-end duds. He stepped in close to Darya and lowered his voice. "Baby, you might wanna help your brother out before his woman hightails it for the hills, or shanks him outta sheer frustration."

"Your brother?" Evette twisted to Sergei. "You never mentioned you had a sister. Or *any* family besides your dad."

"He is not technically my brother," Darya said before Sergei could answer. "But we once navigated the same world, and Sergei looked after me as though we shared blood. And before you take him to task too much—I've never once heard him claim a woman as his own. You must be very special to be the woman to do so."

Great. This woman wasn't just perfect.

She was *nice*.

And clearly had exceptional taste in fashion.

"Well, he does have a way of making a girl feel special," Evette said. "Overwhelmed at times, but special nonetheless." She turned enough to give Sergei a look that she hoped would let him know they had serious discussions ahead of them, then faced Darya once more. "So, are there food plans included in the night's festivities? Or am I going to have to grill you on where you got that dress and those shoes on an empty stomach?"

"Dinner at August," Sergei said.

Shit.

She'd never been to August before, but Dorothy had shown her a review not long after it had opened—alongside a pricey menu that ranked it as one of New Orleans's most prestigious establishments. In all of two seconds, the room felt like someone had blasted the heat, and her palms went clammy. No way was she dressed for a place like that. "I can't just leave Emerson. He's having friends over."

With guards all over the estate, the copout was a long shot, but it was the only one she had short of saying she had to wash her hair.

Sure enough, Sergei was armed with more of his well-laid, albeit uncommunicated, plans. "The men are here, and Olga was delighted to have a chance to watch over them. She plans to surprise them with snacks in another half hour and a tour of the new game room upstairs."

"You don't have a game room."

"It's *we*. And we do now. It's what the construction crew has been working on all week. The room across from it is the one I plan to give Emerson when he's ready to move."

"It's pretty sweet," Knox added with no shortage of enthusiasm. "Sergei told me what he wanted to do, and I lined out all the options he could go with. Also gave him a stellar list of starter games to load up on." He paused long enough to trade sly looks with Darya before refocusing on Evette. "He got 'em all."

"Not all," Darya quickly corrected. "Sergei pulled all the ones that had a lot of gore and locked them away when he was giving us the tour."

Great.

Her kid was going to a private school, had his own smartphone at seven, and now had the mother of all game rooms with a fully stocked library to boot. "You got them all?" she said to Sergei. "How in the world am I going to keep that boy's head on his shoulders?"

"We will teach him. I told you—he will want for nothing. Neither will you."

"Well, he better want for something, or I'm going to let you deal with him when he turns into a spoiled little turd."

His lips twitched. "Are you asking me to marry you and accept Emerson as my son?"

"What?"

"I accept."

"No!"

Darya giggled. "Oh, we definitely need to talk tonight. And maybe more tomorrow. We could go to Cafe

Du Monde for beignets. The last time I came to visit, I ate two orders by myself."

As a means to sidetrack her from finishing her rant with Sergei, Darya's diversion was spot-on. "You did?" Evette's attention dropped squarely to Darya's perfectly flat stomach. "How? Where'd it go?"

She must have touched on an inside joke, because all three of them erupted in laughter.

"Darya is fond of desserts," Sergei said, the lingering mirth in his voice moving through her like molten heat. "When given a choice, she'll eat it before any entrée."

"When given a choice," Knox said, "she'll eat it before *and* after."

Perfect, nice *and* sporting an outrageous metabolism. Life wasn't at all fair. "Do they pump something special into the water in Russia, then? Because I love dessert, too, but can only take so much before my booty decides to claim its own zip code."

Darya smiled huge and her gaze cut to Sergei. "Oh, I love her. The rest of the girls will, too."

Evette cocked an eyebrow at Sergei. "You've got more sisters?"

"Five more," Sergei said, "plus two mothers and eight brothers."

"Nine," Knox said.

Sergei's head snapped to Knox. "Who?"

"Rex Niland. You remember him—Lizzy's right hand."

Sergei nodded as if the revelation made absolute sense—which, of course, it didn't in Evette's book. She was still stuck on how two mothers could factor into any equation.

Before she could ask about any of it, or maybe demand a flow chart, Sergei turned his attention back to her. "There's also a niece and a nephew, both close to Emerson's age, but we can talk about that more at dinner." He pulled her next to his side and waved Darya and Knox ahead of them. "After you."

Knox shook his head and guided Darya forward, but offered a quick aside to Evette as they passed. "Don't worry, kid. It gets easier. Best advice is just to roll with it."

Before Evie could come up with a creative excuse to address her wardrobe, they were headed out of the house and promptly corralled in a limousine waiting at the front of the house. The trip to the Central Business District was pleasant and laden with easy conversation that at least gave her time to catch her breath and brace for dinner. Or at least she thought she was braced. The minute the car pulled to a slow stop in front of the nineteenth-century building with its elegant spotlights highlighting the French-Creole architecture, her stomach took a nosedive.

Sergei must have intuited her nerves when he helped her out of the car because he let Knox and Darya gain some distance between them before he tucked her hand inside his arm, leaned down and murmured, "Everything all right?"

"Oh, I don't know," she said equally as quiet. "I might have one or two nerves that are giving me fits about going into a restaurant in a dress that costs less than the cheapest entrée." She smiled at the doorman as they passed, then added, "We really have to talk about you giving a girl a decent heads-up. I don't have fifty suits I can just pull from a closet."

He cocked his head to one side. "I do not have fifty suits."

Men.

Seriously.

They just didn't get it.

Darya did, though, and apparently had exceptional hearing because she moved in close to Evette the second Sergei stepped away to speak with the maître d'. "He might not have fifty suits, but he can afford them. Which means he can also pony up for you to have a shopping trip or three."

"Oh, no," Evette said. "He's crafty enough as it is. I'm not letting him use my love for clothes to burrow in deeper."

"Oh, that's right!" Darya's smile got bigger, openly delighted. "Sergei told me you're planning on a career in fashion. We'll have so much fun."

"So much fun doing what?" Sergei said.

"Spending your money." Knox winked at Evette and guided Darya behind the maître d'. "You ask me, if she's made it over a month dealing with you, then she's earned her own credit card."

If they'd been anywhere else, she might have argued. But the gleaming hardwood floors, rich mahogany walls and soaring columns replaced all of her thoughts with sheer wonder. They passed through a room with antique mirrors and spectacular crystal chandeliers and entered a two-story room where countless wine bottles lined the floor just above them. The whole thing was so fantastical, she found herself seated at an isolated table for four and sampling a red wine that smelled divine before she even remembered how nervous she'd been.

"He's right," Sergei declared as soon as the sommelier departed.

Knox chuckled and Darya nodded.

Evette didn't have a clue what they were talking about. She lowered her voice and cast glances at all three of them. "Who's right?"

"Knox," Sergei said.

"About?"

"You should have clothes. Darya will take you shopping."

"She'll do no such thing. I don't need clothes."

"You do." He shifted his attention to Darya across the table. "She is not accustomed to extravagance, but you will teach her."

"I can spend money just fine," Evette said. "It's spending unnecessary money I won't do."

"Oh, it's necessary," Darya said. "Very necessary."

"How so?"

Darya pursed her mouth, considered Sergei for all of heartbeat before her smile crept into place and she winked at Evette. "Therapy."

Evette opened her mouth to argue.

Knox cut her off. "It won't do you any good. Russian women are ruthless when it comes to fashion and spa trips. And God help you if she calls in for backup from Sylvia and Ninette."

"Who's that?" Evette asked Sergei.

"My adopted mothers."

Right. So here she was, arguing about unnecessary shopping sprees in a five-star restaurant while her kid was home and overdosing in a gamer's paradise. Clearly, she wasn't getting out of Wonderland anytime soon.

Might as well get some intel while I can.

"Fine," she said. "If we can't talk reasonably about spending limits, maybe you can explain how you've got two mothers, a horde of sisters and even more brothers."

She'd expected something bizarre. Or at least a tale as head spinning as the rest of the night had proven to be. Instead, the story spanned the length of the meal and completely warmed her heart. Apparently, Darya and Knox were part of a family built by choice—six original brothers (who now tallied nine) who'd all come from meager or difficult upbringings, but had banded together as a common unit and built each other up. Six of the men had wives—one of them Evette had just heard on the radio a few days ago. The two mothers were actually the real mothers for two of the men, but they'd happily assumed the motherly role for the whole group.

Darya set her dessert spoon on the side of her now empty crème brûlée bowl, reclined against her seat back and rested a hand on her stomach. "That was divine."

"Seriously, girl," Evette said. "I don't know where you put it." She'd had the same sumptuous lamb entrée Darya had, but had barely managed three bites of the rich spumoni Sergei had insisted she get for dessert. "After that meal, I'll have to fast for two days to fit into my jeans."

"Nonsense!" Darya tossed her napkin to the table. "We'll just work it off tomorrow while we're spending Sergei's money." She pushed back from the table and stood. "I could use a stroll to the ladies' room, though. Care to join me?"

Any kind of walk sounded lovely if it meant finding more space for her meal to settle in her stomach. Even if it was only to the restroom and meant she'd have to make the trek next to an icon of beauty. "Sure."

Like she had been throughout the night, Darya made their time alone comfortable, her gracious and genuine nature making Evette forget about the differences between them and settle into the conversation easy. So much so that, when they were both done washing their hands and had shifted to freshening up their lipsticks, Evette dared to try her hand at gleaning deeper insight into Sergei. "You said you and Sergei used to move in the same circles?"

"Mmm-hmm. In Saint Petersburg. I was Yefim's assistant at one time." She paused in painting her lower lip and locked gazes with Evette in the mirror. "You know who Yefim is?"

"The man who introduced him to his boss." Evette frowned at her own reflection. "Anthony? Alex?"

"Anton." Darya gave her a knowing smile before she went back to putting the finishing touches on her perfect red color. "He really must trust you if he's told you how he came into the life he leads. To my knowledge he's never told anyone save those who work closest with him."

"It wasn't a pretty story. Seven years old is too young for anyone to make a decision like he made."

Darya tucked her lipstick inside her clutch, faced Evette and leaned one hip against the vanity. "Perhaps. But it's not an uncommon one. And Sergei made a very good life for himself."

"What about you? How did you end up adopted by an amazing family in Texas if you were in Russia?"

Her expression softened and sadness crept into her exotic bright blue eyes. "I caught the attention of a very powerful man. An *avtoritet* who worked for a rival *pakhan*. You know what these words mean?"

She'd picked up many words in the first month she'd worked for Sergei and even more in the last few weeks, but a refresher course never hurt. "*Avtoritet* is like a captain, right? Like Kir and Roman?"

"Yes. And the *pakhan* is the *vor*, or boss."

"Like Sergei is today."

"Exactly." Darya's expression sobered a bit. "Most Russian men have a different way of interacting with women. They are direct. Gentlemen in all ways—at least in all the ways you'd want them to be—but driven to claim or possess the woman they've chosen. They will court you. Anticipate your needs and treat you with exceptional honor and care. Most importantly, they do not take no for an answer."

"You mean it's not just Sergei?"

The honest yet very blunt question drew a huge smile from Darya. "Oh, I suspect Sergei is more formidable than most. But yes, this is their way of courting. To show you that they will provide for you. Protect you."

"And this fella you caught the eye of?"

Darya's eyes turned frigid. "Ruslan is a discredit to the men of Russia. He was the scourge of the earth. A man who felt he answered to no one and the vilest of souls. Everyone knew it. Just as everyone knew that I would never escape his attention and that I would suffer greatly if I fell under his control."

"So, what? You ran away?"

"It wasn't as easy as that. Running alone wouldn't

work. Ruslan was too powerful. Too connected. He would have found me eventually. So, Sergei staged my death. Made it look like Yefim and I had both been attacked, but I was killed. My body, of course, was unidentifiable." She pulled in a slow breath. "And then I ran. Assumed a new name. A new vocation."

"And then you met Knox."

"Yes," she said on a contented sigh, her whole face lighting up. "And then I met Knox." She paused a moment, fond memories and gratitude obviously moving through her thoughts if her expression was any indication. She shook her head as though to clear whatever she'd been remembering and straightened. "So, tell me. How can I help you?"

"Help me?"

"You know." She motioned toward the dining room beyond. "With Sergei. I have worked with men like him. Lived among them. They are formidable creatures. Unrelenting when they've found what they want." Her grin turned ornery. "And Sergei's definitely found what he wants in you."

It sounded so good. Like *Cinderella* and *Pretty Woman* all rolled up into one. Only her Prince Charming carried a gun and had one hell of a dangerous reputation.

But no matter how good it sounded, she was still having a hard time believing the whole thing wasn't a pipe dream she'd be woken from in the most abrupt way possible. "How do you know? I mean, he's only known me a little over a month. Most men take ages to make a commitment. But Sergei started putting things in motion almost overnight. Doesn't that seem weird to you?"

"For Sergei?" Darya shook her head. "No. Not at all. He's a man driven mostly by his instincts. And I can tell you that I've never seen those instincts fail." She paused and cocked her head. "I know we've barely known each other more than a few hours, but may I make a suggestion?"

Evette chuckled, a little of the insanity borne from the wild ride she'd been on since the day she'd been fired mingling with the tone of it. "Are you kidding? At this point, I'd love any kind of input."

Darya's soft smile was similar to the ones she'd earned for years from Dorothy and her mother—one of patience and understanding. "Maybe what you need to be asking yourself isn't why Sergei is moving so quickly, but what's holding you back."

The softly spoken statement struck deep, so similarly striking the same chord Dorothy had hit on, she'd be a fool to ignore it.

"How do you feel about him, Evette? Do you enjoy being with him? Feel happy? Safe?"

The questions stunned her. Rattled everything inside her. "I don't know. I've been so busy trying to figure out why he's doing what he's doing and trying to keep up, I haven't thought about it."

"Haven't thought about it, or haven't let yourself?"

Outside the restroom's quiet haven, muted voices, laughter and classical music served as a reminder that the world was still in motion. That people were still going on about their evening and enjoying the moment with their family, their friends or their lovers.

Unfazed and unaware of the frozen moment that held her.

The complete stillness inside her and the uncomfortable silence that went with it.

"I don't know."

But didn't she?

With her father's death, she'd ignored her feelings through wild teenage antics that had driven her mother crazy. With her mother's death, she'd ignored them with booze and parties.

Maybe focusing on the whys behind Sergei's actions was just another way to avoid her emotions. A cleverly disguised mechanism to keep herself safe.

As if she'd heard Evette's thoughts spoken aloud, Darya nodded, turned Evette toward the exit with a hand at her shoulder and opened the door with the other. "Well, my friend. I think maybe that's a good place to start."

Chapter Nineteen

Pretty lights against a clear night's dark backdrop, a belly full of exceptional food and hours full of adult conversation and laughter. Evette couldn't remember the last time she'd had such an experience. Maybe snippets here and there at parties with family or friends, but never a real double date like she'd had tonight.

Her hands lay folded in her lap, one of Sergei's big hands covering them both. In the darkness of the limousine's interior, the tattoos on the backs of his knuckles and those that disappeared beneath his shirtsleeve were more like shadows than ink. Once upon a time, they'd ignited her curiosity and served as a warning.

Dangerous man ahead. Proceed with caution.

Yeah, she'd ignored that warning, hadn't she? Had stormed right past it, sat down at his table and opened a big old can of worms.

Would she change it?

If she could do that day all over again, would she take a different route? Avoid Sergei completely?

No.

Not one second.

The answer was so firm—so bold and confident—she almost flinched beneath its vigor. Which begged the question—why? What was it that had driven her that day? That kept her moving forward now? If she was really so nervous about who he was and the activities he was involved in, what was it that prevented her from finding a different job, packing her things and moving her and Emerson elsewhere? Yes, the money and the security that came with it were luxuries, but she'd gone without lavish things most of her life. Emerson was where he needed to be school-wise now, too, so there was literally nothing stopping her.

Except Sergei.

Leaving means leaving him.

Despite the solidness of his body next to hers and the warmth from his hand, she shivered.

His fingers tightened around hers and he shifted his attention from the houses sliding by outside to her. "You are cold?"

"No." Rattled and confused, yes, but that wasn't something she was ready to talk about, so she shifted to a safer topic. "I don't understand why Darya and Knox didn't just stay at your house. It would have been a lot more comfortable than a hotel."

"Perhaps they wanted to give us space." His gaze roamed her face, his dark blue eyes more like black in the dark confines of the car. "You've been quiet since dessert. Is something troubling you?"

That.

That right there.

In the few hours since Darya had asked her what she liked about Sergei, she'd quietly categorized many things about him that appealed to her. His confidence. His intelligence. His loyalty to those he considered family. And his skills behind closed doors were categorically off the charts.

But it was the protector in him that called to her the most. He was always aware. Always watching not just what was going on in her physical world, but the emotional realm as well. Watching and readying himself to step in and provide her whatever strength, protection or comfort was needed. It made her feel safe. Not just important, but cherished.

Her father had been that way for her mother. Maybe he hadn't been able to deliver at the same financial level as Sergei, but he'd always been there. Rubbing her feet after a long day at the diner. Jumping in to help her when she'd overextended with volunteer work at church. Taking Evette out on Saturday mornings and afternoons to give her mom some much-needed alone time.

"Evette?" Sergei prompted when she didn't answer.

Could she talk to him? Should she?

She cleared her throat and focused on his hand atop hers. "When we went to the restroom, Darya asked me what I liked about you. How you made me feel."

"An interesting topic for such a venue." The humor in his expression ebbed, then he seemed to consider whether or not he wanted to continue. "What did you say?"

"I told her I didn't know." She forced her head up, her voice raspy against the smooth purr of the engine. "But I don't think that's really true. I think it's been easier for me to ignore the good things and focus on all the reasons why I shouldn't be with you."

He stared at her, silent, his features void of all clues as to his thoughts.

"There are a lot of reasons why I shouldn't be with you," she said on a near whisper. "Or at least reasons why other people would say I shouldn't be with you. But when I think about it—about doing things over or leaving here—I can never find the gumption to actually pull the trigger."

The hard lines in his expression softened. "And why is that, do you think?"

Truth.
Give him the truth.
Give yourself the truth.

"Every time I'm with you—every time I see you—it's like my whole body recalibrates. Like it shifts to a heightened, more efficient frequency. I've never been so aware of a person as I am with you. Even from the first time I saw you in the diner."

He nodded. One simple, slow dip of his head that seemed to be an acknowledgment and an encouragement to continue.

"I'm not afraid of you," she said. "Listening to people at the diner, or even hearing some of the things you've told me, common sense says I should be, but I'm not. I feel safe with you."

"Because I would annihilate anyone who dared to hurt you or Emerson." He lifted one of her hands and kissed the back of it, the casualness of the move belying the ferocity of his statement. "What else, *solnyshka*?"

Behind her sternum, it felt as though tiny fissures wiggled out in all directions, warmth and brightness seeping out from behind the minute cracks. Once she spoke the truth, she wouldn't be able to hide it anymore. Not from Sergei or herself. "I trust you."

Such a simple statement. One she hadn't really evaluated, let alone planned on sharing out loud. But it was the deepest, most sincere compliment she could give a person. The one trait she rarely believed in with others. "Aside from Mom and Dorothy, I don't think I've ever been able to say that about anyone else. People tell you they'll do something, then bail at the last minute. Tell you something you want to hear so you'll give them something they want. They'll look you straight in the eye and feed you a load of bull without a bit of remorse.

"But you don't. When you say something, you mean it. Honestly. Openly. Even when it's ugly. You told me about your past and how you came to live your life and you did it without any justification or sugarcoating. You just laid it out there for me and let me make my own decisions." Her throat tightened, the rest of the words clogging in the narrowed confines. "There are a lot of things I like about you. Enough that I'm afraid to look at them all. That I'll get used to them—or worse, take them for granted—and then lose them."

The car slowed and turned into the driveway, the movement making her torso sway into his.

He steadied her with a hand at her shoulder, but waited until the car came to a stop before he answered. When he finally did, his voice was as low and solemn as distant thunder. "I cannot promise you that you will never lose me. My life is dangerous. Anger or rivalry may earn me a bullet or a well-staged accident at any time. As word spreads, you and Emerson will become bigger targets as well.

"But I will not waste days that I could be with you allowing *what might be* to keep you from me. It would be better for me to have you in my life for only a limited time than to not have you in my life at all. *That* is why I give you the truth. Because I will not have the time you are with me sullied by dishonesty. You will know all of me. Even the parts I detest myself."

"Wow." Not the most intelligent or thoughtful response she could have given after such an admission, but it was honest. It was also an opening to steer them into much less serious conversation and, considering how much she had to noodle on, something a little lighter was extremely welcome. "You do realize you're probably breaking about fifty different mob boss rules spouting wise and beautiful stuff like that."

The car door opened on Sergei's side, but he ignored it and smiled down at her. A gentle smile that said he knew why she'd veered them off course and wasn't about to fault her for it. "Does it get me farther into your good graces?"

"A sexy-as-sin man who can get my engine running *and* seduce my mind? Um, yeah."

His thumb skimmed along the back of her hand. "Then breaking them is worth it." He tugged her toward him as he slid toward the door. "Come. We need to see how Olga held up against Emerson and his friends."

Shoot.

She'd been having so much fun and then had spent the whole ride home swimming in the deep end of her own thoughts, she'd forgotten all about Emerson's friends. She stepped out of the limo, leveraging Sergei's solid hold to keep her balance. For the most part, the neighborhood was quiet, only the dim hum of road noise from the main thoroughfares three to five blocks away in any direction. Two guards stood stationed at either corner of the raised porch.

"Don't your neighbors wonder why you've got men outside your house twenty-four/seven?" she asked.

Sergei opened the front door, stepped to the side and waited for her to go through. "Do you think they'll actually be curious enough to come and ask?"

"Ha!" She grabbed his hand and pulled him slightly behind her. "Good point!"

Inside, all was quiet. Not at all the raucous din she'd expected from four boys holed up in a state-of-the-art game room. Then again, it was nearing eleven, which had to be curfew time for even boys Jeb's age.

They climbed the stairs, her heels a much more abrupt sound against the wood surface than the soft pat of his loafers. The subtle scent of popcorn hit her in the hallway and dimmed lights from the game room spilled out onto the thick rug along their path. The closer they drew to the room, the louder the sound of Jimmy Kimmel's voice on the television grew.

Inside, Olga sat sleeping in a big brown leather recliner and Emerson lay stretched out on his side on the matching leather sofa, a navy blue and maroon plaid blanket stretched over his body. The guard stationed at the poker table just opposite the doorway looked up as they entered, closed his computer and stood.

The sound startled Olga from her sleep and her sudden movement made the recliner shift forward so quickly it was a wonder she wasn't catapulted from the seat. While she coughed and sputtered for a moment, she managed to get the footrest down with a little more control and got to her feet. "You are home. Did you have a good night?"

"It was lovely," Evette said, then realized maybe the woman had intended the question for Sergei. She looked to him and raised her eyebrows.

Sergei grinned down at her before he shifted his attention to Olga. "It was a very good night. Thank you for taking care of the boys."

"It was my pleasure." The smile on her face indicated she really meant it, but her usually crisp uniform looked like it had been through the wringer and the gray hair she normally kept in a tidy bun was more what she'd expect to see on a woman who'd survived a tornado.

On the couch, Emerson didn't budge.

Evette lowered her voice anyway. "Did the boys behave?"

"Oh, yes," Olga said with a bob of her head. "At least until Emerson fell asleep. Then the little hellions took it upon themselves to explore the house while I went down for snacks. I found one of them in your office and the other two in your bedroom, so I asked the men to take them home."

Sergei shared a look with his guard. Neither of them appeared outwardly tense or concerned, but there was a whole lot of manly nonverbal communication moving between the two of them.

Whatever the topic of their silent conversation was, the guard ended it with a casual "The house is clear."

Sergei nodded and faced Olga. "Very good. Go. Get some rest." He turned to the guard. "You, too."

Both of them hustled toward the door, but Olga cast Evette a sly smile as she passed, a knowing gleam in her eyes that said she was reading all kinds of sordid details into what might happen after she left Evette alone with Sergei.

Sergei must have caught it, too, because he chuckled as the two disappeared into the hallway. He splayed one hand at the small of Evette's back and pulled her in for a tender and too-brief kiss to the top of her head. "Go to our room. I'll take care of Emerson."

He stepped away and turned for the sofa, but Evette caught his wrist and held him back. "Sergei, we can't."

"Can't what?"

She widened her eyes in that *you know* expression that spanned most language barriers and motioned with her head toward Emerson on the couch. "I'm not leaving him in the carriage house alone. What if he needs me?"

"What makes you think he'd be in the carriage house?"

"Because that's where we live?"

A self-satisfied smile curled his lips, a telltale smugness that she'd come to realize meant that he wasn't just a few steps ahead of her, but leagues. "And his new room has been renovated and completely prepared for him. He already knows something is going on between us. Why not let him use the room tonight to let him get accustomed to the idea."

"Seriously?"

He cocked an eyebrow. "You said you trusted me, yes?"

She had. Not even ten minutes ago. So, she nodded.

"Then trust me in this, too." He used her grip on his wrist to pull her closer and cupped the side of her face. "It will work out. As much as you're afraid of the two of us, Emerson has no such fears." He pressed his lips to hers, inhaled deep, then murmured against her mouth, "Though, if it makes you feel more grounded, I have no problem with you helping me get him to bed."

Trust.

Such a simple concept and yet so difficult to exercise. But her son smiled a lot these days. Even laughed and was playing with other kids—even if those kids did make her suspicious and nervous. And most of those behavioral changes had come as a result of Sergei being in their life. Of the people he surrounded himself with.

She smoothed her palm up and down Sergei's sternum and whispered, "Okay."

The smile he gave her as he pulled away was soft, but full of praise and appreciation. "Why don't you go ahead of me and pull the bedding down?"

Right.

Teamwork.

Good plan.

She hustled across the hall, not quite sure what to expect, but found out quick enough Sergei had hit the décor out of the park. It was like her son's room was a cross between a space-age haven and a spread from an L.L. Bean catalog, complete with navy blue walls, steel gray curtains and a soft gray flannel comforter she'd have a hard time getting Emerson out from under on a cold morning.

God, was she really considering this?

She wiped her suddenly clammy hands on her hips and stepped back from the bed. Logic insisted that the floor was firm beneath her, but it sure felt like there was a huge stretch of unknown in front of her. Like she was just one step away from plunging into some unseen abyss.

Footsteps sounded in the hallway and Sergei stepped into view a second later, her son still sound asleep in his arms and nestled close against his chest.

He'd be your partner, too.

The thought moved through her mind as soft as a spring breeze. One of those subtle realizations that snuck in quietly but swept away the shadows with it. She couldn't move. Couldn't look away. Could only marvel at the ease with which he tucked her son in bed, pulled the covers up over him and leaned in to murmur something in his ear.

A dangerous man. One who'd all but admitted to killing.

And yet he treated Emerson with care and tenderness.

Sergei turned and caught her staring. "I can't decide if that look means you're ready to run from me, or you've uncovered some groundbreaking discovery."

Oh, it was groundbreaking all right. Just not in the way he probably meant it. And with so many truths creeping into the light, the whole situation felt unbalanced. Tilted to the point she could tumble over at any time. "Tell me what you like about me. Why you want this."

His expression sobered, the gravity of her question clearly striking deep. He studied her a moment, glanced at Emerson curled beneath the blankets, then rounded the end of the bed where she watched and waited. "Come." He turned her toward the door with a hand at her back. "I will tell you what you want to know."

Only a single lamp glowed in his room, the soft buttery light spilling from the small sitting area adding a sultry richness to the lavish furnishings. Unlike the guest room, this space practically hummed with his energy. As if merely by occupying it, he'd left traces of himself behind. Boldly marking it with his power and determination the same way he'd left his mark on her.

Behind her, the door clicked shut.

"Take off your dress, Evette."

She spun, her gasp mingling with the unexpected thrill his command stirred in her belly. "I thought you were going to answer my question."

"I am. But I'm going to show you, too." His gaze swept the length of her. "Now take it off. Shoes, too."

Oh, boy.

Sergei in sweet mode was tempting, but Sergei in demanding mode always fired her up. She squared her shoulders to him and planted her hands on her hips. "Are you bossing me?"

"Yes." A knowing smirk crept onto his face. "Are you going to listen?"

"Heck, no. If I gave you an inch, you'd take a mile."

The smile deepened and he prowled forward. "Exactly." He pulled her to him none too gently, one of his hands splayed just above her ass and the other firmly cupping the back of her head so she couldn't look away. "You said you're not afraid of me, *solnyshka*, but the truth is, you have tremendous courage. It's intoxicating. It tells me I will never have to worry about you standing your ground with me."

"Me?" She laughed and smoothed her hands over his shoulders toward his neck. "Are you sure we're talking about the same girl? Because I promise you, I'm plenty afraid of just about everything."

"I said, courageous. Everyone has fear, but not everyone is brave enough to walk through it." He cocked his head and grinned. "That's another thing I love about you."

Love.

Not like, but love.

Most men shied away from that particular four-letter word at all costs, but Sergei wielded it unapologetically.

"What's that?" she said, more than a little curious what admission would go with it.

He hugged her tight with one arm low on her back and slid the other to her waist. "Your laugh."

It was the only warning she got. A second later he tickled the tender stretch along her side and her sharp laughter bounced off the walls as she wiggled and tried to escape his hold.

By the time he stopped, she was breathless and completely languid in his arms, her whole body humming from the playful moment. She sighed and rested her cheek against his chest. "That was evil."

"Perhaps." He cradled her head in his hand and kissed the top of it. "But I never had that sound in my home before you. You can't blame me for wanting more of it."

She pushed against his chest until he relented in his hold enough to let her lift her head and meet his stare. "Baby, you gotta stop. You keep saying things like that I'll end up weepy."

The look on his face said he wasn't buying it. "You said you wanted to know why I wanted you as my wife."

"Yeah, but you're turning my heart into mush."

A wolfish gleam danced behind his eyes. "You mean you don't want me to tell you how I love your boldness? How you've proven repeatedly that you'll do anything to provide for and protect the people you love?"

Tears welled in her eyes. She tried to choke the surge of emotion back, but the strength behind the tears was too much and they spilled down her cheeks. "Sergei—"

"All right," he said softly as he wiped one tear away. "No more talking." He repeated the gesture on her other cheek. "But there is one more I want to show you. One I don't want you to forget."

Before she could answer, he tugged the tie on her wraparound dress free. He peeled the clingy fabric to one side and skimmed his hands along her waist, searching for the inside fastener.

It didn't matter whether his touch was functional or seductive in nature. Her body never failed to still beneath it. To cease processing all other stimuli save the point of his contact with her and fully appreciate the sensation. Tender. Rough. Protective. Claiming. The drive behind it didn't matter. Only that he was connected to her and there was no other feeling that required her attention.

He slipped the button free and gravity did the rest of the work, pulling the other half of her dress so it hung at her side. His fingertips traced the curve of her hips and up along her ribs. A delicate touch provided by roughened hands.

She sighed and closed her eyes. While she tried for a teasing tone, her words came out husky and breathless. "I take it this demonstration is something carnal in nature?"

"Very." One of his hands slipped behind her and pinched the clasp on her bra. "Though, now that I've seen what you had on under your dress, I'm incentivized to prove my point quickly."

So, he liked that did he? "I'll make a note of that for my shopping trip with Darya tomorrow." *My man likes silk and lace demis and racy thongs. Good to know.*

She opened her eyes in time to watch him toss the one fancy bra she owned to the floor and frowned. "You know, for a guy who likes fancy bras and panties, you sure chucked that one fast."

"I like taking them off you even more than I like seeing you in them." He crouched in front of her and nuzzled the black silk covering her mound. "And remember I'm paying for the trip tomorrow, so I'd appreciate if you bought enough that I have ample opportunities to do both in the near future."

His hands coasted down the outside of her legs then tapped one ankle. "Out of these shoes, my bride. I want you steady on your feet for what I have planned."

She obeyed his prompt and lifted one foot for him to slip her pump free. "Hmm." She lifted the other foot for him, and he repeated the action. "Every time you have plans that concern me, I end up flustered, overwhelmed and in a general panic after the fact."

With the dim lighting and his face in line with her hips, she couldn't make out the expression on his face, but his voice was thick with humor as he slipped her panties down her legs. "I can safely say that these plans are guaranteed to leave you smiling and sated." He stood and gave her that devilish grin that always did her in. "If you're not, I did it wrong."

He stepped back and motioned her toward the side of the bed. "Stand there."

Interesting. He'd always been on the commanding side when they were intimate, but there was seldom distance involved. In fact, from the time one of them initiated contact, they were always connected somehow until reality forced them to be otherwise.

Still, the mystery was fun, and he'd already delivered a magically exceptional night, so she shrugged and padded to where he'd pointed facing the mattress. "Like this?"

"No. Face me."

She did as he asked, and he crooked his fingers to move forward. "A few steps forward." He nodded when she reached the spot he wanted and loosened his tie. "Perfect."

So tied up in seeing him carry Emerson to bed and tucking him in, she'd missed the fact that he must have shucked his suit jacket in the game room. Rather than set his tie aside, he kept it in one hand and worked the buttons at his wrists and down the front of his shirt. All the while, his gaze drank her in. Studied her openly and unabashedly.

Her skin sparked beneath the attention. Began to hum with that sweet electric buzz that typically was reserved for his touch. "What are you up to?"

"Making sure you add a particular quality to your list. One that's been on mine since the first day I touched you." He circled behind her and lifted the tie so it dangled to one side of her face. "And I'm making sure you have no distractions so that you absorb every second."

Before she could so much as gasp, he draped the silk tie across her eyes and cinched it behind her head. The fabric was cool and soft against her skin, and the lack of visual input immediately heightened every other input. The crackling energy of his presence behind her. His earthy, masculine scent. The soft whoosh of his leather belt sliding free and the rustle of clothing.

Quiet settled and her senses stretched for more inputs. Air whispered through the vents, warding off the chill of the cooler night, but there was nothing else. No clue as to what he was doing or where he now stood.

"I'm here."

His voice was a velvet stroke issued from directly behind her. An instant anchor in the middle of a gray void. "What are you doing?"

"Looking at you. Giving you time to forget everything except the two of us and this moment."

She smiled despite her nerves. "Sugar, I forgot everything but us the second you touched me."

"So, you feel that, too?" His voice shifted, paired with his soft footfalls on the thick carpet as he rounded to the front of her. "That's good. What I'm going to ask of you will make more sense, then." A muted creak sounded. "Your touch grounds me. Reminds me that I have something good and precious for the first time in my life." The warmth of his body only inches from hers feathered along her skin just before he lifted her left hand. Cold metal with a solid weight to it glided over her ring finger.

His ring.

She'd seen it only the one time standing in his office, but recalling the beauty of the huge cushion cut with the smaller diamonds haloed around it was as easy as breathing. "Sergei."

"I want you to wear it, Evette. Starting tonight." He lowered her hand, but trailed his fingers from her wrist up her forearm and over her shoulder until he cupped the side of her neck. "I want you to feel its weight on your hand while I'm touching you." His other hand firmly clasped her hip and pulled her against his hot, hard and 100 percent naked body. "Want that weight to remind you of our connection when I can't physically be there to ground you." His lips ghosted across her parted lips and he traced a path with his fingers down the valley between her breasts. "To remember you are my sun." Lower to her belly and teasing circles around her belly button. "My light, and my angel."

The muscles low in her abdomen fluttered and she sucked in a ragged gasp, the faint dusting of hair over his pecs tickling her palms as she braced herself for balance. The hypnotic depth of his voice and compelling touch pulled her under. Opened wide that secret place inside her she'd never known existed until he'd come into her life. Connected with her on the most primal level where sensation and instinct ruled every action and reality had no bearing.

"That's what I love most about you, *solnyshka*. Your response to me. The bond between us." Rather than dip his fingers lower as she wanted, he explored her. Her hips. Her thighs. The length of her spine. The curve of her shoulders and the backs of her arms. Caressed every inch of skin with a leisurely reverence that wiped out everything except him. His voice. His scent. His power and how it coiled thicker and tighter around her.

The soft brush of his beard whispered against her cheek and the low rumble of his words near her ear sent delicious tremors down her back. "I knew you were special when I met you. Knew you were good where I was evil." His lips brushed the tender curve where her neck and shoulders met. "But when you danced with me." A tender lick followed by a soft kiss. "When you wrapped your arms around me and first felt what flows between us right now—I knew." His arms tightened around her and his voice dropped to a dangerously low pitch that sent a wild spin through her stomach. "You're mine."

His teeth sunk into her neck and her cry filled the room, the unexpected aggression and animalistic claim ripping the last shred of caution from her.

She *was* his.

She'd always felt it.

Been aware of him at a level she still didn't understand and couldn't explain or describe even if her son's life depended on it.

But it was there. Thrumming with energy all the time. Greedy and hungry for more.

He cupped her ass and lifted her. Where his voice had been a low, gentle rasp before, now it was urgent and thick with demand. "Legs around me."

The instruction was completely unnecessary, her arms and legs wrapping around his neck and hips on pure, sensual reflex before he'd even finished his sentence. His cock pressed against her belly, hot, hard and blatant in its promise of what was to come.

In only seconds, the mattress was beneath her back, the soft swoosh as the plush surface gave way to their weight and the cool, crisp sheets a stark contrast to his muscled body and delicious weight blanketing her front.

"Sergei." She tried to pull him closer. Arched her neck and prayed for more of his lips against her skin. The wet glide of his tongue against hers or even more of his possessive bite. Anything to slake the thirst he'd created. The urgent demand pulsing at her core.

The silk tie covering her eyes slipped free instead.

In the room's dim lighting, his features came into focus slowly—a ferocious predator with the sexual appeal of a dark god. Rugged. Manly. Utterly determined to take and claim what he wanted for his own.

His palms found hers and their fingers laced together as naturally as the force that flowed between them. His eyes locked on hers and his hands tightened, the bite of the ring on her finger a potent reminder of where things were headed. Of everything that could be hers if she dared to let go.

"You said you trusted me. Said you knew I would not lie to you." Anchoring his knees between her knees, he used his thighs to splay her legs wider and stroked the length of his fierce shaft along her clit. "Reach for that trust now. Take what I offer, and I promise you that the only thing that will ever take me from you is death."

There it was. The unabashed truth in his words.

His world was dangerous. For him. For her. For her son.

It was a huge leap of faith. A chasm that had already swallowed her whole with the loss of each parent and spit her back into reality transformed in ways she'd never recover from.

But she was strong. And if she'd learned nothing

else from the time she'd had both of her parents alive and thriving, it was that love was a beautiful thing. A chance worth taking no matter the cost.

She undulated against the length of him. Held his stare and accepted the moment. The risk and all the challenges that went with it as the powerful connection between them surged higher. "Yes."

His eyes darkened and a throaty growl rumbled from deep in his chest. One shift of his hips and his shaft nudged her entrance. "My bride." The tip of him notched inside the mouth of her aching sex and his pelvis pressed forward. A gloriously slow movement that stretched and filled her perfectly. Burned the moment so deeply in her memory, not even the death she so feared could erase it. "All mine."

He set a rhythm. Easy at first, yet purposeful. The velvet hard length of him perfectly stroking inside her drenched and eager sex and building her need higher. Forging a promise. Honing the strength of it until she felt it in every fiber of her being. Knew to the very core of her that life would never be the same from this moment.

She was his.

Protected.

Cherished.

The space behind her sternum tightened and the burn that always came before her tears danced across the bridge of her nose.

But this time she didn't try to fight them. Only held his steady gaze and let them spill down each temple as she accepted the truth. Surrendered to it.

As if he'd read her thoughts, his harsh features softened, but his thrusts deepened. Intensified in pace and power until all she could do was hold on and let the fire consume her. Let it burn away the past and leave her clean and ready for the future.

He shifted the angle of his hips, the head of him brushing the sensitive stretch inside her.

So intense.

So perfect.

A fit beyond description. A sensation that defied logic and reason.

Release rushed toward her, the exquisite tightening of the muscles low in her belly and a sharp rush of blood through her veins stealing her breath.

She forced her eyes to stay open. To hold his gaze as the beauty of her orgasm swept over her.

And then she was gone.

Her eyelids slipping shut and her voice crying out as the waves swept through her. Sent her flying so far beyond the here and now that the only thing she could process was the weightless pleasure, the delectable tingle in her fingers and toes and every pulse of her sex around his shaft.

His throaty growl coiled around her. Mingled with the warmth of his sweat-misted skin and taut muscles against her. "That's it, *liubimaja*. Take it. Know who you belong to. Accept it." His words turned ragged and his thrusts stabbed deeper, his pelvis pounding against hers. "Mine. My bride."

He surged forward and planted himself to the hilt. His cock jerked inside her and a ragged sound ripped up the back of his throat.

She opened her eyes and whimpered at the image that greeted her. His head thrown back, his dark hair framing his rugged features and the muscles along his throat strained to the point they showed each corded detail.

But it was his expression that stilled everything inside her. His closed eyes, his slack jaw and parted lips, the tips of them slightly lifted. As if behind his eyelids, he looked on heaven only to find he'd been granted an eternity of happiness.

It was stunning. A raw vulnerability given by a man who showed weakness to no one and that gripped her with such ferocity she would have fallen to her knees had she been standing.

This man—this fearsome man—trusted her. Wanted her and believed in her enough to let down all his barriers. To show himself completely in the most intimate of moments.

His chest heaved on each labored breath and the muscles along his shoulders, arms and belly clenched to show their unbelievable definition.

She tried to pull her hands free from his, needing the feel of his body beneath her palms almost as much as she needed air.

But his grip was too strong. Too desperate.

She tried again and forced raspy words past her throat. "Sergei. Let me feel you."

While the message didn't seem to penetrate at first, her voice reached him enough that he opened his eyes and trained his wide gaze on her.

"Please." She wiggled her fingers as best she could, the weight of his ring on her finger still foreign, but a welcome reminder of what they'd shared. "I need to touch you."

With a grunt that would have sounded almost petulant under any other situation, he slowly released her hands and braced himself on his forearms.

She stroked him. Set free the need to pet and caress the beast she sensed still dancing near the surface and savored the hard press of his body against hers. The brush of his lips against her neck and shoulders. The thick weight of his hair between her fingers and the slow, languid rolls of his hips against hers as he brought them both back to reality.

His tongue swept across the skin at her neck. "You will not regret this, Evette." His hot breath whispered against her skin and his low vow sent tremors down her spine. "I promise you. You will not regret trusting me. Not ever."

It was a dangerous pledge. One where life could make liars and fools of them both.

But she didn't care.

Dorothy was right. She'd walked into the arena, waved her red cape and earned the attention and devotion of a predator.

"I believe you, Sergei." She wrapped her arms and legs around his neck and hips and hugged him with all she had in her. Forced every bit of emotion and hope he'd fueled in her since the time she'd sat down at his booth into her actions and words and committed herself completely. "I'm right there with you. And you're mine every bit as much as I am yours."

Chapter Twenty

Sergei loved his life. Had never once regretted getting into the car with Yefim or his decision to follow Anton all those years.

But right now—lying with Evette spooned against him, her sweet scent filling his lungs and the buttery glow of the early morning sun showcasing her skin—he wished for at least a moment or two of a simple life. One without danger. Without constant threats and the need for vigilance and guards.

Building a family in his world came with a price. One often paid by the innocent women and children in the way of lost privacy. Many times, he'd seen the strain tear relationships apart. Watched mothers take their children to isolated locations simply to escape the never-ending threats.

True, many of his peers honored the age-old custom of keeping wives and children out of the crossfire, but times were changing. Egos had grown too inflated and the practice of patience tossed aside in favor of an instant-gratification era.

Evette drew in a long, leisurely breath, then sighed it out and wiggled her pert ass against his cock. "I don't know what you're thinking about, but it's making a big enough ruckus I heard it all the way in Snoozeville."

That I'd never let you walk away. Would give up every interest and dime I own to keep you and our children with me before that happened.

"I'm thinking that I find waking up next to you even better than falling asleep in the same place," he said instead. He skimmed his lips over the curve of her exposed shoulder and kissed his way to the sensitive spot low on her neck that always made her sigh and gently raked his teeth across it. "I'm also thinking that I'm going to enjoy breakfast with you far more than I'm going to enjoy breakfast with Olga."

Evette snickered at that, her whole body shaking as she tried to contain her laughter. "Is that your subtle way of saying you've given Olga the day off and expect me to hustle downstairs and whip you up some food?"

"No, it's my way of telling you I'm looking forward to making breakfast with you and knowing the whole time you have nothing on beneath my robe but what you're wearing right now."

"I'm not wearing anything right now."

"I know."

She rolled backward enough to shoot him one of those sassy *don't-be-a-smarty-pants* smirks he'd come to love. "I can't go down there in only your robe."

"Why not? How would you spend Saturday morning in your kitchen?"

"In *my* robe. Where there aren't at least four or five men guaranteed to come walking in for coffee refills at any given time." She rolled back to her side and snuggled back into him like she couldn't quite get close enough. "Besides, it's better if I'm dressed before Emerson comes down anyway."

"No. This is your home now. If the men bother you, then we will use the carriage house for them to get their coffee in the morning from now on, but you will not be inconvenienced or forced to be uncomfortable where you live." He ran his thumb across the top of the diamond on her finger. "And we will not pretend with Emerson. Even if we tried, he would know better. You would know this if you stopped and thought on it for a moment."

Her gaze locked on to the ring and she grew so still it seemed even her breathing had stopped. "We're really doing this, aren't we?"

He splayed his hand low on her belly and marveled yet again at how perfectly she fit against him. "Yes, *liubimaja*. We can take time on the wedding if you like and plan whatever affair pleases you, but I will not sleep another night without you beside me."

She worried her lip and shifted the ring with her thumb. "That's a new one—*liubimaja*. What does that mean?"

He wondered when she'd catch on to the change. Since moving in, she'd been quick to query him whenever he introduced a new word or Russian custom, but she'd been slower to inquire on that one. Ironic, considering it was one he never thought he'd ever offer a woman. "It means, *my love*. Or more aptly, *my true love*."

She peeked over her shoulder, an uncustomary shyness in her eyes as she peered up at him. "Do you mean that?"

So sweet.

Pure sunshine with an indomitable spirit and a heart bigger than Russia.

He rolled her to her back and covered her with his body, waiting until she met his gaze before he answered. "There is no other that has ever touched my heart as you have, Evette. No other that I have trusted to share it with as I have you."

Tears filled her eyes, but her lips lifted in a shaky smile. "You know, for a guy with a bad reputation, you sure know how to use sweet words."

The tears spilled down her temples, and he took his time tenderly wiping the tracks they left behind free. "Yes, well you must not tell anyone. It would lessen my effectiveness greatly and hamper my ability to provide nice things for you and my son."

"Oh my God." The exclamation was little more than a whisper, but the power behind it generated more tears than he had a prayer of catching so he simply stroked her hair and gave her time to process. "You just…your son?"

"Unless Emerson has a problem with it. Or you."

"Babe." She wrapped him up and hugged him to her, her whole torso shaking as her emotions moved through her. It took her several moments, but when she finally spoke again there was laughter mingled in with her raspy voice. "Seriously. You're really, really good at being sweet. But I promise. I won't tell. Even if I don't need the nice things."

"You may not need them, but you will have them." He kissed her cheek and lifted his head enough to meet her eyes. "Now, if Emerson's the early riser you've implied he is, I suspect we'd be wise to get downstairs before he beats us there."

She sniffled and swiped her knuckles along her temples. "What time is it?"

"Almost seven."

Her eyes popped wide and she froze for all of a heartbeat, then pushed at his chest. "Holy crap, we've got thirty minutes at best."

Turns out, Evette could seriously hustle when she put her mind to doing something, because she had her teeth brushed, her hair de-ruffled, his robe on and both of them downstairs in under twenty. A half a pot of coffee was already waiting for them, the first half consumed by the men who'd come on shift at six, two of whom stood just beyond the far kitchen window, their backs to the house while they casually traded conversation.

Evette poured Sergei a cup of straight-up black coffee, handed it off, then set about making her own. "So?" She scooped three spoonfuls of sugar, then topped it off with a goodly amount of half-and-half. "What should we make for breakfast?"

"What's normally for breakfast when it's just you and Emerson?"

She blew across the surface and sent the steam skittering into nothingness. "Depends." She took a careful sip, paused to consider the flavoring, then leaned her hip against the countertop, still cradling her mug with both hands. His robe was ridiculously large on her, but the navy blue color looked exceptional against her skin. "I usually surf the net until he gets up and let him decide. Sometimes it's Pop-Tarts or Lucky Charms. Sometimes it's bacon and pancakes."

The saints help him. If Emerson proved to have a sweet tooth, too, Sergei would have to up his bouts sparring with Kir and Roman to fit in his suits. Sergei guided her toward the table. "We'll wait, and I'll hope for the latter."

"You know, you don't have to humor him. Just because I always gave him the choice before doesn't mean that's the way we have to do it going forward."

He pulled out her chair. "It's not about humoring him. It's about keeping some things normal in the middle of a transition."

She stood beside the seat rather than sit and gazed up at him with such tenderness the space behind his sternum ached. "You're still being sweet."

And she was still being adorable. Enough so his entire reputation as a cold and efficient killer would be shot to hell if either of the men outside turned and saw what had to be a love-struck expression on his face. He cocked an eyebrow and tipped his head toward her chair. "Give it time, *solnyshka*. I'm a man, so I'm bound to rile you sooner or later."

The next twenty minutes were a slice of unexpected domestic heaven. If anyone had told him upon moving to New Orleans that he'd ever spend time huddled around a kitchen table and perusing the internet, drinking coffee with a woman like Evette and waiting for a young boy to arrive and determine their breakfast menu, he'd have laughed out loud. But here he was—completely content in the moment and planning out what they'd like to do together after Evette's shopping trip with Darya like they'd been together years instead of days.

It was just after Evette had brushed his ankle with her ice-cold feet and he'd made her shift in her chair and tuck them in his lap that Emerson padded into the room on near-silent feet. So silent, in fact, that Evette likely wouldn't have even realized he was standing in the opening between the kitchen and living room watching the two of them if Sergei's attention hadn't drifted over her shoulder.

She twisted as soon as she noted Sergei's distraction, but could go only so far with Sergei's grip on her feet. "Hey, kiddo. You ready for breakfast?"

Emerson studied the two of them. Noted her robe and Sergei's casual jeans and T-shirt. Then her feet in Sergei's lap. He grinned like a kid who'd just been handed front-row, third-base seats to the final game in the World Series. "Looks like I'm not the only one who had a sleepover!"

And just like that—any potential awkwardness in the transition was over. Emerson proclaimed sleepover days deserved pancakes and bacon, and the three of them left a mark on the kitchen making their feast that Olga would no doubt complain about for days.

But it was a breakfast unlike any he'd ever had.

Innocent.

Warm.

Happy.

The bacon was gone and what was left of their second helping of pancakes swimming in a ridiculous amount of syrup on each plate when the muted *chunk* of the front door opening and closing drifted beneath Emerson's tales from the night before and footsteps sounded on the hardwoods from the foyer.

Reality.

Carried, no doubt, on the backs of his *avtoritets*.

But he couldn't hide from his responsibilities forever. And, given the sad, albeit understanding knowledge that crept into Evette's warm gaze, she knew it was time to surrender the moment as well.

She straightened a little taller in her seat, cinched the belt on his robe and slipped from her chair, taking her and Sergei's plates with her as she stood. "Grab your plate, Emerson, and help me clean up."

"How come Sergei doesn't have to clean up?"

Right on cue, Kir and Roman strolled into the room, their casual jeans and Henleys appropriate for the morning he'd shared with Emerson and Evette, but strangely out of character for his men.

Evette jerked her head toward the two of them, set the dirty plates on the countertop and opened up the dishwasher. "Because he's got business to do and I've got a shopping trip to get ready for. If I'm gonna make it in time, I'm gonna need more than one set of hands and you've got two new rooms upstairs to say thank you for. So, you're it."

Kir and Roman surveyed the room with a mix of wry humor and open shock, but it was Kir who voiced his surprise aloud. "What happened here?"

"We made breakfast!" Emerson hopped out of the tall chair he'd all but bounced on all morning, one hand holding his plate and the other loaded up with dirty silverware. "Sleepovers mean pancakes and bacon, so we loaded up."

Roman grunted at the news and kept the rest of his response to a knowing smirk.

Kir wasn't nearly so covert. He frowned and zeroed in on Sergei, his Russian accent intentionally thick. "Sleepovers. This must be a word I do not understand correctly."

Cocky bastard. Kir always had been one to push the

envelope, but if he didn't watch it, he'd have not only Sergei on his case, but Evette as well. Sergei stood, taking his nearly empty coffee mug with him. "Perhaps not, but I believe you're familiar with the word *ramifications*."

The message hit its mark and Kir wiped the grin off his face. Mostly. "Yes, this one I'm familiar with."

Sergei nodded, finished off his coffee on the way to the sink and set it on the countertop alongside the other dirty dishes. He pulled Evette to him and kissed the top of her head. "You will come and find me before you leave and when you return home."

"Okay," she murmured quietly.

"You will keep the men with you."

"Of course."

"And you will spend an inordinate amount of money."

Her head snapped up and her eyebrows were pinched so tightly they formed a sharp V. "Now, that one I can't promise."

"Promise you'll try."

Emerson sidled up to the other side of her at the sink, snickered and unloaded the two pans they'd used into the soapy water. "Good luck with that."

"You guys cut it out. There's nothing wrong with being frugal." She rolled up on her toes and landed a quick kiss to Sergei's lips. "Go do fierce businesslike things. I'll report back when we're done."

Unwrapping his arms from around her took significant discipline. Enough so, he suspected he would have failed had he not had two men and a seven-year-old watching his every move. More difficult still were the steps he had to string together to carry him out of the room and up the stairs to his office.

If Kir and Roman noted the strain moving through him, they didn't show it. Merely followed him as they would have any other morning, but stayed suspiciously quiet.

Or at least they did until they were behind closed doors.

"Emerson's friends are working for someone," Roman said without preamble before Sergei even reached his desk. "Last night the guards found them in the house without Emerson with them. A search turned up bugs."

Sergei nodded and took his seat. "I suspected there was more to tell than Olga shared. Reggie said the house was clear, so I trusted that you'd dealt with it."

"Four removed," Kir said. "Two from your office, one from the game room and one from your bedroom."

"Destroyed?"

Roman shook his head. "Relocated to the guest rooms no one but service crews enter. Destruction could have tipped them off to us having found them and we wanted your feedback first."

"Good." Sergei focused on Kir. "I suspect you've run checks on the boys by now. Any idea who's using them?"

"The parents have no ties to anyone that might be interested in us. Both have jobs, but they're barely over minimum wage. All three boys are at the school on scholarships. No history of trouble outside of skipped classes on occasion."

"So, money would be an easy motivator for them." Sergei shuttled his attention between the two men.

Both met his stare directly, but the tension in their bodies said there was still something riding them. Something they weren't looking forward to sharing. "I take it you've formed a theory on who's behind bringing the boys into play?"

Kir looked to Roman and gave him a minuscule nod.

"You remember we had someone mention Carl being seen with Alfonsi," Roman said.

Sergei dipped his chin.

"Evette said they all went to the same high school as well. It was her badge that was used to enter a law office and caused her termination. The boys approached Emerson only days after Carl learned she was working for you. He's reported as showing with large sums of cash after time away. Alfonsi is known for using blackmail to get what he wants." Roman paused only a beat, but it was enough to show he wasn't looking forward to sharing the rest. "What if Carl works for Alfonsi?"

It made sense. The steps they'd taken against Alfonsi and his businesses had happened well after the boys had started courting Emerson, so it wouldn't be a reactionary measure. While Knox's research hadn't been able to produce any financial ties between the two, funneling cash through Alfonsi's many businesses would be easy enough and Evette had definitely confirmed the history between them all. With the bugs still functioning in his home, confirming the relationship would be easy enough to prove out. "It's possible. Though, it may also be that Labadie is a free agent who sells to any potential buyer."

The tension in both men eased.

Satisfied he'd heard the worst of what they had to

share, Sergei reclined back in his chair and crossed one leg over the other. "And how is our meddling colleague, Alfonsi, today?"

The same satisfied smirk Kir had sported the day of the news broadcast crept back onto his face. "One of his captains reached out yesterday. He wants a meet."

Even better news. If he'd rattled Alfonsi enough to want a meet, it might mean the hothead was teachable—or controllable. Either was better than outright warfare. Especially with Evette's uncle's involvement in the mess and Evette and Emerson just now adjusting to becoming a part of his world.

Outside, the high grasses, plants and crepe myrtles that lined the crystal-clear pool wavered on a slight breeze. In the summertime, they boasted a riot of colors—whites, reds, oranges and purple—but right now they were simply a peaceful green. That was one of the things he loved most about his new home. The weather might get cool, but it was never sufficient to send the trees and plants into hibernation. Certainly nothing like the cold he experienced in Russian winters.

"How do you want us to proceed?" Roman asked, nudging him from his thoughts.

Once upon a time, he would have refused any request for a sit-down at this juncture. Would have driven his message home until his competition was obliterated or begging for surrender.

But he loved his new home.

He loved his new family.

And with that came the need to exercise caution and reason.

"I meet with Henri on Monday," he said. "If our obstacles to closing the deal have truly been removed, then I'll agree to the meet. Until then, we use the bugs to our advantage and ferret out if Carl is working directly with Alfonsi, or trolling for information to sell."

"And how do you plan to do that?" Roman said.

Sergei pulled his attention away from the peaceful scene outside, focused on his men and allowed himself a smile. "We give Evette's uncle what he wants—information."

Chapter Twenty-One

What an amazing weekend.

It was the first thought that had greeted Evette when Sergei's alarm had gone off this morning and had echoed over and over again since then as the two of them had started off their first workweek together. Never in a million years would she have thought the simple task of getting ready in the same bathroom or watching her man don one of his amazing suits would have been as enjoyable as it turned out to be, but she was still floating. Running her morning errands with a stupid grin on her face and soaking up the sunshine like the day had been custom made to reflect her happiness.

At ten o'clock the temperatures hadn't quite made it to the sixties, but she didn't care. The tourists who normally flooded the French Market on North Peters Street over the weekends were nonexistent on a Monday, which gave her plenty of space and time to meander through the different merchants.

The moment was perfect. Her heart was settled. Her mind calm for the first time in…well…maybe ever. So much so that she'd even acquiesced with a simple smile and a kiss to Sergei's cheek when he'd suggested one of his men drive her to the market rather than her taking public transit.

This was her life now. She'd accepted it. And fighting either the perks or the drawbacks was nothing but wasted time and energy. A point Darya had driven home on their whirlwind shopping trip Saturday.

She took her time navigating various booths. Even stopped and marveled at a selection of custom-made Mardi Gras masks before finally heading toward the vendor she'd made the special trip for—a sweet Cajun lady Dorothy had introduced her to several years ago who made all of her spices from scratch and packaged up all kinds of seasonings for everything from gumbo to shrimp boils.

As he'd intended it to, the ring Sergei had given her hung heavy on her finger. A reminder. Not just of their unforgettable night, but of the morning after with Emerson.

She rounded the last aisle of the market, spied the lady she'd come to visit and raised her hand to wave—but stopped dead in her tracks when a familiar face caught her attention. Or more to the point, four familiar faces—three of which had no business being out of school and a fourth who had no reason to be around the other three.

But there they were. Uncle Carl and Emerson's three older friends chatting it up just as happy as could be. The two younger boys were mostly giving their ice cream cones the majority of their attention, but the pack leader, Jeb, was totally focused on her uncle and talking with a slew of hand gestures.

"Miss Labadie." Tony's curt voice sounded a second before he stepped in front of her and blocked her uncle and the boys from view. "Perhaps we should head back to the front of the market for a while. Your vendor looks busy."

She sidestepped Tony for another look.

Reggie moved in beside Tony to form a nearly perfect wall, but Evette pushed through them in time to spy Carl handing Jeb a pile of money, ruffling the boy's already mussed hair and guffawing big enough she heard it all the way across the lot.

Evette's sudden movement must have caught Carl's attention, because he looked up, locked stares with her and went perfectly still. Gone was the jovial smile on her uncle's face. Replaced with consternation and, perhaps, even fear.

Reggie turned her with a steady hand at her shoulder. "Forgive us, Miss Labadie, but we need to take care of something. Please come with us."

She could have argued. Probably would have if her thoughts weren't spinning fast enough to make reality a hazy nuisance. Instead, she plodded where they led, her body on autopilot and the hum of patrons at the market overloud in her ears.

Money.

Uncle Carl.

Older boys and their sudden interest in Emerson.

Carl had wanted to meet Sergei and she'd said no. Had cut off all contact with him after Dorothy's street party. Then the boys had shown up on Emerson's radar only a few days later.

Why was Carl paying them?

It made no sense.

The boys wouldn't be able to get Carl an audience with Sergei. At best, Carl might be able to stage some accidental run-in with him, but nothing more. And her guards had gotten her away from Carl as soon as she'd seen him.

Why?

She shook herself free of her thoughts and looked to each of the men on either side of her. They'd been relaxed and somewhat jovial all morning, but now they were alert and seemed to have the single-minded focus of getting her back to the car. "You're keeping me away from Carl."

Reggie kept his gaze trained dead ahead, but Tony glanced at her for a second. He never said a word, but the truth was right there in his eyes. They *were* keeping her away from Carl, which meant Sergei had ordered them to do so. Another why she didn't have an answer for. But she intended to get answers. Lots of them. Just as soon as there was no one around to overhear.

Tony opened the car's back door for her, and she slid into her seat. All of five seconds later, the guards' own doors slammed shut in near unison.

As if nothing had happened, Reggie turned from the passenger seat and asked, "Is there somewhere else you'd like to go?"

"I'd like to know why you kept me away from my uncle." The measure of her voice was even enough she was pretty damned proud of herself. Not so much as a hint of the adrenaline lighting her blood on fire bled through the tone.

Reggie looked to Tony.

Tony met her eyes in the rearview mirror and shrugged. "We were given orders. No contact with Carl Labadie for you or Emerson unless Mr. Petrovyh is present."

"And when did you get those orders?"

"The night you returned from the block party," Reggie answered. "Kir was the one to initially share the instruction, but Sergei told each of us one-on-one the following morning." He paused and pinched his lips together as though uncertain if he should continue. "Your uncle upset you, Miss Labadie. Mr. Petrovyh made it clear we were not to give him the chance to do so again."

So, it was just her man being protective. And with the way she'd responded to seeing her uncle, her guards had no doubt interpreted the worst. But that still didn't answer why her uncle was paying young boys who should be in school.

"Is there someplace else you'd like to go?" Reggie asked again. This time there was a plea beneath the request, and as intimidating as her fiancé could be, she couldn't quite blame him. What didn't seem to be there was any immediate concern about her uncle or what he'd been doing in the market with three young boys. As fast as they'd blocked her from his view, it was entirely possible neither of them had even noted the kids.

She shook her head. "Just take me home."

Tony put the car in gear and navigated the streets, both of the men maintaining their silence. While neither of them pulled out a phone for a call or a text to clue Sergei in to the details of their encounter, she had no doubt they'd be doing so as soon as they got a chance. Definitely *not* a good idea until she had an opportunity to figure out what was going on. Sergei had a penchant for biting first and asking questions later.

In her back pocket, her phone buzzed. She slipped it free and checked the notifications.

Carl: Where are you? We need to talk.

Like hell, they did. Everything in her said the smart thing to do was to stay away from her uncle. At least until she'd had a minute to think things through.

She tucked the phone back in her pocket and stared out the side window, the buildings and people beyond streaming by unheeded. Her thumb tapped an unsteady rhythm on the armrest, the pace oddly matching the ragged beat of her heart. Carl had always been an odd one, coming into money—allegedly from those trips to the offshore oil rigs—and spending it almost as fast when he got home. He was also a mooch known for showing at her apartment at the worst times and taking forever to head home, but this was beyond weird, even for him.

Her phone buzzed again.

And again.

Typical Carl. Always demanding attention until you gave him what he wanted. Kind of like a two-year-old tugging on your shirt hem, only bigger and with more annoying habits.

The night of Dorothy's street party drifted through her thoughts. What he'd accused her of. How he'd wanted to meet Sergei because of his connections.

Connections.

That was it.

He'd said the same thing about her cleaning job. And he hadn't just been shocked at the fact that she'd been fired, but panicked, too.

It was *her* card that had accessed a lawyer's office. And Carl had been at her house that weekend. Not once, but twice. Had he been the one to use it?

For what? He shouldn't need anything from an attorney's office.

Although, attorneys were privy to lots of private information. What if it was information he'd been after?

Whatever the reason, the timing for him being the one to use her card made sense. And if information was what he was after…whatever the reason… Sergei's house would have even more.

Shit.

Shit, shit, shit.

The car came to a halt in her driveway.

The smart thing was probably to get out, go about her business and let her thoughts simmer for a while, but taking that approach felt wrong. She scooted to the middle of the back seat and leaned in closer to Tony and Reggie. "Sergei said he had a meeting this morning. Do you know when he's due back?"

Tony palmed his phone faster than a teenager who'd been grounded from all electronics for a week. "I can call him and find out."

"No." She scooted backward and shook her head. "No, if he's in a meeting I don't want to bother him. I can talk to him when he gets back." More like the *second* he got back. If information shared in his house had been exposed, he deserved to know it ASAP. But if she called in the middle of business, she could cause him problems that way, too.

She patted her fingertips on her thighs and exhaled slowly, no longer giving a damn that both of her guards were watching her with open concern.

Okay. So, she had to wait a bit to talk it through with Sergei and see what he thought. She was smart. She could deal.

God, but she wished her mom was here. Her mom couldn't stand Uncle Carl, but she'd known him a very long time. Had even been friends with him before her dad died. Then she'd mostly shut Carl out. Been cold and distant whenever he'd come over.

A shift.

After her dad died.

True, her mom wasn't alive to guide her, but then her mother wasn't the only one who'd been adamant about avoiding Carl.

She snapped her head up and zeroed in on Reggie. "Take me to Dorothy's."

Chapter Twenty-Two

The trip to Dorothy's was insufferably slow, a process further exacerbated by three trips around the block to find a parking space. Thankfully, the string of texts from her uncle had finally tapered off to nothing about halfway there, the last one stating simply...

Once I explain, you'll understand.

Finally, Tony slid into a spot just down the street.

Evette yanked the door latch before he could get the car in Park.

Reggie must have anticipated her eagerness, because he was out of the passenger seat and falling in lockstep beside her as she strode toward the diner's front door. "You know, Mr. Petrovyh is just looking out for you. If you're upset, you should just call him. He won't mind if you interrupt him."

Oh, she was going to talk to him. But the more she'd thought about it on the drive over, the more she'd determined the prudent action would be to make sure it was in person without a gun in reaching distance. Particularly, if Sergei deemed that the security of his home had been breached. "I'm fine. I just need to talk to Dorothy for a bit, then I'll head home and see if he's done with his meeting."

Tony's quick footsteps sounded behind them just as Reggie stepped in front of her and pulled the diner's door open for her.

The bell overhead gave a happy jingle and a handful of the construction workers who'd pushed three tables together for an early lunch looked up from their meals to note the latest arrival.

On the floor, the two waitresses bussing tables and taking orders twisted enough to make eye contact with Evette. Both offered smiles as soon as they recognized it was her, but it was Matilda, a woman who'd been waitressing for Dorothy off and on for at least five years, who spoke.

"Hey, Evette." Matilda straightened from wiping down the now empty four-top and jerked her head toward the kitchen. "If you're looking for Dorothy, she just headed back for an order."

"Thanks." Evette motioned toward Tony and Reggie, who'd thankfully lingered near the front door. "You mind getting these two something to drink?"

"Nope, not at all." She looked to the men and her smile got a little bigger. "You two can take this table. You want coffee or something else?"

"Coffee for me," and "Coke," they answered almost at the same time, then ambled over and joined Matilda at the table.

Evette headed to the kitchen, but nearly ran into Dorothy as she rounded the far end of the counter. In one hand she had a large tumbler full of soda and the other a plate with a hamburger and a double order of fries.

"Oh!" Evette backed up a step and smoothed her clammy hands down her hips. "You workin' the floor today?"

Dorothy shook her head. "Nope. Just grabbin' a bite before the lunch crowd shows." She gave Evette a thorough once-over and frowned. "Someone walk over your grave, or something? Haven't seen you that pasty since you had the flu your senior year."

Great. If it was that obvious, then Sergei would probably get the lowdown on that from his boys, too.

Evette glanced over her shoulder and—sure enough—Reggie's fingers were flying over the keyboard of his phone. "I need to talk to you about something." She turned back to Dorothy, a fresh surge of urgency pushing through with her voice. "You mind if we do that while you eat?"

Dorothy's frown deepened and her gaze shuttled from Evette to the guards. "Got a feeling this conversation's not gonna be good for my digestion." She lifted her drink toward the empty corner booth Sergei always sat in. "Let's go over there. I'm tired of my office and it's private."

They settled in, Dorothy doing her usual methodical routine of unrolling her napkin and situating her silverware like she had all the time in the world. Evette focused on not fidgeting. Even went so far as to tuck her hands beneath her thighs while she waited for Dorothy to give her the go-ahead to start.

Dorothy grabbed the ketchup and poured some next to her fries. "Well? What's got you riled up enough sittin' next to you is like lockin' up a race horse in the starting gate?"

"I need you to tell me about Uncle Carl."

Midway through putting the cap back on the ketchup bottle, Dorothy froze, and her stare cut to Evette. "Come again?"

"Uncle Carl. I need to know what you know about him. How he makes his money. Why Momma didn't like him. Anything you can tell me."

For all the years Evette had known Dorothy, she'd always been readable. Her expression able to convey her thoughts without a single word spoken. But in that second, everything shut down. Completely blanked to the point Evette's insides turned ice cold.

Dorothy set the ketchup down right where she'd picked it up, the movement slow and methodical. "How about you start at the beginning and tell me why you're asking?"

Evette laid it out while Dorothy ate. How Carl had visited her house twice the weekend her badge had been used to enter the lawyer's office. What he'd accused her of the night of the street party and how he'd reacted to news she'd been fired. How the older boys had befriended Emerson and been caught milling around Sergei's house unsupervised. How she'd seen Uncle Carl hand over the cash to the boys in the marketplace and how many times he'd tried to reach her *just to talk* after the fact.

"I think he's up to something," Evette said, "and I need to find out what that is. Momma didn't like him, and you've made no bones about you not liking him either. That tells me *she told you* why she didn't like him, and I need to know why that is."

Dorothy pushed her plate aside, barely a dent put in her hamburger and only a few fries eaten. "You told Sergei any of this?"

"No, not yet. He had a meeting this morning, but I'm going back to the house after this, and I'll tell him then. But I need information from you before I do that." She crossed her arms on the table and leaned in closer to Dorothy, lowering her voice. "You know Sergei. If I don't give him the right details, he'll act without thinking, and his actions aren't exactly the *Let's talk reasonably about this* type."

Dorothy's gaze dropped to Evette's hand and a soft smile crept in to place. "I see you took a chance."

As she'd done countless times in the last few days adjusting to the weight of his ring on her finger, Evette shifted her thumb to the metal and wiggled it back and forth. "I am. He's a good man. Hard, but caring. And he adores Emerson. But if someone's trying to use him somehow, then I need to stop it."

"Child, if you're smart, you'll get up from this table, go home, tell your man what you know and wash your hands of the whole damned thing."

"Why? What aren't you telling me?"

Dorothy stared at the table, her lips mashed together so tight it looked like they'd never part again.

"Dorothy, tell me. Sergei's done nothing but look out for Emerson and me and make our lives better. How can I look out for him if I don't have all the facts?"

For long seconds, Dorothy just sat there, her chest lifting and falling as if it took immense concentration simply to breathe. When she finally spoke, the words were low and ragged. As if they'd been ripped from her unwillingly. "Because there's more than just facts here, Evie. There's pain and risk. Lots of it." She lifted her head and locked stares with Evette. "I'm telling you—let it go."

"And I'm telling you, I can't. I won't. Sergei's bent over backward for me and Emerson. I may not have the resources he does, but if you think for a second I'm not going to have his back when it matters, you're sadly mistaken. And let's not forget that I just plain deserve to know if someone who's tied to me by blood is doing something they shouldn't. If you won't share for me, then share for Emerson so I can keep him safe."

The words must have literally hit her like a slap because her gaze shot to her barely touched food and her features pinched as though it hurt to even breathe. She stayed that way for long seconds. Where Dorothy's looks had always given her an ageless beauty, the sadness in her eyes in that moment made her seem frail and utterly beaten.

On a sigh, Dorothy hung her head. "Right before your mom died, she told me she thought Carl had something to do with your dad's death. She said, back before Bobby died, something had been bothering your dad. Your mom thought he was worried about paying the bills at first because he was working lots of extra hours delivering packages, but then one night Carl and Bobby had a huge row outside the house they rented." Dorothy looked up from the table to Evette. "Right after that, his delivery truck went off the road."

"She thought Carl killed him?"

"No. Not at first. Your daddy dying threw your momma completely off center, not to mention how bad the whole thing impacted you. The police said it was a cut-and-dried case of black ice on a back road and she didn't think anything else about it. But then Carl came over one night years later while you were in college. Your mom said he was too drunk to walk straight and started talking about how if her husband hadn't been such an uptight fool and done what he was told to do instead of bucking the system, he'd still be alive.

"She called me crying after Carl left. Word for word, she said Carl had told her, *He didn't need to know what was in those packages. Just needed to make the deliveries and mind his own business.* I told your momma never to bring it up again, but you know how she was. How determined she was to see things through. She said she was going to confront Carl about it the next day when he was sober." Tears welled in Dorothy's eyes, then spilled down her cheeks. Her voice when she spoke again was a broken rasp. "Your momma was dead three days later."

Cold seeped straight to Evette's bones. The shivering miserable kind like what you felt when you'd been stuck in a winter rain for hours and were soaked through. She wanted to speak. Opened and closed her mouth twice before she could force words past the invisible noose around her throat. "You should have told me."

"Why? So you could have more pain on top of everything else? Maybe prompt you to do something stupid and confront Carl and end up dead like your momma?"

Dorothy pinched her mouth shut tight, faced the table once more and braced her hands on top of it. "And, ashamed as I am to admit it, I was afraid if I said a word, I'd end up dead, too." Her head snapped back to Evette. "Then who'd have kept an eye out for you and made sure you stayed away from him?"

The door to the diner opened.

Reflexes borne from years of practice made both of them look.

"Oh, shit," Evette whispered.

"Oh, shit is right," Dorothy answered, the obvious concern at seeing Uncle Carl walk through the diner's door after what they'd just been discussing written all over her face.

Carl spied them in the corner booth, smiled an unconvincing smile and ambled their way.

Dorothy lowered her voice, but the urgency behind her words was no less powerful. "You listen to me. Whatever he says to you, you tell him *nothing*. Believe *nothing*. You understand?"

"It's just a coincidence. He can't know what we were talking about."

"Too damned many coincidences around Carl Labadie, child. That's the whole problem. You best figure that out and keep your guard up." As if it was the only thing she could do to keep from saying more she'd regret, she locked her gaze on her plate, snatched a French fry and stuffed it in her mouth.

Carl waddled up to the table before she'd managed to swallow. "Well, now here's a pair of troublemakers if I've ever seen one."

"Hmph," Dorothy said without looking up. Where she'd been all business seconds before, now her demeanor was back to the usual dry humor that had earned her the affection of everyone in their neighborhood. "Pair of angels, you mean." She snagged another fry, dipped it in the ketchup and looked up just as she took a bite, pure innocence on her face. "What are you doin' here, anyway? Thought you'd be off on one of those big jobs of yours earnin' gobs of money."

Evette had to hand it to Dorothy, the woman was a brilliant actor. Better than Evette had ever imagined and definitely better than Evette was likely capable of.

"No, no. Not for another few weeks and that's only if I get the job I've been workin' on. I actually stopped by hopin' I'd find Evette." Carl stuffed his hands in the pockets of his poorly tailored tan slacks, the untucked gray button-down doing little to hide his girth. His gaze cut to Evette. "Looks like I got lucky."

Dorothy cocked her head and gave him the sassy glower that had made more than one belligerent patron stand down. "You tryin' to tell me my girl finally came to spend a lunch with me and you're gonna try to horn in on it?"

"Well, now that she's hooked up with her fancy digs on restricted turf, a man's gotta do what he can to keep up with his niece." He rocked back on his heels a bit. "You don't mind do you, Dorothy? Just for a bit?"

Before she could answer, Tony and Reggie moved in on either side of Carl. While they didn't show any immediate signs of dragging Carl away from her, they were clearly on a mission.

"Miss Labadie," Tony said. "Are you ready to go?"

It was the perfect out. A chance to get away from her uncle, take time to absorb what she'd learned from Dorothy and share it with Sergei.

Then again, once her uncle got a notion to do something, he rarely let up, and it was clear he wanted time to talk to her. If she gave him that time, she might at least learn more to share with Sergei. Not to mention, she was in a public place with guards watching over her.

It was either swallow back her fears and anger, face

the man who may have been the one to kill her parents and get information Sergei might need, or run away and nurse her wounds.

She'd have plenty of time for tears later, but this chance might not come again. She shook her head and wiped her damp palms on her thighs. "No, not yet." She lifted her chin toward her uncle. "My uncle's been wanting to talk to me about something, so we may as well do it while I'm here."

Tony looked to Reggie. While he did a pretty good job of keeping his uncertainty about the situation masked from the group at large, Evette had been around him enough to know he was about as confident as a man on an ice-covered pond in early spring.

Reggie didn't look much better, and his grip on the phone in his hand tightened to the point she thought he'd crush it.

Sergei.

No doubt they'd already called him. Maybe even told him Carl had arrived at the diner.

"You know," Evette said, going with her gut. "If you wouldn't mind giving Sergei a call and letting him know I'll be late getting home, I'd appreciate it. Or, better yet, maybe he could swing by and pick me up after his meeting?"

Reggie jumped on the opportunity in a heartbeat and nodded. "Of course." He gave Carl a hard stare that could only be interpreted as a warning, then met Evette's gaze. "We'll be just over here if you need us."

Dorothy shook her head in that beleaguered way most weary parents did when their kids had been riding them for a new toy for days, slid out of the booth and snatched her plate as she stood. "Guess that's my cue to skedaddle." She cut between Carl and the table and winked at Evette, the glimmer behind her eyes showing her approval of the tactic Evette had taken. "You don't leave here without givin' me a chance to say hello to that man of yours. Don't get to ogle nearly enough man candy in here. Gotta take advantage of yours every chance I got."

"You got it."

Carl watched Dorothy go, his head cocked slightly. Considering. When she was well out of earshot, he twisted and eyeballed the guards stationed two tables away.

He must have been satisfied the distance between them was sufficient enough to give him the privacy he wanted, because he slid into the booth and murmured, "*Your man*, huh?"

Oh, that Dorothy was a sneaky one. Evette hadn't caught the subtle hint Dorothy had dropped, but Carl had sure copped to it fast enough.

Evette rolled with it, crossed her arms on the table and dug down deep for some of her customary sassiness, making sure the gargantuan ring Sergei had given her was on full display. "Something like that. But if you accuse me of using my assets again, this chat you wanna have is gonna be over before it gets started."

The jab did what she'd intended it to and sent Carl's attention straight to the tabletop, his expression thoroughly chagrined. "I owe you an apology for that." When he lifted his head again, his cheeks were flushed. "I didn't mean it the way it sounded. You'd just caught me off guard with the news of you losing your job and moving."

Bullshit.

He'd seen an opportunity to use her, and he'd let a little of his true self slip out from behind the blubbering goober mask he kept in place for everyone else.

His gaze locked on her ring. "That's a big honkin' ring."

"Too big," she said. "But it makes him happy, so I'm wearing it."

Carl nodded, but otherwise stayed silent. Where he'd played the affable card thus far, a different energy surfaced over the quiet moments. As if his thoughts were too sizable and complex to maintain his facade. All that was left was the indifference of a cold, uncaring man.

Whatever was on his mind, Evette didn't care. Sergei was probably already halfway here, and she wanted information before he walked through the front door. "So, you gonna tell me why you were forking over a big stack of cash to three boys who should have been in school today instead of at the market with you?"

One corner of Carl's mouth lifted in a sardonic grin, and he faced her. "Girl, you've got no idea what you're dealing with. You're a tiny little bleeding fish swimming in a tank full of sharks."

Tiny little bleeding fish, her ass. If anyone was gonna be dinner in the short term, it was Carl.

Rather than set that thought free, she kept her mouth clamped shut and prayed the uncomfortable quiet would get her uncle talking.

Sure enough, it worked. "The people I work for are powerful," Carl said. "They don't like it when people mess up their plans, and Sergei's messed up plenty lately."

"And these people are?"

He chuckled at that. "You really are innocent, aren't you?" Carl's laughter died off and his expression sobered. "You remember Stephen Alfonsi?"

Shit.

He'd been on the news in Sergei's office.

"What about him?" she said.

"Well, it seems your new fiancé has created quite a few complications for him. Wants to shut Alfonsi out of New Orleans."

Good. Just went to show her man had good taste, not to mention a creative streak. "Not sure how that's got anything to do with three little boys."

"Because the best way for Alfonsi to level out the playing field is to know what Sergei's plans are, and when someone in this town needs information, they come to me. Those boys are gonna help me, but now I'm gonna use you, too."

Evette couldn't have stopped the sharp bark of laughter that ripped up her throat if she'd wanted to. "You're joking, right?"

Carl stayed stone-faced, completely emotionless.

"You actually think I'm going to give you information on the man I plan to marry?"

He nodded, a single slow dip of his double chin.

The man was insane. Certifiable stupid and crazy as a damned loon if he thought she'd ever do his dirty work. "And why, exactly, would I do that?"

"Because if you don't, I'll tell Emerson's daddy about his son's existence, and he'll undoubtedly move heaven and earth to take him away from you."

The confidence that had slowly built over the last few moments evaporated in an instant, leaving nothing but an empty dread in the pit of her stomach. "I don't know who Emerson's daddy is."

Carl held her stare, the merciless depth behind his green eyes like that of a hardened executioner. "I do."

Fuck.

Fuck, fuck, fuck.

"Who?"

He smirked and rested one arm on the table. "Alfonsi's son, Stevie Jr."

Evette scoffed and shook her head like she had hundreds of times after hearing her uncle's wild ideas, but a weighty unease pressed atop her shoulders. "Oh, give me a break. I couldn't pick him out of a lineup even if I wanted to. And even if that were true, how the heck would *you* know if I don't?"

"Because I was there the night you met him. It was a big party at a hotel in the Quarter. He hit on you, but you were drunk and full of your usual pain-in-the-ass attitude and brushed him off."

She'd been drunk nearly every night back then trying to drown the pain from her mother's death. But if it was the night she was thinking of—the night when she'd completely blacked out somewhere along the way and woken up back at home with the telltale tenderness between her legs that said she'd been supremely stupid—he was hitting awfully close to home. She'd turned up pregnant a month later.

Not that she was inclined to share any of those details with Carl. "Right. So, if I brushed him off, what makes you think I slept with him?"

Carl's smirk faded and the coldness in his gaze grew as deep and dark as the lowest stretches in the ocean.

"Because I'm the one that gave you something to make you more agreeable."

Her stomach pitched and a cold sweat broke out along the back of her neck. The room around her got a little hazy and, if she hadn't been sitting down, she wasn't entire sure she'd have been able to stay upright. When she spoke, it felt as though the words had sliced stinging cuts along her throat on the way out, and her voice sounded like it came from a tunnel. "You drugged me?"

He shrugged, a matter-of-fact motion that he could have used when asked if he'd been the one to accidentally step on a cockroach. "Just a little something to mellow you out." He huffed out a short laugh. "And boy, did you turn agreeable."

Drugged.

By her uncle.

Her own blood.

And yet, there was no question he was telling the truth.

"Why?" Just asking the question hurt. Made her want to punch and cry and claw Carl and everyone else around her.

But she couldn't. Not yet. Not until she knew the truth. All of it. "Why would you do that? To me of all people?"

"Always good to further favors with a man like Alfonsi," he said. "His son was interested. I figured you two might hit it off and it'd be a win/win for everyone." He huffed out an ironic chuckle. "Given his disinterested attitude the next day, I decided it was a lost cause. But then you turned up pregnant and it put a whole new spin on things." That evil grin crept back into place. "I decided I'd just tuck the knowledge away in case I ever needed leverage against Stevie or his dad. Instead, I'm gonna use it so you'll give me what I need."

It was so easy for him. No signs of conscience. No hesitation. Just cold, calculated manipulation.

That was what stung the most.

He didn't care that she was family. Hadn't cared about her dad or her mother either. He'd just used them and tossed them aside when he was done with them. And if he'd been willing to kill, or have her parents killed, he definitely wouldn't hesitate to carry through on his threats toward Emerson.

The bell over the front door jingled and the energy in the room shifted in an instant. Hummed as though lightning had not only struck, but left the air supercharged with electricity in its wake.

Sergei.

She didn't need to look to confirm her instincts. The testimony was right there on Carl's face—a bizarre mix of challenge and uncertainty making his green eyes blaze to life. Like a crazy warrior eager to enter into battle.

Only the weapon he intended to wield was her.

He schooled his features almost as fast as they'd blazed to life and focused on Evette, his low and menacing voice nowhere near the polite expression he'd donned. "You get any bright ideas about sharing what I've told you with your *fiancé*, just remember— Alfonsi's been in this town a very long time and has dirt on more powerful connections than your man can match. One call to a judge and Emerson will be out from under your control in a heartbeat."

"Oh, I got that message. Loud and clear."

He nodded and slid from the booth, his smile the same fond one he'd aimed at her ever since she was a little girl. The only difference now was that she knew it was insincere. Nothing more than a disguise he'd perfected to earn what he wanted. Standing, he shifted his attention to Sergei as he approached and raised his voice. "Well, now. There's the man of the hour." He winked and shoved his hands in his pockets, either wisely ascertaining Sergei wouldn't shake his hand if he'd offered it, or too chicken to find out. "I hear congratulations are in order."

Sergei laid a possessive hand on Evette's shoulder and squeezed.

To Carl, the simple gesture probably looked to be nothing more than basic affection, but it grounded Evette in an instant. Filled her with his strength and said without a single word, *I'm here and no one will hurt you.*

Evette cleared her throat and spoke into the tense silence. "Uncle Carl stopped by to say hello, so I shared the news."

"She did indeed," Carl said just as light and conversational as could be. "So, when's the wedding? I'm looking forward to celebrating."

Sergei stared at him, his expression detached and indifferent. "When we are married and those invited to witness it are entirely up to my bride."

An answer and yet no answer at all, the words cleverly crafted for more than one interpretation, while the tone behind them zinged with the unspoken message that Carl wouldn't be in attendance.

"Smart man," Carl said, either oblivious to the disgust in Sergei's voice, or too arrogant and full of his own schemes to listen. "Always better to let the women run with those things and just knuckle down until the whole process is over with."

Sergei cocked one eyebrow, the look he aimed at Carl one reserved for idiots and fools.

At least that much must have gotten through, because Carl rocked back on his heels and said, "Right. Well, I'm off." He faced Evette. "Glad I finally caught up with you, kiddo. Let's plan on having dinner next week. You can fill me in on how the wedding plans are going."

Translation: *You've got a week to find dirt on Sergei.*

Nodding her head almost killed her, and keeping her venomous tongue in cheek when she finally found the strength to talk took Herculean discipline. "Looking forward to it."

Carl's smile deepened, evil satisfaction beaming behind his eyes even as he turned his gaze on Sergei. "Good to see you, Sergei."

And with that, he ambled off, his gait and demeanor that of a man without a care in the world.

Fool.

Beside her, Sergei turned and studied her features. Awareness flashed behind his blue eyes and the beast that always hovered close to the surface seemed to lift its head. "He upset you again."

Upset.

What a laughable way to put it.

More like upended her past and future and dredged up every shred of shame and pain she'd ever felt along with it. "I'm not upset. I'm *pissed*."

The bell over the front door chimed, indicating

Carl's departure, and her lungs filled for the first time since he'd walked in.

Sergei must have noted that response, too, because his low voice lost all pretense of softness and patience. He held out his hand to help her from the booth. "You will tell me."

Using his grip to stabilize her adrenaline-shaken body, she slid from her seat and met his stare head-on. "First we get my son, then we talk."

Chapter Twenty-Three

Sergei pulled his BMW into the driveway and put the gearshift in Park, the calmness of his actions in stark contrast to the acidic unease prickling beneath his skin. Whatever had happened today between Evette and her uncle, it had her uncustomarily silent and her body locked up tight enough it seemed she might shatter at any moment. The only time she'd acted even remotely normal had been when she'd been face-to-face checking Emerson out of school early, and she'd dropped that pretense the moment Emerson had slid into the back seat.

"This is so cool." Apparently clueless to the turmoil roiling in the front seat, Emerson popped open his car door and hopped out. "You almost never check me out of school early. But for a movie? That's awesome."

Evette cast Sergei an uncertain glance before she pasted her happy expression back into place and opened her own door. "Well, I said a movie *after* Sergei and I take care of something. And it's not *that* big of a deal. You're only missing a few hours."

She shut her door and started toward the carriage house. While they'd slept every night since Darya and Knox's visit in the main house, not all of their belongings had been moved as yet, but Sergei still found her destination surprising.

Emerson slid in next to her, practically dancing between steps. "Do I get to pick the movie?"

Sergei trailed them both. Until he knew more about what had her so upset, the best he could do was follow her lead with Emerson and be ready to wing it if she stumbled.

Evette stopped outside the carriage house door and ruffled his head. "You have to because I don't have any idea what's on, and Sergei would probably pick one of those action flicks that make me nervous." She straightened and jerked her head toward the door. "Now, go. Superheroes are fine, but if you could find a comedy, I'll buy you chocolates to go with your popcorn."

Emerson nodded, opened the door and marched through with all the focus of a soldier tasked with an important mission. "Got it. I'll text you as soon as I find a good one."

The second he shut the door, Evette's smile dropped, and she hustled toward the pool rather than the house. Her voice was barely above a whisper and every word came out clipped and urgent. "I thought of something on the way home. Can you have someone watch over Dorothy? Don't let her know. Just have someone close in case she gets into trouble."

Sergei snatched her arm and tried to redirect her toward the house, the implications that there would be any kind of physical threat resulting from her run-in with Carl insisting he get her safely inside. "What happened?"

Evette dug in her heels. "Not in there. I think your

house is bugged. That's why those boys were being friends with Emerson. Carl was using them."

Everything inside him stilled, the predator Anton had groomed him to be from an early age poised and ready to attack. "How do you know this?"

"Because I saw him at the market paying them off. That's why he came looking for me at Dorothy's. He saw that I saw him, and I wouldn't answer his text messages. I guess he knew better than to come looking for me here, so he took a chance and came looking for me down at Dorothy's."

He could have taken a chance.

Or he could have tracked her.

Her purse hung on one shoulder, a tiny thing compared with the ones Darya always wore, but the first expensive thing she'd reported buying on her shopping expedition. He pulled it off her shoulder, gripped her arm again and steered her toward the house.

She put one foot in front of the other, but only because he didn't give her any choice. "Sergei, didn't you hear what I said? And give me back my purse. Emerson said he'd text me."

"There are no bugs in the house. At least none where your uncle will hear anything. My men found them and moved them." He opened the back door and barked at the man standing just five feet away. "Find Kir and Roman. I want them here. Now."

Not waiting for a response, Sergei kept them moving, not stopping until they were behind closed doors in his office. At his desk, he unzipped her purse, rooted out her phone and powered it off.

"What are you doing? I need to talk to you, and I

don't want to do it where Emerson can hear. If I don't answer his texts, this is the first place he'll come."

Sergei pulled his own phone from his suit coat pocket and started a text to Emerson. "I never replaced your phone. I should have." He hit Send and tucked it back in his pocket. "Now, Emerson will text me instead."

Comprehension settled on her face. "Carl tracked me?"

"Possibly. You've had the phone for some time, yes? And he could have accessed it when you were not aware?"

Her gaze shifted to the floor, though it was clear from her dazed expression that her thoughts were somewhere else. "Shit. I'm so stupid."

"Not stupid. Learning." He guided her to one of the two chairs in front of his desk and nudged her backward until she sat. "Now, tell me why I'm putting a guard on Dorothy and why you pulled your son out of class early for a *movie*."

Slowly, she lifted her head. In all the time he'd known her—watched her traipsing in and out of Dorothy's diner and interacting with her son—he'd never once seen her look so bleak. So lost. Her voice was strained when she spoke. "I think Carl killed my mom and my dad."

Of all the things she could have led with, those were the last he'd expected. That her uncle was a blackmailer with dangerous connections, he'd expected. But murderer? He couldn't fathom it. Carl didn't have enough predator in him to take a life. He was a bottom feeder. A vulture who lived off the misfortunes of others. More likely, their deaths were the results of his failures. Or perhaps at his request. No doubt carried out by Alfonsi's men. "Explain."

She did, systematically working through the day. How she'd seen Carl at the market. All the details Dorothy had shared and how Carl had shown up and admitted to using the boys.

Her words trailed off and she dropped her head, staring at her fisted hands in her lap.

"It doesn't make sense," Sergei said. "Why would he admit what he'd done?"

A teardrop landed on her lap, leaving a darker spot on the faded surface of her jeans. Another followed. Then another.

"Evette." Her name came out harsher than he'd intended, but her pain was a palpable presence between them. One laced with the jagged bite of razor wire and sharpened spikes.

She lifted her head, the tracks of her tears marking her beautiful skin and leaving splotchy red spots on her cheeks. "Because when he found out we were engaged, he decided I'd be a better source."

More blackmail.

Carl's stock in trade.

Heat blossomed in his belly and his trigger hand itched to connect with the gun holstered beneath his jacket. "What does he have on you?"

A broken sob ripped up her throat and her shoulders shook as the tears slipped free, but she held his stare. "He knows who Emerson's father is. Said he'd tell them and that they'd use their connections to take him away from me."

"You said you didn't know who Emerson's father was."

"I don't. I don't even know if he's telling the truth, but if he is—he's right. They could pull strings with the courts and have him taken away from me." She stood. "You have to believe that I would never do what he's asked me to do. Never. I knew the second he told me that I would share everything I know with you, but you have to help me protect Emerson. I know you're newer to New Orleans, but you have to know someone in the court system. Someone who'll fight their claims and keep him safe. Right?"

At first her question didn't register. Couldn't get past the fact that she'd not only trusted him enough to share every horrifying detail she'd learned, but that she believed in him enough to look to him to resolve it.

And he would.

Permanently.

Just as soon as he knew where the threat was centered. "Who is it?"

She shook her head, openly confused. "Who's what?"

"Emerson's father. Who does Carl believe it is?"

Her lips trembled. "Alfonsi's son, Stevie."

Another surprise. One that seemed to have left Evette openly shaken. "Is it possible?"

A fresh wave of tears sprang forth, obvious shame weighting her head until it dropped forward. She gripped the lapels on his jacket and leaned in, her voice a near whisper. "You remember I told you how bad I was after Mom died? How I partied a lot?"

Rather than answer with words, he straightened and pulled her against him, giving her the strength she seemed to need.

She pulled in a long breath broken by more sobs.

"According to Carl, Stevie hit on me at a party." She paused a beat and fisted her hand against his chest. "I blew him off, but Carl thought if we got together it might be good for his relationship with Alfonsi, so…" She lifted her head, her eyes puffy and lashes spiked with wetness. "He put something in what I was drinking to make me more agreeable."

His hands tightened on her shoulders on reflex, the instant, demanding need to feel Carl's throat beneath his bare hands nearly consuming him before he could check it.

"I remember waking up one morning, not remembering who I'd been with, but knowing I'd been with someone. I thought I'd blacked out." She mashed her lips together for a moment, then finished it. "When I turned up pregnant a month later, Carl said he decided to keep what he knew quiet in case he needed leverage against Alfonsi or his son. But now he wants to use it against me to get information out of you."

Fury lashed him.

Burned his insides with the fury of flames straight from hell.

His woman had suffered.

Doubted herself.

Been compromised by her own blood and forced into raising a child on her own as a result.

Carl Labadie was a dead man.

Alfonsi and his son, too.

He channeled his rage. Closed his eyes and willed his emotion into something more useful to her in her pain. Hugged her tighter to him and stroked the length of her spine with all the gentleness he'd craved as a child, lost and alone after his mother's death.

No one would touch her again. Or Emerson. No matter the DNA involved, Emerson was *his* son. Would always be his and protected with the same tenaciousness he offered Evette.

Only when the tremors racking her torso finally slowed and she lifted her head enough to dash her tears with the back of her hand did he speak. "Your uncle will not bother you again and no one will ever take your son away from you. I'll see to it."

She met his gaze, the dimness of her hazel eyes further cementing Carl's fate. "You can't promise me that. If he's really Emerson's dad, he can argue he has rights. Courts are much more supportive of men these days."

Honor her with the truth.

Always the truth.

In his gut, he knew it was the right action. Even the strategist in him warned of the consequences if he hid his actions and she learned of them later.

Because the truth always came out—one way or another.

He studied her features. Let the pain mark his soul so he'd remember it while he carried out his task even as he'd reveled in the light that came with her smiles and tender touch. "Evette, my world is not like the world you've lived in. You know this. This case will never make it to court because I will handle it before it does."

Her breath caught and her eyes widened. "Handle it how?"

"Those deeds are not for you to know. I would never risk my actions, or knowledge of my actions, falling back on you."

"Sergei—"

"*Nyet.* This is not a topic we will discuss. It will be dealt with."

She swallowed hard and peered up at him with stark fear in her eyes. "I'm not sure I can live with how you're going to deal with it."

"You shared knowledge with me. You shared your fears with me. In this life, that is how it must be. Any consequences that come from the actions I take are mine alone. You are innocent."

Her stare never wavered as she processed what he'd said. He expected her to argue. To push her point or demand an alternate course. Instead, she whispered, "And what about the risks to you?"

His chest grew tight and the muscles in his belly clenched. The many experiences she'd given him since the day she'd sat down at his booth—her touch against his skin, her passion, the faith she'd shown in coming to him today and the beautiful smiles she beamed at him each and every day—they were nothing short of amazing. But knowing she worried for him—truly cared for his safety—was beyond humbling.

He cupped the side of her face and traced the line of her tears with his thumb. "I told you, *liubimaja.* There is no risk I will not take to secure your happiness or protection."

A knock sounded at the door, the abrupt rap making Evette jump inside the circle of his arms.

He pulled her close to him and tucked her head against his chest. "Enter."

The door opened and Kir and Roman strode through. One look at Evette tight against him and their steps slowed.

"You needed us?" Kir said.

Sergei nodded and guided Evette's gaze toward his with a finger at her chin. "Go help Emerson pick out a movie. Do not leave the carriage house. I will come to you after I talk to my men."

She knew.

Understood clearly the actions he would put into play the second she walked out of his office.

Whether or not those actions would drive an insurmountable wedge between them going forward remained to be seen, but standing there—staring up at him with her big, beautiful, trusting eyes—she seemed to accept the truth.

He kissed her forehead, letting his lips linger on a prayer that it wouldn't be the last one he shared with her. If it was, at least he could live with the knowledge that she would never again suffer the threats or pain she'd felt today.

She pulled away, twisted enough to nod at Kir and Roman, then padded quietly to the door.

No goodbye.

No reassurance.

And when the door shut behind her, it seemed as though the room dimmed despite the sun bearing through the open window.

Think about the consequences later.

Now is for action.

He shook off his doubts and circled behind his desk, grabbing Evette's phone as he went. He tossed it to Kir and sat in his chair. "Get Evette and Emerson new phones. Check that one and Emerson's for any signs of tampering or tracking."

Kir nodded and tucked the phone in his pocket. "What else?"

"We alter tomorrow's meet with Alfonsi."

Roman frowned and glanced at Kir. "I thought this morning's meeting with Henri went well?"

"It did," Sergei said. "But the situation has changed. What location did Alfonsi pick?"

"Muriel's on Jackson Square."

Very public. Far more public than suited his needs. "His son is his first captain, yes?"

Roman nodded.

"Good," Sergei said. "Change the location. Someplace remote."

Understanding settled in both of their expressions and they straightened from their casual stances.

Sergei kept going. "Alfonsi will be allowed two captains. The two of you will be mine. But there is a new stipulation." He volleyed a look between them they'd have had to be blind to mistake. "If he wants the meet, he brings Carl Labadie with him."

Chapter Twenty-Four

Concrete floors, metal walls and no windows. As isolated locations went, the old warehouse near Michoud Canal was perfect for the moments that lay ahead.

Sergei opened the door to the crude office that had been built into the far corner of the building. A circa 1960 wood desk sat toward the back wall, a gooseneck lamp still lit on one side of it from when his crew had scanned the building an hour ago. Another floor lamp that had probably once graced someone's home was also illuminated next to three file cabinets along a side wall. Even with the lights aglow, there was no shaking the environment's dreary feel.

Then again, he could just be projecting the disquiet that had gripped his own home since yesterday onto the antiquated space. He'd taken Evette and Emerson to the movie after he'd spoken to his men—some animated selection that Evette had seemed as disconnected from as Sergei had been, but that Emerson had enjoyed immensely.

He'd hoped the distractedness would scatter when they got home and settled into a dinner routine, but Evette's quietness had continued throughout the night. Not angry or petulant. Just pensive. As though the jury of her mind was so deep in deliberations she couldn't quite engage with the world around her beyond going through the motions.

The question was what sentence he'd be handed down for his transgressions.

Whatever the outcome, he wouldn't stray from his course. He'd spent most of the night reviewing his options. Stared into the darkness of his room, listened to Evette's slow, steady breaths and savored the fit of her body against his as he considered alternate outcomes.

There were no others.

Not with men like Carl or Steven Alfonsi.

They would always be a danger to Evette and Emerson and that was unacceptable—whether it cost him the greatest light and peace he'd ever known, or not.

He rounded the desk and pulled the wood desk chair out from under it, its old wheels grating a protest as they trundled against the dingy floor. "How far out are they?" he said to Kir, who waited with Roman by the office door.

The response was as short and clipped as all of their other conversations had been since yesterday afternoon. But then, his men had been with him long enough to know when his mood was volatile and knew to tread lightly until the beast was pacified. "Five minutes."

Sergei sat in the chair, his seat, the desktop and the two guest chairs in front of it the only items in the room not covered with a thick layer of dust. His men stood on either side of the front door, their feet braced shoulder width apart and hands clasped loosely in front of them. Their suits were as immaculate and fine as his own. "And Carl?"

"They picked him up shortly after they left Alfonsi's compound," Kir said.

Roman stared straight ahead, the mega-short cut he kept his dark blond hair in and his detached, cold expression making his features sharper. Meaner. Both men had taken the knowledge he'd shared about Carl's actions toward Evette deeply personal, but Roman in particular seemed eager for blood.

"You will let this play out," Sergei said to him. "I will not return to Evette without knowing the truth. Their actions will tell us what we need to know."

The muscles at the back of Roman's jaw twitched and his lips mashed together as though he wanted to protest, but he managed a curt nod.

"Good," Sergei said.

Beyond the office, the metal door they'd left unlocked opened, then slammed shut, the sharp clash of it ricocheting through the tall building like a gunshot.

"It seems our guests are here." Sergei motioned his men into play. "Go. Let us finish this."

On sheer numbers, it was a risk sending Roman and Kir alone. Particularly, if Carl was carrying a weapon. But all of them had agreed Carl didn't seem the type to be versed in physical confrontations of any kind, and that the best way to get Alfonsi to lower his guard would be to show some degree of trust from the start.

Voices echoed through the door, a mix of Alfonsi's abrupt delivery and Kir's accented grace. Footsteps followed and Carl's voice joined into the mix, his usual inane chatter growing more intelligible the closer they got. "…but Muriel's would have been a sight more comfortable."

"Well, now," Alfonsi answered Carl. "You know

how our Russian friends are. Can't do business without over-the-top drama."

Drama indeed. Either the man was a complete idiot, or had balls the size of Texas.

Alfonsi's second captain, Drake, entered first, followed by Stevie Jr., then Alfonsi himself. To their credit, they'd come respectfully dressed in suits as well. Though, if Sergei had to guess, it was to cover the sidearms hidden beneath their jackets more than a show of respect.

Carl waddled in a second later, scanning the environment like he'd never been in a warehouse before and couldn't quite fathom why he was there to begin with. Per usual his wrinkled shirt was untucked and his pants poorly pressed—if they'd ever seen an iron at all. What was most concerning was the windbreaker he'd worn. True the weather was colder than normal today, but jackets weren't his norm, which meant he might well have come armed after all.

Kir and Roman moved in and flanked the front door, resuming their impassive stances.

Sergei stood and forced a businesslike pretense. No small feat when everything in him craved the sound of Carl's pain-filled screams bouncing off the metal walls. He focused on Alfonsi. "My apologies for the crude environment. What I have to share today is of a deeply sensitive nature. Certainly not something any of us would want shared in a place where others might overhear." He motioned to the two chairs in front of Sergei's desk. "Please. Have a seat."

Alfonsi moved in to take one of the chairs.

Carl started to the take the other, but Stevie Jr. stopped him with a frown and moved into place beside his father. Drake stood to one side slightly behind Alfonsi and clasped his hands in front of him.

"So." Stevie unbuttoned his coat, sat and crossed one leg over the other. The casual way he'd reclined against the seat back was not only disrespectful, but left his jacket gapping open to show the strap of a holster. "We've removed any blocks to you completing your deal with Henri Trahan. How about you call off your dogs and let us get back to business?"

Crude.

Demeaning.

Pompous.

All traits the boy had no doubt learned from his father. Though, the insufferable delivery seemed to catch even Alfonsi Sr. off guard because he slowly turned his attention to his son and glared at him. After a wordless scolding, he turned a regretful smile on Sergei. "My apologies. Stevie hasn't yet learned the finer points of conversation and relationship building."

Meaning he was as impulsive as his father.

Sergei forced a smile. "It is an art." One he'd learned and mastered long ago. His gaze cut to Carl, who'd taken up standing next to the file cabinet, both of his hands jabbed into his windbreaker. His lopsided smirk said he found the whole interaction utterly amusing.

We'll see how long your amusement lasts...

Forcing his attention back to Alfonsi, Sergei cleared his throat. "We're here today to talk about a truce. I've come upon some information that must be addressed before any such agreement can be reached."

"This is bullshit." Stevie sat upright and braced his hands on the armrests as though he meant to stand.

"We came here to talk about getting back to business. Not get the runaround."

Alfonsi stilled his son with a hand on his forearm. "Be quiet." He glanced at Drake, then turned his gaze back to Sergei, more patience in his voice than Sergei had thought possible from such a hothead. "Please. Continue."

Sergei laid it out, keeping his voice impassive as he shared only the details he wanted Alfonsi to be aware of. Carl's use of Evette's badge to access the attorney's office. How he'd openly insulted Sergei's fiancée and how he'd hired three young boys to plant bugs in Sergei's home. "There is also significant evidence to implicate Carl Labadie in the death of Evette's parents—either by his own hand or at his request."

"Now, just hold on here a second," Carl said, pushing away from the wall and yanking his hands from his pockets.

Roman had the blubbering fool backed against the wall and his hand at Carl's throat in a heartbeat, choking back whatever else the man hoped to say.

Drake, Stevie Jr. and Alfonsi wisely kept their respective places, but tensed.

Sergei cocked his head and kept going as though nothing had happened. "I'm sure you can understand why an affiliation between Carl and your family would cause me considerable concern. How can there be trust between us if there is someone untrustworthy inside your circle?"

Alfonsi chuckled and seemed to force himself to relax. He shook his head, but broke eye contact as he did it and shifted in his seat. "Yes, I can see where that would cause you concern. Trust is important between two men such as us." After a moment, he met Sergei's stare once more. "I assure you, Carl is no part of our family."

Carl's gurgling gasp at the pronouncement said Roman had loosened his grip enough to let him breathe and that Carl had grown smart enough to keep his arguments to himself.

"He's a friend from back in the day, for sure," Alfonsi added, "but he doesn't work for me. If you've got a beef with him, I understand, but I've got no skin in that game."

The man was a fool. An idiot who truly had no ability to think beyond what was right in front of his face.

Sergei held his stare and calmly uttered, "Prove it."

One beat.

Then another.

Finally, comprehension settled on his adversary's face.

Stevie Jr. seemed clueless. Drake at least seemed to grasp what was going on and let his hands fall to his sides, obviously ready to go for a gun. Alfonsi's gears were churning as well, an unmistakable panic flaring behind his eyes. He cleared his throat, stood and smoothed his hand down his tie. Rather than follow the normal protocol for a man wearing a suit, he left his jacket unbuttoned. "Of course. We'll see to that and arrange a meeting after."

Alfonsi motioned for Stevie to stand.

"Now," Sergei said before junior could do as his father indicated, clearly still lagging behind on the real gist of the conversation. Sergei stood to accentuate his point. "Here."

Carl resumed his struggles, his face turning a motley red in his newfound eagerness to escape.

Alfonsi looked to Carl, then Roman, then back to Sergei. He knew he was stuck. Knew the paths left to him were limited and that he'd have to choose. One way left at least a hope of breathing a day or two longer. The other would mean fighting his way out, and the odds of success would land on whoever had the faster trigger.

Sergei knew the second Alfonsi made his decision simply based on the pasty color that blanketed the man's face.

Alfonsi cleared his throat and nodded. "Stevie. Stand up."

Stevie took one look at his father's face, stood and stepped out from between Alfonsi and Carl.

Straightening his shoulders, Alfonsi slid his hand to the weapon stored beneath his coat and spoke to Roman. "Let him go."

Roman shoved Carl hard enough the back of his head rebounded against the wall and stepped out of the way.

Alfonsi stared at Carl a moment, lifted his weapon and took aim. "I'm sorry, my friend. But this is business."

Carl's eyes widened. "You gotta be kidding me. After everything we've been through? After everything I've done for you?"

There it was.

The truth.

In the face of death, it always came out.

Alfonsi knew it, too, because he turned at the last second and aimed his gun at Sergei.

But Sergei was ready, gun in hand and aimed at Alfonsi.

The blasts that followed were deafening, rattling the building with the overwhelming report of six firearms discharging nearly all at once. The weighted thunks of bodies hitting the concrete floor followed and the scent of gunpowder and blood filled the tiny space.

Carl stood trembling beside the file cabinets, one hand braced to keep himself upright as he took in the sight of Drake, Stevie and Alfonsi splayed out on the floor. Their blood slowly pooled around them, but then shots to the head were always the worst.

Sergei set his gun on the desk, cold satisfaction at the disbelief on Carl's face and the insatiable need for vengeance he'd held at bay for the last twenty-four hours rising up like a ravenous beast finally uncaged. "As your friend said, we Russians do love our drama."

Carl's head snapped up, his gaze cutting first to the gun on the desk, then to Sergei as he shrugged out of his jacket. He opened and closed his mouth, but nothing came out. As though his mind were too scrambled by the ugly truth of his predicament to cooperate with reasonable speech.

"Surely you didn't think my men and I wouldn't be prepared for this outcome." Sergei shrugged off his holster, unbuttoned his cuffs and rolled up his shirtsleeves.

Carl's focus dropped back to the gun.

Sergei stepped between Carl and the desk, blocking his last hope for survival from sight. "My bride has suffered much pain because of you. Her father's death. Her mother's death. Loss of her job." He paused long enough to remember the pain on Evette's face. The shame as she'd shared what she'd learned. "Rape."

He stood right in front of Carl. Breathed in the acrid fear pouring off him and let it feed the animal inside him. "I'm actually pleased Alfonsi chose you over me…because your punishment for what you've done to her and Emerson will be far worse by my hand."

Chapter Twenty-Five

The bad thing about a still, quiet night was that there was nothing to distract a woman from her clamoring internal debates or the fear flooding her body. Seated on the back porch's padded lounger, Evette pulled the Sherpa blanket she'd brought with her to wait for Sergei's return tighter around her shoulders, tucked her knees up close to her chest and fiddled with the ring on her finger. The pool's glassy surface mirrored the perfectly clear sky and the moon's crescent outline.

So neat.

Every shrub, tree and flower perfectly manicured. Every chair, cushion or decorative accent around the pool in its place.

But life wasn't like that. Life was messy. People were messier. Relationships—well, she didn't have the first damn clue how to navigate them. Hadn't really ever given them much of a chance. For a woman just trying to find her way through one for the first time, she'd picked a doozy of a partner. No simple churchgoing man with an eight-to-five job for her. No, sir. She had to go and fall in love with a man who lived and died by an entirely different rulebook than most.

One who'd probably killed for her today.

It had taken her all day yesterday and most of today to admit that truth to herself. To truly hold the knowledge close and ask herself if it was an action she could live with. If she could live with a man capable of such an act.

At the end of the drive, the carriage house lights glowed bright, the ones in Emerson's room promising her son was still head down, busy with the task she'd given him. He was a smart boy. He knew something was wrong with his momma. Knew that things between her and Sergei were off-kilter. But he'd kept his questions to himself. Had simply offered her hugs and bright smiles in a way that said he had faith they'd work it out.

Such a good boy.

So strong.

Balanced.

Wise.

How the heck he'd turned out that way, she couldn't fathom. He sure hadn't been conceived under the best of circumstances, so maybe he'd just been brought into this world a fighter.

She sighed and the chill outside sent her breath dancing on a puff of white air.

Definitely not a tidy life.

Headlights swept across the front of the carriage house and the unmistakable purr of Sergei's BMW broke the silence.

The tension in her shoulders ebbed for the first time since she'd watched him leave midmorning, but a fresh wave of adrenaline rushed in behind it.

This was it.

Right or wrong, Sergei had made his choices, and now it was time for her to make hers.

The car door shut with a muted *thunk* and while footsteps sounded on the concrete, there appeared to be only one set of them.

Sergei rounded into view, spied her seated on the corner of the porch and scanned the space for guards almost as quickly.

"I asked them to either wait inside, or join the guys up front," Evette explained before he could ask. "I wanted the quiet."

He took the steps to the raised area and stopped. Where he'd left dressed in one of his finest suits, now his hair was pulled back in a ponytail and he wore a plain gray T-shirt, jeans and boots.

Clothes for hard work.

Dirty work.

This was his life. Who he was.

He stood there, his face an impassive mask. But in the time she'd known him—seen past the hard image he projected with everyone else and touched the vulnerable heart of him—she'd learned to read him. Knew that behind those dark blue eyes of his, he was waiting. Bracing himself for her judgment.

After what he'd done on her behalf, making him wait any longer was cruel.

She stood and paced a little closer, but kept herself out of arm's reach. "I'm glad to see you're okay. I thought you'd be home much sooner."

Rather than address where he'd been or why he'd been so late, he glanced through the kitchen windows behind her. "Where is Emerson?"

She dipped her head toward the carriage house. "Packing."

For the barest moment, pain flashed behind his eyes, but he covered it quickly and drew in a long inhale. "I see."

No, he didn't. But she'd get there soon enough. And when she did, she needed to be sure he understood completely. "Will I ever see my uncle again?"

She'd crafted her question over the last several hours in such a way she'd get a definitive answer.

He answered it without hesitation, his gaze rock steady on hers. *"Nyet."*

"And Stevie Jr.?"

"Will never lay claim to Emerson."

Never.

No question at all.

And that gave her all the information she needed.

She stepped closer, slowly sliding the ring off her finger beneath the blanket. She handed it to him. "I need for you to take this."

His lips mashed together, the power behind the action so powerful she thought his jawline might snap.

"It's too big for me, Sergei. If you want me to wear it for special occasions or when you have bigwigs over to your house, I will, but I'm really a simple woman. I'd rather have a simple band to match who I am."

He moved so fast she never saw it. Only felt his iron grip on her outstretched hand as he yanked her to him and the demanding press of his lips on hers as he claimed her. Consumed her even as his relief and gratitude spilled through her.

The right choice.

The easy, quiet thought slipped through her mind, carried on her mother's voice.

He loved her.

She felt it in every touch. Saw it every time he looked at her. Heard it in his voice when he spoke her name and had shown he would do whatever it took to protect and provide for her and her son.

And whether his actions were wrong or right, the truth she'd finally come to realize was that she loved him too.

Completely.

She pushed against his shoulders, forced her mouth from his and rested her forehead on his chest. "I'm not leaving you, Sergei."

He squeezed her tighter to him, his voice low, ragged and breathless. "Then why is my son packing?"

His son.

God, she'd never get tired of hearing that. Not ever.

She lifted her gaze to his. "Because when I came to my decision, I wanted to show you that I meant it, so I moved the rest of my things this afternoon. I needed something to keep Emerson busy while I waited for you, so he's packing his now."

His Adam's apple bobbed, such raw emotion etched in his rugged features as he spoke, she felt them to her soul. "I need you to be certain, *liubimaja*."

She cupped each side of his face. Reveled in the soft brush of his beard against her palms and the warmth of his body against hers. "I am certain. Right or wrong. Good or bad—I accept you. All of you. Just as you are."

His hand between her shoulder blades slid up and cupped the back of her head, and when he spoke, his voice vibrated with emotion. A vow offered not just to her, but to the universe. "You will not regret this. Not ever."

"No, handsome. I won't regret it." She rolled up on her toes, coiled her arms around his neck and whispered against his lips. "I'm yours every bit as much as you are mine. And I intend to spend a very long time showing you what being loved feels like."

Epilogue

Maybe going back to college full-time with a kid wasn't such a great idea.

Evette sighed, closed the spiral notebook she'd been taking notes in during class and stuffed it in her backpack. Most parents were smart enough to get their bad grades *before* their kids went to school, but here she was—twenty-eight years old and struggling through a full course load complete with statistics—while her kid was studying for math tests of his own. Kinda hard to push the old *you have to make good grades* spiel when her own curriculum was kicking her ass.

She stood and filed out of the auditorium-style classroom amid all the other beleaguered-looking students. On the bright side, she had all of spring break to prep for the tests that would hit after the time off, and it didn't hurt that her husband of nearly three months was a whiz with all things numbers and wickedly skilled at finding ways to motivate her.

The same giddy happiness that always bubbled up whenever memories of her Christmas wedding came to mind brought a goofy smile to her lips. One she knew darned well the other students hustling down the hallway would view as odd, but she didn't care. Tough schedules or not, she was happy. *Beyond* happy.

"Mrs. Petrovyh!" The eager albeit slightly harried-sounding masculine voice came from the hallway on her left. As short as she was, it took another two heartbeats before the owner of the voice came into view—the counselor she and Sergei had met with when putting together this semester's courses. The counselor's cheeks were flushed as though he'd run most of the way from his office, and the pale blue tie he'd paired with his plain white oxford was slightly askew.

Evie shifted out of the immediate flow of traffic and faced him. "You're a long way from the quiet halls of the admin building, Mr. Peterson. Everything okay?"

"Oh, yes. Yes, yes." He glanced at his feet, then shuffled in place and smoothed his tie. "I just…um…"

Oh, boy.

Another request.

By now, she'd mostly accepted people would always approach her as an intermediary for Sergei—at least where the shy, innocent types were concerned. From the looks of things, Mr. Peterson was about to join the ranks of those seeking an introduction.

She waited, keeping her silence as Sergei had coached her to do.

Mr. Peterson cleared his throat and lifted his head. "I was…um…wondering if I might ask you for a time when I might speak with your husband about something."

Bless his heart. He really did seem to be a nice man. Hopefully, one who just wanted to ask Sergei for a donation of some kind, or for some investment advice. Regardless, Sergei had made it clear that certain parts of his life were 100 percent off-limits for her own protection. So, she stepped in closer, lowered her voice and delivered the simple message she'd been getting a lot of practice sharing. "I'm sure Sergei would be happy to speak with you. But I think it would be best if you arrange any conversations directly with him."

Mr. Peterson's eyes widened and a mix of panic and pleading washing across his face. "You're sure?"

"Yes. I'm sure." She hesitated a second. Not helping someone when they reached out went against everything in her, but—as Sergei had pointed out months ago—if she'd been brave enough to talk to him directly, so should anyone else. "He gave you his business card when I enrolled, didn't he?"

Chin slightly tucked and gaze locked to hers, Mr. Peterson nodded.

"Do you still have it?"

Another nod. Though, this time there was the stirring of comprehension behind his eyes.

"Then, perhaps, a good first step would be to call him and arrange a time to meet?"

He exhaled hard and his words followed on a rush. "He'd be okay with that? With a phone call?"

"Of course he would."

"That's good." A tremulous and uncertain smile crept across his face. He jerked a quick nod. "I could do a call. I just didn't want to offend him. You know?"

"I understand completely, but he's a lot less difficult to offend than you might think. I'd say go for it."

He dipped his head to Evie. "Thank you very much for the advice. Enjoy your spring break."

"I will. You too."

Rather than head directly to the exit, Evie paused

a moment and watched him go. The determination in each of his strides and the solid squaring of his shoulders.

Funny how being a mobster's wife wasn't a whole lot different from being a politician's wife. Minus the grueling election process and obligatory butt kissing, of course. But what she did reflected on Sergei. And the truth was, Sergei was making a seriously positive difference in some of the worst of New Orleans's neighborhoods. Yes, she knew there were questionable things he and his men had done to clear out the uncontrollable thugs who'd plagued their streets, but he'd also done a lot to rebuild their community. Including being a very visible presence at her church and a variety of charitable organizations.

She pushed open one of the double doors that led to the wide circle drive outside Tulane's Gibson Hall. The sun was blindingly beautiful and the green of the manicured lawn around her just beginning to deepen beneath the slowly warming days.

So much promise.

Just like her life.

As usual, a presence moved in beside her as soon as she cleared the building's front stoop, but rather than gain a greeting from one of her usual guards, it was Sergei's voice that coiled around her. "My bride comes out of school smiling." He wrapped an arm around her waist and pulled her tight to his side. "It makes me wonder if perhaps she's found an instructor she finds more appealing than her husband."

Evette couldn't help it. She laughed loud enough the sound of it ricocheted off the other buildings and she threw her arms around Sergei's neck. "There are no other men more appealing than my husband." She gave him a resounding kiss right there for everyone to see, not giving two damns what anyone thought. When she pulled away from his lingering lips, her breath moved a little unsteady and her voice was a heck of a lot thicker than it had been moments before. "Besides, why would I look for an instructor when I have my own private tutor who excels at finding creative methods for motivation."

His smirk was as self-satisfied as always, but there was a peace behind his once-jaded eyes these days. As if in the days they'd spent together he'd slowly come to believe that maybe—just maybe—he might finally have some permanent sunshine in his life. He opened his mouth to no doubt fire off some superior-sounding quip, but her son's voice cut across the parking lot before he could speak.

"Are you guys coming or what?" Emerson shouted across the distance.

Evette twisted in Sergei's arms and laid eyes on her son. "Why isn't he in school? And, more importantly, why does he have his head poked out the top of a limousine?"

"You cannot be a seven-year-old boy and not take advantage of such an opportunity. As to why he's not in school, you've been known to let him out a few hours early for a movie. I assumed checking him out for a special occasion for the same length of time would be permissible."

"He's only seven for twenty-four more hours. And spring break isn't a special occasion."

He cocked an eyebrow. "You haven't been with me for a spring break."

Oh, Lordy.

Considering special occasions for Sergei thus far had ranged anywhere from specialty ice cream runs to extravagant shopping sprees, there was no telling what he had in mind this time. Especially with Emerson's birthday on the horizon. "You do understand that I'm trying to raise my boy not to have a silver spoon in his mouth."

"You could gift Emerson with a thousand dollars to spend a day and he would never be spoiled."

He had a point. Heck, knowing Emerson, he'd open an investment account first thing and make enough to retire before he hit eighteen.

Maybe sooner.

Sergei turned her and guided her toward the limo. "Come, we have a long way to go before we celebrate."

Yep. Something told her this particular occasion was going to be a doozy.

A quick glance at the driver's seat said Reggie was on driving detail, and Mikey waited by the limousine's back door, his feet braced hip width apart and his hands clasped together in front of him. It would have been an intimidating pose, but given the grin on his face, Evette was pretty sure the only person who didn't know where they were headed was her.

Rather than lead her to the back seat, Sergei steered her to the rear of the car.

The trunk popped open as soon as they got there, and Sergei held out his hand. "Your backpack, please."

Evette shrugged it off her shoulder and handed it over.

Sergei lifted the trunk, revealing four suitcases.

"Um…" Not just four suitcases. Four *big* suitcases. "Are we going somewhere?"

"Well, it is spring break."

"Which is seven days long. Not twenty."

Sergei slammed the trunk and grinned. "Never let it be said that I don't travel prepared." He motioned to Mikey standing next to the now open back door. "After you, my bride."

The ride to wherever they were going took them west and away from the city. Sergei managed to look just as calm as ever, but with every mile, poor Emerson looked like he was about to explode from an overload of excitement.

"I take it you know where we're going?" she said to him.

He jerked his head up and down, but kept his lips clamped tight. As if he was too afraid to let his mouth have free rein for fear he'd let the surprise slip. Despite his silence, his smile never dimmed, and his eyes gleamed with mischief.

Why she was surprised when Reggie steered the limousine onto the airport exit she couldn't say, but it sure made her blood move a little quicker. "Okay, so we're flying somewhere?"

"While I know you're supportive of public transportation," Sergei said, "I'm afraid that particular conveyance isn't an option where we're going."

Evette tried to frown at him, but did a poor job pulling it off. "You're on a roll with being awesome, Mr. Petrovyh. Don't ruin it being a smart-ass."

"If I ruin it, I'll find a way to make it up to you, Mrs. Petrovyh."

Mrs. Petrovyh.

Hearing it never got old.

And while it sounded really freaking awesome when other people said it, the way it rolled off Sergei's tongue was still hot as Hades.

The limousine cruised down the airport roads, but rather than turn toward the terminals where she normally went to drop people off or pick them up, Reggie steered them down a different street. Moments later they pulled up to a heavily guarded gate.

After a quick chat with someone on an intercom, the gate slid open and Reggie steered them through.

Seated on the bench opposite Evette and Sergei, Emerson turned, stood on his knees and leaned on the partition that separated the passenger cabin from the driver's seat so he could watch through the windshield better.

And wowza, had he been smart to get a good seat.

Evette craned her head for a better look out the window closest to her. "Is that a private jet?"

"You could call it a private jet, yes. But my recommendation when talking to Trevor is that you refer to it as a Gulfstream. He'll tell you 'private jet' is too rudimentary for one of his babies."

A Gulfstream.

She'd always wondered why rap stars sung about them in songs, but seeing one up close and personal kind of put things in perspective.

The door to the plane was open and the steps built into the door extended for people to board. A red carpet was rolled out in front of it and Reggie steered them so her door was lined up at the other end. Before she knew it, Emerson and Sergei were already out and standing on the tarmac. Sergei extended his hand to her. "I can't leave you here, *liubimaja*. And even if you tried to stay, Darya would just march down here and pull you out."

The mention of Darya jolted her out of her stupefied state like not much else could have. She took Sergei's hand and stepped out onto the concrete. "Darya's here?"

He nodded toward the plane.

Sure enough, standing at the top of the staircase was Darya, looking fabulous as always in a pair of skinny jeans, a loosely crocheted pink sweater that hung off one shoulder and a matching pair of heels that no doubt cost a fortune.

Two older women stood behind her, one with luxurious silver hair well past her shoulder blades and another with dark cherry hair cut in a sharp bob.

Ninette and Sylvie.

"My girls!" Evie took off at a run for the lowered plane, Sergei and Emerson's combined laughter quickly falling behind her. "Oh. My. God!" she huffed, hurrying up the tall stairs to the front galley where they all waited. "I thought I was gonna have to wait until summer break before I could road trip to Dallas to see you guys again."

Out of breath and humming on an overload of adrenaline, she wrapped them up one at a time in huge bear hugs. Talk about two powerhouses. As soon as word had reached the Haven crew that she and Sergei had settled on a holiday wedding, Ninette and Sylvie had shown up along with a slew of other amazing women and had demonstrated in short order what it meant to be a part of a boisterous and loving, albeit very large, family. Shopping. Planning. Plotting. They got in on all the prewedding gyrations and even managed to coerce Dorothy into attending their impromptu bachelorette party. Truly, age seemed to have no bearing on either one of them and their confidence was off-the-charts intoxicating to be around.

The redhead, Sylvie, stepped out of Evie's hug, but kept a firm grip on her shoulders and pointedly eyeballed Evette's belly. Her Scottish brogue was just as thick as ever, but light and full of humor. "Och. It's been three months. I was hopin' you'd surprise me with a wee one. Ninnie and I need more babies to spoil."

Ninette grabbed Sylvie by the crook of her arm and pulled her back. "Oh, for God's sake, Sylvie. Let the girl have her honeymoon first." She aimed a sly, conspiratorial wink at Evie. "We'll give her at least six months. Then we'll give her a hard time."

"Oh, no. I've got a degree to finish first. No way am I mixing statistics or any other math class with morning sickness." She peeked over Ninette's and Sylvie's shoulders to the opulent cabin beyond with its dove-gray leather upholstery and gleaming mahogany wood accents. Clearly, the word *Gulfstream* was another term for *over-the-top luxury travel*.

Not finding anyone else in the open seats, she turned to Darya. "Where's Knox?"

"Not his kind of trip, I'm afraid."

The cockpit door opened and Trevor ambled out just as Emerson and Sergei reached the top of the stairs. At six foot three with shoulder-length blond hair, a buttondown, faded blue jeans and boots, Sergei's brother-by-choice was the embodiment of what a Viking would look like if he took up ranching. He held out his hand to Sergei. "The crew getting your stuff loaded up?"

Sergei nodded. "Another five minutes and we'll be ready to go."

Oh. That reminded her...

"Ready to go where?" Evie asked the group at large.

All-out laughter and a good number of snickers rounded the group and Ninette steered her back to the cabin. "Come on, girl. You might not have gotten a lavish honeymoon over the holidays, but you're gonna get a doozy makeup trip."

"I can't believe you haven't told her yet," Darya said to Sergei behind her.

"No way," Emerson chimed in. "Surprises are the best."

Evie gingerly settled into one of the swivel seats by a window and caressed the butter-soft leather armrests. "Are all planes like this?"

"You've never flown before?" Sylvie said as she and Ninette took the two seats across from her.

"No. Never."

"Well, prepare to be ruined for public modes of air transportation for life, then," Ninette said, "because this is definitely not what to expect on your average plane."

Emerson stretched out longwise on the sofa along the opposite wall and crossed his arms behind his head with a satisfied sigh. "I could get used to this."

Sergei took the open seat next to Evette and Darya sat at the far end of the couch. Darya tapped Emerson's feet. "Feet down and buckle up first. There's a bed in the back you can nap in later if you want."

That got him upright fast. "There is?"

Trevor pulled the main door shut with a firm thunk and did some extra latches that made it look like he was locking them all into a spaceship. Once done, he lifted an eyebrow and aimed what looked like a silent question at Sergei.

Sergei nodded.

Evette couldn't contain herself anymore and blurted out, "Is anyone gonna tell me where we're going that requires a trunk full of suitcases?

Sergei cocked his head, the delighted spark in his eyes making the blue lighter than normal. "I suppose I could have packed lighter, but I doubted you'd have appreciated a leaner number of options for a trip to Milan."

Milan.

At least that was what she thought he'd said.

It was also possible she'd misheard under the whir of the huge Gulfstream's engines.

"Did you say *Milan*?"

He nodded and a round of chuckles filled the cabin.

"As in *Italy*?"

This time his lips twitched as though he were fighting back laughter. "You did seem to grasp I'm quite good at motivation. How better to give you the impetus to study for your exams when we return than to give you a true buyer's experience in one of the fashion capitals of the world?"

Holy. Freaking. Crap.

"I'm gonna get to see how retail buyers work in Italy?"

"No, you're going to *work* with other buyers in Italy. In between celebrating Emerson's birthday and sightseeing with your new extended family, of course."

She couldn't help it. She let out a *whoop* loud enough Trevor had to have heard it behind the closed cockpit door and scrambled out of her seat and into her husband's lap to wrap him up tight.

God, she was happy.

Spoiled freaking rotten and living an amazing, fairy-tale life, too.

But mostly so unbelievably happy half the time she wondered how her body contained it all.

"Hmm," Sylvie murmured. "Do ye think Trevor would get his panties in a twist if he knew the lass was out of her seat and considering a trip to the bedroom?"

"I happen to know for a fact that boy has broken the seat belt rule a time or two himself," Ninette answered, "so, if he says anything, we'll just tell him to stay in the cockpit and mind his own business."

Emerson giggled, and she was pretty sure everyone save Sergei thought she was crazy as a loon.

She didn't care. Just snuggled in closer to Sergei, closed her eyes and thanked her lucky stars for the day she'd been fired. Yes, she'd lost her mom and dad. Lost her way and struggled through some dangerously rough times after.

But she'd survived.

Survived and found her way to a new family. A new life. And more love than she'd ever dreamed of having.

The plane taxied toward the main runway and Sylvie, Darya and Ninette shared opinions on what sights they should take in first.

At the end of the runway, the plane paused.

Evette tilted her head back and studied her husband. "Milan for spring break, huh?" she whispered.

"Indeed."

The engines revved and the plane moved forward, slow at first and then gathering tremendous speed.

Her heat did the same, joy and excitement for the many adventures they'd share together in the months and years to come like champagne bubbles whispering through her veins. "I'll give you one thing, Mr. Petrovyh. You definitely know how to sweep a girl off her feet."

* * * * *

Reviews are an invaluable tool when it comes to spreading the word about great reads. Please consider leaving an honest review for this or any of Carina Press's other titles that you've read on your favorite retailer or review site.

To find out about other books by Rhenna Morgan or to be alerted to new releases, sign up for her newsletter at http://rhennamorgan.com/newsletter/.

Read on for an excerpt from Knox and Darya's story, Tempted & Taken.

Acknowledgments

His to Defend was written near the tail end of an extremely difficult time in my life. Never have I relied upon the expression *One Day at a Time* so much as I have the last twenty-four months.

That said, I've also been surrounded by some amazing people who not only encouraged me, but believed in me when I couldn't believe in much at all. Lucy Beshara, Jennifer Mathews, Juliette Cross, Dena Garson and Duane Magnauck—thank you so very much for listening and being steady sources of support.

Cori Deyoe and Angela James, I cannot thank you enough for your patience, understanding and wisdom over the last few years. Writing books is tricky enough in the middle of a steady, happy life. Having the two of you as my writing anchors in the middle of a life overhaul was the best blessing I could have been given.

For my Romantics—you guys are not only the best cheerleaders and promoters a girl could ask for, but are a great escape to simply hang with day to day. Thank you for sharing a slice of your life with me.

And, of course, many hugs and kisses to the three people I love most in this whole world—the love of my life, Joe Crivelli, and my daughters, Abegayle and

Addison. Thank you for letting me be me and showing your support day after day. With the three of you in my life, I am undoubtedly the luckiest girl alive.

About the Author

Rhenna Morgan is a happily-ever-after addict—hot men, smart women and scorching chemistry required. A triple-A personality with a thing for lists, Rhenna's a mom to two beautiful daughters who constantly keep her dancing, laughing and simply happy to be alive.

When she's not neck-deep in writing, she's probably driving with the windows down and the music up loud, plotting her next hero and heroine's adventure. (Though trolling online for man-candy inspiration on Pinterest comes in a close second.)

She'd love to share her antics and bizarre sense of humor with you and get to know you a little better in the process. You can sign up for her newsletter and gain access to exclusive snippets, upcoming releases, fun giveaways and social media outlets at www.rhennamorgan.com.

*Want to read more about Darya and Knox?
Check out their story in* Tempted & Taken,
*now available from Rhenna Morgan
and Carina Press*

One week Darya had waited. Waited, watched her every step and worked herself ragged. Outside the rearranged Post-its on her desk, not once had she glimpsed any indication Ruslan or anyone else had found her. In fact, her life had settled into its usual routine so easily she'd wondered if maybe she hadn't imagined leaving things askew on her desk.

Regardless, the time to meet Knox was here and hopefully, the leg up she needed to go with the introduction. Parked in front of a single-story building with plain-Jane concrete walls, she stared up at the brushed chrome Citadel Security sign and rehashed the pitch she'd spoken aloud at least twenty times a day. Cool air pumped from the car's vents against her clammy skin, barely making a dent with all the adrenaline coursing through her veins.

The clock on the dash flicked from 1:54 p.m. to 1:55 p.m. Either she could sit here until straight up two o'clock and let her anxiety climb all the way up into the stratosphere, or she could pry herself out of her car and hope a slightly early arrival showed an extra level of professionalism.

She popped the handle and shoved the heavy door

open, swinging her resale Jimmy Choo–shod feet out onto the concrete parking lot. What the tan pumps lacked in pizzazz they more than made up for in accentuating her legs, especially paired with the matching pencil skirt that ended just above her knees and the delicate ivory camp shirt with its mandarin collar. Putting the outfit together had been both a joy and a welcome distraction, a brief trip back to a time when she'd been able to enjoy fine fashion instead of constantly trying to blend in.

Before her hand connected with one of the glass entry handles, the click of a lock being released sounded. She pulled the door open and a wave of chilled air to make her Challenger's AC seem weak blasted across her skin. Even with the ample light spilling through the double doors and windows on either side, it took her eyes a second to adjust from the bold midday sunshine.

A pretty blonde dressed in jeans and a T-shirt stood from behind a curved reception desk stained a soft ebony and accented in soft chrome. Her eyes were an enviable green and her hair styled in a tousled pixie cut. She reached across the tops of three monitors arranged in a perfect semi-circle and offered her hand in greeting. "You must be Jeannie Simpson. I'm Katy, Knox and Beckett's assistant. Can I get you something to drink?"

Two or three shots of vodka would be nice. God knew she needed something to loosen up her tongue. While the outside of Knox's building had been nothing short of plain, the inside was jaw-dropping high-end contemporary. Like Katy's desk, the walls on either side of her were dark—not quite black, but charcoal gray, and fashioned from some kind of metal rather than paint. The wall behind Katy's desk, however, was a beautiful dove gray that added extra depth to the limited space. Classy yet edgy cylinder pendant lights with frosted white glass hung above either end of her desk, and two impenetrable steel doors flanked her on either side. "If it's not too much trouble, water would be nice."

"No trouble at all." Katy cocked her head, curiosity glimmering behind her assessing gaze. "Your accent is amazing. I'm guessing Russian?"

For a second, Darya's thoughts flatlined. With limited daily interactions beyond her normal routine, it was seldom she met new people. So much so she'd forgotten the need for explanation. "Yes," she said, realizing all too quickly Knox would expect the same. "Not too hard to understand I hope."

"Not at all. It's actually beautiful." Katy punched a few buttons on her computer and waved Darya to the small seating area to one side of the front door. "Just give me a minute to grab your water and let Knox know you're here."

"Thank you."

"Don't mention it." She splayed her hand on a black screen beside one heavy door and a heavy clunk that sounded on par with a bank vault being released resonated through the room. Only then was Darya left alone in the intimidating environment.

Slowly, she paced toward the iron-colored leather couch and the oblong marble coffee table. Sitting was out of the question, not if she wanted to exude any kind of calm. She might be technically alone in the room, but the cameras anchored in every corner made it relatively certain there were eyes on her somewhere. She squeezed the handles on her briefcase a little tighter and pretended to study the landscape outside one picture window. What really held her attention was the glass itself, multiple layers thick and no doubt capable of stopping bullets. But then such measures made sense for a security company. As did the secured doors. At least she hoped that was the reason for such stringent measures. The last time she'd been in such a tightly controlled environment was the day she'd met Ruslan, and her world had gone from pampered to hell in all of five minutes.

The door *kachunked* behind her.

Darya turned, the pleasant smile she'd intended for Katy evaporating along with all the air in her chest. Instead of Katy strolling through the large door, Knox ambled her direction, a smile in place potent enough to disarm the most jaded woman and a bottle of water loosely gripped in one hand.

And he was gorgeous. So much more than what the pictures she'd scrounged up promised. More intensity. More charisma. More *everything*. Like in all the photos she'd seen, he wore faded Levis and military-style black boots. His T-shirt was a deep gray that accentuated his lean, but muscled torso, and tattoos peeked out from each sleeve.

It wasn't until he moved within reaching distance and held out the water he'd brought her that the white graphic on the T-shirt registered—a classic Impala and the phrase, *Get in, loser. We're going hunting.*

"You like *Supernatural*?" she blurted.

His smile deepened and he wiggled the bottle still in his outstretched hand. "Not even officially introduced yet and you're already scoring points for good taste." A rugged leather watch with a thick camel-colored band covered his wrist, while a darker brown cuff and two smaller bracelets made of turquoise and red shells circled the other. Total rock star.

She took the water, wishing she could press the ice-cold plastic against her flaming cheeks, but juggled it with her briefcase instead and offered her hand for a formal introduction. "Sorry. I'm JJ."

His grip engulfed hers, the warmth of the contact and the way he leisurely perused her from head to toe scattering her barely resuscitated thoughts. "Not a thing to apologize for from where I'm standing." His gaze settled on hers, the impact of it stoking grossly inappropriate thoughts. Vivid, carnal and deliciously wicked thoughts. His voice lowered and rasped with pure sexual promise. "I'm Knox."

Oh, yes. Definitely dangerous territory. Absolutely the worst trespass her mind could make with plans to pitch her future so close. She forced herself to relinquish his hand. "I'm very pleased to meet you."

His beautiful gray eyes sparked with mischief and he grinned in a way that said he hadn't missed the huskiness in her response. He sidestepped and swept his hand toward the door, but rather than use the movement to add more distance, he splayed his hand at the small of her back. "How about we get out of the lobby and give you a chance to get your bearings before we talk shop?"

Walking was good. Distance would be even better. Although, for the first time since she'd started wearing heels, she wasn't sure if she could put one foot in front of the other without looking like a newborn deer.

Behind the industrial steel door, the air was even

colder, the steady draft tunneling between the glass walls on either side of her gently lifting the hair off the back of her neck. "You must really hate July in Texas."

"My servers hate July in Texas. I learned to tolerate it like every other native before I left the cradle."

Behind the glass, server racks stretched tall and wide in precise rows. Her heels clicked against the industrial tile, mingling with the steady hum from the machines. "This is all for your security company?"

"Some of them. The rest support the traffic from my apps."

Well, that was silly of her. The very reason she was here and she'd not been smart enough to realize he'd need a sizable infrastructure to support the business he'd built. She slowed her steps, appreciating how the wires ran in neat rows up the back of each stack then disappeared into the iron racks above. Combined with the soft blue light emanating from the ceiling can lights she felt a bit like she'd entered a sci-fi flick. "It's quite overwhelming."

He chuckled and placed his hand on yet another bio scanner beside a black wood door. "Overwhelming is when a server goes down and pissed off customers start calling in." The lock released and he opened the door for her. "There've been a few drills I'd liken to an electronic version of a needle in a haystack, but hey. Nothin' like a challenge to keep a man sharp."

For some reason, the image of Knox knee-deep in a challenging situation sent a charge through her strong enough to power half the machines they'd left behind. True, he was handsome, but nothing captivated her more than a man's intelligence. Considering Knox had both in spades, it was a wonder she'd been able to string more than three words together, let alone remember her name.

She trailed behind him into his office. It had the same contemporary feel as the lobby, only less intimidating in its colors. A soft gray chenille sofa and two club chairs covered in a matching patterned fabric were arranged near a window on the far side of the room. In the center was what she assumed was Knox's desk, though it was far more unconventional than the standard arrangement. Where most people chose to arrange their furnishings with their back to the wall and a bird's-eye view on the entrance, Knox's wide steel desk faced an astounding number of monitors mounted on the far wall, each of them streaming what she assumed was live footage from a number of businesses. Even more impressive were the four oversize computer monitors arranged in a semi-circle in the center of his desk.

In the monitors hanging on the wall, people went about their daily activities, innocently working, drinking and eating without so much as a clue they were being watched.

The muted tap of fingers on keys sounded and the screens went dark.

"They're a distraction until you get used to them." Knox spun his sleek black office chair around, rolled it toward a smallish collaboration table on her right and motioned to the guest chair behind it. "Have a seat."

She did, unpacking her laptop from her briefcase as she did so and setting it on the tabletop.

Directly across from her, he leaned in, rested his forearms on the brushed chrome surface and cupped one fisted hand with the other. "So, you mentioned a business opportunity. What's on your mind?"

So much for easing into the topic. And had she really referred to it as a business opportunity? Now he'd think she'd pulled some kind of bait and switch to earn his attention. She cleared her throat and smoothed one hand across the top of her computer. "Business opportunity might not be the right way to describe it."

His expression blanked, the warmth and lighthearted mirth that had shone in his beautiful eyes chilling in an instant. As though she'd not only angered him, but disappointed him as well. Without the vibrancy in his gaze, his eyes looked tired. Pinched and weary around the edges as though he'd gone for far too long without rest.

She forged onward, drawing from the countless rehearsals she'd spoken out loud while pacing her apartment. "You remember when I first reached out to you—when I emailed you on my tracking services—I mentioned I'd learned your name from someone you'd mentored."

He nodded, though the movement seemed cautious. "Jason Reynolds."

"Yes." She fidgeted in her seat and curled her fingers around the farthest edge of her laptop. "Jason's told me many stories about you. About the men you call your brothers and how you've made a successful career for yourself. He holds you in very high regard."

"Not sure how that plays into a business opportunity."

This was it. In the grander scheme of things, it wasn't nearly as big a risk as taking on JJ's identity or fleeing Russia, but it could still catapult her future. She pulled in a slow breath and held his commanding stare. "It's important because I want you to mentor me."

His eyes widened, a little of the emotional barricade he'd put up easing as he spoke. "Jason's a coder."

"I know. He's the one who first gave me the idea."

"And you know him how?"

"He comes to visit his grandmother every Monday. At a retirement home. His grandmother isn't very talkative, but he always comes and brings his computer. He told me you've been known to teach people with an interest and, if they do well, give them a leg up."

"I teach people with *talent*. No matter how much interest a person has doesn't mean they can be successful in the long run."

Emboldened, she sat a little taller and leaned in. "I can't tell you if I have talent, but I can promise you I'm tenacious. I've already completed two of the self-teaching courses you recommended to Jason and have started a third."

He reclined against his chair back, one arm still draped atop the table while the other rested casually at his hip. It was a relaxed pose, but the intensity that crackled around him said she'd be a fool to assume he wasn't assimilating each and every detail to the nth degree. "You're looking to expand on the skip tracing?"

Always stick to the truth, JJ had coached her. *Or as close to it as you can get.*

"I'd like to move away from that business," Darya answered, "to build a career that's less reliant on companies but is still transportable." Realizing the unintended kernel she'd left uncovered, she clarified, "So I can travel."

For several seconds, he merely studied her, the quiet

amplifying until it droned as loud as the servers in the other room.

"The skip tracing is good," she said, needing to fill the silence. "With my contracts, I can keep a steady income, but I don't like the feel of it. I don't like finding people who don't want to be found. I don't want to worry that they'll learn who found their information and take their anger out on me."

Without moving so much as a muscle, his entire demeanor shifted. A shrewd observer one second and a lethal predator on alert the next. His voice was deceptively smooth. "Has that happened?"

Not exactly. Not to her anyway, but it *had* happened. "Once. A collection company wanted to locate a man past due on his car payments. He was living at his ex-wife's address in a town only thirty minutes away. The company secured the car, but the collector inadvertently mentioned who had located the debtor's new residence."

"And?"

She shrugged, recalling the none-too-pleasant altercation that had happened only a few months after she'd gone to work for JJ. "People who lose their possessions tend to be very angry. They also want someone to blame for their misfortune, and this man in particular wanted to voice his displeasure. In person." She paused for a minute, looking for the right words to help him understand without exposing too much of her own predicament. "I don't want to experience that again. I want to create something. To build a career where my success will be limited only by my abilities."

He pulled in a slow breath, sighed as though he questioned having scheduled the appointment and sat up in his chair. "You realize there's a lot more to this than syntax and technique, right? Even with persistence, you need damned good ideas and a hell of a lot of luck if you want to be more than just a hired coder."

"I will make my luck."

His eyebrows hopped high and his lips curled in a sly grin. "You quoting me because you believe it, or to let me know you've done your homework?"

"Because I believe it. This isn't the first time I've taken risks, and I doubt it will be the last, but every person has to make their own way. If the path doesn't exist, it's up to every individual to make one. You took your love of music and movies and made a niche for yourself. I can do the same."

"You use my app?"

Her and everyone else eager to find new leads for their playlists or Netflix binges. Lystilizer had originally focused on music only, but had been expanded to include movies a little over a year ago. The algorithm behind it was amazing, evaluating each user's individual libraries and making spot-on recommendations for new purchases. "I use it all the time."

"Music or movies?"

"Both."

"Favorite band."

That drew her up short. "Can you actually narrow your favorites down to one?"

One corner of his mouth twitched. "Fair enough. How about your top favorites in the last six months?"

"Halsey, Eve to Adam and Chris Stapleton."

He cocked one eye and crossed his arms across his chest, but his grin was playful. Clearly, he not only loved music, but he was familiar with a broad spectrum of genres. "Alternative, rock and country. That's a heck of a spread. I'd have pegged you as a top forty girl."

She shrugged. "I like music that fits my mood. Why limit yourself to only one format when you can explore many?"

"True." He cocked his head. "So, what about movies?"

For a second, she ducked her head, then remembered who she was talking to and shook off her embarrassment. What difference did it make what he thought of her burning through pop culture lists off IMDb? "*The 40 Year Old Virgin* and *The Princess Bride*."

His smile deepened. "'Wuv,'" he said, imitating the clergyman near the end of the movie. "'True wuv.'"

"'You killed my father!'" she fired back with her own impression of Inigo Montoya. "'Prepare to die!'"

He laughed loud enough to fill the room, the rich rumble of it soothing away the remnants of her fears. "A classic. I'll bet I could drop at least twenty-five quotes inside of five minutes. Maybe less."

"I'm watching *Airplane* next. Jason says it's insanely old, but has just as many quotes, if not more."

His laughter died off slowly, and while none of the suspicious tension she'd picked up on before returned, he studied her through slightly narrowed eyes. As if she were a puzzle he couldn't quite put together. "How long have you lived in the States?"

Every time someone asked that question all she wanted to do was bolt, but denying her heritage wasn't an option. She'd long ago accepted her accent was too prominent to eradicate it without serious training, but that didn't mean she was comfortable opening doors that might lead to more questions.

The tattoo on his forearm drew her attention. Bold and drawn only in black ink, it resembled a tree but with a tribal style and surrounded a rugged H in the center. A mark with purpose, yet nowhere near as sinister as the tattoos she'd become all too familiar with in Russia. Was Knox dangerous? Absolutely. Her instincts with people were seldom wrong and for Knox they insisted he had an intellect not to be trifled with. She'd even uncovered rumors of he and the men he called brothers having ties to criminals. But sitting with him now—watching him and interacting with him—she sensed fairness. Honor and determination paired with an indomitable courage. If she expected him to take a chance on her, he at least deserved the same willingness in return, even if it gave him a lead toward discovering who she really was.

She took a deep breath, straightened her spine and fisted her hands in her lap. "I left Russia about two and a half years ago."

Tempted & Taken *by Rhenna Morgan,*
now available wherever ebooks are sold.

www.CarinaPress.com

Copyright © 2017 Rhenna Morgan